The Fatal Messenger

THE FATAL MESSENGER

A Medical Thriller

MARCUS SHORE

NEW YORK

LONDON • NASHVILLE • MELBOURNE • VANCOUVER

THE FATAL MESSENGER

A Medical Thriller

Published in New York, New York, by Morgan James Publishing. Morgan James is a trademark of Morgan James, LLC. www.MorganJamesPublishing.com

Proudly distributed by Publishers Group West®

Morgan James BOGO™

A **FREE** ebook edition is available for you or a friend with the purchase of this print book.

CLEARLY SIGN YOUR NAME ABOVE

Instructions to claim your free ebook edition:
1. Visit MorganJamesBOGO.com
2. Sign your name CLEARLY in the space above
3. Complete the form and submit a photo of this entire page
4. You or your friend can download the ebook to your preferred device

ISBN 9781636984179 paperback
ISBN 9781636984186 ebook
Library of Congress Control Number:
2024931355

Cover Design by:
Formatted Books

Interior Design by:
Chris Treccani
www.3dogcreative.net

Morgan James is a proud partner of Habitat for Humanity Peninsula and Greater Williamsburg. Partners in building since 2006.

Get involved today! Visit: www.morgan-james-publishing.com/giving-back

ACKNOWLEDGMENTS

Without Murphy Hooker I may never have finished writing *The Fatal Messenger*. He is a talented writer and wonderful person. Great thanks to Terence Witt, an accomplished author, entrepreneur, fellow tennis addict, and good friend, for reviewing the entire manuscript and for his invaluable and insightful edits. Susan Lom completed the first full edit of my draft, and I am grateful for her expertise and patience with me throughout the process.

Many thanks to Kevin Anderson and his team of editors and support staff. Ian Corson introduced me to the team at Kevin Anderson and helped me realize the possibility of reaching my goals.

My wonderful, lovely wife gave me the patience and support I needed while writing the manuscript, and my kids were a fun sounding board to keep the story moving and exciting.

As always, thanks and praise to the Lord for giving me the gifts of being a husband, father, brother, friend, doctor, surgeon, and writer.

And finally, special thanks to Isaiah Taylor for believing in my manuscript and Emily Madison, Jim Howard, Lauren Downey, Molly Riggs, Lisa Hollingsworth, and Naomi Chellis at Morgan James Publishing who made this project possible.

DISCLAIMER

The Fatal Messenger is a work of fiction. The characters and incidents in this work of fiction are used solely for the writer's imagination. I greatly admire SpaceX's brilliance and commitment to space and planetary exploration. Holmes Regional Medical Center is an excellent center for patient care in Melbourne, Florida. The University of Central Florida is a premier university with an outstanding medical school. The Shanghai Cooperation Organization is an existing entity, but this manuscript is completely fictitious.

PROLOGUE

Los Angeles, California

C hristmas Eve in the City of Angels and Sheila Roust was running late again. Maybe it was just exhaustion, but she hadn't been able to sleep more than a few hours a night since returning from Sarajevo last summer. That was nearly six months ago. Since then, outside of her fellow students in the Aerospace Program at the University of Southern California, no one in Los Angeles knew her true ambitions, or her brilliance.

Normally energized, tonight Sheila felt disassociated, almost robotic as she applied coats of mascara to her lashes. Prekrasnyy genie, beautiful genius—that was what people called her growing up in a poor farming village, hours outside of Moscow. With a body for sin and a mind that would make a grown astrophysicist cry, she was putting the final touches on her greatest work—her own carnal self. Despite a surplus of God-given talents, Sheila knew that the sparkling pools of blue—or green eyes, depending on what color she wore—were her most powerful weapons. As a teen, she quickly learned she could make any hot-blooded Russian boy, man, or woman fall under her spell by gently lowering her eyelids and deeply staring into her "victim's" eyes. It was an effective trick. But only if her suitors could see them.

Sheila stopped applying. "No one marries goth girls," she muttered, dabbing at the mess she'd made; she didn't want to scare off potential suitors. After all, she would only be in America a short time longer, and Sheila needed to find a marrying man or be deported back to Russia. To blend in, when she arrived in California last year, she picked up the local Valley Girl

1

slang by watching Hollywood movies from the eighties and used it to mask her intellect from Americans. But no matter how Sheila spoke English, her combination of brains and beauty stood out among the superficial Los Angelinos.

Most recently she had attracted the attention of the "X-Man," her nickname for Xander, her semi-regular boyfriend and star linebacker for the USC Trojans, who was due to arrive any minute. They had dated through the fall semester, but it was far from love. Love was only an algorithm to her. Truth be told, Sheila could barely tolerate Xander. He was merely a means to an end.

"I don't care what Xander says." She squinted at her reflection, scrunching her face to make herself look as ugly as she felt inside. Sheila recovered, giving the mirror her best wide-eyed pouty ingenue look that made everyone she'd met crazy.

Her left eye was red and irritated. Blurrier than usual. *What have they done to me?* she thought.

Sheila was furiously teasing out her auburn hair in front of a gold flake mirror when her iPhone blared "Nuthin' but a 'G' Thang."

"Hold the horses. Coming!" Sheila shouted to herself.

It was a missed call from Xander, who was on time for a change. Sheila could hear his car speakers' rap music blaring through her apartment walls. She kept teasing anyway, irritated at his lack of consideration for her.

Xander moved to plan B and laid on his horn.

"So mature," Sheila exclaimed as she gave her outfit a final *zhush* in the mirror, grabbed her phone, purse, keys, and scooted out the door, double locking it on the way out. Long limbed and self-assured, she nimbly strode down the winding outdoor stairs surrounding her condo, skipping steps along the way.

Reaching the street, she smelled the sweet night-blooming jasmine. It was one of her favorite things about living here; sadly there wasn't much else.

"Lovely," she observed, slowing a moment to breathe it in.

Xander obnoxiously revved the engine of his USC Trojan red Cadillac Escalade and turned the stereo up to annoy her snotty neighbors, as if his roaring quad exhaust wasn't enough to do so. He rolled down the passenger window. Sheila saw Xander was bumping to the music, wearing his cool face.

"S'up, pretty woman? You're lookin' fire. Ready to get freaky wid it?"

Sheila took another deep breath of the jasmine. "We don't have fragrances like this where I am from."

"You don't even wear deodorant. Get in."

Sheila frowned at Xander while soaking in the warm December night a moment longer, gently swaying to the rap beat of Kendrick Lamar. A few feet away, on the other side of the winding road, sat a nondescript white Chevrolet Impala with tinted windows. Even to the untrained eye, something was off about it. Old Chevys did not belong in the canyon. The Impala was the color of the night-blooming jasmine, yet its presence was so discordant, almost spectral. The muffled sound of classical music was barely heard through its closed windows, drowned out by the Escalade's rap music.

Eagled-eyed Sheila prided herself on being hyper-aware of her surroundings—but she was off tonight, distracted by Xander's overpowering cologne. Sheila never saw the car before slipping into Xander's Escalade and kissing him on the right cheek.

"Oof." She cringed. "Drakkar Noir? Or night-blooming jasmine? No contest."

"You know you live for that Noir, baby," Xander replied.

The X-Man put his SUV in gear and peeled away, taking his jarring music with him.

The moment the canyon was quiet again, the white Impala started up its engine and followed them down to Sunset Boulevard. Only the night owls perched in the eucalyptus trees could hear the classical music coming from inside the car. It was Franz Schubert. The dark one.

Tripp Bolthouse's ninth annual "Holiday In Hell-A" party at his home high above the Hollywood Hills had a waiting list a mile long. When Sheila and Xander arrived in the ultra-swank Trousdale Estates neighborhood just below Mulholland Drive, the scene was as Hollywood as it gets and as intoxicating as any drug for the starry-eyed sycophants on the guest list. Sheila was not one of those celebrity chasers. Too poor to see any of the new American movies or television back in Russia, she was more impressed with Tripp's mid-century John Lautner–designed home. Never had she dreamt of fame or fortune in Russia; Sheila only wished to survive the winters— but now that she was surrounded by it, she could not stop thinking about the chasm between the classes at the party. There were stars, servants, and wealthy hangers-on. That was it; nothing in between.

Kind of like the Russian caste system, she thought as she sipped vodka and watched them all, fascinated. *Who can I marry here to get this house?*

"Sheila, gorgeous!" an amped-up Tripp chirped, greeting her with kisses on both cheeks. "I've cued up that industrial techno you love."

Bolthouse hugged it out with Xander. Tripp paid Xander as an off-the-books employee at Bolthouse Productions, his party promotion company. Though technically illegal, paying college football stars helped bring in the bridge-and-tunnel crowd from the LA suburbs. Plus, since the X-Man loved to "get faded," he and Tripp thought, why not make a little cash doing it.

One of the most popular DJs on the west side, Tripp knew how to put on a show, and this party was popping off. B-list celebrities and industry types mingled with the beautiful people of Hollywood as well as an assortment of hangers-on who bought their way into the party like trust fund babies, tech CEOs, plastic surgeons, social media influencers, yoga instructors, and aspiring movie producers. Sheila didn't recognize any of them but could tell just by looking at the crowd which ones were celebrities, even if her vision was getting worse by the minute. After her Lasiks treatment in Bosnia over the summer, she had thrown away her contacts, but her left eye was never the same. Her vision was permanently blurred. The constant ache progressed to pain most evenings—and since she had no health insurance, she used alcohol to numb the pain. After four Stolis and soda with a twist of orange, her pain diminished but her vision became even blurrier, and she couldn't stop rubbing her eye. So she looked for Xander to take her home, but she had lost track of him shortly after they arrived when he began flirting with every female USC fan who approached him.

Sheila passed through a pair of large sliding glass doors leading to the pool. She narrowed her eyes. *He's screwing two high school girls.*

She walked to the edge of the pool's Jacuzzi and crouched down behind Xander.

"Having fun?" she quipped.

"S'up?" Xander said, pulling one of the girls onto his lap.

"Can I see you girls' ID?"

"These are my fans. You're barely legal, right? You been crying, racoon eyes?"

Sheila's mascara was running in her bad eye.

"Maybe I miss Russian winters. I could count on them."

"You can count on me, babe."

"You're totally hot," one of the anorexic bikini models oozed to Sheila, still wrapped around the X-Man's torso. "Join us. Water's perfect."

Sheila slowly poured her drink on Xander's head.

"Seriously?" Xander laughed.

"I'll leave you three to it. Don't call me again."

Xander jumped out of the pool and chased her down. "Where you think you're going?!"

"Don't touch me!" She pulled away from his iron grip but resisted striking him.

"It's a party. X-Man's just giving them what they pay for!"

"Stop referring to yourself in the third person!" Sheila cut back. "Ublyudok." ("Douchebag" in Russian.)

Xander eased up. "Wait. Wait. I'll drive you, babe. Don't be like that."

A group of USC fans, watching them argue, started chanting, "X-Man! X-Man!"

Sheila kept walking. "I'll get an Uber. Enjoy your fans."

Xander threw up his hands. "Fine! Ain't no cell service up here, stinky whore!"

She didn't flinch, even when the X-Man's fans cheered her exit. She wasn't going to let her semi-regular boyfriend seduce other women right in front of her, even if she couldn't care less. She had values, as twisted as they might be. Click-clacking her high-heeled Louboutins out of the Bolthouse Estate walls, she teetered down the long brick driveway, passing by the front gate, more incoming cars, and three valets who hit on her by offering to drive her home themselves.

"Grow up, boys." She grinned, marching away to catcalls and whistles.

With no bars on her phone, Sheila began the short trek up to Mulholland Drive, where she knew she could get service and order an Uber. "Must be insane, dating a football player," she complained as she walked past a row of luxury cars: black Porsches, yellow Ferraris, purple Lambos—and one very ordinary white Chevrolet Impala.

"Stupid Sprint. Worst coverage ever."

The Impala started its engine. Sheila was too busy rubbing her left eye and looking at her phone to notice she was being followed. Until Sheila felt that familiar creepy feeling.

She was being watched.

She looked up from her phone and felt a pair of halogen headlights turn on behind her. She looked down; her shadow was cast on the road where it was not before.

Is Xander messing with me? Rather than ignore the car, she turned to confront it as the Impala slowed to a stop ten feet behind her.

"Pedestrians have right of way, idiot!" she snarled.

The Impala didn't move. They were in a standoff.

Sheila turned back and kept walking.

The Impala followed.

When Sheila stopped, the Impala stopped behind her.

Sheila wheeled around. "Not funny! You in there, Xander?"

The Impala revved its engine and flashed its high beams on her.

"Go on. Get a good look!" she bluffed. "I'm calling the police." When Sheila walked away and pretended to call 9-1-1, it dawned on her. Xander would not be playing games in an old clunky car. She could feel her heart thumping in her chest.

Inside the Impala, the driver stared at Sheila from behind the dark tinted front windshield. With Sheila's taunts drowned out by a string quartet playing Schubert's "Death and the Maiden" on the car stereo, he calmly fastened a pair of brown leather driving gloves and gripped the steering wheel.

Sheila continued to walk away. The driver turned up the music and stepped on the gas, jamming the car violently into her back. Sheila didn't have time to scream as she rolled over the hood, then the roof, tumbling down into the nearby jasmine bushes.

The Impala stopped.

Sheila lay there motionless and helpless, bleeding all over her favorite flowers.

"Sweet jasmine," she moaned, taking short breaths.

A pair of recently polished dress shoes stepped out of the car. She heard violin music she vaguely recognized, trying to lift her head. Blurry-eyed, her mascara bleeding down her party dress, she saw a black van pull up next to the car. Two men opened its back door. Sheila tried to get up and run but couldn't move. As she felt herself losing consciousness, she heard footsteps coming her way. She knew the men in the van were not there to help.

The Impala's driver stood over her crumpled body.

"Such a shame," he said, leaning down to admire her.

"Suh uhva beth," she spewed, spitting blood in her attacker's face.

He wiped his cheek with a handkerchief and shook his head. "Now, now."

The two men from the van fastened sets of handcuffs around Sheila's wrists and ankles, hog-tying her, before harshly scooping up their beautiful, wounded prey by the metal cuffs.

Sheila's mind raced. *I can't believe it; they are going to kill me.*

She shouted, "Noo! Rape! Somebody! Help me."

But no one in the posh Trousdale neighborhood would open their doors. The men calmly deposited her in the van. Seeing her life flash before her eyes, Sheila got a look at her kidnapper's face.

"*Who are you?*" she whispered. The driver of the Impala gave her a terrifying smile, then slammed the back of the van on her muffled screams.

1

Melbourne, Florida

"I was gator hunting, swear on my life."

Tom Romero lied as badly as he smelled. Everyone in the trauma center knew he was lying but Anna Gentle, a registered nurse and head surgical scrub technician for eyes, was the only person to call him on it. "Not unless that reptile was packing a shotgun."

One o'clock in the morning, Christmas Eve, Tom had been medivacked by helicopter to the trauma center at Holmes Regional Medical Center in Melbourne, Florida. The skin on his face, shoulders, and chest was embedded with shotgun pellets. One had penetrated his left eye and his retina. Dr. Jake LaFleur was the ophthalmologist on call.

"Will it ruin my moneymaker, Doc?" Tom asked.

"Um, probably not," Dr. LaFleur replied. "How do you make a living again?"

"Swamp tours. That's where I'm dumping those girls' bodies once I get outta here."

"Listen, you, I'm making a citizen's arrest if you keep talking trash," Anna warned.

"You want me to save your eye or not, Mr. Romero?" Jake asked sternly.

Tom quieted down. "Yes, sir. And yes, ma'am. I do."

"Then let us work," Jake said. "This will hurt a lot less if you cooperate."

The trauma surgeons at Holmes had already removed numerous pellets from Tom's face and scalp. He winced at the impending pain as Anna rolled his bed into the pre-op area to see Joe Katz, the anesthesiologist on call.

"Katz here will get you all set up," Jake said in a soothing doctorly tone.

Jake and Anna washed up for surgery in silence, both wishing they were somewhere else but at work. Anna glanced at Jake's hands.

"Lose any more weight and you'll disappear," she commented.

Jake, a burly thirty-five-year-old Louisiana native who enjoyed action movies and jambalaya, pulled the waist of his scrubs from his body like he was in a Nutrisystem ad with Marie Osmond. He'd shrunk his belly eight inches but still wore triple extra-large scrubs for comfort and luck—and to remember.

"Seventy pounds and counting," he said. "I'm off the remoulade sauce for good."

Inside the operating room, Jake and Anna conferred briefly with Joe Katz about the anesthesia cocktail, a mix of desflurane and nitrous oxide, given a likelihood of a nontrivial amount of alcohol in Tom's blood. Joe administered it to Tom through an inhalation mask, as Anna prepared the surgical equipment.

"Still training for the Disney Marathon?"

"I am," Jake sighed. "But holidays are rough. Ever had tofu dressing?"

Tom cringed at the thought under his plastic sedation mask. As the effects of the anesthesia gas took hold, he recalled how he had ended up in surgery on Christmas Eve.

Gripping a fifth of Jim Beam wrapped in a brown paper bag, Tom slipped out of his rusted yellow Ford pickup and stumbled through a curtain of hanging Spanish moss to his secluded trailer near State Road 520 and the St. John's River in Cocoa, Florida.

Covered in a film of sweat and dew from the misty rain, the scruffy Florida native thought he had returned from his late-night booze run long before his old lady would get home from her shift at the Wal-Mart Supercenter. But no, there was Sarah, waiting at the top of the trailer's metal stairs, arms folded. "They let you off early?" Tom asked. He checked his wrist. Only the pale phantom of a waterproof Timex remained.

"Nope." She pointed to the bag. "That mine? *Gators bitin*?"

Tom had told Sarah he was going alligator hunting with the boys. Actually, he'd spent the evening at The Lone Gator, a swamp-side bar less than a mile away.

"Had a big one but the dirty thing ate my bang stick."

Tom stepped up onto the metal stairs. Sarah stiffly blocked the screen door. She sniffed his shirt, a mixture of sweat, liquor, and cigarettes. He pushed his way past her.

"Where'd you catch Janet?" Sarah asked, pointing to the other woman in their kitchen.

Tom squinted at Sarah, trying to think through the bourbon he consumed. Behind her, a scrawny redheaded woman came into view, awkwardly pulling down her spandex skirt, hair mussed, makeup smeared.

"Sorry, sis," the redhead said, "didn't know he was your beau." They were co-workers at Wal-Mart and she had made her way from the bar to Janet's trailer when she found out Tom was her boyfriend.

"He ain't no more," Sarah corrected.

"Look, sugar puss." Tom fumbled for an excuse. "Me and the boys just stopped off at the Gator for a ceremonial drink. That one needed a ride."

"Janet don't live near here. We work together, dummy." Sarah smirked.

Tom sifted through his wasteland of memory. "I know. That's why I offered."

"You fed me full of Fireball shots," accused Janet.

"Did not," Tom said. He didn't notice Sarah had picked up the Mossberg Model 500 20-gauge shotgun she kept stashed by the door for protection.

"Git," Sarah ordered. "Never show your face round here again."

Head swirling with alcohol and Mexican dirt weed, Tom set his bag of bourbon on the side table and gingerly stepped backwards out the front door, hands raised.

"Okay, just lower your weapon, Sarah Connor."

Tom stepped back onto the slick metal stairs and slipped, sending him boots-over-head onto the muddy ground. Sarah and Janet cackled.

"Serves you right!" they chorused.

"See what you did!" Tom seethed, covered in mud. "I *live* here for Pete's sake!"

Sarah slammed the trailer door and locked it. "Not anymore, fool."

Tom stood up and kicked the sawgrass. "Shoot!" He stomped over to the side window and heard loud mocking hoots inside. He peeked in and saw Sarah and Janet cracking open the Jim Beam he'd just bought for himself. They both gave him the middle finger salute through the window.

"You ain't disrespecting me," Tom shouted. "I pay my bills!" He stalked over to his pickup and grabbed a large red and silver hand axe from the flatbed and yanked it from its sheath.

"I'm in the doghouse? We'll see about that." He stormed back to the front door, full of impotent rage. His first swing of the axe shook the flimsy trailer door with a crack of thunder.

The women jumped like two rabbits. "He's losing it!"

Sarah grabbed her shotgun. Janet ducked under the kitchen table.

"I pay rent to stay in this dump!" Tom growled through the door, pulling the axe head free and delivering a second blow that split the door, loosening it from its hinges. Tom's bloodshot eyeball peered in through the gash, seeing Sarah pointing the shotgun right at him, hands trembling.

"You don't have the guts," he sneered.

Sarah pulled the trigger without thinking—the door exploded in aluminum dust. The kick sent her flying back into the kitchen table and over Janet, who was crouched down, fingers in her ears. Outside, Tom lay flat on his back, moaning under an old live oak. A thick stream of blood was pouring from his mangled face. Tom felt for his crotch. With his manhood intact, he opened his eyes. His face was on fire and his vision was even worse than before. He carefully felt where his left eye used to be.

"You shot my eye out!"

———•———

An hour into surgery the shotgun pellet was still embedded in Tom's left retina. Jake had to close the corneal entrance wound and remove the natural lens before the pellet could be accessed.

"Looks like a cannonball on the surface of Mars," Jake said, staring at the large monitor suspended over the surgical bed, which had the latest ALCON Ngenuity imaging system that allowed the entire OR staff to observe Jake's maneuvers in the eye. Beside Jake sat a five-foot tower that encased a state-of-the-art vitrectomy system.

"Nice work, Doctor L," Anna observed from across a side table covered with sterile instruments.

"Now comes the difficult part," Jake said softly behind his mask. He was concerned that removing the pellet could lead to extensive hemorrhaging from the choroid or retina—potentially leading to an obscured pellet, destruction of the vision cells, and a potentially very bad surgical outcome. Removal of all intraocular foreign bodies is always considered urgent since an object in the eye could introduce bacteria and lead to a devastating infection. Metallic foreign bodies can also be toxic, leading to blindness.

"Time to deliver the baby. Anna, hand me the foreign body forceps." Jake extended his open palm, never taking his eyes off the monitor.

"Reminds me of the dart you removed from that college student's eye last week," Anna said. "Slow and steady now." Anna had been working at the Space Coast Eye Institute since its inception, ten years before Jake arrived. Twenty years older than he, Anna had taken him under her wing and helped him navigate the difficult transition from residency to private practice. She also helped him manage his boss, who she had worked with for twenty years.

Jake increased the magnification on the monitor and focused directly on the shotgun pellet embedded in the retina. "Turn up the LED light to one hundred percent."

"Shine some light on the situation, shall we?" Anna made the adjustment, illuminating the retina so Jake could see the grasping claw of the device once it entered the eye.

"Steady now," Anna needlessly reminded him.

Jake worked without the faintest tremor as he positioned the instrument above the metallic foreign body. Anna watched the monitor as the claws of the forceps slowly moved to the pellet.

"Here we go," Jake said as he depressed the handle of the instrument and the grasping claws opened like an old arcade game he'd played when he was a boy. He carefully positioned it around the pellet and closed the claws. "Got it," he said calmly, lifting it from Tom's retina and slowly out of his eye.

Jake returned his gaze to the hole in the retina made by the pellet. A retinal artery was pumping blood into the eye.

Hemorrhaging. Worst-case scenario.

"Increase the intraocular pressure to sixty," Jake said sharply.

Anna, witnessing the bleeding on the monitor, already had one hand over the pressure control and the other reaching for the diathermy probe. The increased pressure slowed down the bleeding but an ooze continued to fill the eye and creep under the retina.

"Diathermy," Jake said, opening his hand to accept the instrument from Anna.

He placed the diathermy probe into the eye and positioned it over the hemorrhaging vessel. The fluid in the eye was blood tinged and cloudy. Visualization was becoming difficult. He slowly cauterized the vessel, but the leak continued. His ability to see was almost gone as the eye filled with blood.

I have one more chance to stop this bleeding.

He placed the probe over the vessel again and activated the cautery as the bloody fluid in the eye completely blocked his view.

"Anna, hand me the extrusion canula." He placed the instrument into the eye and began quickly removing the fluid and blood. As the air filled the eye Jake could observe the damaged area. The bleeding had stopped.

"Beautiful maneuver, Doctor L," Anna replied with a long exhale.

Jake let out a long breath too.

A save.

Jake finished the procedure by lasering the retina and placing a long-acting carbon tetrafluoride gas bubble in Tom's eye to keep the retina stable for the six-week healing process. He stood up and snapped off his surgical gloves. Anna removed the surgical drapes covering Tom. Jake looked down at Tom Romero—unconscious and intubated—and shook his head.

He'll be fine, he thought, *but he'll need at least two more eye surgeries, one to replace the cornea and the second to give him a new lens.*

"Who brought him in?" Jake asked Anna.

"His girlfriend, apparently," Anna replied. "The person who shot him. She's in the waiting room sitting with a deputy sheriff."

Jake gave Anna a quizzical look. "Guess that's true love these days."

2

Austin, Texas

Christmas Eve in central Texas was cool and clear. Scott and Gus, two buddies who had just finished their first stressed-out semester of medical school at the University of Texas, parked Scott's khaki Jeep off Barton Springs Road, south of downtown Austin. They lifted the mountain bikes their parents just bought them from the back of the SUV. The goal was to ride past the funky tree-lined neighborhoods on South Congress Street to Zilker Park for a night of illegal camping and drinking, while breaking in a box of Cuban Cohiba cigars Scott's girlfriend gave him for Christmas.

Rather than endure the endless verbal battles between his MAGA-hat-wearing uncles and far-left-leaning cousins back home in Coeur d'Alene, Idaho, Gus convinced his roommate Scott to spend this year's vacation unlike any other students at UT—by staying in town and camping outdoors. The state capital, known for its great restaurants, the South by Southwest film + music festival, and their city motto "Keep Austin Weird," was also home to hundreds of miles of mountain biking and hiking trails, which Scott and Gus planned to explore. Even though they both dreamt of being wealthy physicians one day, they were still just two broke students living off Top Ramen. So, to save some money, they planned to bathe in the freezing Barton Springs in the morning to "commune with nature" and take advantage of some clean water since their dorms were closed for the week.

The temperature was supposed to drop below forty-five degrees, but the bottle of Whistle Pig bourbon they brought along would keep them warm. It already had, as the pair sped through pitch-black woods, snaking along the banks of the tree-lined ravines that lined the Colorado River and heading toward their illegal campsite in the park. Scott stopped his bike at a sharp left leading to a steep downhill trail that would take them around a cluster of Volkswagen-sized boulders. Both experienced mountain bikers, they wore headlamps and easily handled the bumps by letting their front forks take the brunt of the impact. "If this is as cold as winters get now, think I'm into this global warming," said Scott, who was from Albany, New York, and was used to zero-degree Christmases.

"Definitely digging this nice weather. Back home in Idaho it's five below!" Gus huffed as he rode hard past Scott, then came to a quick stop.

"Smell that?" Gus asked.

"Yeah. Smells like a skunk, or some dead animal."

Gus cranked down on his pedals and took off down the trail.

"Slow down!" Scott pleaded.

"Just follow me, I can hear Barton Creek. We're close!"

Focusing on sounds of the creek, Gus ran over something big in the dark—*BADUNK*! Tree roots, maybe; maybe big tree roots.

"What was that?" Gus shouted, hitting the brakes, barely staying on his bike.

"You hurt?" Scott asked.

"Nah. Hit a moose or something."

"A moose? Did you hit your head?"

"No. Bring your light, I can't see." Gus shook his headlamp, hoping it would brighten up. "This headlamp is hot garbage by the way. It went dead already. Scott!"

"Coming!" Scott rode over to Gus with his TREK headlamp piercing the woods like a mini klieg light. "It could be that dead animal we've been smelling," he said, directing his headlamp to Gus's "moose." He caught a glimpse of what looked like a mannequin someone had discarded on the trail.

As Scott rode closer, he realized what it was.

"Whoa. *It's a body*," Scott said gravely.

"Not cool!" Gus said. "Stop messing with me."

"I'm not." Scott peered down with his headlamp at a woman who was facedown. Gus looked over Scott's shoulder.

"You better not be joking." Then Gus saw her. "I didn't do that!"

"Shh, calm down," Scott pleaded.

"Don't tell me to calm down. That's a freaking dead person!"

"She may just be passed out."

The woman appeared to be around their age, half-clothed and abandoned in the middle of the bike trail. Scott shined his headlamp over her
and saw blood on her clothes. She had thick shoulder-length brown hair
and was wearing burnt orange cotton shorts and a white UT T-shirt with
the fall football schedule on the back. Her left foot had only a white ankle
sock; her right foot, a sock and a white K-Swiss sneaker.

"Think she's dead, dude," Gus intoned.

"We should call the police," Scott said calmly. The odor was horrendous.
He opened his backpack and found an N-95 mask to put on.

"Deep breaths. I'm calling 9-1-1," Gus announced, then frantically
searched his backpack for his phone and mask while Scott inspected the
woman like a junior medical examiner.

"That's not hiking gear she's wearing." Scott touched her lightly on the
shoulder.

"Stop playing CSI," Gus shouted.

Scott nudged her harder. No movement. He felt for a pulse on the side
of her neck. Nothing.

"Yeah. She's cold… Looks like a student. May have been in a fight. See
the defense wounds on her hands?"

"I can't find it; did I lose it?" Gus emptied his pack, searching for his
phone.

"I'm turning her over," Scott said.

Gus and Scott looked at each other with dread after Scott slowly rolled
her onto her back. They recoiled. Her eyes were missing.

"Whoa! Animals must have gotten to her."

In the eye cavities were thousands of swarming ants.

Gus felt sick. "I can't take this, man. I'm outta here!"

"Squeamish," Scott said. "And you wanna be a trauma surgeon?" He
pointed to a trail of large brown ants that disappeared under her hair and went
into her ear. There was a second line of ants crawling away from the woman
heading toward an ant hill. They were carrying pieces of something.

Shaken, Gus stumbled over to lean against a tree but tripped over a
black tin can and fell awkwardly on his left side. It was a blackened Folgers
coffee can. He peered inside and saw two round black objects, like burnt
marbles. Gus felt burning bile creep up his throat as he realized the eyes,

missing from the woman's face, were probably inside the can. He dry heaved into his mask uncontrollably.

"Let's get out of here!" Gus wasn't joking around.

"Where? Dorm's closed," Scott stated bluntly. "Do we know her?"

Scott stared at the burned eyes, then the woman. Dazed, his mind processing what he was seeing, he picked up a branch and tried to brush the ants off her, but more emerged from under her skin and eye sockets. Suddenly, her face erupted with thousands of frenzied ants. Scott jumped back stomping his feet, trying to crush the invaders as they began to crawl toward him.

Gus's face was the color of green tea. "Stop poking her with a stick! *Oh no.*"

Gus vomited ramen all over Scott.

"Not on her!" Scott instructed, jumping back and leading Gus away from the body. Scott pulled out his iPhone and made the call.

"Nine-one-one, what's your emergency?"

3

Sarajevo, Bosnia and Herzegovina

Elena strode up a cobblestone street just after dark. It was the kind of ancient road built six centuries earlier during the Ottoman Empire that had been stained with blood ever since. The biting wind from the Dinaric Alps made her close her jacket and stay alert. She knew she was on dangerous ground crossing an Orthodox Christian neighborhood on her way to her adopted family's home. Since the cease-fire in 1995, much of the hate had been driven out of the center of Sarajevo—the city many still call Europe's "little Jerusalem"—to Republika Srpska in eastern Sarajevo, but many xenophobic enclaves remained in the hillside neighborhoods surrounding the Bosnia and Herzegovina capital. In these areas, the oldest in the city, instead of sniper alleys were found homes, cafes, and bodegas; instead of refugee camps there were "Sarajevo roses," red-stained mortar-shelled memorials the locals called "pawprints." But racism still teemed under the surface of everyday life here.

Stepping past a pawprint, Elena remembered the warning her adopted father, Abi, gave her as a little girl: "Even with your God-given disguise, tread lightly among them, my lamb."

Old Muslims like Abi saw genocidal embers flickering in every Serbian eye, but Elena hadn't survived this long in Bosnia living in fear. She passed by a familiar jewelry store, where the old shopkeeper glared hatred at her through half-closed eyes. *Almost home*, she thought.

Elena sensed somebody tailing her. She was used to attracting attention from men. Ducking around a corner, she upped her pace past a few out-of-work factory laborers smoking on their stoops. They catcalled her at every long-legged step. Elena ignored them—young Serbian men never recognized her as half-Muslim. Trained to be a chameleon by Abi, she could look and speak like a Serb when it worked to her advantage. The beauty of her features, brown hair, fair skin, and superior mind had granted her passport into almost every ethnic circle in Sarajevo. She'd also mastered five languages, which had proved essential for survival—amplified by her feline instincts.

The hair on the back of her neck stood up.

Elena slowly inched her right hand into her Louis Vuitton knockoff bag, clenching her slender fingers around the cold brass knuckles her uncle had given her. The footsteps came closer… She stopped and spun around to confront whoever was following her.

It was just two dirty-faced boys, aggressively begging for money. She shooed them away, "Povesti u šetnju." ("Take a hike," in Bosnian.) The boys jeered like the men on the stoops they were unquestionably working for—a familiar racket run on tourists.

Guess I look like an American tonight, she thought. *Must be the bag.*

No one in Florida knew that Elena had been orphaned in a refugee camp. She didn't include it on her university application to play on the hearts of the admissions department—she didn't have to with her high marks. But she still had nightmares of the bombs, the dead children, and the dirty green walls of the orphanage. It perched like a haunted house on top of a ridge at the upper edge of Logavina Street, where they put the little ones. She couldn't walk past it as an adult; it still felt so real. Many Orthodox Christians had fled to Belgrade after the war, and many Muslims had scattered to all parts of the world, particularly families whose homes were in Orthodox neighborhoods. Not Abi. Elena's adopted family still lived in the same war-damaged home. Abi and his wife, Jula (a Croatian Catholic), had simply patched over holes where mortar shells slammed into their kitchen and planted flowers to fill the others. Their refusal to leave embittered many of their Orthodox Christian neighbors. When they were younger, Abi and Jula tried small gestures of kindness, like sharing the beans, onions, and chard from their garden, which had sustained them during the war. For some of their Serb neighbors, it was an olive branch. For many others, it was a thumb of the nose.

Abi and Jula were inspirations to Elena. Mixed families were slowly being squeezed out of the hillside residential neighborhoods; blatant ethno-nationalism was on the rise again, here and around the world. Of the eight Muslim households in her extended family where Elena once played as a child, today in the hills only two remained—Abi's and her uncle Amir's. Their two homes had stood side by side for forty years. Elena turned the corner and saw the charred remains of one of those homes. The memory cut through her like a blade.

She lifted the smoke-stained collar of her coat and held her stomach tight...

Only forty-eight hours ago, Elena had turned that same corner and witnessed her family wailing on the street by Uncle Amir's house, which was swallowed by a thick black smog, its orange roof painted red by the raging red flames. Cutting through the onlookers, Elena had rushed to Abi, Amir, and their sons, who were tirelessly pouring buckets of water on the inferno that was threatening to take down both their family homes.

"Give me a bucket!" she shouted while dipping her scarf in water.

Abi wiped his brow. "We are nearly out of water. The neighbors do not help."

"Where is Mia?" Elena anxiously scanned the crowd for her six-year-old daughter.

"With Rahima, she is safe," Abi said. "We all are."

"Where are the fire trucks?"

"Jula called them." He grimaced. "We are the wrong color."

Abi went back to dousing the flames with a wooden bucket. It all felt so futile to Elena; a familiar rush of anger coursed through her. The Serbian fire trucks would not come to their aid, and the Muslim fire trucks would not dare enter a Serb neighborhood. The same thing would occur if a Christian house were on fire in a Muslim community. Still, it felt like an act of war against her family. She squinted into the smoke and wrapped the wet scarf around her mouth to breathe. She found her adopted mother pushing through the crowd.

"Mia is safe!" Jula said, out of breath. "Aunt Rahima has her."

"Mama," Elena cried out. "Who did this?"

"Look around." Jula's eyes said it all. "Take your guess." Elena turned to her younger cousin Fatima, who was standing numb on the curb with her three sisters, watching their lives burn. Elena wrapped her arms around them.

"You will be safe in our home."

"How long till they set fire to Abi's?" Fatima exclaimed.

"A poison chalice carries our water," Jula seethed. "When it comes at all."

"Get back! Let it fall!" Abi and Amir shouted as the second floor of Uncle Amir's house collapsed, the embers lighting up the December night. Watching her uncle's home crump to ash, Elena's brown eyes filled with rage—the same vengeful flickers Abi saw in the eyes of his Serbian neighbors who were watching from their windows, doing nothing. Elena stared at her Christian neighbors passing on the street in their winter coats and track pants and felt a rush of uncontrollable rage. "You have comrades on the brigade! Call them!" She glared at a young Serb man who was laughing and talking on his phone. "One of you did this!" she screamed.

Elena's phone buzzed. It was Mikal. She composed herself before answering the call in her native Bosnian, her voice wavering with emotion.

"I am outside Uncle Amir's house...*all ashes*...just like they wanted."

"They can't burn the entire city," Mikal said. "Sarajevo is Muslim now."

"Not in my neighborhood on their Christmas Eve. What am I thinking, leaving Mia here!"

"You're doing it for her, never forget," Mikal comforted her. "She's brave like her mother. Let me take your mind off it. We will celebrate your last night."

"That is the last thing I need."

"Just one drink," he insisted. "Get you back before curfew. I'm already here."

"What?" Elena squinted into the night air. "Where?" She pirouetted. Mikal showed his face ten meters away, standing beside his black BMW 750, holding a bottle of champagne like he was in a car commercial. "Sneaky boy," she replied, trying to hide her sadness. A good-looking young Bosniak, Mikal had lost his parents in the war like Elena, which had drawn her to him.

"I am full of surprises," Mikal said, walking closer. "Your uncle will have to move to a Muslim neighborhood." Elena admired his olive complexion and thick groomed eyebrows, like the actor Omar Sharif. She noticed he'd cut and dyed his raven hair into a close-cropped blond velvet, complementing his brilliant green eyes.

"Look at you. New hair. New you?"

"Something like that," Mikal said.

"I should try that... That smile though... it's quite sinister." She gave him a flirty smile.

Abi peered through his living room window at the young couple on the street. He opened the front door and called out, "My lamb!"

Always an obedient little girl, she did not reply to her father, as was customary. Abi frowned. "You go *with him* when your family's home burns and Mia awaits you?"

Guilt washed over Elena's face. She turned to face her father.

"I'll be back. Tonight. I promise."

She walked toward Mikal. Abi shook his head. *You are not safe with him, my lamb.*

4

Los Angeles, California

"So much for a silent night," muttered Sergeant Taggart, stepping out of his police cruiser wearing the Santa hat his kid made him as a dozen black-and-whites swarmed the ten thousand block of Benedict Canyon Drive.

"Nice cap, Taggart," a cop remarked. "Where's your sleigh?"

"Promised my kid I'd wear it."

The entire Beverly Hills Police Department was gathering in the exclusive neighborhood because a jogger had found a dead woman in a jasmine hedge only four streets up from the old Sharon Tate house on Cielo Drive. According to the department's database, there hadn't been many murders in Benedict Canyon since the millionaire Robert Durst shot Susan Berman on Christmas Eve in 2000. Maybe that's why Taggart noticed the neighbors weren't exactly being forthcoming this morning, mostly watching the officers invading their community from behind closed curtains and padlocked doors.

Not even the jogger who called in the tip would go on the record.

This didn't surprise a veteran like Taggart. Since the Charles Manson murders fifty years ago, folks here had lived far quieter, more guarded lives than Roman and Sharon ever did, hoping not to get murdered by some dirty hippies. Understanding the canyon's history when it came to murder, BHPD sent Mike Lu, one of their most discreet homicide detectives, to investigate. Detective Lu carefully stepped under the yellow police tape, through the jasmine vines, and rolled the body onto its back.

"Her name was Sheila Roust, aka Svetlana Roustamov," Sergeant Taggart said flatly. "Was an SC student. Russian descent. We found her student ID."

Sheila's body was found four miles from her condo in Beverly Glen canyon and even farther from Tripp Bolthouse's Christmas Eve party in Trousdale, which was the last time anyone saw her alive.

"Victim's face has been butchered," Detective Lu observed, inspecting Sheila's body and face, jotting in a small notebook.

"Yeesh. Girl's got *no eyes*," exclaimed Sergeant Taggart.

It looked like someone had burned her eyes out with a hot poker.

"I may just be a beat cop, Detective. But this ain't no suicide," Taggart said.

"Understatement of the morning," Lu said, shining a flashlight on Sheila. "Who does this to a young woman? Crazy buck wild killer? Maybe… More likely, an angry boyfriend, or husband… A lot of family crime happening today."

"This ain't no hit-and-run, either," noted Taggart.

"Correct…" Lu confirmed. "You have clearly got an amazing grasp of the situation, Sergeant."

5

Melbourne, Florida

"Make way, VIP coming through!" boomed a familiar baritone. Anna cracked open the OR door and saw their boss, Dr. Stephen Landry, pushing a wheelchair into the pre-op room conveying an orange-haired college kid with an armful of tattoos and a fishhook in his eye. An aging Ken doll with a fake tan and glowing teeth, Dr. Landry hustled him into the pre-op room past Samantha, a registered nurse, who jumped back before he ran over her foot. Jake stepped out of the OR and coolly walked toward his boss's thunderous voice.

"Jake, you're here!" Landry hooted. "This is Congressman Parker's son. He took some shrapnel on the boat. Say hi, Kip."

"Fix this!" Kip Parker shouted in agony.

"Steady, Kipper, steady," Dr. Landry instructed. "Just lie down and we'll be right with you, mm-kay?" He gently stretched Kip out on a gurney. Jake frowned; he'd hoped not to hear Dr. Landry's voice today.

"Jake's the *second*-best eye surgeon in town," boasted Landry.

Across the tiled floor, Anna Gentle wheeled Tom Romero into the post-op area. He was coming out of his anesthesia earlier than most.

"That those skanks?" Tom slurred.

"Settle down," Anna said. "We're all done. You'll live."

Anna pushed Tom's gurney past Kip's like two listing ships in the night.

"Just finished an emergency surgery," Jake explained. "Shotgun pellet."

Landry pulled Jake to the side of the hall.

"That's nice. Can you do Kip now?" His Cheshire cat grin reminded Jake of a TV game show host. "Or do I need to find a new partner?"

Jake detected traces of tequila and nachos on Landry's breath.

"Steve, will you let him finish with Mr. Romero?" Anna chimed from down the hall.

Jake nodded. "She's right. Let me wrap this up."

Landry whispered, "That swamp trash? He even have insurance? I'm talking about a *congressman's* son here."

"He's got insurance. He's also a veteran. I'll see Kip in a minute," Jake insisted and walked down the hall to join Anna and Tom.

"Good for you, Jake," Anna said. "I'll take care of him."

While Anna laid into Dr. Landry for his unprofessionalism, Jake wheeled Tom to the recovery room. "You're out of the woods, but here's the deal. You have three weeks of recovery ahead of you, in the facedown position," he advised Tom.

"Oh gawd," Tom moaned. "They'll kill me for sure."

"Doctor LaFleur?" interrupted Samantha. "His family is waiting in the recovery room."

"Whose family?" Jake asked.

"Tom Romero's, er, girlfriend and her friend are here. I think they're *stoned*."

Jake sighed. "This ought to be good."

Jake found himself back in the OR with a disgruntled Anna at his side. This time Dr. Landry hovered over his shoulder, breathing his hot stinking breath down Jake's neck. After working for Landry for five years, he was used to blocking out the six-foot-five cartoon character, but this was not how Jake envisioned his career turning out. While recruiting him, Dr. Landry was on his best behavior. Jake actually thought he would be treated like an equal—but the busier Jake's patient load became, the more erratic Landry grew. Over the past two years, Landry began lashing out verbally while micromanaging the staff, including Anna and Jake, his so-called number two. Jake was resigned to having a smiling tyrant for a boss (until the tyrant finally retired). He focused on carefully removing the fishhook from Kip Parker's eye.

"Appreciate you being my hands today, LaFleur," Landry whispered.

"I'm your hands every day," Jake uttered under his breath.

"I heard that," replied Landry, still inebriated.

Anna didn't mince words. "Well, my kids are alone on Christmas Eve, Steve. And I'm here working on another casualty from one of your booze cruises."

"I adamantly object to that characterization, your honor," Landry joked.

Anna and Jake knew Landry's checkered history better than most. His passion was no longer his work, it was schmoozing VIPs on his fifty-five-foot yacht he christened *The Eye Cruiser*. It was decked out with Italian leather couches, an imported antique oak bar, huge OED screen TVs in every room, a dance floor, and an obscenely decorated master cabin with a rotating bed. "I will confess," Dr. Landry said, "we started fishing but weren't catching anything so Amber decided to make margaritas. Next thing we knew, Kip's catching a fishhook, and our Christmas Eve was ruined."

"*Your* Christmas. How many drinks did you feed young Kip?" Anna asked.

"Kid's fine," Landry joked. "Jake will take full responsibility if he dies."

Joe Katz, the anesthesiologist, interrupted. "You said this man had *one* drink."

Jake shook his head. *How did I end up working for this blowhard?*

The Space Coast Eye Institute had started out as a small one-office, one-doctor practice until Landry joined the staff. During his first year, the founder of the practice had died of a sudden heart attack, and Landry took over. He rebranded the practice as an "Institute," and it grew exponentially under his stewardship. A gifted surgeon and medical practitioner, Landry was a superlative self-promoter, so for eighteen years, he had been known as the best retinal specialist in Melbourne. But Dr. Landry lost his fastball five years ago, yet he still believed no one was better at examining eyes than him. Self-delusion was strong with Dr. Steve Landry. Jake felt the aging dinosaur was incapable of retiring gracefully. The straw that broke the egomaniac's back was when other doctors began referring patients directly to Jake, which threatened Landry and made him even more obnoxious.

"You all hear?" Landry announced proudly. "I applied for the Mars mission."

"Aren't you a little, uh, ripe for space travel?" Jake asked.

"I'm thirty-nine," countered Landry.

"Didn't we celebrate your sixtieth last year?" Anna jabbed.

"Check this out." Landry did a quick pose from his bodybuilding days. "Edward can't turn this down."

"Sure about that?" Jake replied.

"Hey, Steve." Anna changed the subject. "Look at the slender digits on Jake."

"My hands cross-train," Jake said as he removed the fishhook with his usual precision. "The Disney Marathon is next month. Got ten more pounds to go."

"Didi will regret leaving when she sees you strutting around," Anna said warmly.

"You run marathons?" Landry erupted in laughter. Then his phone rang. "Gotta take this. Jake, I'm counting on you." Landry breezed out into the hall. "Congressman? Yeah, he's here. Kip's gonna be fine. I got my best man on it," he whispered.

Jake glanced at Anna. "Maybe his boat will sink one day, with him on it."

"Keep dreaming," Anna replied.

Jake chuckled. He suddenly felt an odd tightness in his chest that wasn't because of Dr. Landry. His heart was beating like he was already running a marathon. His hand began to tremble. He immediately removed the instruments from Kip Parker's eye and leaned back in his chair.

"Everything all right?" Anna asked, wiping Jake's sweaty brow.

"Think so... Just having some discomfort."

Jake felt short of breath. He knew it was tachycardia, and it wasn't the first time.

Was it fatigue or stress? Could be either. With no wife or kids, he had been on call all week for the trauma center. Anna watched silently for a moment, then looked worriedly at Joe Katz.

Joe walked over to Jake.

"If you need to take a break, I can keep the patient stable... Just, take five."

Jake knew he only needed a few more minutes to finish up.

"No. I'm fine, let's wrap up. Lock the door. Don't let Steve back in."

He leaned forward and his instruments reentered Kip Parker's eye.

Jake finished the procedure with no more idle chatter. He couldn't help but think about his father, who suffered his first heart attack at fifty; the senior Dr. LaFleur was also an overworked, overweight physician from Baton Rouge who loved rich food. Jake thought about all the work he'd put in to avoid having an early heart attack. Since medical school, the junior Dr. LaFleur had tried to lose his extra tonnage with dozens of diet programs—from Weight Watchers to Atkins, high protein to low protein, from no carb to the Paleo diet. They all worked initially but as soon as he lost the water weight, they fell apart; or maybe he did. He blamed the diets in his twenties but came to realize there is only person who is ultimately responsible for sending him to an early grave—himself. Jake relied on the breathing exercises he learned since he began doing yoga to steady his hand. He thought about his ex-wife, Didi, who left him for a cross-fit instructor last year. Jake recalled how his heart ached when she left him, much like the sensation he was experiencing now. They were only married for two years but they dated during most of his four-year ophthalmology residency. When they met, Didi was overweight like him. Friends called them Mike & Molly behind their backs (from some TV show Jake never watched). The wisecracks still hurt just the same. Then two years into Jake's residency, Didi suddenly started shedding weight, doing Pilates, running, yoga. She became extremely fit, while the hours Jake worked made it impossible for him to keep up. The more she lost, the more Jake gained.

Then a week before Jake's thirty-fourth birthday, while he was repairing a routine retinal detachment, one of his operating staff made a minor mistake, which snowballed into a major complication. The circulating nurse tripped over the electrical plug of the vitrectomy machine, causing it to shut down, so what should have been a forty-five-minute surgical case turned into a frantic two-hour debacle. That incident set off Jake's first mid-surgery bout of chest pain, a false alarm.

He relied on that memory to power through his work on Kip. But he couldn't help but psychoanalyze himself: Maybe this episode was simply residual heartache? Maybe he was still grieving over Didi, and it wasn't anything? He'd have it checked out afterwards, but he wasn't going to quit on a patient in the middle of surgery unless he dropped dead. So far, so good.

6

Sarajevo, B&H

Mikal's idea of a celebration left Elena cold. She was in no mood to spend her last night in Sarajevo partying with her boyfriend's crew, but here she was. The pulsating music in the hip downtown spot called "The Club," hidden in the basement of Titova 7, a former government building in Titova Square, was too loud for her ears. Elena interned at an aeronautics company in America so she knew what a rocket engine sounded like. *This garbage is more head splitting*, she thought. Unlike most young people in Eastern Europe, Elena couldn't stand nightclubs with their smoke machines, laser light shows, and large crowds. The chaotic energy triggered her PTSD and memories of war and suffering. But she let Mikal have his night. She was grateful for all he'd done for her and Mia. Elena smelled the collar of her winter coat; the putrid smoke from the house fire still followed her as Mikal pushed her through the large space packed with dancing Bosnians (mostly Serbs and Croatians) high on vodka, Red Bull, and synthetic party drugs.

Mikal found the back of the club and led her up a set of stairs to a VIP room that overlooked the dance floor where the DJ was spinning.

Mikal sniffed Elena's coat. "That a new scent you're wearing?"

She cracked a courtesy smile. "Nemoj biti šupak." ("Don't be rude" in Bosnian.)

"You can speak English with me," Mikal said. "You're practically an American now." Inside the VIP room, he had bottle service set up on a white leather sectional sofa. Two of his friends, whom she'd never met, were already drinking with two beautiful girls who couldn't be more than eighteen years old. She thought Mikal's friends were dubious, dressed in black with closely cropped heads; they appeared to be Bosniak, like Mikal. The girls were of uncertain heritage, Russian maybe. Elena frowned.

"Nice prom dates your friends have. Take me home."

"What home?" one of Mikal's friends replied in Serbian. "The home that burned?"

"Screw you," she shouted over the music. "Who is this idiot?" she asked Mikal, gesturing with her chin at the unknown guy.

"Don't listen to him," Mikal said. "Dani has a sick sense of humor. Look, just stay for one drink... One? For, how they say, old times' sake. Who knows when we will meet again?"

"Don't say that, stupid." Elena softened. Mikal took her coat and handed it to the bottle service girl, then softly embraced Elena. Over her shoulder, Mikal stared at his seated friends; his smile morphed into a sneer. Elena reluctantly sat down and took a drink of water to calm her nerves. She nervously glanced at the time on her phone.

"I want time to say good night to Mia."

"It's early still. You'll see her. First, drink. I will not take 'no' for an answer." Mikal smiled. "It's Dom. Your favorite." Elena took a champagne flute and dutifully clinked glasses with Mikal and his friends while he made a long-winded toast that she couldn't hear over the music even if she cared. She downed her champagne and thought of her family wailing in the street, and the bastards who set the fire who were going to get away with it.

"The timeless quality about Sarajevo I selfishly find so charming"—Mikal was finishing his speech—"is actually the mark of a failed economy. Lucky Elena here has found her way out."

The table of men gave off droll chuckles.

Elena sized them up, head tilted. "You all look and talk alike," she observed as she poured herself another glass of Dom and took a sip.

Mikal stopped chuckling.

Elena was amusing herself. She liked to stir things up when she was in a vengeful mood. She thought her comment made the men feel dismissed, or like flunkeys, which was her intent. Mikal's friends shifted uncomfortably in their plush seats and took sips of Beluga vodka like they were being secretive. A few moments later, an athletic young Serb with long wavy hair turned around to regard Elena, the beautiful woman sitting back-to-back with him. Half-drunk, he said in a cool whisper, "You. Gorgeous. What you are doing with these Bosniak losers?"

Mikal spat back a Serbian insult. "Jebi seronja."

The tall Serb stood up slowly, casting an intimidating shadow. Mikal's grey eyes turned as black as a shark's. He stood up, wearing the defiant look that came from his time as a teenage soldier in the Bosnian army, a look that terrified Elena.

"Can't you see?" the Serbian smirked. "She doesn't want to be with you." Mikal did not move.

The Serbian spit at him. When that got no reaction, he threw a lumbering right hook. Mikal gracefully evaded the punch like a matador, throwing the hulking Serb off-balance. He delivered a forceful open-palmed blow to the Serb's solar plexus, which doubled him over and left him gasping for air. He calmly grabbed the Serb by the shoulders and sent him flying backwards with a powerful knee to the face. Elena couldn't watch. When she opened her eyes, Mikal was standing over the bloody Serb with his fist raised. One of the man's female friends came to his aid. "It's over! Leave him alone!" she shouted in Serbian.

Elena grabbed Mikal's cocked elbow. "Enough!"

Mikal's face softened. He lowered his clenched fist.

Elena scanned the crowd, stunned to see no bouncers; none of the Serb men in the room moved to help one of their countrymen bleeding on the floor at the hands of a Bosniak.

Elena grabbed her bag. "Too much testosterone. I'm out."

Mikal's friends laughed like they were watching a pay-per-view sport, still sitting with their arms calmly draped around their young dates. "Let's go," Mikal said blankly to Elena. He curtly waved to his friends, threw some Euros at the bottle service girl, and grabbed Elena by the arm, pulling her out of the VIP room, down through the crowded dance floor.

He stopped near the bar. "Wait here," he said over the music. "I'll get us water."

She watched Mikal closely. He cut through the swell of people and spoke with the bartender like they were good friends—as if beating the daylights out of another human was an everyday event for him. The bartender handed him two bottles of water and they shook hands. Without paying for them, Mikal returned to Elena. He took a long swig from one bottle and twisted the cap off the other, handing it to her.

"You'll be dehydrated for your flight. Drink," he instructed.

Elena knew that some girls in Sarajevo might like a violent, overprotective man, but she was done with him; she'd already seen too much of it in her life. "What *was* that back there?" she asked, grabbing the water bottle and taking a long drink.

"What? He was rude to you." Mikal shrugged, his jovial nature long gone.

"Macho man. You could've killed him."

"He still breathes. He spit at me, and our people. He deserved what he got."

"Whatever. Take me home."

"I'll get the car," Mikal said. "Meet me out front."

Mikal left her and made his way up the stairs to the exit.

Outside, Mikal pulled up to the front of Titova 7 in his BMW. Elena got in the passenger seat. She had seen his shark eyes before. *No point getting into a heavy breakup conversation that could get ugly—it isn't worth it*, she thought. *I will be in America tomorrow and that will be that.*

"Mia may be asleep now," Elena said. "I still have packing to do."

Mikal glanced at her water. "Drink or you'll be hungover for your flight."

As they drove through the dark historic Sarajevo streets, she finished the bottle, thinking of a way to say goodbye without getting into a long, dragged-out conversation. Suddenly, she felt dizzy. nauseous. Her mouth tasted salty.

"I don't feel so good, Mikal. Pull over."

"Champagne dreams," Mikal said in a monotone voice. "Nearly home."

"Think I may be sick." Elena put down her window and let the cold wind hit her face, hoping it would sober her up. For a moment, she thought the dizziness had passed, but then it grew worse. Her vision blurred and began to spin. Confused, she looked at Mikal, who was driving with a strange look on his face. She tried to ask him what was happening, but no words came out. Elena reached for the handle of the passenger door but could barely raise her hand.

She heard Mikal say in a distant voice, "Dom and you don't mix. Close your eyes and sleep it off." Elena wanted to escape, but she had no strength. Focusing on taking deep breaths, she let her head fall back on the leather headrest.

Elena closed her eyes, feeling the night air from the Alps wash over her. She slipped into darkness listening to the hum of the wheels on the road.

Melbourne, Florida

Christmas Eve came and went before Jake, Dr. Landry, Joe Katz, and Kip Parker wearily exited the glass doors of the trauma center. Day was beginning to break across the Florida sky. No one said a word, not even "Merry Christmas." Jake had mercifully sent Anna home hours ago to be with her kids. "Need a fat blunt," Kip said, rubbing his bandaged eye. "Feel me some glaucoma coming on."

"Lay off the weed, Kip," Jake advised. "And don't mix alcohol with the prescribed medicine."

"Yeah, uh, sure thing, Doctor J," Kip said. "Happy Hanukkah or whatever."

"Thanks. But I'm not Jewish," Jake replied.

Jake turned toward his car. Out of his peripheral vision, he noticed a slow-moving figure in a garish floral Tommy Bahama shirt lurking behind a parked Mazda. He narrowed his brown eyes. It was a salty-looking man who—when spotted—shouted, "You will atone!" in their general direction. Jake gave Kip a perplexed look.

"That geezer ain't talking to my ass," Kip said, pulling out his cell phone.

The wind-scorched man approached them. He looked drunk.

"Can I help you?" Jake asked.

"One of you can," said the salty dog, wiping his mouth.

"Red?" Dr. Landry asked.

Red DeRanger was the freckled fishing guide Landry had hired for his booze cruise on Christmas Eve. "We paid you. What do you want?"

"You tried to pork my wife on your yacht!" Red seethed.

"Pork? C'mon. Getting high on your own supply, Red? Amber and I were just dirty dancing with your wife. And so forth. Havin' some fun."

"You lie!" Red lunged at Landry with a rusty filleting knife. Landry turned away to protect his face; Red's thin filleting blade barely missed his neck.

Landry dove for cover. "I never touched her!"

Red thrust his knife at Landry again. Out of nowhere, a wall of human flesh blocked his path. Jake administered a rabbit punch to Red's larynx, causing Red to drop the knife. He then put Red in a choke hold. The fisherman let out a gurgle, grabbing at Jake's thick arm.

"Drop the knife, Red," Jake said in his soothing professional doctor voice.

The filleting knife clattered harmlessly on the pavement. Jake released Red, who dropped like a sack of rotten fish guts. Cowering behind a car, Dr. Landry cautiously poked his head up like he was in a foxhole. "Well, that sobered me up."

Joe Katz looked at Jake, then down at Red; he couldn't believe his eyes.

"You a karate man, doc?" Kip exclaimed, doing a karate pose.

Checking Red's vitals, Jake said, "I started Mayweather boxing workouts last month."

"Word! Word!" Kip threw back his head and howled at the image as a black Mitsubishi pulled into the parking lot to pick him up.

"Nice reflexes, LaFleur," Katz said, exhausted, and kept walking to his car.

Landry jogged over to Jake and held up a high five. "Didn't realize you fat boys could move that fast!" Jake looked at Landry's lingering hand for a few seconds, then gave it a little pat, just to get him to stop. "That's my partner!" Landry exclaimed.

"I'll gut you both," Red rasped in pain from the pavement.

"Shut up!" Landry kicked the knife away. "I should call the police on you, Red! Or have Jake drop you off the causeway into the Indian River."

Red wheezed, holding his throat.

"Should we take him in the hospital?" Jake asked. "Can't just leave him here." Landry draped his arm around Jake and led them to their cars, stepping over Red.

"Oh, yes, we can. Forget it, Jake... *It's Florida.*"

As soon as Jake heard Landry butcher the last line from the movie *Chinatown*, he stopped walking. His heart still racing, he felt his chest tighten again.

"You all right, buddy?" Dr. Landry asked.

Grabbing his chest, Jake dropped to one knee a few feet away from Red. "Can't catch my breath."

The two injured men remained on the pavement for a few minutes while Dr. Landry checked their vitals. Soon, Jake's chest tightness resolved and his heart rate returned to normal. Red's breathing remained shallow and wheezy.

"Come inside with me, Jake," Landry said. "I want to check your heart rate."

Jake protested, but Landry wouldn't take "no" for an answer.

"Can I come inside, too?" Red croaked.

Dr. Landry led Jake and Red into the ER and ordered them both to lie down on two unoccupied beds. The nurse helped Landry hook Jake up to an EKG machine. The results showed mild changes in his ST segment, perhaps signifying a myocardial infarction. Dr. Landry called the front desk to alert them he was checking Jake in for observation.

Red DeRanger was released with a bruised larynx.

Jake spent the next twenty-four hours in the Holmes hospital being tested for various cardiac anomalies. As he lay in a hospital bed waiting for a cardio-stress test, he kept thinking about his father and his recent divorce: *Did Didi cause this? Do I need to see a therapist?* He picked up a *Sports Illustrated* and thumbed through it. His eye caught an ad for the Disney Marathon he was training for—he gazed at all the toned bodies in the ad, then studied his own reflection in a framed mirror on the opposite wall. Jake didn't see an athlete looking back at him; he saw an overweight, overworked man in a hospital gown. He felt mortal. Angry. Alone.

But in the wake of playing hero in the parking lot, Jake felt a surge of defiance. He didn't want to die early like his dad. He wanted to fight. He wanted to live. He made a pact with himself—*If I drop dead at the finish line, so be it. But I swear I'm running that Mouse Marathon. Or I'll die trying.*

8

Austin, Texas

aw enforcement in Austin were baffled by their gruesome discovery. By 7:24 a.m. on Christmas morning every creature was stirring in Zilker Park. Gus and Scott were long gone, replaced by a slew of cowboy-hat-wearing investigators with buzz cuts from across regional jurisdictions including the Texas State Troopers, the Austin Police Department, Zilker Park Rangers, UT Campus Police—and Jim Bullock, the Travis County coroner, who looked to be in charge of the crime scene.

Or maybe Jim just cared more.

Bullock knew most of the other officers assumed the body was the work of some crazed junkie and wanted to be home opening presents with their families. But not Bullock. He was driven to solve every homicide in Travis County and had been for twenty-five years. It was his job, and since Austin had been a relatively peaceful place to live throughout his career, each homicide he encountered felt like a perverse puzzle for him to personally solve. Bullock would never admit it, but this type of grisly murder was the kind of novelty that got coroners book deals, particularly when a beautiful UT grad student with no eyes gets murdered and dumped In Zilker Park.

"Reckon she died from a fractured skull, approximately forty-eight hours ago," Bullock said. "Clear homicide if I ever saw one."

"And on the Lord's Day, too," muttered a fresh-faced officer. "Oh, the humanity."

"Nope. Approximately *forty-eight* hours, two days ago," Bullock repeated bluntly.

"Right," the rookie cop said, looking at his watch. "I'll put that in the report."

"You do that," Bullock commented.

Behind Jim, a swarm of officers buzzed around the victim's body, still lying where Scott and Gus had found her in the bloody T-shirt, shorts, socks, and one sneaker. Bullock took notes while instructing the crime scene photographer to shoot specific evidence.

"Woman's eyes have been removed," Bullock observed, pointing with his ballpoint. "The coffee can over there has two charred objects that may be them."

"Who would do something like this?" the junior officer asked.

"It's a sick world," Jim said.

Behind him, the lead detective, John Davis, from the Austin Police Department, put down his walkie-talkie. "Jim. Get this. The Beverly Hills Police Department is looking for a perp with the same MO… Say they got a fresh body on the ground that matches our young woman. No eyes. They're sending us a report."

"Don't say." Jim gazed over at the body. "We may have found ourselves an early serial killer."

Bullock was old enough to remember that one of the deadliest mass murders in U.S. history happened here when he was a boy. He should, since he drove past the University of Texas Clock Tower every day on his way to work at the Travis County Coroner's Office. That's where, in 1972, an architectural engineering major named Charles Wittman climbed to the top with his marine sniper rifle and started picking off his fellow students like frogs in a pond. To Jim, the tower was a 307-foot-tall symbol of what horrors a single deranged man can unleash on a peaceful town. Every day at noon, the tower still played "The Eyes of Texas Are Upon You," by a carillon of fifty-six bells ending with twelve strikes.

Bullock couldn't help but notice those same bells faintly rang out just as his work was interrupted by two agents from the Federal Bureau of Investigation, who were already poking around Zilker Park and collecting evidence. It had been almost sixty years since "The Tower Sniper" shook the nation, so Bullock and the local police were not used to seeing Feds in their business. Pridefully, they felt like they were being bossed around their own crime scene by two female agents "like they owned the place." Considering that the FBI had jurisdiction over interstate crimes, they did. But FBI Agents Jane Rizzo and Tami Thorn weren't there to win any popularity contests or prove themselves to any of the local shields. They were there to catch a killer, full stop.

"Was cozy in bed a few hours ago," grumbled Thorn, in a crouch, examining the dead woman.

"Deal with it. When you got no kids, no hubs, you get the call," retorted Rizzo.

Jane Rizzo, a twenty-year veteran of the FBI, could deal with most anything, even in a war zone. A former army sergeant who won a Bronze Star in Mogadishu in 1993, Rizzo had a pair of brass ones that were as big as any of the local police eating pastries in the park. Brave, blunt, ballsy, and mostly by the book, Rizzo looked like the older Italian cousin of her hero, gold-medal-winning soccer star Megan Rapinoe. Rizzo loved to psych out opponents by telling them how (being a former star athlete herself) she was a dead shot just like Rapinoe, but with her feet, hands, and a Glock nine-millimeter pistol. Rizzo's pat line: "I'm a crack shot, three times over. Beat that."

Few in the FBI could.

Jane's partner, Agent Tami Thorn, wasn't into petty competitions; she resided high above that realm. An erudite African American from Queens, New York, with a double PhD in computer science and linguistics, she had survived and succeeded by outworking and outsmarting people her entire life. Pegged as a brainiac code breaker and cybercrime specialist when the FBI recruited her, the Bureau had recently paired her with Rizzo, their resident female action hero, to help get her investigative feet wet—a hole in her otherwise sterling resume.

To date, Tami had shined in the classroom but had yet to have a collar she could claim or fire her gun in the line of duty. Her bosses were betting that sharpshooter Rizzo would break her in. The FBI notoriously did not develop their female agents; Rizzo and Thorn knew it and were determined to beat the odds. They had both been top of their class at Quantico, albeit fifteen years apart. Both were sharp as tacks and never sick at sea.

Yet despite their many talents, they had been passed over for promotions in the years since their auspicious starts. Rizzo had been waiting for her big break for almost twenty years.

"I'm dealing fine. How are you?" Thorn volleyed, sensing her partner's irritability.

"Just tired," Rizzo said, checking her messages. "Listen up. UT Campus police confirms, victim's name was one Uma Gloten. Twenty-one years of age. Unmarried." Rizzo scanned her bio: "Grad student, majoring in aerospace. High marks…"

"Interesting. Miss Gloten was also interning at SpaceX's rocket testing facility near Waco. Says she wanted to be an astronaut. Big brain on this one," Thorn said. "That's Edward Menard's company. He's an eccentric."

"All billionaires are, I hear," Rizzo said dryly.

"Menard owns Tesla," Thorn added.

"Then the world, right?" Rizzo joked.

"Mm-hmm. Baby momma's that Grimes chick, too," Thorn said. "They both gonna live on Mars. Leave this ol' world behind."

"What is a Grimes?" Rizzo shot Thorn a look while inspecting the contents of the burned-out coffee can.

"Pop star. Shaves her eyes when she's depressed."

"We got some crispy eyeballs in here," Rizzo said. "Hold up. Austin to Waco? That's one long commute."

"Hundred miles north on I-35, about three hours round-trip," Thorn confirmed.

"Must be one important internship," Rizzo replied.

"Meh. Got an aunt who commutes that far," Thorn said while peeling off crime scene gloves. "Travis County coroner nailed the time of death though. Miss Gloten died approximately fifty-two hours ago. And you chewed that poor man out 'cause he wasn't being cooperative."

"Who, warm and fuzzy me?"

"Also, appears Miss Gloten was not a U.S. citizen. She's here on a student visa the past eighteen months."

"Curious if she traveled anywhere in the past year."

"On it," Thorn replied.

"Got a feeling about this one," Rizzo said.

"You want your Cielo Drive so bad." Thorn knew all about Rizzo's ambitious streak.

"The other dead woman was found just a few blocks from the Tate house, right?" Rizzo replied. "If you gotta work Christmas, let's at least make it interesting."

9

Sarajevo, B&H

Elena sat up disoriented in her queen-sized bed. *What just happened?* Her foggy mind raced to catch up. She looked over at the Little Mermaid alarm clock with brass bells that Abi and Jula had given her for her ninth birthday. It was 8:30 a.m.

Her flight was in three hours. She was next to her sleeping six-year-old daughter, Mia, with her familiar curly dark brown mop of hair. Elena had no memory of how she got here.

Did he bring me up here? Did he wake Mia? Did Abi see him?

She had never gotten blackout drunk in a nightclub before. Mikal had also never entered her home during their intense but on-and-off yearlong relationship—she'd always stayed downtown at his flat. Confused, Elena gently kissed her daughter on the forehead and quietly made her way to her family's shared bathroom on the second floor.

She was still wearing her outfit from last night, but nothing else in the house seemed out of the ordinary. She heard her mother, Jula, making breakfast downstairs for her cousins as she inspected herself in the mirror. She had large black circles under her eyes as a result of not removing her makeup before bed. She checked her body for injuries and saw no cuts, bruises, or scratches, but her head was on fire, as were her bloodshot eyes. She remembered drinking only two glasses of champagne last night, and then water from Mikal, and then…*nothing*.

It was an unfamiliar, disturbing feeling for a woman who prided herself on being always in control.

She heard the words her father had pronounced many times and even repeated last night—*be suspicious of Mikal*. Like many young Muslim men she knew who had survived the Bosnian war, Mikal was a very private person who was distrustful of strangers. He wasn't comfortable around family environments since he never had one himself—and that always bothered her. They had even quarreled about it on several occasions. Mikal had once confessed that he did not know how to act around happy families but wished to have a family of his own one day.

Somehow she never believed that was true.

Because of his aloof demeanor, Abi was certain the young man was hiding something. Elena had found it odd that Mikal had no digital Internet trail, and no one in the city seemed to know how he earned his money, which seemed abundant whenever he needed it. Abi had even heard rumors that Mikal had a "militant side," whatever that cryptic comment meant.

Elena had given up trying to get Mikal to open up and assumed his remoteness was simply a result of growing up in a refugee camp. So, as charming and sexy as he could be when he was in the right mood, he was ultimately an unsolvable puzzle who was prone to violent outbursts, and Elena distrusted and disliked that type of person. Maybe because she had been a lot like him before Mia was born.

She stared at her reflection... The jarring memory of Mikal beating the Serbian man in the club resurfaced as she brushed her teeth and washed her face and took four aspirin tablets. She was disappointed in herself. "Glupa" ("clod" in Bosnian), she accused to her reflection.

She thought about her trip. Elena's conscience was torn over leaving her daughter in a home that was nearly set ablaze two nights before. She'd already been away from Mia for much of the year studying for her graduate degree in Florida and had regretted missing her sixth birthday in November. *Does she understand why Mommy's leaving?* she wondered. *Could she at her age?* She feared Mia would grow up to resent her if her plans to bring her to America after she graduated and got a green card failed, so she was determined to make it work, at whatever cost, to assure herself and Mia lasting security and acceptance.

She listened to her cousins talking downstairs. *Will this house that withstood mortar fire during the war be standing when I return?* She heard her mother moving about the kitchen cooking and looked at her phone, running through her to-do list. She didn't have time to feel guilty or analyze what Mikal might have been up to last night. She had to finish packing.

She had to be strong for Mia.

A single mother, she felt she had no choice but to get her education and not rely on any man but Abi to help raise her daughter. Mia's birth father, a charming Italian whom she met while studying for her undergraduate degree at the University of Sarajevo, had returned to Italy six weeks after she gave birth and had refused to play any role in her daughter's life. She felt Mia was already showing signs of anxiety, sucking her thumb and not letting Elena out of her sight when she was home. *Poor sweet thing*, she thought. Elena had spent the past two weeks assuring Mia that she would be back for her once she got her education, and they would both leave Sarajevo to live in America. One day. One day.

"Mommy?" she heard her daughter call out. "Can we have cherry crepes for breakfast?" Mia was half-asleep, tugging on her arm. *The most beautiful girl in the world*, she thought. They shared the same hazel brown eyes with matching yellow-flecked irises.

Her eyes welled as she picked Mia up and kissed her. When Mia was a baby, Elena had read that when you have a child, you give part of your soul to them.

Elena felt that deeply in this moment.

"Mmmm, fruit crepes with sweet cream. Let's see what Baka is cooking."

———●———

At 10:00 a.m., every member of Elena's extended family was congregated outside her home to see her off. The elders of the family stood next to the rubble of Amir's burned home and did their best to ignore the painful memory that still smoldered, even as Abi and Amir saw their Serb neighbors watching them from behind closed curtains. Abi and Jula did not want Mia to feel abandoned, and they encouraged the little girl to see Elena's departure as positive.

"Mother is going on an adventure," Jula said to Mia. "How exciting!" Jula turned to Elena, who was wearing her stoic refugee face to hide her pain. "Be careful, my darling. I read that Florida is full of crazies." Elena knew that the "land of the free" could be a hostile place to people who looked like them, but she would never worry her family. She brushed it off.

"It is nothing. I can handle their kind of crazy."

Abi gave his daughter a long embrace.

Jula could see he beamed with pride. Elena was on her way to becoming the first girl in their family to earn a graduate degree, which was an achievement Abi, who came from a farming family, could never dream of a few years ago when he was a young man.

"You have the heart of a lion, my lamb," Abi said. "Make us all proud."

"I will, Papa." She hugged Abi tightly. She did not want to let him go. She feared she might never see him again as she wiped away her tears. She turned to Mia.

"Bring me back something from Disney World?" Mia asked.

"I shall," Elena said. "One day soon I will bring you to see Jasmine herself."

"But I want to meet the Little Mermaid," Mia said.

"Ariel lives there, too! Mama must finish her education first. I will be back for you."

Tears streamed from both of their eyes. Elena composed herself. "What are we?"

"Strong like lions." Mia gave her mom a resolute face and a tender smile.

"That's right. You mind Baka and Djedi, you hear me?"

Mia nodded, her upper lip quivering.

Just then, a black BMW pulled up.

Abi frowned and leaned into Amir. "That's the one that dropped her off last night."

Mikal stepped out of the car in a stylish black suit and waved politely to her family.

They did not wave back.

Not wanting to make a scene, Elena pretended that she knew Mikal was coming. "You can cancel the taxi, Papa," Elena said to Abi. "I forgot he was taking me." She hugged her parents and all of her relatives and Mia one final time.

"I love you, Mama," Mia said tearfully.

"I love you too, baby." Eyes glistening, she grabbed Mia for one last hug.

Abi and Amir loaded her bags into Mikal's car.

"Watch out for him," Jula said. "The state he brought you home in…" She trailed off.

"We're finished after last night," Elena replied under her breath.

She got in the car and looked back at the life she was leaving behind. Elena held back tears as they drove away. Once they were out of sight, Elena looked at Mikal with cold eyes.

"What are you doing here?"

"What kind of boyfriend doesn't drive his girl to the airport?"

"I am not your girl."

"Elena. I'm *hurt*," Mikal said, feigning offense. "What troubles you so?"

"Um, how about I don't remember how last night ended? … Not sure I want to know."

"You should have eaten. I warned you. After you threw up on the side of the road, I brought you home and Jula helped you inside and up to bed."

"That's it?" she asked.

"You don't trust me?" Mikal asked her without taking his eyes off the road.

"Not particularly. I didn't think I had that much to drink." Elena said, leaning her head back on the leather headrest and rolling down the window. The wind felt good on her face. "So why do my eyes and head feel like they were hit with a hammer?"

"Alcohol," Mikal said coldly. "It's the poison of the West."

"That you forced on me," Elena shot back.

For the rest of the drive to Sarajevo International Airport, Mikal and Elena bickered like lovers who knew their days were coming to an end. She sensed something shady had happened last night but Mikal did his best to convince her that she was imagining it. When they arrived at the airport, Elena stopped arguing.

"No more words, okay?" she said, collecting her purse.

"Elena, my love. Don't go away mad," Mikal said coolly as he got out, popped the boot of the car, and handed her bags to the sky cab at the curb. He seemed completely unaffected by her anger as he leaned in for a goodbye kiss.

Elena let him peck her on the cheek.

"I am going to miss my flight," she said curtly and pulled away.

Mikal watched Elena quickly make her way into the airport.

He picked up his phone and dialed.

"The messenger is on the way… Pick her up."

(10)

Los Angeles, California

FBI Agent Tami Thorn stood smoking under a canopy of Benedict Canyon trees less than a mile from the old Tate-Polanski house. She blew a thick plume of smoke from her e-cigarette that obscured the remaining Beverly Hills Police Department officers still at the murder site. Thorn looked up from her phone and saw all eyes on her.

"Smoking is prohibited at a crime scene, ma'am," said Sergeant Taggart.

Thorn knew the rules but blew another plume anyway.

"I'm vaping. It's been a long day."

Agent Jane Rizzo made her way through the crime scene after conferring with Detective Mike Lu and two members of the FBI's Los Angeles division. Only police tape remained where Sheila Roust's body was found twelve hours ago.

Rizzo wore a knowing smile.

"What are you so jacked about?" Thorn asked.

"My hunch is verified. We got a serial killer with an eye fetish."

"You get off on this, huh?" Thorn asked.

"Most field agents do." Rizzo shot her former desk jockey partner a contemptuous glare.

"What do you think he does with the eyes?" Thorn asked.

"Why so certain our perp is a man?" Rizzo shot back, even though she knew most serial murderers were male.

"'Cause other than Aileen Wuornos, serial killers are predominately—"

"Old news," Rizzo said. "Any DNA results yet?"

"Working on it. Found this: Uma Gloten, plus this victim here—Svetlana Ileana Roustamov aka Sheila Roust, twenty-eight, also unmarried—were both young, attractive, Russian exchange students in the U.S. on temp visas: Gloten at UT/Austin, and Sheila here at the University of Southern California."

"Beauty and brains on both of them," Rizzo said.

"The house Sheila partied at last night is also nearby. In the Trousdale Estates."

"La-de-dah," Rizzo chirped. "Definitely want to pay that home a visit."

Rizzo and Thorn turned off Mulholland Drive and drove down a winding palm tree–lined street to the Trousdale Estates. The morning LA smog was beginning to lift over the Bolthouse estate as they pulled up to the gate. Rizzo didn't wait for Tripp's hungover guard lounging behind the twelve-foot hedges and electric security gates to invite them in. She preferred the element of surprise to keep suspects off-balance, so she found an opening in a side gate and decided to waltz right in. "You ever do anything by the book?" Thorn commented.

"Depends on the book." Rizzo grinned, ducking under the gate.

They walked unchallenged up to the front door of the famous John Lautner home. Rather than ring the bell, Rizzo started calling out for Tripp to show his face. "Hey, Mr. Bolthouse? It's the ghost of Christmas past!"

FBI guidelines did not approve her tactics, but Rizzo felt her badge was all the invitation she needed to poke around in places she wasn't wanted.

"Nice joint." Rizzo observed the impressive wall of polarized paned windows on the front of the house, which reflected a shade of blue. "Lots of glass."

"Believe this is what they call mid-century modern," Thorn remarked.

Rizzo and Thorn were met at the door by Darcy, Tripp's personal assistant, who wore a short navy skirt, black open-toed wedges, and a white silk blouse.

"Hellooo? Excuse me? You can't be in here, ladies; party's over," said Darcy with a subtle Australian accent. Rizzo thought her straight blonde hair cut to the shoulders and pearl white complexion appeared to put together for the morning after.

"Lovely home—Federal Bureau of Investigation," Rizzo announced, flashing her badge. "Looking for a Tripp Emmanuel Bolthouse. I'm Agent Rizzo; that is Agent Thorn."

"Morning," Thorn replied, eyes glued to her phone.

Darcy's perky expression faded. "Wow, Feds. Okay."

"We're investigating the murder of a woman who was at your boss's party last night. He conscious?"

Rizzo and Thorn were ushered through the house and into the back acreage of the estate, littered with hungover partiers lounging in yurts. Born and raised in New York, Thorn had never seen such a majestic view of Los Angeles, reaching from downtown close to the Pacific Ocean.

"So. This is how the other half lives," she said, half impressed.

Darcy led them to the man himself, sitting in a Jacuzzi high atop the city.

"Mr. Bolthouse, you have unexpected company." Darcy whispered something in his heavily pierced ear. Tripp raised an eyebrow in bemusement.

"FBI," Rizzo announced. "We're investigating the death of a Svetlana Roustamov. She was at your party last night with her boyfriend, Xander Lopez. Got a minute?"

Tripp used a remote control to turn off the Jacuzzi jets. The bubbles quickly dissipated, revealing that Tripp wasn't wearing a bathing suit. "Svetlana? You mean Sheila. Superhot Russian? Loves techno?"

"Miss Sheila Roust, yes. She was murdered after leaving your party. When was the last time you saw her?"

Tripp stood up, proudly displaying his nakedness. Rizzo didn't blink; she had been in locker rooms throughout her athletic career.

"Tragic news. Tragic," Tripp said. "Thoughts and prayers. Dead as in dead?"

"There's just one kind," Rizzo replied. "Answer the question."

"Brutal. Sheila left last night all fired up, before I even played her jam." He walked behind the pool bar and poured himself a mimosa. Rizzo shot Thorn a glance, clearly underwhelmed by this guy's masculinity.

"Was she quarreling with anyone? Was Xander Lopez involved?" Rizzo continued.

"He's always *involved*. But Xander's my boy. He was hitting up some other hos at the party. Excuse me, some other ladies, and Sheila lit out. The jealous type."

"You ever witness Mr. Lopez strike Miss Roust?" Thorn interjected.

"Never." Tripp shook his head.

"Strike anyone?" Thorn pushed.

"Off the field? Can't recall."

"He some kind of professional athlete?" Thorn asked.

"Plays for USC. They don't pay him, but there's ways around that. He works for me part-time; that last comment's way off the record, by the way."

"If you and Mr. Lopez are violating NCAA rules, that's your business," Rizzo said. "We're looking for a serial killer."

"I make it a point never to include serial killers on my guest list. Except the ones who get away with it, right?" He winked.

Rizzo looked up from her notepad like she was about to lose it on this scumbag. She tightened her fist and cracked her neck. Tripp backed down.

"Bad joke. Don't write that down. Look, X-Man didn't kill Sheila. He was here all night. But you should know," Tripp went on, "dude hates cops. If you come at him with pieces drawn? Bring Kevlar. He's got 'roid rage mixed with real pyschopathic rage."

Rizzo nodded to Thorn; it was time to leave.

On the way out, she spotted Tripp's discarded thong bathing suit on the bar.

"Funny," Rizzo said, picking it up with her pen like it was a piece of evidence. "I just feel ordinary rage." She draped it on top of his mimosa.

11

Melbourne, Florida

"You took him out with your thumb? Who are you, *John Wick*?" Dr. Ben Silverman exclaimed in his dry Brooklyn accent.

"Learned it at Mayweather Boxing," Jake said quietly. "No big deal."

He and Ben used their combined girth to push their way into the crowded doctors' lounge at Holmes hospital on the Monday after Christmas. Working on call together for the past two years, Ben and Jake had become as close as two socially awkward doctors could get. They had bonded over their work, their weight, and their passion for food, action movies, and video games, which explained why the pear-shaped psychologist from Brooklyn was so shocked to be the last person to learn about Jake's eventful weekend.

"No biggie? ... I'm stunned. You're a born coward," Ben kidded him. The tables in the lounge grew quiet as the surgeons, nurses, and anesthesiologists who were scrolling their phones looked up and gave Jake a curious look—then went back to eating and scrolling.

"More like 'strategically cautious,'" Jake said under his breath as they warmed up their lunches in the microwave. Ben scanned the room, feeling the vibe in the lounge.

"Word travels fast," Ben observed. "And your best friend is the last to know?"

"Didn't want the entire hospital to find out." Jake shrugged.

"Too late," Ben chuckled under his breath. "You're a local celebrity."

They sat down to eat. Jake stared at his pathetic Nutrisystem "low fat garden enchiladas" and wondered how most of the hospital staff had seemingly heard about the knife attack without any help from Ben.

When prodded for details, Jake explained it was just dumb luck that he subdued Red, but Ben could see his shy friend was different. "Wasn't expecting anything like that from a man who prefers playing *Mortal Combat* to engaging in even the slightest verbal confrontation. Will your fisherman ever sing again?"

"He may warble again. Unfortunately I bruised his larynx and caused a fissure in his vocal cords. But they checked him out. Steve made us go to the ER."

Ben, who was ten years older than Jake, excitedly adjusted his yarmulke so it covered his bald spot. "King Landry made you and the guy who tried to fillet him get checked out?"

"Landry was going to leave him writhing around in the parking lot. But we thought I was having a heart attack, so…"

"You gotta take better care of yourself. Men our size die mowing their lawns at an alarming rate. That's why I remain immobile, whenever possible."

"It was just chest pain," Jake continued. "Reflux maybe. They performed a stress test. My cardiac enzymes were normal. So I'm sticking to my marathon training plan. What else do I have?"

Ben let Jake's last comment hang in the air as he stroked his neatly shaved salt-and-pepper beard. He relished analyzing the psychology behind Jake's current evolution from obese schlub to fit hero. "So macho and svelte you've become. I think all those Bourne movies are wearing off on you."

"Still a passivist," Jake said. "Until someone's charging me with a deadly weapon."

"Or attacking your schmuck of a boss." Ben cough-laughed. "In the fight-or-flight camps, you fight; I, on the other hand, will happily fly."

They ate their tasteless lunches in silence. Ben noticed his friend subtly checking out an attractive oncologist seated beside them who resembled Jake's ex-wife.

"Incidentally. How's your love life?" Ben asked, taking the cue.

"In about the same shape as Red's throat. Fissured."

"Tsk-tsk. Gotta get you back in the game. I want to see your psyche as ripped as your body is clearly becoming." Ben took a bite of a celery stick. "Besides, I need a distraction. Nothing exciting ever happens here but rocket launches and alligator attacks."

"Never should have left Brooklyn," Jake said. "You don't even like the beach."

"I'd be harpooned the moment I set foot on sand!" Ben said with his trademark self-deprecating humor. He watched his friend pick at his enchiladas. He perceived Jake's inner struggles better than most. "My professional opinion? You work too much."

"Did I ask, big guy?"

Ben gestured to the stress lines on Jake's forehead. "Go somewhere. Get your mind off her. You're still a young man. Don't wait. Didi didn't."

After lunch, they ambled down the tile hallway toward the south exit near the parking lot. Ben kept nagging him. "Take a vacation. Have some fun," he said, slightly out of breath, his wide frame wobbling past the younger, in-shape doctors wearing their Fitbits.

"You billing me for this?" Jake turned to Ben. "What about you, bubala?"

"I am no role model for happiness or health. The only treadmill I'm on these days is work, wife, kids, synagogue; it's a vicious cycle. Come for dinner and say 'hi' to the kids. Barb's making her healthy lasagna."

"That's not a real thing," Jake joked.

"You haven't had good eggplant lasagna unless it's made by a Kosher woman." Ben predictably bragged about his wife's cooking, but Jake had been to his house for dinner and it was like eating food from a test kitchen: average on a good day, pretty terrible on others. "You'd be surprised."

Jake admired Ben's devotion to his wife and five children. He wanted their happy, domestic life someday for himself, but not yet. Something inside of him still yearned for passion and adventure. Was he dreaming? Probably. But he had a colorful imagination for a humdrum eye surgeon.

"Sorry, pal. Tonight's my class at UCF and I want to get a run in before my presentation. Also, my mom is flying in tomorrow night and I have to get my apartment looking good."

"Next time," Ben said. "Glad you're not bleeding out on the concrete somewhere."

Jake felt his cell phone vibrate. He looked at the caller ID and saw it was Dr. Landry. He grimaced; the man would not leave him alone.

"Gotta go," Jake announced. "The king is calling. He left me five voicemails already."

"When are you gonna finally leave that guy?" Ben asked.

"Gonna be a partner in six months, I reason... Didi couldn't wait."

"Rumor is she's dating her Pilates instructor," Ben teased.

"Didn't need to hear that." Jake picked up the phone. "*Steve... Yeah*. I feel great. Just leaving, on my way into the clinic."

12

Los Angeles, California

Rizzo gazed at the top of the Los Angeles Coliseum. She had always admired its architecture and history. Built in 1923, it was once billed as "the greatest stadium in the world" and was dedicated to World War I veterans. A veteran herself, Rizzo knew these facts, while her battle-untested partner did not. The agents made an afternoon visit to the Coliseum to see what they could learn from Xander Lopez, Sheila's volatile boyfriend. Today was one of the Trojans' final practices before the Rose Bowl on New Year's Day, so it was off-limits to the media and any non-football observers. Naturally Rizzo walked right in and approached Lopez as he was walking off the field.

"Xander Lopez?" Rizzo stood in the giant man's way.

"Yo, Micah. Get this bimbo reporter off my field!" Xander yelled to a nearby trainer. Rizzo held up her badge in one hand and a photo of Sheila on her iPhone in the other.

"FBI. You know this woman?" she demanded.

Lopez stopped in his tracks. He gave Rizzo a look like he was bracing for bad news as he removed his scarlet helmet and examined the photo on Rizzo's iPhone.

"Yeah. I know Sheila. What she do now?"

Thirty minutes later, Rizzo emerged from the Coliseum's locker room after a one-on-one with Lopez. The 280-pound Adonis was still in uniform, eyes swollen. Thorn could tell by his posture that her partner had reduced the stud to a scared little boy.

"Beat those Buckeyes," Rizzo said, patting the giant on the back.

"Catch the scumbag who did this," Xander mumbled, head down, walking slowly off the field.

"That's our job," Rizzo replied, then joined Thorn at a trainer's table.

Thorn cleared the game of Wordle she was playing on her phone and watched Xander walk away. "I'd like to interrogate *that one*," Thorn said with a mischievous smile. "Looks sad now. What'd you do to him?"

"I showed him a photo of Sheila with her eyes ripped out of her head."

"Harsh. He confess? Because… he's getting away."

"Multiple witnesses back up his alibi. He spent the night in one of Tripp's yurts and didn't leave till after Sheila was found."

Behind them, a white-haired USC special teams coach with creaky knees ambled off the field. He stopped in front of Rizzo and Thorn. The coach stared at Rizzo curiously.

"We are not the media," Thorn said, holding up her FBI badge.

The coach squinted to get a better look. He snapped his fingers. "'The Leg,' right? University of Oregon?"

"They call me Special Agent Rizzo now," Rizzo said, not looking up from her phone.

"Jane Rizzo, yeah. I never forget a strong leg." The coach glanced at Thorn. "You know your friend was the first woman college kicker? Awfully good one too."

"You played college football?" Thorn chortled.

"Looked good in uniform, too," Rizzo replied, disinterested.

"I can confirm that," the old coach said. "She could really hammer the ball. Kicked a sixty-yard game winner against UCLA in '98 that helped us win the Pac-10."

"It was '61. You're welcome," Rizzo said.

"Still kicking? That goalpost's begging to be abused." The coach pointed.

"Nope," Rizzo said. "Blew out the knee, so I joined the Bureau."

"You ain't arresting Lopez, are ya?" The old coach squinted up at the agents.

"Nah, just asking him some questions."

"Good. Ain't beatin' Ohio State without him on the field. Wanna try one now, Legs?" the coach asked with a wry smile.

"You're serious?" Rizzo smiled.

"Of course I'm serious."

Rizzo glanced over at Thorn.

"Go on if it'll make you feel better," Thorn said.

Rizzo thought about it. "Let's go. Make it fifty yards."

The old special teams coach instructed a ball boy to set up the kicker's tee.

"Hell, our kicker can't hit from fifty. Want to make it interesting?" The coach pulled out a crisp hundred-dollar bill from his billfold.

"You're *on,* just make it quick," Rizzo said.

The coach and ball boy stood back to watch as Agent Rizzo slipped off her Tecovas leather urban boots, pulled off her socks, and stretched her legs. She lined up the ball with her eyes, taking five steps back and two steps to the left. She eyed the goalpost intently—then bounded up to the football and swept her bare right foot through the air, arcing the football up and through the uprights as smoothly as any kicker in the NFL.

"Well, I'll be. The Leg lives," Thorn said deadpan, slow-clapping.

"You flushed that!" the old coach cackled, tossing Rizzo the hundred-dollar bill.

"Keep it. Thanks for the kick," Rizzo replied, grabbing her boots and socks and high-fiving the coach. She made her way back to Thorn.

"Should have tried soccer instead of wasting my time in a man's game."

"Sounds like the Bureau," Thorn observed.

"I'd have two gold medals by now," Jane added.

"You're a glutton for punishment, girl."

(13)

Orlando, Florida

You could hear a pin drop in the lecture hall at the University of Central Florida. Jake let the silence linger. He repeated his question.

"What does the acronym LASER stand for?" He knew the simple question would surprise some of the residents, and it did. For the past two years, Jake had volunteered once a month as an adjunct professor and lecturer on the UCF College of Medicine's Lake Nona campus in Orlando. The ophthalmology residency program was only five years old, but it was already considered one of the preeminent research universities in the state and attracted some of the most respected professors and clinicians in their fields. But none of that mattered if Jake's students were half-asleep. Looking for signs of life from his usual lecture spot below the stage, Jake gazed out into the modern amphitheater and its seven semicircular rows of tables full of students. Using a remote control, he turned up the lights to make eye contact with the front rows of young fellows and chief residents in their pressed white lab coats, as well as the second- and third-year residents in the back.

Jake usually enjoyed seeing the enthusiasm of his students—it recharged his battery from the monotony of private practice—but tonight that enthusiasm was in short supply. "Come on! We all didn't have heavy dinners, did we?" Jake patted his stomach and strode up the aisle to shake them from their post-holiday torpor. "We all know how eye surgeons use lasers to treat eye disease. But what does the acronym LASER actually mean?"

One second-year resident coughed in the back.

"I get it... I was you, once," Jake said. "I know that most of you second-year students tend to live by Mark Twain's words." He paraphrased, "'Better to stay quiet and have people think you're a fool, than open your

57

mouth and remove all doubt.' But you third-year residents should know this... shame on you."

He glanced over at his personal favorite, a shy overweight second-year resident who reminded him of himself.

"Josh...?"

The young man cleared his throat. "Um... Light... Amplification by Stimulated Emission of Radiation?"

"Correct! Josh, you never let me down," Jake said with a warm smile. "So. What does that tell us about a laser?" His gaze swept across the sea of faces. "Anyone? Anyone?"

The room barely responded to his lame *Ferris Bueller's Day Off* reference.

He didn't mind—even when his jokes bombed, Jake liked to keep his lectures light whenever possible. He felt more at ease in a classroom setting than in real life, because here he knew the material, and he could talk about it for days. As for casual conversations with regular humans? Too many unknown variables.

"*Think.* The six words themselves will show you how a laser works," he continued.

When no one spoke up, Jake pivoted. "Okay, I'll let you sleepwalkers off the hook since it's Monday after the holidays. But since you all obviously need a refresher on lasers, I will shed some light, pun fully intended, on how we use them in retinal surgery—my area of expertise."

He went on to explain how lasers are used to treat eye diseases. After speaking nonstop for almost forty minutes, he looked up at the residents' faces. Most were paying attention, but a few had their chins on their chest. "At least I kept most of you awake. Next time, I expect all of you to be fully engaged."

Thud! Jake dropped a heavy textbook on a table to wake them up.

"Hear that, Michael?"

The fellow named Michael called from the back. "I hear you, Doctor LaFleur."

"Excuse me. Professor?" A quiet rasp of a voice came from the back of the auditorium.

Jake turned his head to see a man of medium height with short hair and a dark complexion walking down the right aisle. He had a familiar, seasoned swagger to him as he emerged from the shadows. The pocket protector fastened on his white short-sleeved shirt unmistakably identified his old friend, Dr. Farshid Aria. He was a bit greyer than at their last meeting, but his open face and kind smile hadn't aged a day. Jake smiled; as a student, he recalled how he could never correctly identify all of the mysterious instruments in his mentor's shirt pocket. It had even become something of a game over their time together in the lab.

"Wait, everyone! What an honor. I want you to welcome my preceptor from the Johns Hopkins Wilmer Eye Institute, Doctor Farshid Aria—and his mysterious unyielding pocket protector, which may hold all the secrets to the universe. Perhaps, even a pocket laser."

Several of the residents chuckled as Jake ushered Dr. Aria to the front with a friendly handshake. The room gave Dr. Aria a round of applause.

"I was just in time to hear you plagiarize my LASER lecture." Farshid smiled.

"So true," Jake said. "Ladies and gents, you are in the presence of greatness. Dr. Aria was one of the founding fathers of vitreoretinal surgery. I trained with him during my two-year fellowship." He turned back to Dr. Aria. "To what do we owe this great pleasure?"

"I was in the area and saw you were speaking, so I popped in," Farshid rasped.

"Did you hear the crickets I got from these sleepyheads? What am I doing wrong?"

"Ah, don't be too hard on them. I remember a certain retina fellow that didn't know the answer to that question either."

Jake raised his hand like a guilty student.

"We all have those days. Maybe you'd like to finish your lecture for me?"

The students applauded. Dr. Aria hesitated, then walked on stage to finish Jake's lecture with a discussion on Pattern Laser Photocoagulation of the retina using the Pascal laser. While he spoke, Jake looked up at Farshid standing comfortably under the stage lights. His mentor had always been self-conscious about his heavy Persian accent and mild-mannered delivery, so he was heartened to see that his old friend had grown to embrace the spotlight.

At the conclusion of Farshid's Q&A, most of the students exited the auditorium. Farshid shook hands with the few residents who approached him and Jake could tell Farshid was enjoying the adulation.

"That was incredibly insightful," Michael said, shaking Farshid's hand. "I'd never heard it explained quite that way."

"I am happy to have enlightened you," Farshid replied.

"All right. Break it up, everyone. Let Doctor Aria catch a breath," Jake kidded. "Besides, he's not the one you should be buttering up. I still give out the grades."

Michael turned to Jake. "I didn't mean to suggest that you weren't doing a good job."

"Yeah, yeah, tell it to the judge." Jake nudged Michael. "See you next month. Drink a Red Bull before you show up next time. Doctor's orders."

Once the residents had all filed out, Farshid remarked, "A very curious group of young minds."

"Says you," Jake said. "You really opened them up. Like you always did me."

He added, "Did you mean what you said about already having dinner? You look quite famished to these weary eyes."

"Oh. That was just for show. You know I'm always ravenous."

"Well, want to 'grab a bite,' as they say over here?"

"Why, Doctor, you read my mind."

Sumptuous scents of cardamom, clove, and coriander wafted through the cozy back room of the Saffron Indian restaurant in the upscale strip mall on Sand Lake Road. Sounds of the sitar filled the air. Among the vast community of Middle Eastern and South Asian engineers living on Florida's "Space Coast," Saffron was considered one of the most authentic Middle Eastern restaurants in Orlando. During Jake's residency, he and Farshid had dined here often and always felt at home. Jake had not treated himself to a restaurant meal in six weeks, so he took his time ordering in Hindi—one of the four languages he spoke fluently, a skill passed down from his mother.

"Please, sir. Main ordar dena chaahata hoon. ("I want to order.") Dal Makhani, Banjari Gosht, and Bhapaa Aloo, with two Mahkaha Kheers for dessert... Let's go crazy."

"It will be right out, gentlemen," the young waiter replied.

Jake and Farshid looked at each other with warm smiles. They each recognized a familiar soul sitting across from them.

"Your Hindi is excellent," Farshid complimented his young apprentice as he took in the room as if he were seeing it for the first time. Jake watched his old friend admire the Indian tapestries embellished with gold thread, beads, and tiny octagonal mirrors that hung on the textured walls. Then Aria admired its orange glazed floors adorned with hand-knotted Indian rugs and peppered with red silk chairs sporting embroidered accent pillows, as if putting it all to memory.

"This fabric is most sensual." Farshid ran his fingers over the hand-stamped sari table covering. "You know, you are one of the few young Americans I know who bothers to learn about other cultures. But, low-fat dessert? Really?"

"I'm already blowing my diet," Jake joked. "Didn't you know that Mahkaha Kheers is a fasting season tradition?" The two shy and humble men kidded easily.

"What happened to the boy who loved food more than life itself?" Farshid gestured to Jake's shrinking belly.

"Eh. I had a heart episode." Jake sighed. "So, I'm changing my ways. I am off the gravy."

"Good for you. Your Hindi is so sharp, one might take you for a 'foreign devil.' All you need is a tan and a lustrous mustache." Farshid smiled, employing the subtle delivery that often took Jake a few moments to realize he was joking. The two hadn't seen each other in four years but always picked up where they left off, like they had been molded from the same clay. One common trait was that Farshid and Jake had both become doctors to help others, not get rich. It was this shared altruism that had long been a topic of discussion among the two when Jake was learning under Farshid. And in the years since, it seemed to galvanize their long-distance friendship in an industry often plagued by narcissists with "God complexes."

These two were just the opposite. In fact, whenever his teacher failed to receive the recognition he deserved for his work, Jake suggested Farshid had a "martyr complex."

Sighing, Farshid replied quietly, "As your nation's greatest film director, Orson Welles, once said—"*They will love me when I'm dead.*"

Jake wished more doctors had Farshid's motivation and attitude. He trusted him with his health and his life. He couldn't say that about many other people he knew, if anyone.

"You had my class rapt. You looked so comfortable up there."

"I am over my apprehension to the stage. Now, why are you teaching and not doing?" Farshid questioned his friend.

Jake explained, "I'm still practicing, but I enjoy the residents. They didn't show it tonight, but they still have that thirst for knowledge. Medicine is still pure for them… It's inspiring to me. Usually."

"And what you do at work is not so inspiring?" Farshid replied with the soft raspy voice of a man who had smoked since his youth.

"Just pedestrian, I guess. Once all of those residents go into practice for themselves, their days will be taken up with billing codes, Medicare, keeping employees happy, and calling insurance companies to try to convince them to pay, just like the rest of us."

"The opposite of why any doctor chooses to practice." Farshid nodded.

"What about you?" Jake asked. "I heard you were hitting the lecture circuit."

"I am indeed." Farshid nodded again.

"You've been very mysterious. Finally going public with what you've been working on?"

"In a way." Farshid cast his penetrating eyes on Jake. "The biomedical company developing the nano drug delivery system that I have been working on has given me a seat on their board."

"That's fantastic."

"Yes. It is a big breakthrough for how we treat eye disease, so they have me running around the country lecturing about the new treatment with a focus on 'the Nano Solution.'"

Farshid passionately explained his new pet project as Jake listened intently. He greatly admired Farshid's innovative mind; he was one of the few doctors who could come up with an idea in the morning, bounce it around with Jake at lunch, have his team of researchers and mechanical engineers develop a surgical instrument by the next morning, and be putting it to use that afternoon.

"Well, I've seen only great reviews from the programs you've visited." Jake knew how to stroke his ego without sounding patronizing.

"Alas, I fear history is kindest to the charismatic personalities in our field," Farshid said.

Jake knew this was still a sore spot for Farshid, who had never received global recognition for his landmark work. "Still have that simmering martyr complex, I see," Jake kidded.

"Once a martyr, always a martyr," Farshid replied, shrugging, as their food arrived.

They ate in relative silence.

Jake and Farshid had always enjoyed sharing quiet meals together. It was something Jake was never able to accomplish with his ex-wife (or anyone else) without feeling awkward. Not even his buddy Ben, who couldn't shut up during their many meals together.

After dinner, the two doctors shook hands in front of Farshid's rental car. Seeing his old friend always made Jake feel like he was on the right track, even when he felt lost in his personal life, like now. Not a normally affectionate person, something prompted Jake to hug his old friend.

"Thanks for coming to see my lecture. You are a big inspiration to me, you know." Farshid patted him on his wide shoulders. "You Americans have soft hearts. I see you are still a big old teddy bear."

"I plan on being a smaller bear when you see me next, unless I keep pigging out," he said as he held up his doggie bag. "I'd love to see you again if you have time."

"I heartily accept your invitation," Farshid replied. "I shall be here for a few days. You can tell me more about your upcoming partnership with this Doctor Landry."

"That will take a seven-course meal."

Just then, familiar laughter caught Jake's ear. He stopped talking and turned to see a handsome couple approaching them.

"Jake?" Didi stopped in her tracks. His ex-wife wore a red spaghetti strap cocktail dress and high heels; she had an intimidatingly good-looking date on her arm wearing a linen sport coat over a yellow tank top.

Jake's face lost all color. "Hey. Didi."

Didi was taken aback by Jake's appearance. "Wow, I almost didn't recognize you. You look so healthy." His ex-wife was glowing with happiness, something he never saw when they were married.

"Thanks. You too. We just ate at Saffron."

"That's where we're going," Didi replied.

They stood, the four of them on the sidewalk in awkward silence. Seeing her felt like a knife to his heart.

"Remember my mentor from my residency?" Jake gestured to Farshid.

Didi shook Farshid's hand. The hotshot dude smirked.

"Sure, uh. Hi," Didi said, obviously unable to remember his name.

"Doctor Farshid Aria," he said, bowing slightly. "The pleasure is mine."

"Long time no see, Doc. This is, um, Ozzie?" Didi trailed off. Her muscular date, six inches taller than Jake, extended his massive hand.

"Oz. I'm Didi's personal trainer."

Didi and Ozzie gave each other a knowing look. Seeing the passion they had for each other was a blow to Jake's ego. The darker part of his personality that readily took down Landry's attacker wanted to rabbit-punch the massive Pilates instructor in the throat, but he resisted. Jake was a rational man; until Red, he had never been in a fight in his life.

He swallowed his pain and extended his hand.

"Jake," he said. "Nice to meet you. *Oz.*"

A moment of uncomfortable silence followed, until Didi broke the stalemate.

"So good to see you, Jake, keep taking care of yourself."

"You too," Jake said meekly. "Enjoy your dinner."

"We will. And dessert," Oz boasted as they walked away arm in arm. Jake watched them go, looking like someone had socked him in the stomach.

"That is your ex?" Farshid asked, knowing it was. "She looks quite different."

"She seemed weird, right? They looked like they were dressed for a cruise ship."

Farshid put his hand on his shoulder and offered some avuncular advice.

"He is quite handsome, but I sense, an empty vessel. Like her, I fear."

"She actually has a PhD in economics," Jake said. "She's a bright girl."

"Degrees mean little when it comes to matters of the soul," Farshid responded. "You still love her, I can see."

"No. Yes. I don't know. My psychologist friend seems to think so."

"I went through a divorce not long ago, from a woman I truly loved." Farshid sighed. "I can only say, do not let her memory keep you from loving again. The heart is a very resilient muscle."

"My love boat may have sailed. I'd just be happy with a little adventure in my life, ya know? Shake things up while I'm still relatively young," Jake reasoned.

"Be careful what you wish for, my friend," Farshid replied.

(14)

lena's head jerked forward when the US Airways 737 touched down on
the tarmac. Some of the other passengers reacted like they were on a ride
at Disney World—*rookies*, she thought, turning off the Bose headphones
she bought in Rome to drown out the sounds of talkative passengers and crying babies. The "Fasten Your Seat Belt" sign chimed as a clacking symphony
of unlocking seat belts filled the cabin. People stood to grab their overhead
bags and jockey for the exit. Elena enjoyed observing Americans, *always
in a rush*. She had just read a story about a Wal-Mart employee in New
Jersey who was trampled to death by Christmas shoppers that had queued
up overnight for their annual holiday sale. Watching the other passengers
she thought, *if these people knew the atrocities of war, they would be more
considerate*. The rough landing was a fitting end to her twenty-two-hour trip
from Sarajevo to Orlando. She'd been too angry with Mikal to relax on the
Sarajevo to Rome flight but got some sleep after buying a neck pillow at the
Leonardo da Vinci Airport for her flight to New York and then Orlando.
Elena stared out her window, watching the airport workers unload luggage
from the plane. She pulled up the cuff of her blouse to check her faux gold
Chanel watch—it was 10:30 p.m. *Hope Brittany waited*, she thought.

She turned on her cell phone; it buzzed. Three voicemails.

9:00 p.m.—"Hey girl, your Uber has arrived. I'm by the security exit.
See you soon."

Elena hit delete.

9:30 p.m.—"Just heard your flight's late. Don't worry, I'll find some
place to sit with cute guys. I'll be here when you land. You can buy me a
drink."

Elena smiled; she knew Brittany better than she knew anyone else in
America, after rooming together in her first year of graduate school at the
University of Central Florida.

10:00 p.m.—"Girl, take your time; I'm drinking cosmos with a hunk. He says he's an investment banker but he's probably a bank teller. Don't care, free drinks! When you get through security, I'm in the sports bar waiting."

She hit delete and texted back. *Landed. Still here?* No response.

Elena pulled her carry-on bag out of the overhead compartment and exited the now nearly empty plane. The Florida humidity enveloped her like a sauna blanket. Many Europeans thought the Florida heat was overbearing, but she welcomed it; to her, it meant she was following her dreams.

She took off her black knockoff Valentino sports jacket and casually flipped it over her shoulder. Although her legs were weak and her hair was a mess, Elena knew she looked way better than the herd of tired travelers in their sweatpants, T-shirts, and flip-flops. She made a point to dress stylishly whenever she made her American entrance—it wasn't that difficult. On the short walk into the terminal, she was singled out by two mustached Homeland Security officers who had no reason to stop her but asked to see her passport and green card anyway.

She showed them her passport and F1 student visa. She didn't volunteer any personal information, like that her goal was to get a full-time job working through the OPT (Optional Practical Training) program at SpaceX in Cape Canaveral, where she had interned last semester. Homeland didn't bother with any of that. They just wanted to flirt with her. "Elena *Smilovic*? Why aren't you smiling then?" teased one Homeland agent.

"Never heard that one before," she uttered.

She loathed it when men told her to "smile."

She knew if these galoots couldn't properly pronounce her Americanized name, they'd totally butcher her birth name, Emina Ajna Sidran, which is why she changed it before applying to UCF. She also knew it was a red flag to xenophobes. She chose her new name because it seemed cheerful, vaguely exotic, and represented who she wanted to become: *a happy, liberated woman*—all the things she was told back home that she could never be.

One of the Homeland agents handed her back her papers.

"Happy New Year, boys," she said, giving the two agents a flirty smile. *American men are easy to manipulate*, she thought. Sometimes that's all it took. A smile.

Striding through the main terminal, a rush of freedom washed over Elena as she gazed at the palm trees still decorated for the holidays. She'd often dreamt about American palm trees as a girl in the frigid Sarajevo winters, and now she was here—it still felt like a dream. The terminal was packed with weary travelers and noisy kids running around. Five ten in heels, she felt like Dorothy landing in Oz among the munchkins. She wanted to call Mia but knew the six-hour time difference meant her daughter would still be sleeping. Walking past rows of exhibits from NASA, Disney World, and Universal Studios, she glanced up at her favorite poster of a space shuttle circling the planet that read: *IT'S NOT A SMALL WORLD AFTER ALL – The John F. Kennedy Space Center*

Elena passed it every time she landed in Orlando; it made her feel like she belonged, even as she felt eyes on her while she strutted through the airport. She walked past numerous shops and a wide food court before hearing a familiar sound: Brittany's contagious laugh. Elena followed it into the ESPN Wild World of Sports Bar and Grill and spotted her roomie's unmistakable profile at the bar. She envied Brittany's glowing self-confidence. Unlike Elena, her roommate had more friends than she could count. She thought Brittany looked like a young Nubian queen with her flawless skin, curly hair, and regal high forehead—though a Nubian queen who rarely missed a meal. Elena had dubbed her a "voluptuary" last semester one night when they were out partying. Brittany loved that description so much she said, "I'm stealing that line," and she did.

Brittany was sitting alone, talking to the bartender. It was December yet she wore a summer dress that rested comfortably on her shoulders and was low cut enough in the front to show some cleavage, with the bottom cut high enough to show some lower thigh.

"Britt," Elena called out.

"There's my favorite Euro-trash girlfriend!" Brittany slipped off her stool, almost falling to the floor.

"Still a klutz, I see. I owe you one for sticking around."

Brittany threw her arms around Elena. "You can't believe how boring Melbourne's been without you." She gave Elena's jet-lagged appearance a once-over. "Let's have a drink, babe, looks like you need one."

"What happened to your hunk of burning love?"

"Sit down and I'll tell you all about his sorry ass."

Elena could see that her friend would be dancing on the bar after one more drink so she placed her arm around Brttany and guided her away. "Airport bars depress me. Let's get my bags and then we talk about that drink."

Brittany gave Elena a disappointed pout and grabbed her purse.

"Where are you two going?" the bartender pleaded. "I get off in thirty."

"Sorry," Elena replied in an exaggerated Bosnian accent. "But you won't be getting off with us." The bartender threw his hands in the air and laughed, recognizing the futility.

Elena looked for the signs to Baggage Claim A. The main terminal was crowded with holiday travelers plodding intently toward their destinations. It was late, but lines of people were scattered everywhere, at the stores, restaurants, and security lines. Through the crowd, Elena caught a glimpse of an intimidating-looking man, dark complexion, with short-cropped black hair, dark clothes, and black boots who was staring at her from across the terminal. He looked Middle Eastern, maybe—of average height but stocky, like a rugby player. He didn't look happy or appear to be on vacation like the others. He also didn't look to be going anywhere. He remained very still, standing out among the other travelers streaming around him.

The small hairs on the back of her neck rose as their eyes met briefly, then the man looked away and walked into a bookstore. Elena exhaled. Since the war she didn't trust many men, especially ones who looked militant. Was she still seeing phantoms? *Maybe it will never stop*, she thought.

"What's wrong?" Brittany asked. "You look paler than normal."

"Caught a creeper looking at me."

"Big surprise. A guy's checking you out. You're hot, even after twenty-two hours on a plane."

The alcohol on Brittany's breath somehow took away Elena's anxiety; everything felt normal again. "I'm tired of men today. Let's get out of here."

Making their way to the baggage claim escalator, Brittany saw a Starbucks. "Oh. I need a caffeine injection first. I'll get my car and meet you outside baggage claim."

"You sure you can drive?"

"You know me, get me a double cappuccino and I could drive to California." Elena remembered many times when she had seen Brittany sober up faster than the average human.

"I'll come with you. I need coffee too."

They walked into Starbucks. Elena hoped the coffee would help her make it through the hour-long drive back to UCF. She glanced over to where the creepy man had been; thankfully he was gone. She felt silly for overreacting as they ordered two nonfat cappuccinos. The sound of grinding coffee beans and the aroma of espresso gave her a second wind. Coffee in hand, she walked to the creamer station and poured demerara sugar into her paper cup. A large decorative mirror hung behind the station. She grimaced at her reflection. The long journey from Sarajevo showed on her face; the dim overhead lighting accentuated the dark circles under her eyes.

I look like a witch, she thought, running her hands through her limp brown hair to give it some life. In the mirror, she caught a glimpse of the odd man just outside the Starbucks. Her heart rate jumped. *Who is this guy?*

Brittany gave her a hip check. "Excuuuse me," she said, purposely slurring. "I need some sugar, sugar." She could see the tension on Elena's face. "Oh, don't believe that dirty old mirror. You're as beautiful as ever."

"Creepy guy. Six o'clock."

"Where?" Brittany turned to look.

She stopped her. "Don't turn."

Elena looked back in the mirror. The man was gone. She walked out of the café and scanned the terminal; he had vanished. Brittany followed her out, sipping coffee.

"What's gotten into you?

"I'm serious," Elena answered. "This guy stares at me like he wants something."

"They all want something. I'll get the car and meet you outside." Brittany patted her arm and sauntered off, playing toss-catch with her key fob.

Elena watched Brittany walk through the sliding glass doors to the parking garage. Exhausted, she made her way to the escalator, past people hustling to and from airplanes and kids scurrying around wearing Mickey Mouse ears and waving Star Wars light sabers.

Elena glanced in all directions, as she gulped her cappuccino.

She froze; the creepy man was back, talking with a taller man dressed similarly and wearing the same black boots, across the walkway below a bank of televisions blaring CNN. Not wanting to make eye contact, she glanced up at a screen. The CNN chyron ticker scrolled off: *POSSIBLE SERIAL*

KILLER AT LARGE IN WESTERN STATES. The television showed photos of the killer's victims, two beautiful young women.

Elena's heart skipped a beat. She put her hand to her mouth.

Wait a minute, she thought, *I know those girls.*

15

Orlando, Florida

Filled with a growing sense of panic, Elena's mind raced. *Am I in danger?* She quickly joined a group of Southwest flight attendants passing by, laughing loudly. For a moment she disappeared from sight. The two suspicious men looked around the terminal.

"Where did she go?" Khalid said, craning his neck.

Tarek pointed. "There. By those women in blue dresses."

"She must've gone to baggage claim. We'll find her."

Elena split off from the group of stewardesses, making a sharp right toward the escalator, zipping past a fleshy older woman with shoulder-length grey hair who was doting over her adult son.

"Who's been feedin' you, boy?" exclaimed Cindy LaFleur as she inspected Jake's shrinking frame, clacking her tongue.

"I'm off the roux, Mom. Fatty food's my enemy."

"Are you sure you're my son?" Cindy asked. "You've been starving yourself ever since that heifer broke your heart."

"Way to bring that up immediately," Jake kidded.

Jake loved his mom but not her obsession with food. Ben had told him that his mother taught him to "eat away his pain" as a teenager. Whenever there was a problem in life, Jake had fed it, and Cindy was the classic Cajun mother: she was either talking about the meal they'd just had or the meal she was going to make next. Being a devoted son, Jake let his mom poke fun at his shrinking belly. He knew it would only be for a few days. Cindy had flown in from Louisiana to watch him run the Disney Marathon. A retired Tulane professor who spoke multiple languages, she was primly dressed in a navy-blue pantsuit, white blouse, and sensible flats. Cindy suggested they go eat supper at Pappadeaux's.

"Put some meat on your bones."

"It's closed, but we'll grab something…on the way…" Jake trailed off.

He was rendered speechless by an attractive woman passing them with a strong gait. She shot Jake a glance. He thought she looked anxious.

A moment later, two strange men rushed by, apparently following her.

Perhaps it was loneliness or the spy novels he devoured, but Jake decided to follow the woman to make sure she wasn't in danger—and also to admire her beauty a moment longer.

"Guess we better motor before everything's closed."

Jake brusquely grabbed his mother's hand, who complained in French, "Tout comme ton père," she said. "Les médecins sont toujours pressés." ("Just like your father. Doctors are always in a hurry.")

Jake and Cindy fell behind the two men following Elena, through the crowd and onto the escalator. Jake marveled at how this beautiful agile woman navigated the crowded escalator. The two men couldn't keep up with her moves. *Maybe this woman doesn't need my help.*

But he couldn't take his eyes off of her. Boarding the escalator, Jake pointed at space exhibits lining the walls to keep his mom occupied. "Vous voyez les expositions de la NASA et de SpaceX?" ("See the exhibits for NASA and SpaceX?" he asked her in French.)

"What the heck is a SpaceX?" Cindy complained in English. "You're walking too fast!"

At the bottom of the escalator, Elena spotted her two orange bags circling on the second baggage carousel. She turned a corner and quickly ducked behind a SpaceX Starship exhibit, where two young children were playing hide-and-seek. Crouching down, she watched the two suspicious men pass by, then circle back.

Her heart racing, Elena texted Brittany: *Meet me at pick up area now!*

She put her phone away.

A little boy in a NASA Space Camp T-shirt had stopped playing and was standing beside her, looking at her curiously. "Are you an astronaut too?"

"*I'm cosmonaut,*" she said in her thickest Bosnian accent. "Boo!"

The kids ran away. Lights flashed and a horn blew. The turnstile began to move. More luggage arrived, including those from Cindy's flight from New Orleans, which came down on the first carousel next to Elena's. Elena's heart pounded as she looked for the two men.

They were gone.

Fascinated, Jake watched Elena slowly emerge from behind the SpaceX exhibit, then beeline it past him to get her bags. *I knew she was in trouble*, he thought, half amused at the scene being played out before him. He gently guided his mother, who was in the middle of describing the grillades and grits she was going to make him, over to Elena's baggage carousel.

Jake reached Elena as she was leaning over to pick her bags off the carousel's moving surface. The two suspicious men brushed past them and walked through the exit doors. Elena peered the area 360 degrees and darted through the sliding glass doors into the humid evening with her orange bags slung over her shoulders, scanning the cars for Brittany's maroon Lexus.

"Son, there's my suitcase," Cindy said, pointing at the conveyor belt in front of Jake.

He placed the luggage on its wheels, grabbed Cindy's hand, and dragged her outside to pickup area C.

"What's the big rush?" Cindy demanded.

Elena was standing curbside, looking for Brittany's car. A black van was slowly rolling toward her. Jake saw Tarek extend his arms to grab Elena from behind.

His internal alarm went off. *Holy cow, this is real.* He instinctively stuck out his right foot and tripped Tarek, causing him to stumble into Khalid a few feet away from Elena. The two men cursed at each other in Farsi, which Jake recognized. Cindy reached down to help the men to their feet.

"Goodness, my son can be a clumsy oaf. You two hurt?"

Cindy gave her son an incredulous look. Jake could hardly contain a smile.

Elena looked back at the toppled men. Her eyes met Jake's. Rattled, she thought, *I must be exhausted to let them get that close to me.* She ran to pickup area G and called Brittany. Voicemail.

Prokletstvo! She's probably roaming around the garage drunk, looking for her car. Out of her peripheral vision, Elena saw one of the creepy guys was back, ten meters away and walking quickly toward her. Next to him a black van was moving along the curb.

She glanced inside the van—the taller man was driving.

Should I scream? Or level up and throw fists with these creeps? She looked around; reunited families and lovers were greeting each other, but the crowd was thinning fast.

Elena walked quickly the other way.

The stocky man called out, "Elena! Elena!"

Hearing her name sent chills down her spine. The man had an accent Elena recognized as Middle Eastern; she'd heard it many times in Sarajevo since the war ended. She felt in grave danger for the first time on American soil.

She looked over her shoulder—the man was now less than twenty-five yards away. She walked faster and prepared to use her duffel bags as bludgeons, then run.

Another car, a white Chevy Impala with tinted windows, raced past her, double-parking at an awkward angle fifteen yards in front of her. *Now who is this guy?*

The white Impala's passenger door slowly opened, as if inviting her to jump in.

She considered it as she looked over her shoulder.

Tarek was ten yards away, still calling her name. *How does he know my name?* Jet lag had caught up to her, her eyes throbbed, she was a sitting duck.

A maroon Lexus RC screeched up beside Elena with its passenger door open.

"Lanie, jump in!" Brittany yelled.

Elena jammed her bags into the open back seat window and dove into the passenger seat. "Drive!"

Brittany got a look at the man. "He's ugly as hell!"

"Step on it!" Elena shouted as Tarek's menacing face filled the passenger window. Brittany floored it and the Lexus jumped away from the curb and sped off.

A second later, the black van pulled up next to Tarek.

"Get in," Khalid said through the open window.

Tarek jumped in and slammed the passenger door in anger. "We have to get her tonight."

The black van tore off after them, passing right by the parked Chevy Impala, which did not move. The driver of the Impala unhurriedly closed the passenger door.

Seconds later, pulling Cindy along, Jake arrived and watched Brittany's Lexus vanish with Elena in the passenger seat. He didn't notice the van following behind it. The driver of the Impala covertly observed Jake for a moment, then slowly pulled away from the curb.

"You trying to give me a heart attack just like your father!"

Jake sighed, looking at Cindy. "Thought I saw someone I knew... Let's go eat."

16

Cocoa, Florida

Brittany's Lexus tore out of the arrival-loading area of the airport, heading east to Melbourne. The waning moon and lack of traffic made Route 528 darker than usual. Along the roadside, whitetail deer grazed in the brush, lifting their heads at the oncoming headlights. Brittany gyrated in the driver's seat of her brand-new Lexus sedan, listening to Lizzo. Elena looked back nervously; she saw headlights a long way back.

Brittany smiled. "Stop stressing, we dusted those fools."

She unbuckled her seat belt and tried to reach in the back. The car veered right, skidding over the gravel in the emergency lane.

"Watch the road!" Elena said, grabbing the wheel.

Brittany regained control of the car. "Oops. Grab a couple outta the cooler, will ya?"

"You have alcohol tolerance of a Bolshevik," Elena said.

"Yeah, but that's why you love me." Britt smiled.

"Those galoots are still chasing us," Elena guessed.

"Not anymore. C'mon, I can't reach."

Brittany reached behind the seat again; the car rolled to the right again.

"Okay, just drive, Boris Yeltsin." Elena turned around and kneeled on the soft, tan leather seat. She found the cooler on the floorboard and grabbed two beers. Through the rear window she saw headlights growing dimmer in the dark. *Maybe Brittany's right*, she thought.

"There you go," Brittany cooed. "Pop 'em open and let's start the party." Elena opened the beer bottles and reluctantly handed one to Brittany. She sat back and thought about palm trees and warm days on the beach, then remembered the news broadcast showing the picture of the two murdered girls. She knew them from Sarajevo. They were friends of Mikal. She met them one evening at the club. Elena pulled her cell phone out to call Mikal.

Her phone battery was dead.

"Jebati!" she cursed in Bosnian, tossing her phone away.

"I understand you're scared, but don't hurt the upholstery," Brittany said and turned up the pounding bass. "My ride's clean as hell."

A few minutes passed before Elena heard someone laying on their horn behind them. She shuddered. A black van was approaching on their left. Elena turned off the radio.

"What you doing?" Brittany asked, her beer resting between her legs. "I love that song."

"Look out your window." The van was beside them.

Tarek had his head out the passenger window, yelling "Pull over!"

"Those *are* the same guys," exclaimed Brittany. "I hate toxic jerk-offs who won't take '*NO*' for an answer." Brittany gripped the steering wheel and pursed her lips. "Hang on, *momma's got a heavy foot tonight!*" Elena buckled her seat belt as Brittany flipped the switch from party girl to ferocious brawler. "Who does he think he's messin' with?"

Brittany hit the gas and jumped her car up to ninety miles an hour.

The van fell behind but quickly caught up, riding their back bumper. "Must be a V-8 under that hood," Brittany observed as they flew by a sign for the Route 520 exit in one mile.

"Get off at 520!" Elena instructed.

"I know what I'm doin'!" Brittany slowed down to seventy and let the van pull up next to them. Tarek signaled for them to pull over. Brittany blew him a kiss.

"Later, loser!" She hit the brakes and made a hard-right turn.

The car skidded onto the 520 exit going seventy miles per hour and fishtailed through the emergency lane. Brittany struggled to regain control as the Lexus smashed into the guardrail, flipping over onto its roof and sliding down a grassy incline.

Passing the Route 520 exit, the van screeched to a stop in a cloud of smoke, backed up to the exit, and turned down the exit ramp. Shattered glass on the road shimmered as the van's headlights lit up the crash scene; smoke and the smell of burnt rubber filled the night air. The guardrail on the right side of the exit was mangled. They drove past it and came to a stop farther down the ramp. The men got out of the van and saw the Lexus on its roof.

"Get her out. The car may burn," Tarek yelled from the van.

Khalid shined a flashlight into the wrecked car, its wheels spinning helplessly. The interior cabin of the car was filled with smoke. He saw Elena hanging upside down on the passenger side suspended by her seat belt, her airbag limp on the dashboard. He turned his light to the driver side. Brittany was not in her seat belt. She was lying upside down with her face pressed against the roof. Her head was sharply twisted and her eyes were grotesquely wide open. *Broken neck*, he thought.

Elena gradually opened her eyes. Her sight was blurred. Her head was pounding as blood rushed to her head; the airbag's explosion left the familiar smell of burning gunpowder in the car. Her arms were stretched down over her head. She tried to move them, but they were too heavy. It seemed easier to push them up than down.

She shook her head gently to try and clear her vision. It was dark but there was a bright light flashing behind her and small square chunks of safety glass sparkled everywhere. All of her senses began to kick in. The seat belt was digging into her thighs, her shoulders ached, her neck and face hurt, and her eyes were stinging. She realized she was still in her seat belt, upside down. She began to panic. She pushed hard against the roof of the car and tried to slip out from under the belt.

Khalid saw movement from Elena.

"She's alive. Shine the light on Elena," instructed Tarek as he hopped out of the van.

Khalid shined his bright light in Elena's face, causing a shock of pain behind her eyes. She turned away from the light, but she couldn't see out of her right eye.

She saw the driver's seat was empty. "*Brittany!*"

She reached over and touched Brittany's bare arm. A wave of dread hit as Elena struggled to unbuckle her belt. It clicked open and she fell to the roof. She was lying next to Brittany; her best friend's blank eyes stared into the distance, a look of death she'd seen too often in Bosnia. She tried to scream but her throat was dry. Nothing came out. She felt a tug on her left leg as the two men pulled her out through the broken passenger window, away from the car. They stood above her, calculating their next move.

"Put her in the van," Tarek ordered Khalid. "Leave the other one."

Elena tried to crawl back to the car. "Britt," she moaned.

A new pair of headlights approached from behind.

"Quickly." Tarek picked Elena up by the shoulders; Khalid grabbed her legs.

The headlights stopped fifty feet behind them. A sturdy middle-aged woman in blue scrubs and pink Crocs emerged from the passenger seat. "Stop! You can't carry her like that!" The woman raced down the incline, out of breath. "Never move an accident victim! You could be causing more trauma! I'm an ER nurse!"

Tarek and Khalid placed Elena on the ground. They looked at each other; they didn't want to speak, the less they spoke the better. Khalid walked to the van as the nurse shouted.

"Joe, get down here!" She turned back to the men. "My husband's calling 9-1-1!"

She checked Elena's pulse. "Honey, can you hear me?"

Elena's voice was barely audible. "Brittany's in there... Help her."

"Okay, hon. Just try to be still, help is coming."

The nurse glanced inside the burning car. "Joe, there's another girl in there!"

"Get away, it may blow!" Joe scrambled down the incline to help.

Tarek followed Khalid to the back of the van. "They called police."

"I've got ears," Khalid snarled, opening the back of the van and grabbing a CZ-57 automatic rifle. They looked at each other without speaking. It was understood; the woman had seen them, so she must be eliminated.

As the Lexus suddenly exploded in a ball of fire, the two men shielded their faces.

Tarek peered down the highway. A flurry of red and blue flashing lights was approaching, less than a mile away.

"We've got company." He ran back to the van. Khalid racked the rifle and walked down to the burning car as the two Samaritans were gently moving Elena away from the fiery crash site.

"Put her down," Khalid ordered, rifle raised.

The ER nurse froze. "Joe...he has a very large gun."

The Samaritans lowered Elena and stepped away, hands raised.

"We don't want any trouble, now," Joe pleaded as sirens pierced the night air, distracting the would-be abduction. Joe reached behind his back and whipped out a silver snub-nose .44. Aiming the gun at Khalid, Joe stood as he was taught in his concealed weapon carrying class, feet shoulder width apart and knees slightly bent.

Surprised, Khalid calculated the odds. The man's hands were shaking; he knew a handgun would be inaccurate from the twenty yards that separated them. He smiled, aiming his rifle as the sounds of emergency sirens grew closer. Red and blue flashing lights bounced off the highway and moved down the exit ramp.

Tarek backed the van up next to Khalid. "It's over. Get in!"

Khalid considered shooting the Samaritans.

"*Get in*," Tarek insisted. Khalid lowered his rifle and leapt in the back of the van.

Closing the double doors, Khalid and Joe locked eyes. Khalid wore a diabolical smile. He wagged his index finger at Joe as the van zoomed away.

Seconds later, a cavalry of rescue vehicles pulled up to the crash site. A half mile up the road, the black van fled into the night, headlights off. Khalid dialed his cell phone from the passenger seat.

"We have a problem."

(17)

Los Angeles, California

The red planet was flickering just below a crescent moon the evening FBI Agents Jane Rizzo and Tami Thorn paid a visit to the headquarters of SpaceX, at 1 Rocket Road, a few miles east of the LAX airport.

Earlier in the day, Rizzo had been interviewing Sheila's teachers, neighbors, and circle of friends, while Agent Thorn and Detective Lu chased down leads from the anonymous tip hotline that was set up after the killing—but they had come up empty. As the Bureau's Behavioral Analysis Unit (BAU) at the National Center for the Analysis of Violent Crime (NCAVC) back in D.C. rushed to develop a psychological profile of the killer, an impatient Rizzo was pushing Thorn for forensic evidence they could use and running on shredded nerves.

"What do you want me to say?" Thorn asked as they approached the entrance. "Both local coroners say no DNA. No fibers, no prints, no blood, no semen. He's a ghost in the night."

"Don't buy it; keep on their asses," demanded Rizzo. "Or we'll be off this case before we sleep in our own beds again." Rizzo stomped off ahead of her.

"Lay off the caffeine," Thorn called out, shaking her head.

The agents needed some downtime after working a seventy-two-hour jag with little sleep, but under growing pressure from FBI Director David Kohl to find the killer before he struck again, they got the break they were looking for: a Vice President and Director of IT Security, Edward Menard had agreed to meet with them. The agents had been hounding him ever since Rizzo discovered both murdered women were interning at SpaceX when they were killed—albeit in different SpaceX facilities located in totally different states—but it was a lead worth checking before they retreated to their hotel rooms to collapse for a few hours.

The glass door entrance of the SpaceX complex in the Hawthorne neighborhood of Los Angeles glowed like a white monolith when lit up at night as they entered the building. Thorn, reading from a google search on her phone, updated Rizzo on the man who founded SpaceX.

"South African; born to a Canadian mother and South African father. Moved to Canada when he was seventeen. Economics degree from Wharton. CEO of SpaceX, PayPal, Tesla, Hyperloop, and now Twitter. Worth hundreds of billion smacks. He's also colonizing Mars."

"Mars, in his spare time? Must be nice," Rizzo said.

"I read this novel in college called *Project Mars* by Wernher von Braun."

"Wernher von who?" Rizzo replied, completely uninterested.

"Braun. You know, 'the father of space travel'?"

"Oh. Him," Rizzo said sarcastically. "Why am I listening to this?"

"Well, his book was about humans colonizing Mars… Guess who their leader was?"

"I give up."

"Some dude named Elon…" Thorn smiled. "Coincidence?"

Rizzo looked at her. "You really are a nerd."

They were greeted by Gemma Arbor, Menard's genteel British executive assistant. She offered a limp handshake to both agents—who hadn't showered in a day or done laundry since they arrived in LA—before leading them through SpaceX's multi-level, open-aired office complex enclosed by floor-to-ceiling glass windows to see her boss.

"See that red dot?" Thorn pointed as they walked past a window. "That's Mars."

"Our future home, if all goes according to plan," Gemma remarked.

Rizzo glanced up, uninterested. "All I see are planes. What's it like working for a company that wants to go to mars?"

"SpaceX is a visionary," Gemma asserted. "Like Apple, it inspires something akin to religious devotion from it's acolytes."

"You one of the acolytes?" Rizzo asked Gemma.

"We all are," Gemma chirped, gesturing to her co-workers on the floor. "We *believe*." Gemma stopped outside a large glass-walled conference room. "Here we are. You may notice all of our conference rooms are named after rocket scientists, astronauts, and engineers."

Gemma pointed to the placard photo of a bald scientist named Robert Goddard.

"Never heard of him," Rizzo cracked. "How about Wernher von Braun?"

Gemma positioned her face a few inches from a bio-login sensor next to the Goddard placard. The sensor scanned her retina and the sliding door opened.

The agents looked at each other.

"Is SpaceX into eyes?" Thorn asked. Gemma stared at her.

"We value our privacy," Gemma said. "IP is everywhere, as you can imagine."

The three women entered the room. The motion sensors shut the doors behind them, causing the glass walls of the conference room to go opaque.

"Sweet trick," Rizzo grumbled.

Thorn sat down, placing her laptop on the smoked glass oval conference table. Rizzo paced, gulping the morning's third cup of black coffee from the Coffee Bean.

"Must be a stressful time," said Rizzo. "Working so late the week after Christmas. Being in the middle of a space race."

Gemma looked Rizzo up and down, silently appraising her travel-worn appearance.

"We view it as a tremendously exciting time," she replied archly.

"I wonder," Rizzo speculated. "Have you heard about 'The Eye Torcher'?"

The agents looked at Gemma, who scoffed. "What on earth is 'The Eye Torcher'?"

The killer they were chasing had become a national news story; he was even given a catchy nickname by the *New York Post*: "The Eye Torcher" because he removed and torched the eyes of his victims. The nickname had caught on like wildfire in the tabloid media. But apparently not deep within SpaceX's hallowed halls.

"Don't follow the news much, do you?" Thorn asked.

"Frankly, I don't have time…" Gemma sniffed. "My head is in the sky."

"You do know why we're here, right?" Thorn asked sarcastically.

Gemma bristled. "You'll have to ask Mr. Menard about all that… Here he is," she gushed.

In strode a tall, somewhat exotic-looking man in his early fifties with a handsome face, short-cropped hair, and intelligent eyes that looked like he wore a constant smile. "Apologies for being tardy to your wild goose chase," he said, clearly annoyed to be taken away from his work.

"FBI. Agent Jane Rizzo, and that's Agent Tami Thorn," Rizzo said.

"Yup." Thorn nodded.

"Hope we didn't spoil your holiday."

"I don't take vacations," Menard replied with a trace of his native British accent. "Vacations will kill you."

"You sound like our boss," Thorn said. "We worked Christmas, too."

"Last time I took one, one of our rockets exploded," said the executive, politely shaking both their hands with a brilliant smile. "So, I stopped taking them. Shall we sit down?" Gemma left the room as Menard opened his MacBook Pro. "Don't need my lawyers here, do I?"

"Just a few routine questions," Rizzo said, looking at her notepad. "Says here you work for the richest person in the world. SpaceX must feel invincible having all that money."

"Hardly." He laughed. "The challenges of our extraordinary efforts keep us grounded."

"That your daughter?" Rizzo asked nodding to framed picture on his desk of a young woman standing next to a sporty EV.

"My beautiful companion, Alexandria." He said annoyed at the question.

"Right," Thorn said. "Do you drive an electric car? I hear they can blow up."

"Not anymore," Menard said. "EV makers fixed that glitch years ago. As for our rockets." He chuckled. "They still go *boom* occasionally."

Rizzo cut the small talk. "As you know, we're investigating the murder of two young women who interned for your company."

"Here in Hawthorne, and in your rocket testing facility in Texas," Thorn added.

"Yes. Yes. 'The Eye Torcher' the press calls him; I did some research after you rang. I want to help in any way possible."

"Did you know either of the victims? Uma Gloten or Svetlana Roustamov?"

"I rarely interface with interns."

"You'd remember them," Thorn interjected.

"Both were beautiful. May have had slight Russian accents," Rizzo added.

"I don't make it a priority to know the interns." Menard said, scrolling through the two dead women's dossiers on his laptop screen.

Menard cleared his throat. "For whatever it's worth, I can tell you they were both student interns working on our rocket engines. Ms. Roust assisted our Starship team on its Raptor engine here… and Ms. Gloten on Starlink's Falcon engine in Texas."

"Explain Starship and Starlink?" asked Rizzo.

"Starship is the largest spacecraft ever conceived. It's quite remarkable, looks like a work of art." Menard explained how it will make space travel affordable for private citizens. "It's fully reusable and powered by thirty-two Raptor SN47s, the Holy Grail of rocket engines. Starship will take passengers to the moon, Mars, and beyond. I'm surprised you haven't been following our exploits."

"I hadn't till now. Never saw *Star Wars*, either," said Rizzo.

"Either you work too much, or we need a new PR firm," Menard commented.

"She works too much. Are you flying Starship to Mars anytime soon?" Thorn asked.

"Depends on what you mean by soon," Menard said. "We aim to establish a colony by 2040 with eighty thousand people. And since Mars's atmosphere lacks oxygen, all transportation will have to be electric: electric cars, electric trains, Hyperloop, electric aircraft."

"All the things you do, right?" Thorn asked.

"No law against cornering the market on another planet." He smiled widely.

"Yet," Rizzo said.

"So that's why your boss is called the 'Imperator of Mars.'" Thorn said.

"He's a true visionary." Menard admired. "In a few days, we're actually launching Starship's first trip around the moon at the Port of Los Angeles. One hundred lucky civilians. You should tune in. Or look to the sky on New Year's Day."

"A ticket on that must cost a pretty penny," Thorn said.

"If you have to ask, you can't afford it," Menard said with a smile.

"What's the project Miss Gloten was working on?" Rizzo asked.

"*Starlink*. The most expansive satellite network ever made. We're giving the world free Internet! You may have heard about the project at the beginning of the Ukrainian war. We supplied Internet to Ukraine when the Russians invaded." Menard pensively shifted his stare. "We're launching another round of fifty at Cape Canaveral the same day we're launching Starship. That's why we're all such busy little beavers," he concluded.

"Two launches on the same day?" Rizzo said.

"Space travel needs showmen, too."

"Rumor is your satellites could be used for spying," Thorn prodded.

Menard laughed. "Spying? *For whom?*"

"I dunno. CIA. NSA. Russia. China. Take your pick."

"The FBI is misinformed, Agent Thorn, 'we come in peace' here. Mostly."

Gemma walked in, interrupting their conversation by handing Menard a zip drive and a handwritten note.

Menard grew visibly agitated. "Excuse me. Would you mind stepping out for a moment? Gemma, bring our guests some herbal tea with the blooming tea balls while they wait."

"Coffee for me. I don't drink anything that has blooming balls in it." Rizzo stood up.

While they checked their phones in the hall, Thorn said matter-of-factly, "He's holding back on us. We received intel last year that the CIA's contracting satellites to spy on other countries. They ain't sharing it with us though."

"Where'd you hear that, rook?"

"I got my sources. Menard's satellites are ruffling some feathers in the Agency," Thorn said. "Not to mention astronomers who can't see the stars with his space junk in the way."

"If there's so many, why don't I have free Internet?" Rizzo asked sarcastically.

Menard walked briskly out of the conference room. "Come with me. There is something troubling I want to show you. We've been going through security tape since you alerted us to our connection to the murders. We've found your Miss Roust on her last day."

"I have to see this," Rizzo said.

Inside SpaceX's security command center on the ground floor, the two agents and Menard stood before a massive bank of security monitors that covered the entire 533,000-square-foot facility. Rick Reynolds, SpaceX's linebacker-sized chief of security, led them through what he had found.

"This is where Ms. Roust somehow got into one of our highly secure areas," he said.

Menard turned to Rizzo. "Someone's getting sacked for this, I assure you."

The security chief shifted uncomfortably in his chair as Menard and the agents stood behind him. They were all glued to the monitor that was playing video footage of Sheila in a white lab coat, making her way through the Raptor Rocket Testing Facility. Unchallenged, she passed on to Berth 240, where the massive Starship MK17 was docked, a sleek stainless steel alloy rocket with wings like something out of a 1960s science fiction movie.

"Whoa. That thing's big," Thorn said.

"Looks like a skyscraper," Rizzo said.

"It's our sixteen-story masterpiece," Menard crowed.

In the video, Sheila wound her way around to the back of the ship's rocket boosters, where six Raptor engines were being serviced by a group of quality control engineers. The team was so focused on their work that none of them noticed Sheila duck behind a bank of supercomputers.

The security cameras lost her.

"You have other angles?" asked Rizzo.

"Just these twenty-six," Reynolds replied, his arm sweeping the air as he indicated the bank of screens in front of them..

"How can we still have blind spots?" Menard exclaimed.

"I'd be more concerned about the security of the Raptors, sir." Reynolds pointed to the screen. "We can't track what she did for six minutes and twelve seconds before exiting. *Here.*"

The video cut back to one of the two secure exits. Sheila casually walked out using her own eye on the retina scanner, unnoticed by anyone on the mostly empty floor.

"How??" Menard was apoplectic. "She didn't have clearance!"

"It's a major breach. I am on it, sir," said Reynolds.

"You better be, Rick! We launch in four days."

"You ever heard of anyone using someone else's bio-login?" Rizzo asked.

"In our fortress?" said Menard. "Inconceivable. There must be a glitch in the software."

"I've seen fake fingerprints before," Reynolds said, "but never fake eyes."

Agent Rizzo took charge. "Take us to the spaceship. Let's see what Sheila was up to when she evaded your 'fortress's' cameras."

18

Lightning crackled from a powerful thunderstorm that had swept in to blanket the night sky over Los Angeles. Ominous grey clouds obscured Mars, further dampening the moods of Edward Menard, his corporate counsel, and his chief of security. Gripping oversized SpaceX umbrellas, they marched Rizzo and Thorn through the rain to the center of campus, to investigate the twenty-six-story tower where Starship was docked.

Alarmed by the legal ramifications of a security breach days before SpaceX's double launch of Starship and Starlink, ever-nervous Milton Franklin, JD, was growling in Menard's ear, strongly advising him not to welcome the help of the FBI.

"We need to keep a lid on this," Franklin said under his breath. "Inviting the Feds in is a mistake."

Menard listened to his counsel while overriding the retinal scan bio-login security with his personal key card, to allow the FBI to enter the secure area. He got on the intercom, and in a booming voice, ordered everyone out. Agent Thorn noticed none of the engineers exiting the facility dared look their boss in the eyes as they passed—she speculated they knew something had gone wrong and were hoping they were not going to be blamed for it.

"Level with us, what do you think Roust was up to?" asked Agent Rizzo. "Could she have gotten her hands on a security key card like that one?" She pointed at the card in Menard's hand.

"You don't have to answer her questions," Franklin implored.

"Please, stop being a lawyer for one minute. It can be excruciating." Menard held up his key card. "This is the only one in existence, so no." Menard glanced away. "As for a motive I wonder could it be corporate espionage, IP theft from a competitor, a hostile nation."

"What hostile nation would want to get in here?" Rizzo asked.

"The better question is: which one wouldn't?" Menard replied, eyebrows raised.

"We're wading into murky waters," Franklin interrupted. "Speculating on who did this could trigger an investigation."

"Milton. *Enough.*" Menard turned to Rizzo. "You wouldn't do that, would you?"

"*Never*," Rizzo replied with mock severity.

"That's settled then," said Menard.

"She was being facetious," stressed Franklin.

Menard ignored him, gesturing to Rick Reynolds, chief of security. "Audit the retinal scan database. I want confirmation of every employee's bio-login identification. Find out whose ID she used!"

"Already underway," Reynolds replied, wiping rain from his thick mustache, hoping to keep his job and retirement pension after today.

Inside the complex, the group retraced Sheila's steps, passing multiple Falcon 9 rockets and Raptor, Merlin, Kestrel, Draco, and Super Draco engines in their storage bays. Rizzo's gut told her that Sheila's breach was somehow connected to the Eye Torcher case. She couldn't prove it but she knew from her years in the field that when someone is murdered right after committing a felony, the events are usually related. Gulping down the last of her coffee, Rizzo remembered going three days without sleep on an Army Ranger mission in Afghanistan that fell apart and wondered if she could repeat that feat twenty years later without anyone getting killed. She knew she might have to.

The group arrived at Berth 240, the twenty-six-story hangar where Starship MK17 was docked.

"Here we are," Reynolds said. "The scene of the break-in."

"Behold, the eighth wonder," said Menard, admiring Starship like a proud uncle. It was even more spectacular in real life—a sleek, shimmering work of space technology powered by thirty-two methane-fueled Raptor engines.

Even Rizzo was taken aback by its size. "Impressive."

"It still has that 'new car' smell. So does our Mission Control," Menard said, leading the group into a lofty glass-walled colossal room full of cutting-edge aeronautics technology located next to the spacecraft.

"Our new nerve center rivals NASA's in Houston or Cape Canaveral." Menard walked Agents Rizzo and Thorn down the left aisle of the dimly lit amphitheater past four abandoned rows of twenty workstations, equipped with forty computer monitors (two for each engineer).

"This is where our CORE team of engineers will monitor every space flight and measure the performance of the components on our crafts." Menard gestured to the Big Board, a wall of supercomputers and, above them, ten flat-screen jumbo monitors, each showing live shots of Starship with time-coded countdown tickers on the right margin of the screens. "When we broadcast our double launch on New Year's Day, these shots will go out live to millions of people around the world. It will be the most compelling reality series ever produced."

"I prefer a good book, myself," Rizzo replied.

"We installed glass so our employees can watch, and cheer," Menard explained, leading the agents down to the front row. There, two twenty-five-year-old software security engineers were clacking away on laptops that were ported into the supercomputers' USBs.

"This is Dan Mopac and Mike Davis," Reynolds said, introducing the two young men, who were dressed more like college students than engineers—in untucked plaid shirts, messy hair, and blue light-blocking computer glasses—contrasted to Menard, who wore a black button-down Prada shirt and soft black leather Gucci loafers.

"Mike and Dan here head our cybersecurity team," explained Menard. "They're running an audit on our network, looking for any suspicious patches in our code. They're also performing tests on all the open network jacks close to where our intern went 'off the reservation' to identify irregularities, viruses, trojans—any sign of a system hack. Boys"—he turned to the auditors—"this is the FBI…"

"Hey," said Dan, not looking up from his laptop. "So far, so good."

"And over here is where our trespasser, Miss *Roustamov*," Reynolds said, stressing Sheila's last name like he despised all Russians, "disappeared from our cameras for six minutes. We think she may have gone in there." He pointed to a tall but narrow ventilation shaft that ran behind the wall of computers and monitors.

"One of your urban tunnel prototypes?" Thorn asked Menard, referencing his stalled project to create a subterranean highway system under Los Angeles.

"It's a cooling duct to keep our mainframes from overheating," Menard explained. "When we do combustion tests, it can get broiling hot in here."

"Have to be rail thin to squeeze in there," Agent Thorn said, inspecting the duct.

"Roust was supermodel skinny, remember?" Rizzo said. "But why would she do that?"

"If the deceased woman was indeed a hacker of some sort, no way she could port into our computers from behind that wall; it's stainless steel," Reynolds said.

"Maybe she used it simply as a way to avoid your cameras and get to the exit, after doing whatever she was sent here to do?" Thorn speculated.

"Where does it lead?" Rizzo asked.

Reynolds gestured to Starship. "Over to the rocket ship."

"You surmise she spent *six minutes* in this air duct?" Menard questioned Reynolds.

"Where else could she have gone?" Reynolds replied. "Unless she crawled on the floor and knew every blind spot for all twenty-six cameras, not to mention how to elude the twelve engineers on the floor that evening. Conceivably, she could have come out the other side of this and avoided that camera…" Reynolds pointed to a security camera on the south wall.

"And *that camera*"—he pointed to a security camera on the southwest wall—"and perhaps found a way to the door, but she must have moved like a dang cat burglar."

"I want in there," Rizzo said, shining a pocket flashlight into the dark crevasse.

"Be my guest," Menard said, waving his hand. "It's safe."

"I can't stress this enough," Franklin implored, wringing his hands, "but giving them carte blanche to turn this place over without a court order will likely blow up in our face."

"I've dealt with explosions before. I want their expert opinion on this," Menard said.

"All right, let's go then," Rizzo said, gesturing to Reynolds.

"If you say so, ma'am," Reynolds said unenthusiastically as he unlatched the metal door to the vent shaft. He tried to squeeze into the narrow duct, but with the build of a retired high school football coach, his paunchy belly—encased like a sausage in a red SpaceX golf shirt—wouldn't allow it. "Guess I need to lose a few in the new year."

"Guess so. Move," Rizzo said, taking off her brown leather jacket. "I'll fit."

"Good luck with that," Thorn scoffed. "My butt can't squeeze into that sardine can."

"I'll join you," Menard said brightly. "I'm trim enough, I think."

"I'd highly advise against this," said Franklin, his voice rising with each word.

"Then *you* volunteer," said Menard, gesturing to Franklin, who was far shorter than anyone else in the room and barely weighed 140 pounds.

"I'll pass," Franklin said meekly. "Notorious claustrophobic."

"Go make yourself useful then." Menard waved him away.

One after the other, Agent Rizzo and the head of the Vice President and Director of IT Security, squeezed into the narrow cooling shaft and began to inch their way through it like they were shimmying along a narrow ledge. Every step they took reverberated on the metal floor. After a few steps, Rizzo noticed Menard was breathing heavily. "You a notorious claustrophobic, too?"

"Not normally," Menard joked, his fit midsection easily fitting in the shaft. "This is easier than I anticipated."

"Like a TV dinner in here," Rizzo said as the whirring fans on the back wall of the duct blew her brown hair into Menard's face.

Once they had gotten ten yards in, they heard a loud crash of thunder.

Suddenly all the lights in the hangar went out.

The ventilation shaft went pitch black…

"What's happening, Rick?" Menard shouted.

"This normal?" Rizzo asked, resting her right hand on her holstered Glock.

"Of course not!" Menard replied.

"Could be the lightning storm," Rick replied in a muffled voice. "We're checking."

"You do that," Menard shouted, feeling the walls closing in.

A moment later red backup generator lights flashed on, eerily filling the hangar with diffused light. Inside the dimly lit shaft, Rizzo saw a tiny yellow light start to flash on the wall of the duct a few yards ahead. "I see something," she said, inching closer. "A flashing light."

"There should be no lights in here," Menard said.

"It just started," Rizzo said, shining her flashlight on it.

Upon closer inspection, it was seen to be a small black device duct-taped to the front wall of the shaft.

"Looks hinky." To Rizzo, it looked like a walkie-talkie with a yellow key-pad. Menard inched over to the device, which was now at eye level between him and Rizzo. He frowned.

"This is not our tech," said Menard. The device was connected to a black USB cord that emerged from a hole in the shaft's stainless-steel shell. "*Unbelievable*," said Menard. "Who installed a *backdoor port* into our mainframe? I need to examine this in better light."

$$\text{(19)}$$

Rizzo and Menard emerged out the other side of the ventilation shaft; the lights in the hangar had powered back on. A red-faced Menard rushed back to the group clutching the device; Rizzo trailed behind him, giving Thorn an 'I told you so' look.

"We're back online," Reynolds said. "Lightning hit the tower. The system was reset."

"Forget the weather, our intern was a bloody hacker," Menard said, out of breath, slamming the device down on a stainless-steel desk. "She left this rootkit, connected to our system."

Mike stood up, stepping away from the small black box. "You disconnected it? I, uh, don't think that was a good idea."

"Why not? It's corrupting our network!" Menard exclaimed. "Who would authorize the installation of a backdoor port?"

The hangar grew silent.

"In the ventilation duct?" Dan asked. "*No one.* Someone would have needed to drill through five inches of steel to get to it."

The group gathered around the table to inspect the device.

"Explain a rootkit to us idiots in the room," said Rizzo.

"Malware," Thorn replied. "It infects a database. Allows an attacker remote access."

"This one looks Chinese," said Reynolds, pointing to the manufacturer's logo on the top right of the black box.

"China." Thorn turned to Rizzo. "They'd benefit from hacking into Starlink."

"Speculation," Franklin declared. "I think you ladies need to leave."

"*Ladies?*" Thorn raised her eyebrow. "How about federal agents?"

"Milt. Can it. They stay." Menard turned to Reynolds. "I want the names of the contractors who built that ventilation shaft."

96

"This rig's only a few months old," Reynolds said. "I know we outsourced the construction."

Menard thought a moment. "They could have installed it without our knowledge when it was built. Tell me that the contractors were well vetted."

"I have to ask," Reynolds said. "I'm sure they all went through background checks."

"You're sure, are you?" Menard exclaimed. "Do your job, Rick!"

Mopac looked up from his laptop and raised his hand. "Mr. Menard…"

"What is it?" Menard replied tersely.

"I, uh, found an unauthorized desktop sharing service installed on this network jack…"

Everyone turned to Mopac, who was sitting at the computer terminal at the far end of the table that faced the wall of larger screens.

"Is this an inside job?" Menard asked in a huff, taking over Dan's chair and clacking away at the computer keyboard himself.

"Appears to be a coordinated effort," said Dan. "Someone inside had to be part of this, besides the intern."

"How did they get into our network?" Menard asked. "We hardened the install with a restrictive hot base firewall rule set two weeks ago! It should have prevented anything like this happening!"

Mike leaned over Menard's shoulder as he accessed the database. "We also performed a whitelisting install to block unauthorized apps from running. But this jack could've been breached before that."

"There are spies among us," Menard said, steaming. "I've been betrayed!"

Dan inspected the rootkit. "It appears someone is accessing log data from the backdoor port. They're using an account from a member of the code architecture team."

"Who?!" Reynolds asked Mike, who was furiously scouring the network for breadcrumbs.

"Appears to trace back to a software engineer on our Raptor team," Mike replied. "Xang Xi."

Menard rubbed his head. "Never heard of him. I want him detained when he comes in."

"Too late. He resigned on December twenty-third," Reynolds said, checking their employee roster from his phone.

"Same day Uma Gloten was murdered," Thorn said to Rizzo with a raised eyebrow.

"Find him," Menard shouted. "I want him prosecuted for corporate espionage."

"Sir...sir?" Mike stammered, pointing to the wall of monitors. "*This is bad.*"

Everyone looked up at the ten monitors on the wall. The live shots of Starlink had disappeared. They were replaced by an endless stream of pirate code furiously cascading down every monitor in the hangar like a digital waterfall, signaling a corrupted system.

"This is bad!" Dan echoed. "Very bad!"

Panicked, Dan and Mike ran to check all the computers in the room. "Every jack in the network is sequencing rapidly! They're in!"

"What do they want?" Menard shouted. "You assured me the patch we installed would only run trusted code!"

"They could've signed their own firmware and bypassed the patch," Dan said, eyes wide.

"Christ." Menard's face went pale. "What did they do?"

Dan scanned the code as it whizzed down the screens. "Appears they're targeting the Raptors...triggering a controlled burn in all thirty-two high-combustion chambers. It's scheduled for January first, right after Starship's liftoff."

"How!" Menard shouted in disbelief.

"By overwriting our stabilizing firmware with a malicious version that would—"

"Disable all the fail-safes," Menard said, finishing Dan's thought. "They want to blow up Starship and all our passengers... *Look.*" Menard pointed to the thrusters at the bottom of the rocket. "They're firing up on their own."

"Removing the device may have triggered it to go off now instead," Mike said.

"Shoot. They're forcing a controlled burn to 1000 bar chamber pressure," Dan said.

"It won't hold, we only tested up to three hundred and thirty!" Menard rubbed his forehead.

Everyone turned to look at Starship as its engines began to heat up; the Raptors roared like the creature they were named for. Menard swallowed his fear and spoke slowly:

"We have to stop this. There are thirty-two Raptors under that hood. If they blow and each one would set off a blast the size of two Hiroshimas… sixty-four atomic bombs."

"That would level the entire city," Thorn said, alarmed.

"I've heard enough." Rizzo started dialing. "Calling the bomb squad."

"LAPD won't know how to disable this," said Menard.

"You just said 'atomic bomb.' It's our jobs if we don't report it," Rizzo insisted, "…and our lives."

"We can do this ourselves," Mike said, typing furiously on his laptop. "All we need is to get to the hardware security modules on Starship."

"Mike's right!" Dan said, turning to Menard and Rizzo. "Then we can disable the corrupted devices ourselves and override the controlled burn."

Menard looked at Dan and Mike, who both nodded.

"Do it!!" Menard roared. Dan and Mike bolted out of their chairs and sprinted over to Starship as the engines began whirring to full capacity.

"Do not call the authorities!" shrieked Franklin, lunging for Agent Rizzo's cell phone. "We are a private company! We handle our own security!"

"Too late. Already done," Rizzo barked. "You touch me, you go to jail."

"You best step away from us," Thorn warned Franklin, who raised his hands and moved away from the agents. Menard turned to Agent Rizzo.

"Just tell the cops to stay out of their way. Everyone else, *out of the building!*"

20

When the sun came up the next day, Los Angeles had not been wiped off the map, and the city's residents had not been pulverized. The morning of December 29 began like any other day for most Los Angelinos, who had no idea how close they came to becoming victims of the largest blast ever seen in the continental United States.

The Los Angeles Police Department's Bomb Squad had arrived at SpaceX Headquarters at 1 Rocket Road at 10:23 p.m. on December 28, five minutes after Agent Rizzo called it in but, as Edward Menard had predicted, they were not equipped to respond to the complexity of the threat. Their bomb-sniffing dogs and detonation experts could find no bombs planted in the complex nor any explosives at all. The bombs were the thirty-two corrupted Raptors themselves.

The only thing standing in the way of the hackers accomplishing their mission was the fast work done by SpaceX's cybersecurity duo, Mike Davis and Dan Mopac, who located the hacked hardware security modules on Starship and disabled them before the forced fatal combustion tests on the thirty-two Raptor thrusters had reached their breaking points. When the rocket thruster smoke cleared, a visibly rattled Edward Menard breathed a sigh of relief and promised Mike and Dan they would both receive promotions and fat end-of-the-year bonuses for their heroism—if they signed NDAs to keep the story under wraps; of course, they would.

The handful of local news outlets who (after monitoring their police scanners) had arrived on the scene were told it was simply a "false alarm" by the LAPD spokesman. This spared SpaceX's reputation, as well as avoiding the LAPD's Bomb Squad from getting raked over the coals by the media for being profoundly ill equipped to handle twenty-first-century terrorism—if that indeed was what this "prank" was. With the threat averted, Agents Rizzo and Thorn still weren't sure what they had just experienced as they drove north on the 110 freeway, heading back to their downtown hotel at dawn. They were left to speculate what all this drama had to do with the Eye Torcher, if anything.

"Maybe it's not a serial killer we're chasing," said Rizzo, wearing a dazed look as she drove the black Chevy LTD rental car.

"You suggesting the Torcher's part of some larger terror plot?" Thorn asked, half-asleep herself.

"Uh-huh," Rizzo said. "You heard those guys. They wanted to blow up Starship and its passengers on New Year's Day. Menard just triggered it early when he disconnected the device, like a dumbass."

"Funny, I had the same feeling…that we've stumbled onto something bigger," Thorn said. She continued, "Menard should delay that launch of his till we figure out what in the world is going on."

"Let's bring him in tomorrow and see what he thinks," Rizzo said.

"You mean today?" Thorn said, yawning.

"Right," Rizzo said, squinting her eyes into the eastern sunrise. "Today."

"Think he's had enough of us all up in his business yet?" Thorn joked.

"Yes. He's been an open book so far. Seems to relish the attention."

"That's 'cause we charming as hell," Thorn said. "For a couple of dirty cops."

"Don't remind me," Rizzo said. "I need a shower."

Thorn lifted the front of her shirt to her nose. "That's what fear smells like, girl."

"You haven't smelled fear till you've faced two dozen insurgents attacking your squadron," said Rizzo, staring into the sunrise. "But that lawyer of his almost wet his pants, that's for sure."

"See him run outta there?" Thorn laughed. "Only battle that boy's been in was playing *Mortal Combat* on his PlayStation." Both agents chuckled out of pure exhaustion, knowing the clock was ticking, and they had their own ticking time bomb to defuse before he killed again.

$$\textbf{21}$$

After a shower and some much-needed sleep, Rizzo and Thorn made their way up the stairs to the main entrance of the faded white FBI satellite office on 11000 Wilshire Boulevard near the UCLA campus. They remained convinced that Sheila Roust's murder, only two days after her role in a plot to blow up Starship, was no coincidence.

Rizzo insisted on speaking with Edward Menard immediately about delaying SpaceX's double launch. Rizzo reached out to Gemma Arbor, Menard's executive assistant, who arranged for a meeting later that day. As they passed by the stream of government employees on their way to lunch, Rizzo commented, "These people have no idea…"

"Would've been toast if your skinny behind hadn't found that rootkit," replied Thorn.

"That your attempt at a compliment?"

"Don't get cocky, football star," said Thorn. "Not like you disarmed the thing."

Rizzo pointed to the odd design of their temporary home with its two massive white pillars jutting to the sky. "Is it just me, or is this cement tomb shaped like a 'pause' button?"

"Yeah, maybe," Thorn replied, looking down at her phone.

"Ironic," Rizzo said.

"Ironic, how?" Thorn asked.

"Considering all the red tape they've been throwing at us."

Thorn looked up from her phone. "That your attempt at a joke?"

Although generous with his time the prior evening, Edward Menard opted out of the requested emergency meeting, instead sending his little bulldog Milton Franklin and four other members of SpaceX's legal team to represent him. After last nights near disaster, Rizzo wasn't surprised. She poured herself a cup of coffee from the stainless-steel coffee urn and faced

102

Menard's expressionless lawyers, who were stubbornly seated around an old oak government conference table.

"Who's investigating last night's fiasco then?" Rizzo asked bluntly.

"Ma'am, SpaceX investigates SpaceX," drawled Clint Harris, a broad-chinned Southern lawyer with bushy brown eyebrows and steely blue eyes.

"However, Mr. Menard greatly appreciates your pointing out the intern," Franklin added.

"How about finding the rootkit in the wall that nearly killed us?" Thorn asked.

"That too," Franklin continued, "but our internal team disabled the situation, not law enforcement—so we're classifying it as a false alarm."

Thorn squinted at Franklin. "You sure looked shaken by that false alarm."

"Are we litigating my character now?" Franklin bandied back.

"You sprinted outta there real fast, as I recall," Thorn said.

Franklin ignored Agent Thorn's attempt to get under his skin. "Bottom line: Mr. Menard does not want any more help from the FBI with our private matters. We are not NASA, ladies."

"There's that '*ladies*' thing again," Thorn said.

"You know we can get a court order," Rizzo said.

"Be our guest," Franklin said. "But until then—"

"You got a coordinated group that almost incinerated your spaceship with one hundred passengers onboard," Rizzo interrupted. "Your boss isn't concerned about that?"

"We object to that characterization," Franklin said and paused to listen as Clint Harris whispered in his ear. Franklin cleared his throat. "Let me state, for the record, if that tragic outcome had come to pass, then we obviously would welcome your assistance."

"But we all know it didn't go down that way," added Harris. "So, we will not delay. This is SpaceX's seminal project and they will not see it hijacked by one rotten apple."

"*One rotten apple* almost wiped this city off the map," Rizzo replied.

"The operative word in that phrase is 'almost,' Agent Rizzo," added Harris primly.

"Look, Milt." Rizzo sat down across the table from the lead counsel. "The Raptor's liquid methane engine components. Where is developmental testing done?"

"Our rocket testing facility is in McGregor, Texas," Franklin calmly replied.

"Where you also produce the Starlink engines?" Rizzo asked.

"Correct."

"Also where our other dead girl, Uma Gloten, was interning, right?" Thorn said.

"So you claim."

"What are the odds your other intern, who we also found with her eyes ripped out a few days ago, wasn't involved?" Rizzo asked.

"We're attorneys, Agent Rizzo, we don't do odds," Harris responded archly.

"Roust was murdered two days after being caught on tape planting that rootkit," Thorn said. "Two dead SpaceX interns in twenty-four hours. Both missing their eyes."

"I hear you, but show us the evidence of a plot," demanded Franklin.

"You check the security footage in Texas yet?" Rizzo continued.

"We're auditing our exclusive LAN network that connects all of our facilities," Franklin said.

"Your geek squad disabled the Raptors," Thorn said, "but our analysts believe the hack in Hawthorne could've compromised your network coast to coast. You've considered that, right?"

"We consider everything," Harris gruffly replied.

"Not everything," Rizzo said. "We had to alert you to Sheila's last ride."

Franklin closed his MacBook Air and took off his wire-rimmed glasses, rubbing the bridge of his nose. "Prove the existence of this so-called plot, then we'll talk. But until then, the launch goes as planned... Good day."

As Franklin and his phalanx of SpaceX lawyers filed out, Thorn growled after them, "Thought your boss was smarter than this." She stood up.

"You'll be hearing from us," Rizzo said to Franklin, who turned and gave her a smug look.

"I don't doubt that," Franklin said, locking eyes with Rizzo. When the lawyers left the room, Rizzo crumpled her paper coffee cup and banked it off the wall and into a wastebasket.

"I'd like to drop-kick that little weasel," she said.

22

The two agents made their way across the seventeenth floor to update the man in charge of the FBI's LA team. His corner office was decorated with drab wood paneling and cheap mid-century furniture; to Rizzo, it looked frozen in the 1960s. They barged in on Special Agent Harold "Harry" Hawks (supervisor of the Southern California regional agency for the past twenty years) checking his bleached teeth in a pocket mirror after finishing his brown-bag lunch. His slicked-back pepper grey hair, fake tan, and five o'clock shadow told Rizzo he was a pretty boy jock. She'd been hit on by his kind back in college—but she still felt Hawks could help them get a court order. After the 9/11 attacks, protecting the city from terrorism had been the focus of the Los Angeles office. Under his leadership, the FBI had thwarted numerous terror attacks in Southern California by strengthening its Joint Terrorism Task Force with the LAPD and by establishing a Field Intelligence Group to identify sleeper cells. Rizzo had assured her younger partner that Hawks would be receptive to the latest twist in the Eye Torcher case, but the look on his face told a different story.

Embarrassed to be caught picking his teeth, he quicky stashed his mirror and leaned back awkwardly in the faux leather chair as Rizzo updated him on the events of the past twenty-four hours.

"They're daring us to get a warrant," Rizzo concluded. "We should call their bluff."

"On what grounds?" Agent Hawks asked.

"Menard said it himself. They nearly killed three million people last night," Rizzo replied.

"Okay. But what does that have to do with the Torcher case?" Hawks asked.

"Were you not listening?" Rizzo shot back.

"Don't be cute, Jane," Hawks said. "We have specialists that handle terrorism." Listening to Hawks explain why SpaceX wasn't in "their lane," Rizzo wondered if her reputation for being so impetuous in her younger years was still haunting her.

"Respectfully, sir," Thorn said, calmly stepping in. "The bomb was planted by one of the Torcher's victims."

"A bomb?" Hawks replied skeptically.

"Rootkit…same thing," Thorn replied.

"Not to a seventy-year-old federal judge," Hawks said. "Try explaining that to an old man who can't get his AOL started."

"This is 2023," Rizzo said. "At least let us make our case. How many other dead conspirators are out there?"

Thorn added, "We found two already."

"You prove the Gloten girl in Texas is part of it?" Hawks asked.

"Not yet, technically," Rizzo added.

"You're telling me this 'plot' is only connected to the Torcher by Roust?" Hawks asked.

"Gloten also lost her eyes," Rizzo insisted. "We believe she was murdered by the same killer. SpaceX is launching two rockets in seventy-two hours. Just because we stopped stage one doesn't mean there aren't more strikes planned."

Benji Weir, a redheaded thirty-five-year-old Junior Intelligence Analyst assigned to the case, poked his head through the open office door. "Can I interrupt?"

"You're late, kid," Rizzo said.

Agent Hawks gestured for him to enter.

"Get this," Benji said. "Interpol just reported both of the dead women visited Sarajevo over the summer and were seen meeting with a known terror cell."

"There it is," Rizzo said with a told-you-so expression.

"Boom goes Benji," Thorn exclaimed, giving Benji an awkwardly received high five.

"Both women also entered the U.S. using fake Bosnian passports," Benji continued.

"That all a coincidence too?" Thorn said sarcastically.

"Let me think." Hawks frowned.

"We're not just hunting a serial killer," Rizzo said. "He's getting rid of his accomplices."

"I concur. The chatter we are hearing points to an active terror cell," Benji added.

Hawks thought a moment. "Nice work, Weir. Report it to the Joint Terrorism Task Force, CIA, and Homeland. Rizzo and Thorn, stay on your case."

"Our case? They're the *same case*!" Rizzo exclaimed.

"This isn't your call. Find the Torcher. Leave the rest to the qualified."

"So, we aren't qualified?" Thorn shot back.

"You lack experience, Agent Thorn—and discipline, from what I know about you, *Jane.* Remember you're only on this case because it was Christmas, and you have no families."

"You really know how to make us feel wanted, *Harry*," Rizzo shot back.

"You have forty-eight hours to find the Torcher or I'm reassigning the case to a senior team," Hawks said. "Now stop whining and do your job."

Astounded, Rizzo and Thorn gave each other a look of disbelief.

"You're making a big mistake," Rizzo said and left the office. With a raised eyebrow directed at Hawks, Thorn made an explosion gesture with her hands.

23

Indialantic, Florida

The *Mission Impossible* theme song rang out in the darkened room. Dr. Jake LaFleur's eyes moved rapidly under his eyelids as his ringtone played. He stirred in his king-sized bed, disoriented from being awakened from REM sleep. He let out a quiet groan. He was dreaming he was lined up for the marathon but couldn't move. All the runners were bounding past him, but his legs felt like lead. No matter how hard he tried, he couldn't run. He clumsily reached for his Samsung Galaxy on the bedside table, fumbling it onto the beige carpeted floor. Like most young doctors, Jake never silenced his ringtone, even on his days off. He looked at his clock—it was 1:11 a.m.

"Crap," he muttered to himself, grabbing for his phone and lifting it to his ear. "…Doctor LaFleur," he responded.

"Jake," a man said over the phone. "It's Doctor David Burke at Holmes. I know you're not on call, but—"

Jake cleared his throat. "What's the problem?"

"We have a patient here that sustained an ocular injury from a serious car accident on Route 528. LifeFlight just brought her in. She has extensive bleeding around the eye. I'm going to close the wound but she needs an eye exam to rule out a ruptured globe. I'm afraid she may lose the eye…"

Jake sat up and rubbed his eyes. "Where's Doctor Marks?"

"In Destin… On vacation with his wife and kids."

"Okay," he croaked, "be there in twenty minutes." Jake ended the call and turned on his bedside lamp. He found his glasses and glanced over at the silver-framed wedding photo of himself and Didi on his nightstand. He sighed; he hadn't had the heart to get rid of it since the divorce.

Lumbering out of bed, Jake muttered, "Guess Mom will be eating breakfast alone."

Sleep deprived and slowed by his recent heart episode, Jake made it to the Holmes Regional Medical Center in under twenty minutes. He sipped on a thermal mug of hot tea that his mother had quickly made him; the time was 1:27 a.m.

"Look what the cat dragged in," someone called out in a raspy voice. It was head nurse Wilma Tremond, the elder stateswoman and self-proclaimed yenta of the hospital, manning the front desk. Jake self-consciously ran his fingers through his unkempt wavy brown hair.

"Lost my comb in a fight," he kidded, which was technically true; the last time he'd seen his comb was the incident with Red, which landed him in the hospital.

"It shows. I trust that's caffeinated," said Nurse Tremond, glancing at his mug.

"Green tea. Highest octane," replied Jake.

"Got a feeling you're gonna need it." She smiled.

The theme to *Mission Impossible* rang out from his side pocket. Jake fumbled for his phone—it was his mother again.

"Oh boy… Cindy's in town," he sighed.

"Lucky you. Doctor Burke's waiting." Nurse Tremond pointed to the west wing of the trauma center. "*If you choose to accept the mission, Agent LaFleur.*"

"Very funny," Jake replied, sending his mother to voicemail.

He walked down to the end of the brightly lit corridor, through the silent sliding glass door of Trauma Bay 1. David Burke, the rail-thin supervising trauma physician, was hunched over, checking the vitals of a young woman with a bandaged right eye and bruises on her arms and face. She had stitches above her right eyebrow and an IV bag of fluids hanging over the left side of the bed.

"Doctor LaFleur. Glad you could make it to the party," said Dr. Burke, standing up straight and rolling his shoulders.

"Wouldn't miss it," Jake replied, getting his first look at the patient. *She looks familiar*, he thought.

"Miss Smilovic was in a nasty car accident," Dr. Burke explained. "She suffered burns, a concussion, bruised sternum, and swelling around her right orbital. I put in twenty stitches to stop the bleeding above the right eye… Possible ruptured globe from the airbag—but it's your call, Doctor. I'm still waiting for the results of the CT scan to help rule out an orbital fracture or ruptured globe."

"That's my job.," Jake murmured, calmly reading Elena's chart and sipping tea.

"We have the OR ready for emergency surgery, if needed."

Jake gently touched her shoulder. "Miss Smilovic?"

Elena slowly opened the one caramel brown eye that wasn't bandaged over.

"Who are you?" Elena rasped.

"I'm Doctor Jake LaFleur… You're in the hospital. You've been in a car accident."

"Britt…" she moaned with her thick Bosnian accent. "They killed her."

Jake shot Dr. Burke a concerned look.

"State Police report says it was a one-car accident," said Dr. Burke. "One fatality. A Brittany Todd, the driver of the vehicle."

"Two men. In a black van," Elena said, half sedated from her pain medication.

"We will notify the authorities, Miss Smilovic, and you can tell them what happened, okay?" Jake said, gently removing the gauze bandage to inspect Elena's damaged right eye. "But first…"

Seeing Elena for the first time without the bandage, his vulnerable heart skipped a beat. *It's the woman from the airport*, he thought. *Two men WERE chasing her*. He couldn't believe the coincidence.

"Let me just add, that I believe you, what you remember about the accident," Jake continued, slipping into his most soothing bedside doctor voice, causing Dr. Burke to scrunch his face in disbelief. "But we need you to stay awake while I examine your eye, okay? Just relax so I can take a look."

Elena groaned.

Jake turned off the overhead light and looked through a handheld slit lamp device. He examined her right eye for a ruptured globe, common in a car accident, noting his observations in a voice recorder.

"The good news is no sign of a corneal or anterior scleral rupture. No foreign objects penetrated your eye… No obvious displacement of your lens, no traumatic hyphema."

He placed the device back in its case.

"My eyes have ached since I left Bosnia," she complained. "Both eyes blurry."

"Vision is a gift we take for granted," Jake replied, reassuringly spouting doctorly lines while his mind raced. *What are the odds, seeing her twice? Maybe she's still in trouble? Maybe I can help. ... Wow, she is absolutely gorgeous... Stop it, Jake!* he told himself. *Be professional.* He calmly turned on the overhead light.

"You're going to be fine. I was concerned about an eye rupture or a retinal detachment from the airbags, but it's just a brow laceration and corneal abrasion. You're a very lucky woman; it will heal without surgery... I am sorry to hear about your friend."

"Thank you," she whispered.

"Guess I dragged you out of bed for nothing," offered Dr. Burke.

"Not a problem," replied Jake, unable to take his eyes off Elena.

"I still can't see straight," Elena complained.

"Well. Let's take a closer look at your left eye, then," Jake said, eagerly putting a direct ophthalmoscope on his head to examine her retina, trying to spend as much time near this beautiful woman as he could.

A baritone voice interrupted at the door. "Knock, knock."

Two stern-faced Florida Highway Patrol troopers wearing broad-rim hats, dark green uniforms, each with a Taser on one hip and a .40 caliber Glock on the other, appeared in the doorway.

Jake took off his loupe. "Speak of the devil."

"We'd like a minute with your patient," said Trooper John Monroe through his walrus mustache.

"Come in, officers," said Dr. Burke. "She has quite a story to tell."

The two barrel-chested troopers stepped into the room.

"I'm State Trooper Monroe, and this is Trooper Gavin Wallace. We were first to respond at the site of your accident." The troopers explained how they'd contacted Brittany's next of kin, an aunt who lived in Chicago, and that travel arrangements were being made for her, but they had a few more inquiries for Elena about the accident. Jake saw Elena tense up as they questioned her. He had no idea who this woman was but felt oddly protective of her, which was out of character, unprofessional. "We found a cooler of beer in the vehicle. Were you drinking too, miss?" asked Trooper Monroe.

"Test my blood… I just got off plane, Britt picked me up," Elena said.

"We ran a blood test; she had no alcohol or drugs in her system," Dr. Burke added.

"Good to know," Trooper Monroe replied, writing it down in his notepad.

"Two crazy men in van ran us off the road," said Elena.

Monroe stared at her over his reading glasses. "This is the first we're hearing of a second vehicle, ma'am."

"Ask the couple who stopped to help," Elena replied.

"What couple?" asked Trooper Monroe.

Elena sized up the men in uniform. She'd dealt with corrupt police before in Bosnia and knew her best defense might be to stay silent.

"Ma'am, there were no witnesses at the scene when we arrived," added Trooper Monroe.

"The woman said she was a nurse, that's all I remember…" Elena said, trailing off.

"Did you fly in from Bosnia earlier tonight?" asked Trooper Monroe.

"I have green card," she said coldly. "I came back for my spring semester."

"Says here you're an aerospace graduate student at University of Central Florida… Must be interesting work. Anyone with a security clearance at Cape Canaveral, and all," added Trooper Monroe. "My kids sure love to watch those rockets launch."

"I'm just intern," said Elena. "I get school credits."

"We also found a pair of carbon fiber knuckles in your Louis Vuitton purse. That's a serious weapon. Are you afraid of someone, Miss Smilovic?" asked Trooper Wallace.

"I told you, we saw two men." She shrugged. "In black van. They followed us from the airport."

"This is beginning to sound like a Lara Croft action movie," said a skeptical Trooper Monroe.

Jake cleared his throat. "Excuse me, officers. But, quite coincidentally, I also happened to be at the Orlando-Melbourne airport last night around ten p.m. to pick up my mother. You see, she's visiting for the holidays, and I'm her only child."

"Get on with it," prodded Trooper Monroe.

"Well, I happened to see Miss Smilovic there, being pursued by two men, just like she said."

"You two know each other?" Trooper Monroe gestured at Jake and Elena with his Bic.

"No!" Elena replied.

"No. Miss Smilovic walked by me. She's, uh, kinda hard to miss," Jake said, alluding to her obvious beauty; the troopers nodded. "Anyway, I watched two men following her. I sensed that something was not right."

"I see. So, you can corroborate her story?" Trooper Monroe glanced at Elena.

Jake replied, "My mother can as well. We both saw two men pursuing Miss Smilovic down toward the baggage claim, clear as day."

"Anyone notify the airport police?" asked Trooper Wallace.

Jake shook his head. "No. But I stuck out my foot to slow them down…"

"You tripped up the assailants?" asked Trooper Wallace.

"I accidently tripped them up, I guess." Jake shrugged.

"Well, this changes our report," said Trooper Monroe. "Get a good look at them?"

"Yes, sirs. I'd be happy to describe their appearance," Jake said, looking down at Elena with reassuring eyes. Elena furrowed her brow, trying to focus her one good eye on the kind doctor who was helping her. When Jake's round smiling face came into clear view, she did remember seeing him earlier at the baggage claim.

This didn't look like a killer, she thought. She would sleep with one eye open anyway.

(24)

A few hundred yards away from Elena's room in the palm-tree-lined, three-story cement parking structure of the Holmes Regional Medical Center, Sam Turner, a middle-aged X-ray technician in blue scrubs, trudged out into the early morning light carrying a backpack and staring at his iPhone. He had performed Elena's CT scan an hour earlier and now was leaving the hospital after working a double shift. Sam stopped walking and looked up from his phone, confused. He'd forgotten where he parked twelve hours ago.

"There I am..." he said, finally spotting his red Volvo station wagon. Slowly ambling over to the driver's side, he reached in his pocket for his car keys, not noticing there was a man standing in a shadowy corner of the lot.

Then Sam heard the quickening stride of boots coming toward him.

"Got a light?" asked a deep-voiced, foreign-accented man.

"Huh?" Sam jumped, half-startled, half-asleep. He turned around. "You talking to me?"

The man stepped out of the shadows holding an unlit cigar. He was stocky with close-cropped dark hair and wearing an eerie smile, but his touristy Universal Studios Harry Potter T-shirt momentarily put Sam at ease.

"A light?" repeated the man with a distinct accent. "Got one?"

"No smoking on hospital grounds, pal," said Sam, gruffly dismissing the stranger and turning back to his car. The man stepped forward and locked Sam in a choke hold.

"*Hey*! What are you—?" Sam cried out as the man violently pushed him into his Volvo and jumped in, slamming the door behind him. A muffled struggle could be heard inside the car.

Then silence.

A few minutes later, the stocky man emerged from the Volvo wearing Sam's scrubs. He locked the door behind him and snapped on Sam's ID badge. He sauntered out of the parking garage, lifted a cell phone to his ear, and stared at the ER entrance.

"I'm ready," he intoned.

Less than a mile away from the hospital, a white Chevy Impala was parked outside a Dunkin' Donuts. The driver held a cell phone to his ear.

"Go into the hospital," he ordered, "Find her room. I will be there soon."

$$\textcircled{25}$$

Elena was moved to a private room at the Holmes hospital for further testing later that afternoon. As she was still experiencing blurred vision in both eyes, Dr. Burke asked Jake to return to complete her eye exam. To fit her into his schedule, Jake finished a seven-mile training run at a record pace guaranteeing he could see Elena before getting to the office. He arrived at the hospital clean shaven, in his best-fitting scrubs, and fragrant with the cologne his mother gave him for Christmas. "Hello. Doctor LaFleur again," Jake said, quietly entering the doorway and smiling down at his lovely patient.

"I am Elena," she uttered cautiously from her bed.

"I am Jake. We met this morning," he replied, placing his on-call bag on a stainless-steel table next to her bed. It contained eye charts, dilating drops, a portable slit lamp for examining the front of the eye, and an indirect headset for viewing the back of the eye.

Elena widened her good eye to get a look at him. "...I remember."

"That's a good sign," Jake said, selfishly hoping she remembered him as much as the accident. *I love her accent...*, he thought as he surveyed Elena's injuries in the daylight; she had a bandaged hematoma on her right eye, superficial lacerations on her face, and brush burn marks on her chin, nose, and right cheek, presumably from the exploding airbag. *She still looks gorgeous*, Jake thought as he made small talk about what little he knew of Bosnian culture while putting on his surgical gloves.

"Never been to Sarajevo," Jake said. "I know it's been through some tough times." He unzipped his bag and pulled out a small eye chart.

"Sarajevo was called the 'Paris of central Europe.' Before war," Elena said unemotionally.

"Must've been a wonderful place to live," Jake replied, not knowing what to say next. "I'm going to finish checking your vision. First let's take a look at your left eye." Jake handed her the eye chart. "Start at the top and see how far down you can read."

Elena looked up at Jake; her vision was blurry. He was a bit hefty but handsome nevertheless, with gentle features—*harmless, probably*, she thought, feeling more comfortable as she navigated the eye chart the best she could. Jake assessed her eye movement and pupils, then checked her eye pressure. Everything seemed normal. He set two eye-drop bottles on the steel table.

"I have to place some drops to dilate your eyes now."

Elena hadn't had her eyes dilated since she was a child but remembered they burned.

"Might sting a little," Jake added, gently administering dilating drops to her left eye, then removing her bandage and lifting the upper lid of her bruised right eye and placing more drops. Jake excused himself. After fifteen minutes, he returned to complete the exam.

"Now, Elena." Jake hesitated. "Is it all right if I call you Elena?"

"Get me out of here, and you can call me anything you want," she kidded with a half-smile.

"I may hold you to that." He smiled. "I'm going to look inside your eyes now, okay?" Jake fastened an indirect ophthalmoscope to his head and turned on the headlamp.

"You won't find a soul," Elena commented in her thick Bosnian accent. Jake hesitated to reply.

"Shakespeare said 'eyes are windows to the soul,' no?" Elena said with dry Eastern European humor.

"Not that familiar with Shakespeare's work, but I think that's also in the Bible. *Proverbs*. I'm more into spy novels."

"You know the Bible and you like spies?" she asked, amused.

"…I do."

"Typical American…You remind me of a coal miner, from Tuzla Valley," Elena said, nodding at his doctor's headlamp, while Jake gently opened her left eye and focused the light on her retina where the optic nerve and macula reside; they were intact.

He asked Elena to look up at the ceiling, positioning his lens on the superior part of her peripheral retina. "I'm going to hold your eyelid open. Just let me know if it is too uncomfortable." He resisted stealing a glance at her perfect skin. Her long brown hair somehow still smelled like lilacs even though it was partially matted with crusted blood. Something odd caught his attention inside her left eye…

He almost swallowed his Trident gum.

Had he imagined it? Jake looked again. He hadn't imagined it.

"Elena, have you ever had any problems with your eyes in the past?"

"My eyes have always been strong… Do I have eye disease?"

Laser scars, he surmised. *This woman's superior retina is full of them. Why?*

"They seem perfectly healthy, but have you ever had laser treatment for your eyes?"

"…I have never worn glasses. No laser treatment."

Impossible, he thought. "Ever have a bad accident involving your eyes?"

"Never."

"Are you diabetic?"

"No."

"Have you ever been treated for a retinal hole or tear?" he persisted.

"No… What are you not telling me?"

Jake sensed her growing dismay. "You have quite a few laser scars on your retina."

"Laser scars?" she repeated, confused.

The scarring was visible throughout her peripheral retina; they were white, indicating fresh burns. Jake saw no black pigmentation, which appears a couple of weeks after treatment. The scars were also small, about fifty microns in diameter—highly unusual; peripheral laser scars were usually bigger, being three to five hundred microns. But the most unusual characteristic of Elena's scarring was that they were arranged in a pattern.

"Never seen anything like this," he uttered. "They were likely placed in the past week or so." Jake switched to a higher-magnification handheld lens. Looking closer, the groups of laser spots formed symbols. Or letters.

"Interesting, it looks like writing. Do you happen to speak Arabic, Elena?"

Elena squirmed. "What kind of question is that?"

"I can make out numbers and words… *Fascinating*," he said, lost in the discovery.

"You're hurting eyes." She nudged him away.

"Sorry." Jake turned down his headlamp.

"I would know if I had laser treatment in my own eye." Elena grew defensive.

"I don't mean to disagree with you, but I'm just telling you what I see," Jake replied. "May I examine your other eye?"

Elena gave him a sharp look and slowly nodded.

He walked around to the right side of the bed, removed the bandage, and gently opened her swollen right eye just enough to shine a light through her dilated pupil. Her posterior anatomy was intact and appeared normal.

He asked her to look up, focusing his light on her superior retina.

"Same findings. There are laser scars throughout the entire retina." Jake was amazed at the precision of the laser treatment. He'd performed hundreds of them during his six years of ophthalmology and had never seen anything remotely like Elena's retina before. *Who did this work, and why?*

"You're kind of freaking me out now," Elena said.

"The scars in this eye are in a geometric pattern… It looks like…a *bar code*."

"A bar code?" she repeated. "I call sránje."

"Excuse me?" Jake stood up straight.

"I've never seen an eye doctor before. Is this some sleazy attempt to pick me up?"

"No, ma'am." Jake was taken aback. "Of course not…"

"Were you just smelling my hair?" She frowned.

"Please. Ms. Smilovic." Jake's face turned red. "I'm just your doctor."

"It's okay," she said robotically with a deeper accent. "Lots of men have hit on me."

"Can I show you what I see?" Jake asked, connecting a small black box with a flash drive to his headset. He shined his light back into Elena's eye and snapped several photos. He removed the flash drive and inserted it into his MacBook Air. The iPhoto app opened and blown-up images of her retinas filled the computer screen.

"See there? Those are the laser scars in your left eye."

Elena stared helplessly at the photos, trying to understand what she was seeing.

"That is Arabic," she said. "What does it say?"

"Don't know. But notice how the spots are white? It tells me these have been placed within the past couple of weeks, maybe days." Suddenly, Jake remembered that the Pascal laser had a software program that allowed surgeons to place laser treatments in patterns—but it only had a limited number of pre-set patterns like squares, circles, and semicircles. This work was far more advanced.

"I don't understand," Elena insisted. "How can I see with tattoos on my eyes?"

"They're small and were placed in your side vision; they don't interfere with your central vision. But this explains your discomfort. That, and the corneal abrasion… You say you've been having blurred vision for how long?"

"A few days," Elena replied, trailing off, suddenly deep in thought.

Jake tried to gauge her honesty. *She seems to believe what she's saying. But how could she receive laser treatment without knowing it? Is she lying? But why?*

"Were you really at airport to pick up your mother?" Elena interrupted. She looked up at him skeptically. Jake was caught off guard by the personal question.

"Um, yes, I was… Don't you remember?"

"Maybe… What are you, are some kind of Boy Scout?"

"Yes, actually; Eagle. Who were those two men chasing you?" Jake asked.

"You tell me," she replied suspiciously. "Who the heck are you really?"

"Uh. I'm nobody. I'm just an eye doctor," he said, placing his hand on her shoulder.

"Don't touch," she said, stiffening her body. "Get out. I want to leave."

He removed his hand. "I'm just trying to help you."

Elena became angry, pressing her nurse's emergency button.

"Leave. NOW… Or I scream rape."

Stunned, Jake backed away. "Wait now, Miss Smilovic. I'm sorry I upset you, that was not my intention. Here's my card"—he held out his hand—"if you need anything." She refused and turned away.

Jake placed his business card on the side table, quickly packed up his gear, and left the room. Confused about what just happened, Jake closed the door behind him and slowly walked down the hall, shaking his head. As he passed the supply closet, the door slowly opened. Two dark eyes peered out from the shadows, tracking Jake as he left Elena's room.

(26)

Paranoid. Confused. Aching and exhausted. Elena finally succumbed to sleep after having been awake for nearly forty-eight hours. She dreamt of the movie *A Clockwork Orange*, which she had seen on VHS with her cousins when she was thirteen. In her dream, she was Malcolm McDowell's character listening to a little "Ludwig Van" (Beethoven) on a 45-record player in her childhood bedroom. Suddenly, a group of doctors in white lab coats burst into her room and dragged her out, screaming. The men tied her to a red movie theater chair and forced her eyes open with two tiny gold specula as the Kubrick movie played on the big screen. She tried crying for help, but no words came out. Elena felt the sharp tongs of the specula tear at her eyelids. A large faceless man in a glowing white lab coat and miner's hat loomed over her.

Was it the American doctor? An overhead light blinded her; the veins in her temples pulsated like a beating drum. Beside the faceless doctor, she made out Mikal's face staring down at her with his bleached blond hair, smiling one of his sinister smiles. Her subconscious was telling her something: she had been drugged at that club in Sarajevo; something terrible had happened to her. *It was Mikal*, she thought. *He did this!*

Outside her dream, Elena slept quietly in room 207. The clock on the wall read 3:12 a.m. The second floor of the hospital was empty and quiet. A shadowy figure appeared at her door tiptoeing in a pair of men's shiny brown dress shoes. The figure slipped into the dark room, shutting the door behind him. He stepped closer to her bed, his rubber soles squeaking with every careful step. The figure hovered over her while she slept, admiring her beauty as he skillfully removed the bandage over her right eye and silently sat down next to the bed, as Elena stirred.

"Shhhh, relax," the figure said in a deep accent. "Relax."

Elena tried to scream. A thin hairy hand clamped down over her mouth. "Silence," he whispered, shoving the used eye bandage into her mouth, muffling her. She saw the outline of a swarthy man staring at her; his breath smelled like licorice.

"*There, there…* It's just the doctor paying you a house call." With his free hand the man switched on a bright headlamp, just like Jake's and her uncle Tito's mining lamp back in Tuzla.

Helpless, she felt him peer into her soul.

After a few agonizing minutes, he sighed, turning off his headlamp.

He cursed in French, visibly frustrated. "Your pupil is too small. I cannot see the message." Then "the Doctor" pulled something from his bag. It was a three-inch needle.

He slowly brought the needle up to Elena's left eye so she could see it. He punctured her conjunctivae, causing a small red spot on the white part of the eye. She felt a sharp pain dart through her eye and into her brain as she thrashed about like a hooked fish out of water, unable to scream out.

"I will see you again soon," the Doctor said. "Do you hear me, my lamb?"

Elena writhed as he pressed the needle against her eye again.

"Much pain… Yes?" he asked.

She gasped for air. Tears streamed from her eyes and down her reddened cheeks.

"Calm yourself. Breathe through your nose… You will listen now?"

She took in a deep breath, shuddered, and nodded her head affirmatively.

"You will deliver the message, Elena. Won't you, my lamb?" The man showed her a recent photograph of Mia with Mikal in Sarajevo. "If you break routine, the little girl dies wondering why you couldn't save her. You and Mia will not be spared. You hear? Yes?"

Elena nodded furiously.

"We will be watching." He put away the needle, quietly chuckling to himself.

She told herself, *Wake up, Elena. This must be a dream. Wake up.*

But she was already awake. This nightmare was real.

(27)

Los Angeles, California

Stubbornly refusing to give up her hunch, Agent Rizzo jaywalked across Wilshire Boulevard, dodging traffic in front of the Federal Courthouse building in Los Angeles. An army veteran who served two tours of duty in Africa and Afghanistan, she could spot a coordinated terror plot a mile away and was determined to make the case to her supervisor, Harry Hawks. Although it was very late, she tracked him down still in his office and found him eating a piece of cherry pie.

"You sure eat a lot for a health nut. Sir," she said, dropping a "CLASSIFIED" folder on his desk.

"Low blood sugar," Hawks muttered. "Why aren't you looking for the Eye Torcher?"

"Here's the hard evidence you asked for—ties between the two dead interns." Rizzo pointed at the folder.

"Ever heard of email?" he said gruffly.

"Don't do email," she replied.

He glanced up from his pie. "That explains why you're languishing in the field, Jane."

"Very funny… Here's the highlights: both dead women worked on the Raptor engines. Both helped sabotage them to blow on New Year's Day. I believe both were murdered, to tie up loose ends… The travel logs I obtained from State showed both women also visited Sarajevo in the past two months, and they both used falsified Bosnia and Herzegovina passports to get their visas."

"If they used fake passports, what are their real identities?" Hawks countered.

"Loop in Interpol. Harry, why aren't you more excited about this?"

"I don't get excited," Hawks replied.

"Cracking a massive terror case like this could get you promoted back to D.C. How long have you been running this *La-La Land* operation, anyway?"

"Too long," Agent Hawks replied, sipping coffee. "You've stated your case. Leave."

Rizzo stared at Hawks's tanned emotionless face, wondering how much Botox he'd had. "What happened to the guy who single-handedly took down the Long Beach rally bomber last year? Or the Century City strangler in '18? Or that mass shooter in Burbank in '14?"

"You're doing background on me now?" Hawks asked. "I'm flattered."

"I have better things to do," Rizzo said. "But Benji said your instincts were sharp. When did you lose your fastball?"

"Reverse psychology doesn't work on me," Hawks replied, shoving in another forkful of pie.

"Just level with me. Whose feet do I have to kiss to get a search warrant for all the SpaceX locations? Or authorization to bring in Xang Xi, the man who helped Sheila install the rootkit?" she added. "He's that Chinese national, you know, who's gone missing."

"How about doing simple police work first? Like tracking the dead girls' whereabouts before their death? Or finding the missing eyes of one of the victims?" Hawks replied.

"We're working on that," Rizzo said.

"Work harder." Agent Hawks wiped his mouth. "Look. What do you want to hear? Candidly, I spoke with the D.D., all right? He concurs this has the potential to evolve from a serial killer case into a national security threat. BUT, he isn't ready to turn it over to the CIA and Homeland yet."

"Turn it over? This is my collar!" Rizzo exploded.

"Control your temper. That's what got you in the doghouse in the first place, if your instincts are too dull to ascertain that."

"I ascertained that years ago," Rizzo said sarcastically. "Freakin' snow-flakes."

"We've got enough hotheads, we don't need you throwing gasoline on every hint of a fire," Hawks replied.

"So I punched one informant *ten years ago*." Rizzo shrugged.

"Listen, show me hard evidence of a coordinated terror plot, and you'll get plenty of credit for the bust. If not, you can slink on back to D.C. and let us handle it."

"I'm not letting this go." She persisted. "Benji's got a source at NSA that's tracking the dead girls' cell phones to retrace their steps in Sarajevo right now," Rizzo said.

"That's a start," Hawks said.

Outside Hawks's open office door, they heard a commotion. It was Junior Intelligence Analyst Benji Weir shouting, "You're still here!" Soft around the middle and wearing loose khakis and a wrinkled red polo, he speed-walked into Hawks's corner office.

"Excuse me, sirs?" he said, out of breath. Rizzo gave him a sideways glare.

"Sorry. *Ma'am.* Thought you'd want to know. My buddy at the NSA expedited Agent Rizzo's request to access their 12333 database. *Get this*: they're picking up chatter of an active terror plot that's about to go down on American soil in the next forty-eight to seventy-two hours, coming from… Bosnia-Herzegovina."

"Same place Sheila Roust and Uma Gloten traveled," Rizzo said to Hawks.

"I got that," Hawks snapped. "How are you privy to classified intel, Junior Analyst Weir?"

"Uh." Benji hesitated to explain to his superior. "Agent Rizzo requested it, and all of the intelligence agencies now have complete transparency in data-sharing, sir."

Indeed, in his final days as president of the United States, Barack Obama passed the "FISA Amendments Act and Executive Order 12333." This gave increased authority and levels of power to the National Security Agency to share data on raw "warrantless surveillance" with the FBI and fifteen other U.S. government intelligence groups. Created by President Reagan and amended by President George W. Bush after 9/11, the EO gave FBI operatives working on ordinary criminal cases the ability to search the NSA's information archive, called "12333 Database."

"Don't you have to be assigned to a foreign or counterintelligence operation to access the 12333?" Hawks cocked a suspicious eyebrow at Rizzo and Benji.

"Times are changing, sir," Benji said. "It's a brave new, transparent world."

"Good to know. Makes our jobs easier," Hawks said, putting on his reading glasses and skimming Rizzo's file. "Agent Rizzo, I suppose I owe you an apology. This isn't just a serial killer case anymore. Call Homeland and let NSA know what you discovered. Keep digging."

Rizzo fist-bumped Benji as they about-faced and sprinted out of Hawks's office.

Rizzo paced around Benji Weir's cluttered cubicle on the seventeenth floor. It was 2:55 a.m. and Benji was hunched over his desk searching the FBI database for any other Russian-Bosnian students who might be part of the terror plot. "My eyes are bugging out," Weir complained, digging into a giant bag of Haribo gummy bears.

"You want to be a field agent. This is it, kid," Agent Thorn said.

"Don't those give you cancer, or the runs, or whatever?" asked Rizzo.

"Only the sugar-free ones... Holy crap!" exclaimed Benji, dropping the bag of bears on his desk.

"What you got?" Agent Thorn swiveled her chair around to see his monitor.

"Two matches, who fit the exact profile of Sheila and Uma. Foreign student interns. Same age, same height, same hair color, same ethnicity," Benji said. "One of the Bosnian women is in Baton Rouge, the other touched down in Orlando last night."

Benji looked at Rizzo. "...From *Sarajevo.*"

Rizzo took a closer look at his screen. "Florida Highway Patrol says one was involved in a fatal car accident last night," said Benji.

"Is she dead?" asked Rizzo.

"No. But a woman named Brittany Todd is. Our target was admitted to a hospital in Melbourne, Florida, and is in stable condition. Her name is *Elena Smilovic.*"

"Isn't Melbourne near the Kennedy Space Center?" Rizzo asked.

"Also, Disney World and Cape Canaveral," Thorn added. "...Isn't that also where...?"

She looked over at Rizzo.

"SpaceX is launching it's second spaceship in thirty-six hours," Rizzo said, nodding, finishing her thought.

Rizzo grabbed her jacket and Sig Sauer P226 sidearm.

"Pack light, Tami. We're goin' to Disney World."

"I want to go to Disney World," Benji whined.

"Next time. Alert the Melbourne County Sheriff's to watch her," Rizzo ordered. "And if you really want to be a field agent, lay off the junk food, okay?"

(28)

Melbourne, Florida

Deputy Sheriff Olivine Williams from the Brevard County Sheriff's Department towered over Elena's hospital bed. The thirty-eight-year-old African American officer had arrived at six in the morning to interview Elena. She was tall, heavyset, and rather intimidating in her olive-green uniform and laden duty belt. What stood out most to Elena was the bulky black leather holster containing Olivine's 9mm Glock. Fearing for Mia's safety, Elena's heart raced while being questioned about her police statement.

"One car," Elena nervously corrected Sheriff Williams, who had a sharp eye and sharper ear.

"Excuse me?" Sheriff Williams stopped writing in her notepad.

"Americans have problem understanding accent. It was one car," Elena repeated.

"Oh, I understood you, lady. But it says here, Trooper Monroe from the Florida Highway Patrol states that you told him that two vehicles were involved?"

"The report is wrong." Elena shifted in her bed.

"So, you and the deceased, a Brittany Todd, were not pursued by two Middle Eastern men in a black van as you previously claimed?"

"No."

"And you were not pursued on foot *by the same two men* through the Orlando airport earlier that night?" Officer Williams spelled out what Elena had claimed earlier.

Elena pressed both hands over her eyes. "It's all muddled. The airbag, how do you say, concussed me?"

Officer Williams wasn't buying it. "Well, a Doctor Jake LaFleur appears to have corroborated your story and even provided a description of the two men to Trooper Monroe. He's scheduled to come in to talk to a police sketch artist this afternoon."

"I don't know this LaFleur."

"He's *your* eye doctor, lady; he's standing outside. You both signed an affidavit confirming this information."

"My head hurts… I'm not a morning person. Can you go now?" She looked away.

"Are you aware that filing a false statement is against the law?" Williams asked.

"Arrest me then," Elena replied bluntly.

Williams glanced over at the attending nurse on duty, who just shook her head.

"I just came on duty," Nurse Lyons said apologetically.

"Listen," said Deputy Sheriff Williams, leaning down close to Elena, pointing her pen for emphasis. "I don't know what you're up to, but I don't have time for games, Miss Smilovic. It's the holidays and my kids are off of school, so…" She tucked away her notepad. "Reckon we'll just file this one under 'solved,' then… Have a good day. And off the record? … *Watch your back*."

(29)

Deputy Sheriff Williams left Elena's hospital room at 6:31 a.m. on December 31.

Elena carefully touched the gauze covering her right eye. Both her eyes ached, so she asked Nurse Lyons to close the shades. She drifted off to sleep—until she was jolted awake by the amplified PA system calling a Code Blue in the ICU. She opened her good eye. A man in blue scrubs and a surgical mask was seated on the right side of her bed, stroking her forearm as if she were his pet cat. She stiffened, recognizing his penetrating eyes and thin frame. One of the men from the airport, she thought. This can't be real.

The man leaned close in and a took a long whiff. "Sweet."

"What do you want from me?" she whispered, terrified.

The man stroked her cheek with his coarse fingers. "You know. *You know...* Beautiful Elena. We have eyes on you, always."

She glanced down at her right hand. It was not in restraints.

"Deliver the message," the masked man whispered into her ear.

Desperate, like a cornered animal, she impulsively reached for the ballpoint pen on her side table and jammed it deep into his left ear.

"Arrghhhh!!!" The masked man fell back off the bed, grabbing the side of his head.

Elena screamed for help, leapt out of bed, and assumed a defensive combat posture. While blood streamed out of the thin man's left ear, he playfully wagged his forefinger at her.

"Naughty girl," he said and slipped away into the hall.

Seconds later, Nurse Lyons flipped on the room lights. "Are you okay, miss?"

"What do you think!" Elena looked like a wild animal, grasping the bloody pen like a knife.

At the hospital early to check on Elena before seeing his morning patients, Jake rushed in behind the nurse. "What happened?!"

"He just left!" Elena wailed, scrambling to collect her belongings off a nearby chair.

Jake rushed out into the hallway. Seeing no one suspicious, he returned to Elena's room.

"I checked the halls and didn't see anyone…" he stated.

"Because he's dressed *like you*," Elena insisted.

Jake found Nurse Lyons, searching Elena's bathroom for an intruder. "No one's in here, Doctor."

"Bad dream, maybe?" Jake posited. "PTSD?"

"Must've been some dream," Nurse Lyons said, pointing to the floor. Jake looked down; he was stepping in fresh blood.

"Follow the trail of blood," Elena said. "I broke his eardrum with pen."

"Wow," Jake said, impressed.

"I have to report this to security," Nurse Lyons announced, and she left the room.

"I am not safe here," Elena said, frantically tearing off her hospital gown and shrugging into her white blouse. Jake turned around to give her some privacy.

His back to her, he asked, "Was it one of the men from the airport?"

"Yes." She thought about Mia. "*No… I don't know anymore.*"

Elena looked at her top; it was covered in dried blood. She sighed. Jake turned to face her.

"Look. I can see that you are afraid." He put his hand on her shoulder. "Let me help."

"Hands off!" She pushed him away.

"You're safe now," Jake said. "Security is coming."

"Get out of my way." Elena tried to push him aside. He didn't budge.

"Where are you going? Jake asked her. "Okay, forget it. Hey, I can get you out of here," he offered. This got Elena's attention.

"They're going to release you later today anyway, and I know the back way out."

She stared into Jake's concerned big cow eyes.

Musing, she walked over and stood a few inches from his face. She sniffed at him. She brandished the bloody pen, bringing it close to his face.

"Why should I trust you? Are you an assassin?"

"What? *NO!*" he protested. "I have a heart condition." He extended his soft, thick hands. "Do I look like an assassin to you?"

"You said you like spies," she said, seething.

"That's fiction, not real," he replied. "I'm just a regular, *single* guy."

She gave Jake a long look. *He looks like teddy bear who's in love with me,* she thought.

She dropped the pen and put on her gold watch. She took off her dress shirt and stuffed it back in the plastic bag containing the rest of her clothes that were covered in bloodstains and burn marks. She slipped back into her hospital gown and black boots.

She tried to straighten her hair in the mirror, then gave up. "Screw it."

Elena grabbed her fake Louis Vuitton bag and ripped the bandage off her right eye.

Jake winced at her technique. "You really shouldn't do that."

Elena found dark sunglasses in her purse and put them on.

"You win, cow eyes," she said. "Get me out of here."

(30)

J ake took off his XL lab coat and draped it over Elena's shoulders to hide
her hospital gown. "Follow me," he instructed, opening the door and
poking his head outside. He looked both ways. The hall was crowded for
the morning. An FHP state trooper was roaming the floor; this was a new
development. *Why didn't that trooper check in on her?* he wondered. The state
trooper ambled over to flirt with the attractive nurse in the nurse's station.

That's why, Jake noticed… *Nurse Courtney.*

He gestured to Elena and they made their move. They took a left, drift-
ing silently past the trooper and Nurse Courtney, who were chatting about
their mutual lack of plans for New Year's Eve. Elena had a determined
gait; her leather boots tapped softly on the tile floor as they passed a steady
stream of doctors, visitors, and nurses. No one paid them any attention as
they rounded a corner.

The elevator at the end of the hallway dinged loudly. The doors opened.
A stocky man with a dark complexion and three-day-old beard emerged. He
was wearing a Disney World hat and a colorful leather Disney World jacket
with Goofy and an eight ball on the back. Elena grabbed Jake's arm and
ducked behind his large frame. She peered around his shoulder, focusing
her one good eye on the man, who stood there, tilting his head to the left,
staring at the action in the hall.

Jake felt a bump in his heart rate.

That's one of the thugs from the airport. Jake made a 180, Elena clutching
his arm, and picked up their pace. The stocky man suddenly spotted Elena
trailing Jake and pursued them down the hall.

"There they are," a woman called out.

Through the crowd of people, Jake saw Nurse Napoli pointing them out
to the hospital's security guard.

"Stop, you two!" the security guard ordered.

Seemingly hemmed in, Jake darted over to the stairway exit, pushed the door open, and rushed Elena down the stairs to the first floor, stopping at an orange door with a sign that read: "Private: Doctors' Lounge." He punched in the last four digits of his social security number and the door opened. They ducked inside as Jake closed the door behind them.

"Jake! My friend," he heard a jovial man call out. It was Ben toasting a bagel in the kitchenette. Jake gave him a cursory wave.

"Come. Sit! You have a guest?" Ben gestured them over.

"Hey, pal, you can't bring guests in here," a gruff physician sitting at another table pointed out.

"She's my niece," Jake replied, taking Elena's hand and quickly leading her through the tables of doctors eating breakfast "She's gonna be a radiologist, giving her the grand tour."

They passed right by Ben. "Not now, fill you in later," Jake whispered, his eyes straight ahead.

There was a loud knock on the door.

"Who's banging?" asked a physician, walking over to unlock it.

The now perspiring stocky stalker burst into the lounge, forcefully pushing his way through the crowd of tables in hot pursuit. Ben looked at the man and turned to see Jake rushing to the back of the room. Seeing that Jake was running from this man, Ben stood and maneuvered his large belly into the man's way.

"Excuse me," he called out. "This is the doctors' lounge. Are you lost?"

The stocky man halted and locked eyes with Ben. Ben felt the man searching his face and his blood went cold. The stocky man violently pushed Ben aside, following Jake and Elena as they exited through a door on the other side of the lounge.

The pair jogged down the hallway by the Invasive Radiology Suite until they came to a door that read: "No Entry, Employees Only."

"*Here*." Jake opened the door using his security badge and ushered Elena through it. Just then the thick stranger appeared in the doorway frame, frantically looking left and right.

They had vanished.

He heard a familiar voice. "Tarek."

He turned to see a janitor pushing a laundry cart. It was Khalid.

"That way," Khalid said, pointing. He was wearing stolen scrubs and holding a wad of gauze to his ear. He led them over to the Employee Exit door. They used Khalid's pilfered badge to enter.

Meanwhile, racing down the stairwell at top speed, Elena asked, "Why are you helping me?"

"Eagle Scout, first class," Jake replied.

"You said that earlier… What is this Eagle Scout?"

"We help people. At all times," he said, repeating the Scout motto.

"Konju complex," she replied, following Jake out the ground level exit. Seconds later, Khalid and Tarek raced down the stairs and followed them into the morning light.

Agents Rizzo and Thorn's rented Ford LTD screeched to a stop at the front of Holmes hospital and parked in one of the "Doctors Only" spots.

"Inside," Rizzo ordered, bolting out of the passenger seat and through the front doors before Agent Thorn had time to turn off the engine.

"Wait for backup, why don't ya!" Thorn shouted to no avail.

Rizzo flashed her badge at the front desk nurse and bounded up the public stairwell to the second floor, two steps at a time. She burst into Elena's hospital room, only to find it was empty.

"Shoot." Rizzo checked the bathroom and under the bed. She spotted footprints in a stream of dark red liquid splattered on the tile floor. She reached down and felt its texture. "Bloody footprints, still wet. What the…?"

Rizzo followed the trail of blood out into the hall until it ended a few feet away from her partner, who was already questioning the state trooper and the nurses on duty.

"Only thing in that room are bloody footprints that lead to nowhere. Where is she?"

The FHP trooper and Nurse Courtney gave each other a look. "She was just sleepin' in there last time I checked," the trooper replied. "I only left the door for a few minutes."

"You had *one job*," Rizzo exclaimed, trying to hold back her anger.

"Um, ma'am?" Nurse Courtney piped up, while checking the hospital's database. "Miss Smilovic did not check out. She should still be in there."

"Well, she's not," Rizzo growled.

"I saw them, they went that way a few minutes ago." Nurse Napoli pointed down the hall. "Our security guard took off after them."

Rizzo got on the phone to her contact at the Florida Highway Patrol. "Close off the front entrance and check every room in this hospital. She's on the move."

She gave the trooper a look of disdain.

"I'm awful sorry I let her slip past me," the apologetic trooper said. "But she was in a motor vehicle accident the night before last; I figured she wasn't in any condition to flee and she had been last seen in restraints."

"Keep talking," Agent Thorn said.

"Well, it's mighty curious how she got here. Miss Smilovic told us that two men ran her off the road—killing her friend—after pursuing her through the Orlando airport on foot."

"Did you investigate her claim?" asked Rizzo.

"No, ma'am—didn't have time. She recanted her story she gave to a Brevard County sheriff this a.m. after she and her eye doctor had already told us that it happened…"

"I can confirm that," Nurse Lyons volunteered.

"Squirrely, huh?" said the trooper.

"Yeah. Squirrely," Rizzo replied. "You said her *eye doctor* confirmed it?"

The trooper nodded. Rizzo and Thorn looked at each other.

"She may be in danger," Rizzo said. "What's her doctor's name?"

"Doctor LaFleur," Nurse Napoli said. "Jake LaFleur."

"Awfully nice guy," added Nurse Courtney. "He's not in some sort of trouble, is he?"

"Don't know." Rizzo barked into her phone. "I want an APB put out on them both."

(31)

Indialantic, Florida

Jake wiped his sweaty brow as he sped his old blue Honda through a quiet palm-tree-lined street near Indialantic Beach, a few miles on the beachside, east of Melbourne. Up to now, he had only helped someone evade bad guys in his daydreams. In the aftermath of the hospital jailbreak, he felt terrified, confused, yet more alive than he had felt in years—maybe ever. With his heart beating out of his chest, he checked his Fitbit. When marathon training, he knew his heart rate could reach 150 bpm while running—it was 150 now. Nearing full-on tachycardia, Jake relied on the deep-breathing techniques he had learned in a yoga class as he nervously looked for a black van in the rearview mirror. No one was coming. Yet.

Passing by modest homes built during the early days of the Apollo Space Program with their well-kept yards and patriotically displayed American flags, he looked around, wondering why Elena had led them to this sleepy seaside community. It looked like the perfect spot for a retired Mafia boss, like Hyman Roth from *The Godfather Part II*, to lay low, not a young woman like her. With questions and adrenaline pumping through his brain, he listened for police sirens but heard only the muttered murmurs of NPR's *All Things Considered* from his car stereo.

He glanced over at Elena, who had her window down, feeling the morning breeze on her face. "I missed the sunshine," she said softly.

"How's your eye?" he asked.

"Same."

"Did you recognize that man in the Goofy jacket?"

She looked at Jake. "What is this *Goofy*?"

"Was that the man who came to your room?" His question hung in the salty air.

"Two other men visited me. Not Mister Goofy… He was at the airport."

"Wait." Jake was confused. "*Two men* were in your room?"

"Not at same time."

"But. Whose eardrum did you puncture?" Jake asked.

"Not his… *Pull over.*" Elena pointed to a white two-story Victorian home on the right with a round tower. Its baroque shadow loomed over the other houses on the street as if it had been dropped in from another time and country. Jake parked out front while cautiously noting its front gable, turned posts, decorative brackets, and elaborate spindle work.

"Is, uh, this your place?" he asked, having a strong feeling it wasn't. "They'll look for you here."

"I'm not idiot," Elena said, texting someone. "It's a friend." Jake noticed a figure in the front window watching them from behind parted lace curtains. The curtains dropped. So did his stomach.

"Who's after you?" he demanded, cutting to the chase. Elena didn't answer.

"What does that Arabic writing on your eye mean, or the bar code?" he asked her. Elena said nothing. Jake tried to read her body language. She had the best poker face he had ever seen.

"Just go, Boy Scout." She waved him off. "You've done enough."

"But." He reached over and gently touched her left hand. "What do I tell the hospital? I could get fired."

She looked down at Jake's hand dwarfing hers.

"I never asked you for help," she replied coldly, grabbing her bag and stepping out of the passenger seat. She took off his lab coat, tossed it into the passenger seat, and shut the door.

"Thanks for ride." She headed up the walk.

Jake watched Elena go, wondering if he'd ever see her again. He glanced in the rearview mirror. No one was coming.

This is crazy. This is crazy, he said to himself. He jumped out of the car. "Wait."

He followed her up the walk. She turned around, lowering her sunglasses to see his face clearly. Jake stood there, palms out with a silly half-smile on his face.

"…Must be a masochist," Elena replied, and she kept walking up to the porch. He followed her like an oversized puppy.

(32)

"**E** lena… Aren't you a sight for sore eyes," cooed the frail half-blind old woman who answered the creaky front door. "That a new dress?"

Elena leaned down and let the shriveled lady kiss both her cheeks.

"Maman. It is hospital gown. Long story." She carefully embraced the old woman as if she were made of porcelain.

Who's this? Jake wondered. *Too old to be her mother.* Feeling like a 230-pound ghost he stood there quietly watching the two women greet each other. To him, the strange home looked like some foreign embassy or a doily museum surrounded by magnolia trees, green grass, and humming-birds buzzing the red begonia bushes that lined the wraparound porch. Jake checked to see if there was a foreign flag on its flagpole (there wasn't); by the looks of the place, it had been well taken care of over the years by someone with time and money. Maman looked like she had neither of those assets going for her. Jake's ample stomach grumbled loudly.

Elena gestured at him. "To su kravlje oči." ("That's cow eyes," in Bos-nian.)

Maman chuckle-coughed from a lifetime of smoking. "Come, come." She beckoned them in. "Let me feed you, young man. Sounds like you need brek-e-fast."

"Thank you," Jake said. "I'm Doctor LaFleur, actually."

"A *doktor.*" She winked at Elena. "Pleased to meet you." The old lady in her yellow housecoat led them down a long hallway, thin spidery legs lean-ing heavily on a carved wooden cane. "Call me Maman. Everybody does."

Jake assumed scoliosis caused Maman to be hunched over like a wrinkled question mark. They slowly passed by a series of small, ornate rooms deco-rated with Persian rugs, old framed black-and-white photographs, wooden bookshelves, and dusty antique furniture. The home smelled of mothballs, cigarette smoke, and Biofreeze gel.

Jake took a deep breath to calm his heart rate.

"Maman's the only one I trust here…after Brittany," Elena said with a forlorn look.

Jake sensed Maman must be Elena's relative when they began conversing in what he guessed was a mix of Russian and Bosnian. Maman sat them at a sturdy oak kitchen table and brought over a pot of tea and some pastries.

"Böreks. From the old country." Maman served Jake. "Eat 'em up."

"Looks good, Maman." Jake sipped the Russian Caravan tea and dug into the hot flaky phyllo dough, filled with seasoned ground meat.

Captivated by Elena when they met, Jake had done some light stalking of her by Googling her in his office. Curiously, he discovered Elena had no digital trail at all, but after going down an Internet rabbit hole, he had learned thousands of Bosnian war refugees like her had settled around Orlando since the mid-nineties. Outnumbered by Cuban, Haitian, and Vietnamese refugees who arrived much earlier, most Bosnians who lived on the "Space Coast" of Florida were Serbian, but many others were Croatians and Muslims. Which side of the conflict had Elena and Maman been on? He couldn't tell by their appearance or dialect. *Elena seems to trust this Maman… Why?* His phone dinged. It was a text from Ben.

"U Ok? I'm back home getting work done. Cops were all over the floor! Call my office, you're the talk of the doctor's lounge. FUNN!" (clown emoji)

Jake smiled. He knew Ben loved chaos or at least the kind you see in movies. He thought about what his colleagues must be saying about him while he poured cream in his tea and listened in on Elena and Maman's conversation. He sensed the tenor of their talk had changed. Maman's kindly face had become twisted up in a grimace, her eyes now dark as black opal. Jake paused eating mid-bite, watching intently as the old lady leaned over her steaming teacup and asked Elena in a low gravelly tone, "Vy dostavili soobshcheniye?"

Forced to learn four languages by his mother (including Russian), Jake mentally translated. *"Have you delivered the message?…"* He looked at Elena. *What could that mean?* he wondered.

Jake watched Elena's back stiffen.

"Imam druge misli," Elena replied in Bosnian.

No idea what language that is, Bosnian probably, Jake thought. Maman pounded the table with her little hand, rattling saucers. Jake jumped in his seat.

"Who's this cow-faced man?" Maman asked sternly in English.

"No one… My eye doctor," Elena said. "I was in accident."

"This I know…" Maman replied coldly.

"…You *know* this?" Elena looked up from her tea.

"Remove your glasses," Maman insisted. "I want to see your beautiful eyes."

Elena reluctantly removed her sunglasses, revealing her black eye and facial abrasions.

"Tsk… What a shame about your college friend… Poor thing," Maman replied. "I have a *doktor* I want you to meet… In fact, he is on his way over."

Elena's face went pale. She stammered, "I've got to go to the bathroom."

She grabbed her bag and rushed out of the kitchen.

Jake watched her abrupt exit, awkwardly swallowing his last bite of pastry.

"Um, she's been a little rattled since the accident," he explained. "I'll go check on her."

"Petulant child." Maman walked over to a kitchen phone and pressed a single button.

"Thanks for breakfast, your pastries are delicious." Jake jumped up from his chair and walked down the hallway. The doors were closed and locked. He couldn't find the bathroom, so he walked into the front sitting room and peeked out the window.

Outside, Elena was already at the side of his car opening the passenger door. She looked back at the house and saw Jake at the window.

"Let's go, cow eyes!" she yelled.

Jake exited the front door and quickly paced to his car. Elena appeared pale. He slid into the driver's seat and sped away, heading south.

Elena's hands shook, searching the bottom of her bag for nicotine gum.

"What the heck was *that*?" Jake asked.

"You don't need to know," she replied, her voice wavering.

"I kinda do! I thought you trusted her?"

"Yeah, well…" Elena sighed, then demanded, "Can this piece of junk go any faster?"

"I'm flooring it!" Jake punched on the gas of his old car.

That old woman rattled her, he thought, driving erratically as fast as he could. *What did she say?* It seemed Elena hadn't "delivered the message," whatever that meant.

"Just drop me here," Elena said.

"On the side of the road? I'm not dropping you anywhere till I know you're safe," he insisted.

"Fine." She sized him up. "I will use you as human shield then."

"Human shield—is that a fat joke?" Jake peered sideways at Elena.

"No," she drolly explained with exasperation. "I will literally use you as shield when they shoot."

"Who'd want to shoot you? Does this have something do with your eyes?"

Elena said nothing.

"Okay, fine. Don't tell me," Jake said. "Do you have a car?"

"At my apartment, near campus," Elena replied.

"We can't go there, they'll be all over that... Let me think..."

While they drove in silence, he listened to indistinct words from his stereo set to WMFE, Orlando's NPR. The car's clock read 8:00 a.m. *"Bringing you breaking news from Melbourne-Orlando at the top of every hour! Brevard County Sheriffs are currently searching for a twenty-eight-year-old Bosnian national and University of Central Florida student who is a person of interest in the homicide investigation of twenty-five-year-old UCF student Brittany Todd, who was killed earlier this week in a one-car accident on Route 528..."*

Jake raised his eyebrows, turning up the radio.

"While being detained by the Florida Highway Patrol, Elena Smilovic reportedly fled from Holmes Regional Hospital early this morning in a 2003 blue Honda Accord belonging to local physician Doctor Jake LaFleur, who is believed to be with her."

"Oh no, oh no." Jake's career flashed before his eyes.

Elena clicked her tongue. "American propaganda."

"A police spokesman said Doctor LaFleur aided the suspect in evading both Florida Highway Patrol and Brevard County Sheriffs. If you have seen a vehicle with Florida license plate 93H-2XE or know the whereabouts of Ms. Smilovic, please contact the Brevard County Sheriff's Department or text EYEONCRIME@411."

"What did you do?!" Jake exclaimed.

Elena's face went white. "This is setup, I have not done anything," she stammered. "They are making me patsy, like your Oswald."

"You know Lee Harvey Oswald but not Goofy?" he responded.

They drove in silence. Jake's mind reeled. *Now I'm some kind of fugitive? Who is this woman in my car? Is she evading my questions by hiding behind broken English?* Jake had seen her do it with the police. Her understanding of English (not to mention American pop culture) seemed to go in and out like a staticky FM radio station. The *Mission Impossible* theme song rang out from his lap. Jake fumbled, pulling his iPhone 6S from his pocket.

"Ay-yi-yi." Jake sighed and answered the phone. "This is *not* a good time!"

"Why's it so noisy at the hospital?" asked Cindy LaFleur.

"I'm not at the hospital, Mom."

"What's going on? Are you joining me for breakfast or not?" she entreated.

"Just put it in the fridge," Jake said. "I'm with a patient."

"But I fixed you your favorite. My French toast."

"You know I'm off carbs, Mom. Call you later, and don't turn on the news!" He added, "Just in case."

"In case of what?" Cindy asked.

Jake hung up and drove in panicked silence, trying to think of a next move.

Elena scoffed. "Got momma's boy over here."

"I know where we can go," he said, taking a sharp right turn, tires screeching.

"I just saw you eat carbs, by the way," Elena said with a smirk.

33

Viera, Florida

"**I** don't want any trouble!" Dr. Ben Silverman exclaimed, barricaded behind his front door.

"You told me to call you!" Jake pleaded through the door.

"That's before I got this mishigas text from the hospital telling me you are a wanted fugitive." Ben opened the mail slot and stuck his phone out of it.

Jake crouched down to read the text from the hospital administrator's office updating all staff members about Jake and Elena's morning escape.

"You lose some weight and suddenly you're Harrison Ford?"

Jake stood up, stunned. "Well, this is not good."

"I'm going." Elena turned abruptly to leave.

"Hang on," Jake implored.

"Is that her with you??" Ben peeked his eye through the mail slot to get a better look.

"You know me. I don't even get speeding tickets! Will you please let me explain?"

"She's suspected of murder, you know," Ben said, his one eye admiring Elena's beauty through the mail slot.

"It's totally bogus. Just let us in. I parked in back."

Ben sighed. The mail slot clanked shut.

Jake gave Elena a look of (what he hoped was) confidence while Ben unlocked the chain and swung open the door, his large girth filling the doorway. "I must be meshuggeneh aiding and abetting a fugitive." He waved them in. "Get in here before Ruth sees."

Ben led them down a stairwell to his subterranean office, away from his wife and two young sons, who were eating breakfast in the kitchen.

Lumbering his three hundred pounds down the stairs behind Elena, Ben admired the way she gracefully moved her long, languid body, the polar opposite of him or his equally heavyset wife, Ruth.

Out of breath, Ben deadbolted his office door and wiped sweat from his brow.

Jake introduced them. "This is Elena."

Ben put his hanky away, his pupils dilating with admiration. Elena folded her arms. "Hi…" He grinned. "May I say, your special lady friend is quite stunning…for a wanted criminal."

"Get this straight, boys, I'm not anyone's special lady," Elena insisted.

"Of course not," Ben said, half-humored by his friend's predicament.

"She's my patient. This is one huge mix-up." Jake explained his situation. "When I picked Cindy up at the airport, I saw two men in paramilitary clothes chasing Elena through the airport. They followed her out and ran her friend's car off the road, killing her friend. Then they tried to kidnap, kill, or torture her at the hospital—I'm not exactly sure—but I helped her escape. Simple as that, end of story."

Ben rubbed his beard. "What a *shande.*"

"I saw all this with my own eyes," Jake said. "That's why I helped her."

"I believe you, I believe you. *I think*," Ben said. "What do you want me to do?"

"We need help going underground," Jake said.

"Underground?" He laughed. "What do I look like, the French Resistance?"

"You're my best friend!"

"I see. Okay. You need a *safe house*," Ben replied. "You want to stay in my attic?"

"Is he serious?" Elena looked at Jake.

"No," Jake said. "But we need some place they'll never think to look for us."

Ben thought about it. "Well, I suppose…you could always lay low on Landry's yacht? We know where it's docked, and he has lax security. Putz keeps the key under the mat."

What's one more crime? Jake considered it. *Would he press charges?*

"He's not on his booze cruiser today," Ben continued. "He's at the office and then heading to Disney. His young beautiful wife loves the mouse. He texted me looking for you."

"He texted me, too," Jake said. "Probably not going to be made partner now, anyway."

"Perhaps not, my friend," Ben said. "Remember Red?"

"Oh yeah… I did save the *couyon* from getting knifed," Jake said.

"Who wielded a knife at you?" Elena asked with a raised eyebrow.

"It's nothing," Jake replied.

"What's he gonna do? Call the cops?" Ben said. "They're already after you."

Jake looked at Elena. "You get seasick?"

(34)

Indialantic, Florida

The morning sun broke through golden early morning clouds over the Atlantic, casting a soft light on the two grizzled faces standing guard on Maman's east-facing porch. Tarek wore sunglasses that he had bought at a Sunoco gas station. He was pacing like a soldier and flicking imported Farvardin cigarettes at the hummingbirds buzzing the red begonias that lined the yard. Leaning against a turned post, Khalid, the thinner one, tried on a black velvet cowboy hat that he'd stolen along with three oxycodone tablets from an elderly patient at the hospital. Fitting the hat gingerly over his bandaged ear, he gave a squinty gaze to his partner. "Like Clint East-a-wood, eh?"

Tarek snatched the hat off Khalid's head. "No jokes." He tossed the cowboy hat into the begonias. "Brain is leaking from your ear."

"That good American disguise." Khalid frowned. "When will the Doktor give me medicine?" he whined.

"Capture the girl messenger, and you get relief… If fail…"—Tarek swiped a thick finger across his own throat and stared at the street—"… both of us."

Behind them, a white Chevy Impala had parked behind a black van outside the house.

Inside Maman's dusty study, stocked with a collection of hardbound books she'd amassed over eighty-three years of life, the somber music of Franz Schubert playing on an antique phonograph filled the dry air. The hunched old lady in the yellow housecoat offered tea to the driver of the Chevy Impala. He was a physically fit, below average height middle-aged man with a salt-and-pepper beard and swarthy complexion, and he was seated on an antique chesterfield sofa.

"Schubert... I knew you were coming." Grinning coyly, Maman offered him tea. "Russian...?"

"Most gracious." He nodded, took a sip, and wiped his mouth with a white linen handkerchief.

"The girl is off her routine," Maman said. "Her new friend is upsetting the apple cart."

"New friend," he repeated thoughtfully.

"A *doctor*. Like you." Maman scowled like she was tasting bitter fruit. "But a fat American...with a French name... *LaFleur*."

The bearded man looked contemplatively into his porcelain teacup. He finally spoke in a soft voice. "We must alert our comrades."

"Is that necessary?" Maman coughed nervously.

"We have failing stars on both coasts. But the sweet citrus rose blooms... Make the call."

Maman clicked her tongue, shuffling as she tapped her rosewood walking cane over to a side table decorated with plastic orchids and framed photos of her Yugoslav ancestors. She slid open a bottom drawer and removed a large hardcover book. She opened its leather cover and produced a secure GlobalStar satellite phone, pressed a single button, and handed it to the doktor.

"Here you go, sher."

A foreign male voice picked up after one ring.

"Limadha tatasil by?" ("Why are you contacting me?" in Arabic.)

"Atanawal alshshay mae jidaty." ("I'm having tea with Grandmother.") The doctor replied in Arabic. "You may speak English."

"You're breaking protocol."

"The Florida girl is off her routine," the doktor said.

"Did the you pay her a visit?"

"I did not have the proper tools to read your advanced work...which is exquisite."

"You believe flattery will save you?" the man growled.

The doktor grimaced and cleared his throat.

"Why not take the eyes?"

"She has not fulfilled her duties, as of yet..."

The man grew irritated. "What else?!"

The doktor paused. "Grandmother was alerted by the one watching Svetlana…"

"…*Da. Da?*" ("Yes. Yes?") the man urged, falling into his native Bosnian tongue.

"The 'Starship' concert in Los Angeles has been canceled," the doktor answered timidly.

Loud metallic crashes came from the satellite phone's receiver. He calmly sipped tea; Maman looked on anxiously.

"*Ko nije uspeo?!*" ("Who failed?!") the man demanded.

"She left…unfortunate breadcrumbs. The authorities did not take the red herring."

"Our brothers in Shanghai will be gravely disappointed," the man said, gathering himself into a more threatening tone.

"There is also the matter of Elena's new friend," the Doctor added.

"She was to have no relations in America," the man said.

"The girl is human," he retorted. "She has been here for two years. This one is an obese American doctor. Maman senses he has feelings for her."

A loud "harrumph!" from the other end of the call. "No loose ends—find Elena. Eliminate the fat American," the man ordered.

At that moment 5,324 miles away in an ancient brick loft, Mikal caught a glimpse of his reflection in a window overlooking the Emperor's Bridge and Miljacka River. His short-cropped blond hair and steel grey eyes appeared more menacing in the old glass. He kicked his demolished laptop across the cement floor.

He spoke into the sat phone. "Meet me at the designated location." He walked closer to the window; the orange pink late afternoon sun illuminated his olive-skin face. "*Ne zovi me više.*" ("Don't ring me again.")

"We are on the next flight to New Orleans," replied the Doktor.

Mikal hung up his phone and threw it violently against the brick wall.

(35)

Melbourne, Florida

"Ya'll are barkin' up the wrong tree. Jake's a pussycat," Anna Gentle insisted protectively, watching federal agents and Brevard County sheriffs tear apart Jake's office at the Space Coast Eye Institute. Agent Rizzo intercepted Nurse Gentle, who was five inches taller than her and nosily attempting to inch her way through the doorway.

"I'm jet-lagged, lady. Back off. Let us do our jobs," Rizzo said.

Anna held up her hands and backed away slowly.

After chasing down blind alleys, fueled in part by the media's obsession with the "Eye Torcher" story the past six days, the stress was showing in Rizzo's demeanor. Suspecting that her rocky career at the FBI hinged on thwarting the terror plot that was behind the string of murdered women with missing eyes, Rizzo kept her head down, grinding like it was the fourth quarter of a game that was slipping through her fingers. She glanced at the clock on Jake's office wall and frowned. The SpaceX launches were in thirty-two hours...

Scouring through his belongings in search of clues, Agent Thorn pulled out a book from his bookshelf. "What do we have here?"

She held up a small softcover book with a picture of Saddam Hussein on the cover. Rizzo recognized the book. Every soldier in the Iraqi army had it in the front pocket of their uniforms during the American invasion. Why would Dr. LaFleur have a copy?

"Ever known your boss to be interested in Islamic extremism?" Rizzo asked Anna.

"Don't know nothing 'bout that," Anna said. "His momma's Catholic, though. They can be pretty extreme." Anna smirked.

An excited commotion emanated from the hall.

Dr. Steve Landry barged into the office with glowing pink skin, goggles and a towel around his neck. "What goes on in here?!" He saw the badges and changed his tune. "What seems to be the problem, officers?"

"You own this clinic?" asked Deputy Sheriff Trimble.

Landry gave Rizzo a suspicious glance. "Who's asking? ... You IRS?"

"FBI." Rizzo flashed her badge, sizing up Landry and quickly pegging him as a fool and an unlikely accomplice in a terror plot. "I'm Agent Rizzo. That's Agent Thorn. We're looking for your partner, a Doctor LaFleur."

"Jake?" He turned to Anna. "Where the heck is he? He never showed up today," he explained to the agents.

"You've had no contact with him?"

"No! Didn't even call in, that's why I'm coverin' for his butt. Why?"

"He's a person of interest in an active investigation," Rizzo said.

"...You gotta be kidding me!" Landry scoffed.

"The news said he's on the lam with a patient he treated at the trauma center who killed her roommate," Anna interjected.

"What! Why doesn't anyone tell me anything around here!" Landry asked Anna.

Anna smirked. "'Cause you been napping in your tanning bed all morning." Landry glared at Anna with racoon eyes from his tanning bed goggles. Anna turned away.

"It's a complicated case," Sheriff Trimble interjected. "Lots of moving parts."

"Do you know Doctor LaFleur to be anti-American?" asked Agent Thorn.

"Heck no! I don't consort with commies... I don't even smoke Cuban cigars."

"Jake's no extremist." Anna stood up for her friend. "He's training to run the Disney Marathon; can't get more American than that. Lost a lot of weight recently."

"Perhaps he's fasting for religious purposes?" Rizzo speculated.

"...Ramadan's not for a few months," Thorn corrected.

"He's *Cajun*, not Muslim," Anna said.

Thorn's cell phone rang; she took the call in the hallway.

"Sure got a bookshelf full of suspicious-lookin' literature for a guy who bleeds red, white, and blue," said Sheriff Trimble, reading off titles from Jake's shelf. "*The Quran… Getting to Know Allah… The Essential Rumi…*"

"Quite a collection," Rizzo said. "Must be a smart fella."

"I know for a fact, those Middle East books were gifts," Anna said. "From a Doctor Aria or something. He was Jake's mentor during his retina fellowship. He's an internationally known retina specialist. Travels all over the world and brings these books back for Doctor LaFleur."

"We'd like to speak to this Doctor Aria," Rizzo said.

"You think I take calls around here?" Anna shot back. "Find him yourself."

"Okay, next question. Is it true LaFleur speaks Arabic and Russian?" Rizzo asked.

"That's news to me!" Landry replied.

"French and Spanish too," Anna said. "Helps with internatioanl patients. If you weren't sunbathing in your office all day, you'd know that."

"Funny, a doctor from Melbourne, Florida, being so worldly, huh?" Rizzo said.

Anna squared off with Rizzo.

"His mother was a linguistics professor. What you gettin' at?"

"We believe a terrorist cell may be plotting a strike in this area, and your good doctor may be aiding them," Thorn said.

Anna chortled. "*Seriously*…what you gals been smoking? No way Jake is involved in that."

Landry sat on Jake's desk, in shock, wiping his face with a towel. "I can't believe it… Just a few days ago, he saved me from this crazy fishing guide who came at me with a knife… Took Red out with one blow, like the Terminator."

"Really now. Like Rambo?" Rizzo said.

"Saved my bacon. Gave him a heart attack though. I took him and Red to the hospital after. He's feistier than he looks," Landry added.

"See?" Anna said. "You *should be* investigating some *other* shady characters 'round here." She shot a death stare at Landry.

Rizzo walked over to Agent Thorn in the hallway. "Any contact with the other match in Louisiana?" Rizzo asked.

"Roger that." Thorn hung up her iPhone. "N.O. office has a visual on a Svanna Bortiach: twenty-two years old, Russian national with a temp visa, also an aerospace student who entered the country last summer with a false Bosnian passport."

"Uma. Sheila. Elena. Svanna. That makes four," Rizzo mused.

"But this one flunked out," Thorn said. "Doesn't seem connected. Get this, now she's the college mascot for the LSU Tigers. No affiliation with SpaceX at all, though our boys in Baton Rouge claim some shady characters have been tailing her."

"Another college football connection," noted Rizzo. "LSU's playing Alabama in the Sugar Bowl 'round the same time as the SpaceX launches."

"Could be a coincidence," Thorn said.

"Or not," Rizzo said. "Pack your junk. We're going to Louisiana."

"I never unpacked. What about Elena, and this guy?" asked Thorn.

Rizzo gestured to a framed photo on the bookshelf showing Jake and Ben wearing plastic bibs at a table full of freshly devoured lobsters. "Our 'Doc Courageous' has a defective heart."

"Could be a good Samaritan who stumbled into this mess at the airport. Smilovic has a real pretty face," Thorn added.

"All our dead girls do. Have the sheriffs toss Elena's apartment. She may be the Torcher's next victim."

"On it," Thorn said.

"Also need to visit SpaceX's operation at the Cape. Smilovic interns there, like the others," Rizzo said.

"Except Svanna. You sure we got time for another wild goose chase, Jane?"

Rizzo frowned "Every cop in Florida's looking for Smilovic. If she's relying on this bozo"—Rizzo pointed to Jake's lobster bib photo—"they'll surface."

"You better be right," Thorn replied.

36

Indian Harbour Beach, Florida

Jake floored it across the Eau Gallie Causeway above the Indian River, his blue Honda Accord sputtering like it was on its last legs, but at least the AC blew cold. He glanced over at Elena, red-faced. "Just needs new spark plugs."

"You are really a doctor?" Elena asked.

"Got the degrees to prove it." He grinned at her.

"You have car of Serbian sheepherder," she commented.

"Thanks... Didn't know sheepherders had cars."

Jake pulled into the Eau Gallie Yacht Club parking lot, several miles south of Cape Canaveral and Cocoa Beach. The club was founded in 1907, and the main building was built in 1957. Not much had changed over the past sixty years. The average age of the Yacht Club members had long been Medicare eligible, but after adding an outdoor grill a new pool and promises of clubhouse renovations, younger families had infused new life into the aging club. Jake felt he and Elena could blend in as one of those younger couples and walk around unnoticed. He knew his boss had been a member for years and boasted one of the nicest boats in the marina, decked out with the latest deep-sea fishing equipment, which he never used correctly (or soberly). Jake also knew Steve, much to his displeasure, spent every New Year's Eve in Orlando with his spunky third wife, Amber, who, twenty-five years younger than he and imagining herself a real-life Cinderella, liked to ring in the New Year at the Disney World resort.

"...What is this place?" Elena lowered her sunglasses to get a better look at the club.

"It's actually a lot nicer than it looks. They're renovating the whole place. There's a beautiful marina on the Banana River. My boss has a boat here. He'll be at Disney World all weekend."

"To party with rodent or goofy dog, I presume?" Elena asked.

"Uh, yeah…coast should be clear."

Jake's car sputtered past rows of gleaming Mercedes, Porsches, Maseratis, Cadillac SUVs, and Teslas. Two teenage valets stood outside the Harbor Grill in matching blue shorts and striped crew neck shirts but paid no attention to them as they passed by.

"Lots of NASA bigwigs belong here, like Buzz Aldrin… He went to the moon," Jake explained.

"I do not know this Buzz." Elena watched a buff tennis instructor hit balls to two well-manicured older women on the club's clay tennis court. "Do you have a wife?"

Jake steered into the back-employee parking area and pulled the key out of the ignition.

"Divorced."

His Honda continued to sputter after the engine stopped.

"No wonder you're single," she replied, getting out of the car.

"Just act like you belong," Jake muttered under his breath.

"I have a healthy sense of entitlement," Elena said, strutting confidently behind Jake, who knew his way around after being forced to attend countless pharmaceutical dinners here over the years. He pointed to the biggest yacht in the marina, moored picturesquely in the Indian River.

"There it is… We can lie low here till we figure this whole mess out."

"Can you drive the boat to Bosnia?" Elena asked.

"Highly unlikely." Jake approached Landry's fifty-five-foot Azimut called *The Eye Cruiser*. The yacht looked sleekly sculpted by the wind with a vertical bow and floor-to-ceiling windows. Elena gazed up at the nautical behemoth.

"Looks like a Russian oligarch's boat," Elena said.

"May have been. He got it at a repo auction. *Shoot*. Gate's locked." Jake tried slipping through the dock's slatted gate. "Let me see if I…" His belly got in the way.

"I can." Elena's thin frame easily slipped through the slats.

"Looks like you've done this before," Jake remarked.

She flipped the turn lock and opened the gate for him.

"I have."

They walked up scoffed wooden steps along the port side of the moored boat. Jake stepped onto the yacht and offered his hand to Elena to help her aboard. Elena reflexively stiffened, but as she looked into Jake's eyes, a warm welcoming feeling came over her. She took his hand.

Jake located the key Landry kept hidden under a welcome mat at the stern of the ship.

"His secret hiding spot," he said, making a wry face.

"…Not so secret," Elena said.

Jake opened the sliding glass door, and they stepped inside the sprawling 2,200-square-foot yacht. "Welcome to Shangri-La…"

Decorated by Amber Landry's Miami-based interior designer, the yacht was styled with high shine cabinetry, linen paneling, and omnipresent glass for "exceptional water views." Elena examined the environment like she had never seen such opulence in her life, running her fingers lightly across the Italian tan leather sofas in the lounge, slowly scuffing her heels across the lacquered teak floors, checking out the kitchen, saloon, a dining area that seated eight, four staterooms, a guest double aft, and an additional twin cabin with a Pullman berth. When they entered the lounge, Jake found the thermostat on a panel next to the imported antique oak bar and dance floor and flipped on the air conditioner. He also accidentally turned on the rotating disco ball.

"…Saturday Night Fever," Elena commented archly.

"He thinks he's in the yacht mafia. Went for the whole Colombian drug-running look."

"He succeeded." Elena came to the master stateroom with its rotating king-sized bed shaped like a clamshell. She raised her eyebrow dubiously.

"No funny stuff, cow eyes."

Jake held up his soft hands innocently. "I'll sleep in one of the twin cabins."

"…I feel dirty," Elena said, staring at the bed as she walked toward the door.

"It is very Scarface," Jake replied as he left the bedroom.

"No." She stopped at the door and gestured to her hospital gown. "I need to clean up."

"Oh…" He blushed. "Right. Oh—"

She shut the bedroom door in his face.

"—kay."

Jake left her in the master bedroom and explored the yacht, first checking the fridge—it was stocked. *What am I thinking? Should I turn myself in?* He thought about his partnership at the clinic. *Not till she's safe.* He grabbed a bottle of Evian from the fridge, inadvertently eavesdropping on Elena, who seemed to be running water and making a phone call in Bosnian. Raised to be polite, he walked to the living room to give her privacy, sitting down on a leather sofa, and sipped his bottled water. He turned on the OLED screen TV and found the local news. He groaned aloud, seeing his driver's license photo and Elena's passport photo side by side on the screen.

Must be a slow news day… Cindy's not gonna like this, he thought.

Jake wished at least they'd used a more recent photo where he didn't look so fat. He checked his phone; he had thirty-two missed calls in the past two hours, eight from his mother; he sighed. He knew he hadn't broken any laws—as far as he knew—when he helped Elena escape. They were going to discharge her later anyway, so he felt confident he would be exonerated of any wrongdoing, in time. But what about the PR damage of having his face all over the TV? *Will Landry understand? Will Mom? Will anyone?* he worried. He thought about Elena's beautiful eyes.

"…The Pascal laser," he said to himself.

He picked up his phone and rang Dr. Farshid Aria, whom he was supposed to meet for dinner that evening at a Thai restaurant they frequented years ago. Jake had many colleagues in Florida but few real friends other than Ben that he could trust. Surprisingly, Farshid picked up after two rings.

Jake blurted out, "I'm in trouble." He confided to his mentor, explaining the airport, the hospital, the creepy hit men, the laser message in Elena's eyes, the old lady, and his face on the morning news. When he had finished, there was a long silence on the line.

"What have you gotten yourself into?" Farshid asked. "What did I say last time we met?"

"Be careful what you wish for," Jake remembered. "I know, I know."

"What intrigue," Farshid mused. "But 'deliver it' where, or to whom? … She won't tell you?"

"Not yet…"

"I suppose I can translate the Arabic…but as for this bar code? I could determine if a Pascal laser did the work," Farshid assured him. "But only a computer designed to read such things could achieve your wish."

"Just the Arabic. I realize this is a big favor."

"It most certainly is," Aria agreed. "I am too old for these capers. Can you trust this woman…? Allowing our hearts to guide us can be a fool's errand."

"It's not love. I know it sounds crazy, but I just believe her."

"She is beautiful?"

"Yes, she is…" Jake declared.

"You trust too easily."

"That's what Didi used to say."

Farshid grew silent. Jake assumed he was considering whether to get involved; he couldn't blame his mentor. He stared down at his less-than-round image reflected a hundred times on the mirrored disco floor. He thought about all of the New Year's Eves he had spent at home with Didi when he was too embarrassed to take her out dancing because of his appearance. Now that he was in better shape, he had no dancing partner. It made his heart ache all over again.

What would it be like to dance with Elena? He imagined it all. How her eyes danced suggestively as they moved as one. How her hips felt swaying to the beat… *Man, I need to find someone.*

Farshid cleared his throat, interrupting Jake's daydream.

"You know that I live by God's rules," Farshid said solemnly. "I cannot approve of you breaking the law. But I will help you this once. As your friend."

Jake felt relieved. "Thank you."

"I can come to you, if you wish," Farshid offered.

"Probably shouldn't, for both of our protection."

"Best I do not know," Farshid said, chuckling. "But you are safe, yes?"

"My heart rate's skyrocketing, but I'm fine," Jake assured him.

"Tomorrow morning, I will be seeing patients with residents and fellows in Orlando. We will be working at my colleague Doctor Brennan's clinic at 1282 Sand Lake Road. Come to me. I will help you translate. Bring your lady friend."

"She's not my…"

Farshid interrupted. "And be careful. Vultures are circling… Now, every person in Orlando knows your face."

$$\left(37\right)$$

Elena gazed up at the stars, feeling like an inconsequential speck of dust on the millionaire's yacht. She had slept with one eye open all week and knew she wouldn't sleep soundly again until she was reunited with her daughter and permanently out of this nightmare. She wrapped herself in a teal pashmina she found in Amber Landry's closet, anguish written across her lovely, bruised face. Her pocket buzzed and she glanced down at her iPhone. Two new texts from an unknown European number.

Mikal's burner, she thought. *Katastrofa.* ("What a disaster" in Croatian.)

Jake, wearing Landry's BBQ apron, lumbered along the upper deck, carrying the vodka she'd requested. "You remind me of big teddy bear," she said tartly.

He handed her a double Ketel One and soda in a Baccarat crystal tumbler and smiled.

"I feel like one after eating all that pasta." He smiled.

"You realize now you blowing the 'no carbs' thing."

"Don't remind me," Jake said ruefully. "Want me to check your eye again?"

"*This* will ease pain." She took a big swallow and squinted to read his apron. Her bruised left eye was beginning to open.

"*Ophthalmologists Do It With Precision* ... Is that sex joke?"

Jake looked down. "Yeah. Steve and Amber are kinda, like, swingers."

"What is meaning? 'Do it with precision'?"

"Umm... Eye doctors do it with extreme accuracy, I guess?"

She thought a moment. "I like lovers who improvise," she teased.

He chuckled awkwardly and they sat down in matching teak lounge chairs.

The odd twosome looked quietly up at the starry night.

"...How did we get here, Boy Scout?"

159

Jake sipped his drink. "I'd be at the hospital right now, if you hadn't come into my life." *That came out strange*, Jake thought, but Elena didn't seem to notice.

"It is already New Year in Sarajevo," she said quietly.

"You have family back home?"

"A little one…" She smiled. "Mia…thinks she is Disney princess."

Elena pulled out her phone and showed Jake a video of her and Mia playing in a Sarajevo playground with Abi and Jula. "Mia wants to live here. I tell her America is run by corrupt oligarchs, like Russia, but she does not listen." She cracked a wry smile.

"I like your life," Jake replied. "You're a good—" He paused as his phone vibrated.

He looked down; it was another text from Cindy.

ARE YOU ON THE RUN? THE POLICE JUST LEFT. I TOLD THEM YOU CAN'T BE A TERRORIST; YOU CAN'T EVEN CHANGE A FLAT TIRE! CALL YOUR MOTHER!

"—*Mother*." Jake sighed, pocketing his cell. "Plan to live here after you graduate?" he asked Elena.

She scoffed. "Probably not now that I am *fugitive*. I shall be arrested or deported."

"I've been thinking about that. I may have a plan," he said.

"Cow eyes has plan?" She clicked her tongue skeptically.

The yacht's doorbell chimed. The hair stood up on the back of Elena's neck. Jake looked at Elena, his index finger over his mouth. He switched off the table sconce. Elena eyed the railing, determining how quickly she could dive into the water if the police, or Mikal's men, were closing in.

The doorbell chimed again. They froze. Elena listened for sirens or the cocking of guns but heard only frogs, water, and bad music from the New Year's Eve party going on at the club.

"Yoo-hoooooo…" a woman with a smoky voice called. "Bawdy Broussarrrrrds?!"

Elena relaxed. Jake crept to the stern and peeked over the edge. It was not the police or hit men; it was an inebriated sun-scorched couple standing at the dock's gate holding a bottle of champagne. Jake whispered to Elena, "They'll go away, just be quiet."

"You crazy kids up for a Jacuzzi?!" the man shouted.

Elena cast a worried eye on the tarped Jacuzzi a few feet away from her.

"Well, *farts*… They're not here." The woman sighed. "Swore I saw lights on up there."

"Forget it, sweet cheeks," the man said. "Time's wastin'!" The inebriated couple stumbled back to the party at the Harbor Grill. Jake took a breath and checked his Fitbit.

"Does watch tell you when you are pissing in your pants?" asked Elena in an amused tone.

Jake looked down; it was another text from Cindy. "That was close."

"*Close* is mortar shell in kitchen, where I am from."

"Oh… I'll keep that in mind if I ever visit Bosnia."

Waves of giddy laughter floated over from the club. With midnight approaching, the alcohol being served seemed to be hitting the partygoers' bloodstreams in a tidal wave.

"Didn't know the yacht club got so rowdy. More people may stop by."

"So much for brilliant plan." Elena stood up and extended her hand. "Come. I know private spot. Before more swingers crash the gate…" Jake looked up at her luminous silhouette backlit by the stars. He took her hand.

"Bring the vodka," she said.

(38)

Cape Canaveral, Florida

"I found Landry's keys. They were on the hook near the door." Jake dangled a set of keys, stepping off the yacht. "We'll go incognito." They tiptoed off Landry's private dock and glided past the partygoers, who were too drunk to notice the imposters among their throng. Jake wore his boss's double-breasted navy-blue blazer with gold buttons; Elena had taken Amber's black Lululemon workout tights and a loose-fitting plunge-neck cashmere sweater. They darted across a putting green and beyond the tennis courts until they found the car Landry kept at the club to shuttle his VIP guests around. It was a bright yellow Hummer H3.

Elena raised an eyebrow. "I don't think incognito means what you think it does."

Jake whispered, "My face and license plate are all over the news. Get in, *quick*."

Elena scanned the lot and reluctantly climbed in. "Go!" she ordered.

"Where are we going?" Jake asked, starting the engine.

"It is a surprise," Elena said playfully. She instructed Jake to drive north on A1A twenty-five miles north of Patrick Space Force Station and Merritt Island National Wildlife Refuge.

"I know where you're taking us." He pointed to the metal bleachers along the Banana River that had been set up to watch SpaceX's launch the next day. "I've watched many launches here."

"Not there. *There*." She pointed to a secluded mango grove just east of the gated white SpaceX Complex 40 Launch Pad, which glowed in the moonlight. Jake pulled the Hummer off Centaur Road into a small clearing.

"Is this legal?"

"I see lovers park here sometimes," she said. "Since SpaceX took over this property from Space Force, there are no army men. Just sleepy private security."

Jake turned off the engine but left the radio playing. He calculated the odds that Elena actually might want to kiss him. They were slim, but he set the mood by opening the sunroof and windows, just in case. Elena pulled out the vodka bottle and two small glasses. Jake sat there wracking his brain for something charming and witty to say but only came up with:

"Uh…nice spot… You really work there?" Jake nodded at the complex visible in the distance through the banana leaves.

"Intern. Unless they canceled security clearance." She poured two shots.

Through the sunroof, they saw the vast expanse of stars, which blanketed the sky over the Atlantic Ocean. The lonely doctor's heart raced (but in a good way for once) as the sounds of night toads and rolling surf danced in the salty air. With his romantic skills rusty, he said the first thing that came into his head. "Do you want to be an astronaut?"

Elena didn't reply. *That was stupid.* He groaned. *Say something cool, Romeo. This is your chance.* Her phone buzzed. She looked down at the illuminated screen. Out the corner of his eye, Jake spied it was a series of coded numbers and a photo of her daughter with some good-looking man, smiling together over a milkshake.

She shivered slightly and put her phone away. "…*Cosmonaut*," she replied, hiding her agony, like she'd done so many times in her life. "Get it straight, Boy Scout."

"What's the difference?" Jake quipped.

She stared at the SpaceX complex and downed her vodka. "You ask too many questions."

"Well, uh," he said, "I haven't asked you at all about the men trying to kill you." *Way to kill the mood*, he thought.

She poured another round. "Good… I do not drink to them. I drink to the dead."

Jake looked at his glass. "Can't we maybe…drink to our health instead?"

"Whatever," she said. They toasted and knocked back the shots. "Na zdravlje!"

Jake grimaced. "*Strong.*"

"Puts hair on your chest," she said, wiping her mouth.

"If you say so!" Jake coughed.

"Here." Elena handed him a water bottle. "Chaser."

Jake took a swig from Elena's water bottle. They sat in the dark, listening to the night sounds and the firecrackers going off on shore across the Indian River. Lightheaded from the vodka and being in Elena's pheromonal orbit, Jake flipped around the radio dial and found a New Year's Eve broadcast.

"Just in time for the ball drop." Jake said.

"Falcon 9 Starlink goes up tomorrow." Elena gestured at the launchpad. "The world gets free Internet."

"I read about that. That's good, right?"

"If you think global American surveillance system is good," Elena said coldly. "They are sending thousands of satellites into space. Do you think only to give people access to Netflix?"

"Gee. Never thought of it that way," he replied, feeling the alcohol take effect.

"Naked eye won't know what are stars and what are satellites up in sky after he is done," Elena continued. "Galileo is rolling in grave."

Wow, she's brilliant and beautiful. Say something, you idiot!

"Satellites are junking up the sky, huh?" he asked.

She poured them another round. "I am fascinated with universe."

"Me too." Jake finally got an idea. He pointed to the brightest star in the sky. "Know what that is? …That's the Christmas Star. It's when Saturn and Jupiter align. It only happens every eight hundred years."

Elena shot him a glance and poured another round. "Jupiter and Saturn. They are making love tonight?"

"Yeah. Did you uh…have a date for New Year's Eve before all this mess?"

"That's following train of thought?"

"Sorry."

"I have no American lovers… It was not permitted."

"*Permitted?*" Jake was perplexed. "Man. SpaceX runs a tight ship. I actually don't think that's legal in this country."

"Not him. My ex." Elena felt her bruised eye. "The one who did this."

Jake gave her a fuzzy gaze. "Did *what?*"

"He made me—" Elena stopped short. "I must be getting drunk."

More distant laughter and fireworks bursted over the eastern shore.

Elena focused her intense, almond-shaped eyes on Jake for the first time all night.

"Our time is almost over, Boy Scout." She smiled.

He drank in her luminous beauty inches away from him. With oxytocin (the love hormone) and vodka coursing through Jake, he gave her a goofy smile. "Don't say that. I have a plan."

Elena put her index finger over his mouth. "Stop talking."

She leaned over and slowly kissed him. Jake felt a dizzying rush of electricity through his body as the DJ on the radio counted down the final seconds of the year.

"5…4…3…2…1… Happy New Year!"

Sky-wide blooms of fireworks went off all around them. For a moment, Jake's world seemed perfect.

Suddenly, he felt dizzy, nauseous. His mouth tasted salty.

Elena released her lips and sat back, watching him. A black veil slowly covered his eyes. Jake fell back in his seat and passed out.

"Lightweight," she said. She hopped out the passenger side, walked around the front of the truck, and dragged his large body out of the Hummer, laying him gently on the sandy ground beneath a mango tree.

"Sleep tight, cow eyes."

———◆———

Elena pulled up to the front gate of the SpaceX Complex 40 Launch Pad and flashed her SpaceX security badge.

"Working late, huh? Sweet ride," said an overweight SpaceX security guard.

"Last-minute details for the launch," Elena said, wearing dark sunglasses at night.

"Details, details. What happened to your eye there, beautiful?"

"…Car accident," she responded.

The guard sized her up. "You don't look like any rocket scientist I ever saw."

"Edward Menard hired me personally," Elena said, using her sexiest Marilyn Monroe voice. "I specialize in rocket elevation technique."

"I bet you do." The guard checked his computer. "But this vehicle is not on the log sheet, honey."

"My other car was totaled in the accident. I have security clearance."

"Yes, you do. But this banana boat don't… Gonna have to call it in."

She reached out and touched the guard's arm.

"How about I give you a New Year's kiss, and you just let me in?" Elena leaned against the driver's-side door, providing the chunky guard a clear view down her low-cut cashmere sweater. "I'll be in big trouble with Mr. Menard if I'm late." The guard could see Elena wore no bra. His eyes slowly moved to look up at her face. She bit her lip like a sex kitten.

"A kiss?" His voice wavered.

"For luck," she whispered.

The guard went slack as she pulled him in for a kiss.

The security gate rose slowly. Elena coasted forward and the Hummer purred through the gate.

(39)

Baton Rouge, Louisiana

"We ID'd the dead girls' Svengali! Where are you?" Agent Benji Weir's voice crackled through Rizzo's iPhone speaker while she weaved through New Year's Eve traffic in Baton Rouge.

"Plane was delayed. We're on route to the stakeout. Fill us in," Rizzo shot back.

"On with the task force now. I'll merge you in." Benji put them on hold.

Rizzo glanced at Thorn. "What's a Svengali again?"

Thorn replied, "A charmin' motherfu—"

"*Ladies.*" A baritone voice came on the line. "Tobias Harrelson of the FBI's Joint Terrorism Task Force. Agent Hawks tells me you've been assigned the Eye Torcher case."

"Tell me you got him," Rizzo exclaimed, honking her horn at the car in front of them.

"Not exactly." Agent Harrelson explained how that night across the Atlantic Ocean at 8:42 p.m. Sarajevo time a heavily armed SWAT team comprised of CIA, FBI, and Interpol agents kicked in the metal door of an ancient brick loft on Konak Street across from the Emperor's Mosque, with a search warrant for Mikal Mikalovich.

"Place was trashed," Harrelson explained. "He was either tipped off, one of his men turned on him, or he felt the heat coming. But he ghosted."

Rizzo banged on the steering wheel. "Dammit. Who's the ghost?"

"Bosniak extremist. Cold-blooded sadist. Known for talking women jihadists into suicide missions. Has deep ties to Al-Qaeda. Mikal cut his teeth in the Bosnian mujahideen and was one of the founders of the Active Islamic Youth."

"Dude's a lifer," Thorn said. "Is it the Task Force's assessment Mikal is the ringleader?"

"Likelihood is high," Harrelson said. "All intel points to him. This is what he does—he recruits women who are vulnerable refugees, often orphans."

"Does his MO match the Torcher?" Rizzo barked.

"Taking the eyes as prizes is new, but he's been known to dispose of his messengers once he's done with them. We're sending over a mug shot from his latest arrest in 2014. Interpol's had eyes on him since 9/11—until last night. Serbs call him the 'Sarajevo Svengali.' Interpol believes he's headed to America."

Agent Thorn showed Rizzo Mikalovich's mug shot on her laptop.

"Good-looking devil," Rizzo commented.

"Extremely dangerous cat," Harrelson said.

"Elena in his ring, too?" Thorn asked.

"Elena Smilovic, aka Emina Ajna Sidran," Harrelson reported, "appears to be Mikal's lover. No sign of her involvement in whatever he's plotting."

"Why kill these women? What's the plot?" Rizzo asked.

"Unclear."

"Nothing on SpaceX?" Rizzo asked.

"Negative. Your hunch didn't track with our intel."

Rizzo was too stunned to speak.

"You recover any tech?" Thorn asked.

"Affirmative. Found his rig in a dumpster, laptop in pieces—all wiped. He drilled holes in the hard drives, fried the motherboard, hard drive controller. The DRAM, BIOS ROM, CMOS RAM chips were all found in the microwave. Same for his Micro SD and SIM cards... Though Interpol did find a string you can pull... They've picked up chatter from sleeper cells in Mikal's network the past twenty-four hours. Translated, the messages say the same thing: '*The sweet citrus rose blooms.*'"

"It's code," Thorn said. "Benji, run it through our cryptography DB."

"Wait! Wait, wait." Rizzo's eyes lit up. "Sheila and the USC Trojans... Svanna and the LSU Tigers... *Sugar Bowl. Citrus Bowl. Orange Bowl. Rose Bowl.*"

Thorn followed her train of thought. "He's planning an attack on college bowl games?"

"And getting rid of his accomplices. Benji!" she shouted. "You still there?"

"Still here." His voice crackled over the phone.

Rizzo fired back: "Notify Homeland and Field Intelligence: the Rose Bowl, Sugar Bowl, Citrus Bowl, and Orange Bowl are all possible targets. Lock 'em down! And inform Hawks that Bortiach is a cheerleader for the LSU Tigers; we're picking her up now—will report after she's in custody."

———•———

Rizzo pulled up to a magnolia-lined street a block from a dilapidated two-story Victorian with an overgrown yard near the LSU campus. They parked behind an unmarked FBI van that had been surveilling the property the past forty-eight hours.

"Bowl games *and* rocket ships?" Rizzo pondered. "Don't get the connection."

"They're separate plots, like Hawks said," Thorn replied.

"Menard is gonna have my badge," Rizzo said.

"Nah. You sniffed out the Starship bomb. Saved his ass. And LA, too." Thorn added, "That's some expert detective work even if your hunch didn't pay off."

"Tell it to the brass…" Rizzo groaned. "Bowl games are tomorrow."

"We still got time. *Here.*" Thorn handed Rizzo a stale airport sandwich. The clock on the car's dashboard clicked over to midnight. "Eat somethin'. It's New Year's."

Rizzo stared at the wilted sandwich as if it were a consolation prize.

"…I was thinkin'." Thorn took a bite of hers. "If Elena's Mikal's girl, that lobster-bib-wearing doctor could be on his endangered species list."

Rizzo sniffed her sandwich. "Someone's geo-locating his cell phone, right?"

"The special agent in charge of the Orlando field office said they were."

"LaFleur better be running." Rizzo took a bite.

(40)

Miami, Florida

A balmy Florida breeze escorted a three-engine Dassault Falcon 8X jet as it made a feathery landing at the Miami Opa-Locka Executive Airport, just ten minutes away from the Hard Rock Stadium, home of the Orange Bowl and the Miami Dolphins. At 11:44 p.m. on New Year's Eve, a dapper mustached pilot in a grey ITA Airways uniform stepped down onto the tarmac and popped a Certs mint; moving like a shadow in plain sight, he mixed with a group of international pilots and flight attendants on their way to the airport's "Blade Lounge" for the first of many cocktails on their holiday layover. The good-looking pilot provided a falsified Italian passport and credentials to junior U.S. Customs officer Chuck Sampson, who was stationed on the airfield and too busy eyeing the beautiful Italian flight attendants to notice. Outside the south exit, the pilot found a taxi station. He looked up at the weather-beaten storefronts bordering the southern exit of the airport. *Looks like Russia*, he thought, *piece of trash*. Mikal removed his false mustache and tossed his pilot's hat into a trash bin. He hailed a taxi to the East Coast Buffer Water Preserve a few miles away. At his destination, he overtipped the Cuban cabbie and disappeared into the marshy dark near Highway 27.

Frogs croaked in the bog. Three minutes passed. A set of headlights from a white Ford van approached mile marker 22, lighting up the dark two-lane road. The van door slid open. A giant specter of a man stepped out.

Mikal appeared from the glades and leapt into the van. Inside the vehicle, Mikal's slim athletic frame was wedged between two behemoths (dressed in paramilitary gear) wearing grim faces and (even grimmer) body odor. The motley crew traveled north on Highway 27 in utter silence. Sensing tension, Mikal broke the ice with a congenial offer. "Dykhaniye myaty, comrades?"

170

("Breath mint, fellow soldiers?" in Russian.) The Russian terror cell said nothing. Mikal returned the pack to his breast pocket.

"Gde ostal'nyye kody?" ("Where are the remaining codes?") asked Yuri, the bearded man with a shaved head and tattooed neck, from the front passenger seat.

Mikal handed Yuri his encrypted sat phone. "Tsvetet sladkaya tsitrusovaya roza. Moi angely nosyat kody v svoikh glazakh." ("The sweet citrus rose blooms. My angels wear the codes in their eyes.")

Yuri copied the contents of the sat phone and threw it back at Mikal.

"A gde ostal'nyye?" ("Where are the rest?") he asked.

Mikal cleared his throat. "Doktor seychas izvlekayet odin. Ya sam dostavlyu okonchatel'nyy kod." ("The Doktor is extracting one now. I will deliver the final code myself.")

Yuri turned around and pointed a dirty finger at Mikal. "Vy podrezayete yego blizko." ("You're cutting it close.")

Mikal stared at Yuri, his pleasant expression gone. He snatched Yuri's finger and twisted it violently. Yuri grimaced, his fierce eyes swelling with anger. The beefy agents sandwiching Mikal pressed their RSh-12 (12.7-mm) assault revolvers to Mikal's temples.

Feeling the cold metal barrels on his skin, Mikal released Yuri's finger.

"YA znayu, chto delayu," ("I know what I am doing") Mikal angrily asserted.

Yuri gestured. His men put away the guns. He turned back to the road. "Ne narushayte Shankhayskiy pakt. Vy znayete posledstviya," Yuri warned Mikal. (Don't fail the Shanghai Pact. You know the consequences.") Mikal stiffly nodded calmly as the van passed a road sign that read: "Orlando, 211 miles." He unlocked his sat phone and texted Elena a coded sequence, with a photo of himself and Mia sharing a milkshake. Beneath his charming surface, he seethed.

YA ub'yu etu suku, kogda naydu yeye. (I'm going to kill that witch when I find her.)

(41)

Baton Rouge, Louisiana

Crickets chirped like a symphony of rusty banjos echoing through an old neighborhood north of the LSU campus. Distant firecrackers (early to the party) crackled, as Agent Rizzo wiped sandwich crumbs off her brown leather jacket, staring through a pair of government binoculars. It was almost midnight and still eighty degrees outside, an uncommonly warm winter night. All of the windows in the yellow Victorian that Svanna shared with two other students were closed. The steady hum of the air conditioner's condenser unit muted the night sounds.

Rizzo gestured to the lattice-covered crawl space under the house.

"Can one of your men slip a functional mic under there?"

"Not unless they're the size of a nutria," replied FBI Agent Tom Boyle.

"…A what?"

"Swamp rat. Too small," joked Boyle, explaining that since Baton Rouge was barely above sea level, all the houses were built on cinder blocks to prevent flooding.

"Disgustingly hot weather. Alligators, now swamp rats." Rizzo grimaced. "How do you people live here?"

"You got us Louisianians all wrong, Janey. We got the best food in the country. Best outdoorsman activities, and Southern hospitality. Let me prove it to you, sometime."

She rolled her eyes. They had been having the same conversation about the South for years. Rizzo had met Thomas Montgomery Boyle in 2006 when they were rookies. Jane was the tanned military hero/college placekicking star tracking down a kidnapped heiress in the French Quarter. "Tommy" (as she once called him) was a shy Cajun with a clip-on tie, busting post-Katrina scammers bilking the government of FEMA money. It wasn't glamorous work, but Tom Boyle had paid his dues. Now he was the ASAC (Assistant Special Agent in Charge) overseeing investigative personnel for the New Orleans office, while Rizzo's career trajectory had stalled. The irony was not lost on Jane as the two old friends caught up in the tight quarters of an FBI surveillance van.

Rizzo caught Tom stealing furtive glances at her athletic legs as he mentioned to Agent Thorn how they had once dated when they were young. "Never clicked…least for Janey." It was inappropriate workplace chatter, but Thorn couldn't resist smiling.

Rizzo quickly changed the subject. "Who owns that vehicle in front of the house?" She pointed to the purple Ford Focus with an LSU Tigers decal on the back windshield.

"Registered to Bortiach," Boyle said. "White Impala in back has a bar code on the driver-side back window; it's a rental. Arrived about thirty minutes ago. A man in his fifties, greying black hair, dark complexion, wearing an N-95 mask, toting an old-fashion leather doctor's bag. We sent a picture for identification; doubt we'll get a hit."

"Get me an ID on the rental," Rizzo directed Tom.

"Workin' on it," Tom replied, annoyed. "Stop being so cagey, Janey. Is this the 'Eye Torcher' we're chasin', or y'all really think the LSU cheerleader is a terrorist?"

"Reckon we think both, Tom." Rizzo smiled, laying on a Southern accent.

"Bad juju for the Tigers tomorrow then." Boyle sighed, watching the house through a pair of AGM thermal vision binoculars, which were linked to Thorn's laptop. He picked up his walkie-talkie and spoke into it.

"Movement on the second floor. There appear to be three men and two women. Stand by, team."

"Our tigress is awake," rasped a frail old woman in a thick European accent. Svanna groaned, lifting her spray-tanned chin off her chest. "Another injection, *Doktor*?"

"No more," replied a man with a soft Middle Eastern accent.

Watching the images on the computer screen in the van Rizzo complained, "Still no audio??"

"Sound Shark is having a tough time with the noisy AC unit," Boyle said.

"Who's the shorter figure?" Rizzo pointed to an infrared silhouette on Thorn's laptop—what looked to be an elderly lady with a bun in her hair hunched over someone in a lawn chair.

"Bortiach rents from an elderly woman, Miss Cecily. But that's not her. She's visiting her grandkids," reported Boyle.

Rizzo leaned close to the monitor, trying to read their body language.

———●———

"Gde ya?" ("Where am I?" in Russian) Svanna moaned, straining at the restraints around her wrists and ankles. "Tebe ne nuzhno eto delat'." ("You don't have to do this.")

"Of course, we do, my child," said the Middle Eastern man in the N-95 mask.

Svanna whimpered like she was in a nightmare, shaking her matted brown hair.

"Shhh, child," coaxed the old woman.

"*Where am I?? That's not Cecily,*" she cried out. Someone abruptly duct-taped her mouth. Terrified, she realized she'd been blindfolded, gagged, and tied to a lawn chair still in the half-shirt, ankle socks, and soccer shorts she'd worn to bed. *What do they want from me!?*

The last thing she remembered was coming home after practice, ordering Uber Eats, taking a shower, stealing a puff from her roommate's vape pen, and conking out watching Netflix. She had set her iPhone alarm for 6:00 a.m. It never had a chance to go off.

"Uspokoit'sya zlaya devushka" ("Settle down, wicked girl"), ordered the old lady.

Am I being taken to a gulag?? She felt a cold steel blade pressed to her neck. An orphan born in a Ukrainian refugee camp before migrating to a farming town in central Russia, Svanna had been tortured before. She took a panicked breath through her nose and tried to relax.

"*Good…* Now, let me see her eyes," said the man in the N-95 mask.

Svanna's blindfold was lifted.

She raised her head, blinking several times at her captors, trying to shake the sedative off her sluggish eyelids. Two faces loomed over her, backlit by the light of a whirring ceiling fan.

"There, there. It's just the Doktor paying you a house call. You've been expecting us, no?" Svanna focused on the old lady's face; she was grotesque, like the waxworks museum in Saint Petersburg she once visited on a school field trip. The masked man switched on his headlamp and shined it in her eyes. Svanna thrashed her head back and forth, shouting a muffled, "NYET!"

"No games." He sighed and motioned to Maman. "Hand me the spider." *Spider??* Svanna's mind raced.

A marksman from the East Baton Rouge SWAT team watched the second-floor window through his rifle scope. "I can't get a clear shot. Drapes closed," he reported into his mouthpiece.

"Back off," Rizzo ordered into her walkie-talkie. "No cowboy stunts, we want her alive."

Svanna distanced her mind from the traumatic scene; the glare in her eyes reminded her of the stadium lights she performed under during LSU's football games. Tomorrow, she was supposed to board a charter bus with the other cheerleaders for the ride to New Orleans, to work the sidelines of the BCS National Championship Game at the Sugar Bowl against the #1-ranked Alabama Crimson Tide. It would be broadcast globally. She hoped that her friends back home in Torzhok would see her and she would be discovered by a talent agent or a professional American sports team for her dancing and tumbling abilities. A long shot, but immigrants like Svanna with temporary visas and poor grades exist on such dreams. Now, her aspirations seemed as dark as the shadow of the fit Middle Eastern man with bad breath and thick black hair, looming over her. Adnan fastened the spider, a small metal speculum, between her eyelids. As the device's cold grip slowly forced open her right eyelid, a flood of repressed memories rushed in: the same cold spider crawling on her in Sarajevo, Mikal's smirking face.

Mikal... Etot ublyudok. ("That scumbag.") Svanna hadn't answered his texts in four days. He kept insisting she was to "deliver the message," *whatever that meant.*

Svanna blew him off. She was closing the book on her life dating sketchy rich men in Sarajevo. Her new American beau, Todd, a teacher's assistant in her history class, had advised her to cut ties with her "toxic past." But Svanna had already promised to meet up with the seemingly wealthy Mikal over Christmas break in America.

175

While the other members of her so-called "gold digger" clique at the University of Sarajevo—Uma, Sheila, and Elena had at one time or another all fallen under Mikal's charismatic spell—she never succumbed. Svanna was not a romantic—she was a realist—but she had played along, allowing Mikal to set her up with tuition and a car. She assumed his gifts were payoff so she wouldn't press charges for drugging her at a nightclub the last time they met. Until this moment, she'd had no clear memory of that traumatic night, only a hangover, a few bruises on her neck, and aching eyes. Now it all came back.

He performed surgery on me. But what did he do to my eye? Svanna slowly wriggled her chafed and sweating wrists under the restraints while the Doktor shined a light as brilliant as the sun into her eye.

Piece of junk chair, she thought, feeling the frame of the old lawn chair that she'd bought for three dollars from a yard sale. It gave at every pull; she resolved to fight with the ferocious elephantine force of a dying woman. If this was her fate, she would not go easily. *I will fight to the death.*

———◆———

Rizzo's intuition told her it was time. After determining the infrared figure tied to the chair was almost certainly Svanna Bortiach, Rizzo grabbed her bulletproof vest.

"They're holding her hostage. *Let's go.*"

"Hold on now," Boyle replied. "We haven't gotten the search warrant yet, Jane."

"We have probable cause! C'mon, I'll take the heat."

"…Guess we're goin' in then." Boyle directed the SWAT team to stand by. "Any sign of violence, breach the rez." Rizzo, Thorn, and Boyle strapped on their Kevlar vests as faint New Year's Eve firecrackers burst around them like popcorn in the night.

Rizzo in the lead, the three agents slipped out the back of the van and crept up to the old yellow house, stepping over pine needles onto a wooden porch with a broken entrance light. The boards creaked under Rizzo's step.

She stopped, motioning for Thorn to go to the right side of the house and Boyle around to the back. The police presence went left. Rizzo crouched under a draped window on the front porch, listening for activity. The front door appeared loosely latched; it was probably unlocked, Rizzo decided.

"Front door's open," Rizzo whispered into her hot mic. "I'm going in. Thorn, come to the front and back me up."

Boyle located the white Impala parked in the back alley and checked the back door.

"Back door is locked. I've got it covered," he whispered.

"Stay low, everyone. SWAT team stay put unless needed," Rizzo whispered back.

Thorn unholstered her .40 caliber handgun, Rizzo her Sig Sauer P226. She turned the battered copper doorknob, pushing lightly on the door and stepping into a dark hallway. Something didn't feel right to her. *Feels like an ambush… Like Kabul.* Thorn entered behind her, weapon drawn.

Upstairs, the Doctor examined Svanna's right eye through a hand-held twenty power diopter lens. Black pigmented laser scarring was visible throughout her peripheral retina arranged in the shape of a sequence of eleven Eastern Arabic numerals and an excerpt from the Quran.

"Their eyes were their passports, these girls," he lamented. "Could they follow simple orders? … They misbehave as if they were American!"

"It will all work out, as the good Lord intended," Maman crooned, stroking Svanna's hair.

The Doktor scoffed, then read the detonator code into a handheld voice recorder.

"Thalaatha (3)… Sifr (0)… Khamsa (5)… Sab3a (7)… Arbi3a (4)… Thamaaniya (8)… Sitta (6)… 3ashara (10)… Ithnaan (2)… WaaHid (1)… Tis3a (9)."

The Doctor removed his surgical loupe. "You've done God's work, tigress… Praise be Allah." He shook his index finger. "But another disobedient angel you were, tsk tsk." He gently removed the speculum and caressed her face. "Pity…you may be the most beautiful of them all." Svanna glared up at the him. "You know, you have my daughter's almond eyes." He patted her on the cheek and held up the voice recorder containing the dirty bomb detonator code; he looked pointedly at Adnan (thirty-nine) and Shariff (nineteen), the two members of Mikal's Louisiana-based sleeper cell.

"I trust you will share this with the good people of New Orleans, yes?"

"Praise be Allah," Adnan and Shariff chorused, nodding.

"*The sweet citrus rose blooms,*" chanted Shariff.

"What about the final code?" asked Adnan.

"Leave it to me," the Doktor replied. "Svengali and I will recover the wayward dove."

42

Rizzo crept silently up the carpeted stairs, sidearm drawn. Thorn, Boyle, and the SWAT team fanned out through the dark kitchen and dining room.

"We clear??" Tom asked Rizzo in her earpiece.

"Negative," Rizzo whispered, listening through the second-floor bedroom door. She lightly tested the doorknob. Locked. She could hear the conversation inside the room.

"I trust you are not attending the Sugar Bowl contest," the Doktor asked Maman with sarcasm.

"No. I prefer to watch my stories," she replied.

He nodded. "I'd advise against it." Shaking his finger at Svanna, he said, "You should not either, tigress. But we will see to that." Adnan used a long needle to draw fluid out of a rubber-stopped medicine vial as the Doktor spoke Arabic into a voice recorder.

Her heart pounding, Svanna's life flashed before her eyes. *It's now or never.* She furiously pulled at the arms of the old lawn chair. *C'mon!* She twisted her wrists free. *Yes!* Svanna glanced over at her captors with wild animal eyes, untying her right ankle. She spotted the voice recorder on the table a foot away.

He turned around, surprised. "Tigress. You have not been excused."

Adnan held up a long steel needle. Using all her strength, Svanna darted toward her bedroom window, dragging the rickety lawn chair across the room still attached to her left leg. The Doctor chuckled.

"Spirited girl. Adnan, grab her."

Downstairs, Thorn heard the thudding and clattering coming from the second floor.

"What's up, Jane?" she asked into her mouthpiece.

Svanna let out a muffled scream.

"Going in!" Rizzo stood and shot off the bedroom doorknob. Hearing gunfire, the trigger-happy SWAT team kicked in the front door firing, almost hitting Thorn as she rushed up the stairs. Time slowed down for Rizzo as she heard gunshots discharging downstairs. From the corner of her eye, she spotted a boy of nineteen appear from a room down the hall. Rizzo was taken aback. *Who's this kid? A target or civilian?*

In an LSU Tigers cap and sweatshirt, he looked more like a student; Rizzo motioned for him to go back into his room. Suddenly, the kid, Shariff, pulled out a Glock from his waistband and fired two rapid shots at Rizzo, who ducked, the whiz of the bullets barely passing over her head, as she rolled into Svanna's bedroom, springing back to her feet, gun drawn. Svanna was halfway out the window dragging the broken lawn chair at her ankle. Adnan was attempting to horse-collar her back inside.

"FBI! Freeze!" Rizzo shouted.

Thorn raced upstairs as Shariff barricaded himself in the hallway bathroom. She emptied her gun through the bathroom door and kicked open the door. Shariff was lying like a rag doll in the shower with three holes in his chest, his LSU cap covering his face.

Hearing shots, Rizzo turned her back toward the hall for a split second. Adnan yanked Svanna back inside the room. Using her as a human shield, he held a large handgun an inch from her right eye.

In a firing stance Rizzo held him at gunpoint. "Let her go!" she yelled.

Rizzo saw fear on the man's face; his gun trembled as Svanna cried out for help.

Rizzo softened her voice. "I'm not going to hurt you."

Adnan muttered in Arabic, his hands shaking. Rizzo walked closer, saying the only Arabic words she knew. "Allahu Akbar." ("God is great.")

"Allahu Akbar..." repeated Adnan softly, trembling.

"Just let Svanna go, okay?" Rizzo prompted.

Through the partially open bathroom door behind Adnan, the Doktor fired two quick shots at Rizzo, who ducked and rolled. Svanna bit down hard on Adnan's wrist. He reflexively discharged his gun, exploding the left side of Svanna's face. The force sent her body halfway out the open window. Adnan stood dazed for a moment in the middle of the room, trying to regain his senses. Behind him, the Doktor fired again from the bathroom doorway. Thinking the shots were coming from Adnan, Rizzo and Thorn unloaded five shots into his chest. He fell back, collapsing on the tiled floor... Acrid gun smoke hung in the air.

The SWAT team charged in. "Freeze!!!" They cleared the second floor.

Rizzo cautiously approached Adnan. She bent down to her knees and felt Adnan's neck for a pulse, her pistol still aimed at his head. He was dead.

The bottoms of Svanna's dirty feet were facing Rizzo and Thorn and her head and chest lay over the windowsill. "She almost made it," Thorn said under her breath, inspecting Svanna's body. Her neck was covered in blood. She was lifeless, no pulse.

Rizzo scanned the rest of the bedroom, gun drawn. The SWAT team charged in, ARs ready and aimed straight ahead. "Put the guns down, idiots." Rizzo pushed past the heavily armed men. "Where'd the old man go?"

During the firefight, the Doktor had managed to crawl out the bathroom window.

Thorn heard footsteps pattering on shingles above their heads.

"Suspect's on the roof!" Thorn yelled into her mouthpiece. "Cover the White Impala in the alley!"

Rizzo noticed her shoes were wet. She checked under the bed. An IV bottle was toppled over beside it, its needle dripping fluid. Rizzo's eyes followed the clear stream trickling across the floor over to a closed closet door. Something shifted behind the door.

"Come out with your hands up!" Rizzo aimed her Glock and swung open the closet. She saw Maman's frail frame, fallen back on a pile of Svanna's dirty clothes, her eyes rolled into the back of her head, mouth foaming like a rabid dog, and she groaned.

Thorn crawled inside and inspected the old lady's mouth.

"Heart attack?" Rizzo asked.

"Cyanide," Thorn replied.

"Man down! Man down!" someone shouted downstairs.

Stepping over a pool of blood by the back door, Jane's heart sank. Following the red-spattered trail to the back alley, Tom Boyle lay lifeless on the ground, his head pouring thick red. Captain Riggins, the SWAT commander, met her, helmet off, shaking his head.

"Agent Boyle was covering the back as we entered the front of the house," he told her.

Rizzo kneeled next to Boyle and checked his pulse. "Paramedics!"

"…It's too late," Thorn said.

Rizzo collapsed backwards on the graveled alley and ran her trembling fingers through her hair. "…Tommy."

Thorn gently touched her shoulder. "Jane…"

Rizzo's face contorted in sadness and anger. "Where'd that scumbag go!?"

A young SWAT entry operator announced, "Impala's not in the alley."

"Seriously!" Rizzo shouted. "You let the man jump off the roof, kill an agent, and drive away??"

"Deploy all units. Suspect is driving a white Impala," Captain Riggins shouted into his headset. He turned to Rizzo. "He won't get far. EBR's chopper's in the air."

"*Find him*!" Rizzo roared.

The East Baton Rouge coroner and EMTs wheeled Svanna's body out on a stretcher.

"What about her eyes?" Rizzo asked woodenly.

"They tried to take them out," Thorn said. "Destroying evidence, no doubt."

"Her right eye is intact, but the bullet entered her left temple and exited her left eye," said the coroner. "Forensic lab has it. Doubt there will be anything to get from the left."

Thorn held up a small black voice recorder. "Found this in Svanna's hand… She was holding on to it tight." Rizzo hit play. They listened.

"I will now extract the code from the messenger's right eye," the Doktor was heard to say before reciting a set of Arabic numerals.

"It's a detonator code. I'm sure the Sugar Bowl's the target. I heard them discussing it," said Rizzo.

"*Was* the target. We got the code from Svanna," Thorn said quietly. "She died a hero."

Agent Boyle's body was wheeled out on a covered stretcher in front of them.

Rizzo swiped away tears, watching his body pass by.

"So did you, Tommy," she intoned.

(43)

Cape Canaveral, Florida

L ying face down in the sand under a mango tree, Jake caressed a bottle of vodka like it were his dream lover. The bottle sloshed in his arms; he gently kissed it.

He heard a muffled voice. "Stop cheating."

His bloodshot eyes blinked open. Befuddled, Jake sat up, wiping drool from his round cheeks. Elena tapped him on the shoulder. It was suddenly dawn. He shielded his eyes.

"Were you kissing the vodka?" Elena smirked.

"What? No." Jake pushed the Stoli bottle away.

She sniffed at him. "You have Menard of wild ox, do you know that?"

"…What happened?"

"You fell asleep before we make love under stars."

Jake rubbed his dry eyes. "Really?"

"No… Stupid." She playfully patted his cheek. "You drink like twelve-year-old girl."

"Can't believe I passed out… You sleep any?"

"Let's go, before SpaceX security arrives." She stood up, wiping her hands together.

"Okay." Jake climbed inside the Hummer. "But this would be a fantastic place to watch the launch."

"Launch is tonight. I need to go home."

"Now?" Jake stared at her like a hungover puppy. "What about the police and the, um, guys chasing you?"

"Okay. Forget it, then," Elena said coldly. "I'll call Uber." She stormed out of the mango grove and strode up to Centaur Road to get cell reception.

"*Wait.*" He waved at her. "Elena." She turned around and looked at him. Jake ran a hand through his wild hair while brushing off the sand and straightening the blazer that he had borrowed from Landry. "I have an idea."

Driving down from the Cape on the blustery overcast morning, Jake unveiled his plan to get them out of this crazy mess, beginning with arranging for his friend to translate the Arabic message on her eye.

"You gossip about me over phone?" Elena bristled.

"Look, I trust Farshid with my life," he replied. "He's an expert on the laser that imprinted your eyes, and he's Persian. If he can translate the Arabic, maybe we can barter with whoever is chasing you. Ya know, give 'em what they want?"

"They want me dead," Elena said bluntly.

"Okay, then. We'll go to the police with what we know, and maybe let them protect us?" Jake took her hand confidently. "We can deliver the message… Together."

Elena's face stiffened as she slowly turned her head toward him. "*What did you say?*"

"Sorry." He confessed. "I, uh, kinda…eavesdropped… At Maman's house."

She yanked her hand away. "*How?*"

"I kinda speak…Russian?" He shrugged sheepishly.

Elena pulled off her sunglasses. "That is new development, Boy Scout! Who are you??" She punched him in the shoulder.

"Oww!!" Jake veered the Hummer off Tropical Trail and braked in the berm by the Banana River. A cloud of dust enveloped the vehicle.

"Are you one of them?!" Elena held her fist an inch from his face.

"NO!" Jake held up his hands. "My mom's a linguist! I speak five languages!"

"No American speaks five languages!" Elena shouted back.

"Well, I do! And what do you mean, one of who??"

Elena jumped out of the Hummer, slamming the passenger door. Jake slowly drove along beside her as she stomped up the bumpy road in her high heels. "One of who? Elena! … I'm not your enemy! Can't you see I'm putting my life in jeopardy to help you?"

Elena stared at him intensely through the open window. She looked for "tells" in his lying face… She saw none. She only saw a desperate sincerity.

This teddy bear cannot be Russian assassin, she decided, collecting herself.

She stared through the passenger window. "You must have smart mother," she said softly.

"I do." He felt his heart rate lowering. "…One of who?"

"…Mikal's cult," Elena finally admitted.

"Who's Mikal?"

"My ex." She pointed to her eyes. "The one who did this."

"Were you dating an eye surgeon?"

"No… He paid me hundred thousand Euros to give me to do some job." Her voice wavered. "I needed money for Mia. He said he would tell me later what the job was."

Jake interrupted her. "So, you knew about the procedures the whole time?"

"*You think I'm imbecile!* He drugged me and I think he lasered my eyes when I was unconscious. Then, I saw the TV at airport. Two friends from back home who also spent time with Mikal were murdered on Christmas." She stammered, "With their eyes gouged out… I smell a rat, so I ran."

"Umm. *Elena.*" Jake's face turned pale. "*Is your ex-boyfriend that serial killer on the news?*"

"I do not think so. He's in Europe. I think," she said matter-of-factly. "But Mikal has killed many men."

His heart rate spiking, Jake could barely choke out the words, "That's who's chasing us?" He rolled down his window to catch his breath.

"Don't puke into wind," Elena said. "It will just blow back in your face."

Jake gasped for air. "I'm just…taking all this in."

"I only tell you because grandmother has turned her back… Now I'm all alone."

Jake checked his heart rate. It was racing at 134 bpm. "Elena. I'm having a slight panic attack right now, but you are not alone. You can trust me. JUST GET IN THE CAR."

She slipped back inside the vehicle. Jake hit the gas, kicking up dust in the berm.

"He would have hurt Mia if I refused," she explained.

"Refused *what?*"

Elena wrestled with her conscience. "He made me do something awful."

"I won't judge you," Jake said.

Elena grew silent. "Best you do not know, Boy Scout."

He shot her an incredulous look. "Okay. Fine. *Don't tell me.* Just let me take you to see Farshid. Then I'll drive you to your apartment if you want. I will go to the police alone."

"You may visit your friend… But I'll stay on boat."

"But Farshid needs to examine your eyes."

"*Show him photos you took.* The ones you showed me at hospital."

He thought about it. "I suppose I still have them on my phone."

"I need a shower," Elena said.

Like a soldier in a foxhole fantasizing about his girl back home, the image of Elena taking a bubble bath involuntarily filled his mind. Like always, Jake felt a twinge of Catholic guilt for his latest "impure thought." After subsisting on a strict diet of spy novels since Didi had divorced him, fear, death, and women were all mixed up in his swirling head.

"I'm the one who smells," Jake blurted out. "Sure you don't want me to, uh, stay?"

"And do what, scrub my back?"

"I mean," he stammered awkwardly, "after last night, I kinda thought—I missed out?"

"You smell like ox, cow eyes. Don't behave like one."

(44)

Washington, DC

"Our team discovered something highly unusual in the victim's eyes," began Dr. Elmore Deuterman, head of the FBI's Forensic Science Lab in Washington, D.C., at an emergency meeting of FBI terrorism experts at 7:00 a.m. on New Year's Day.

Agent Rizzo listened to his report, slumped in the back of a sterile conference room at the FBI's New Orleans office on Leon C Simon Boulevard, six miles north of the French Quarter; she was still in her leather jacket stained with Tom Boyle's blood and in shock over the botched raid that had left three terrorists, one victim, and one FBI agent dead.

"Look at this." Deuterman pointed to an image of Svanna's eye broadcast on the Cisco WebEx video call. "We found a message lasered into the retina of the right eye. It's an Eastern Arabic dialect and includes a sequence of numbers and a coded phrase that ends with the words 'the fourth messenger.' Our cryptanalyst team is deciphering it. They anticipate cracking the message within the day, at the latest."

"Don't have that long, Doc," Rizzo said. "It's all going down tonight. Bowl games—"

"And SpaceX," Thorn added, entering the conference room with a cup of green tea to keep her awake. "Our investigation has led us to believe they are targets as well."

"I was under the impression this was about college football games?" asked Antoinette Baker, Assistant Director in Charge, Southern Region, who was in the room with Rizzo and Thorn. A Louisiana native of Creole/English lineage, "Toney," as she was called, had known Agent Boyle for years, like Jane.

LA's Assistant Director in Charge Harry Hawks joined the call from his stylish mid-century home office in Topanga Canyon and stated, "If I may, Assistant Director…"

Sensing his fiery subordinate was in no shape to speak to the team, Hawks summarized Rizzo's "dubious theory" that the serial killer, known as the "Eye Torcher," was a cleaner for a terror cell plotting to blow up the two SpaceX launches on New Year's Day. Hawks ended his grandstanding by commending Agents Rizzo and Thorn for their heroic work averting a disaster at the SpaceX facility in Hawthorne just seventy-two hours earlier. He also unconvincingly reasserted his belief that the incident had nothing to do with the Torcher case.

Rizzo and Thorn raised their eyebrows at his stubborn refusal to accept the truth.

"Thank you, Harry." Baker politely smiled, then turned to the agents in front of her. "So, is the Sugar Bowl a target, or not?" Baker tapped a pencil on the conference room table.

"It is if you believe the chatter Interpol's picking up," Thorn offered.

"The Superdome's already in lockdown. Convince me we are not wasting resources on a wild goose chase," Baker persisted.

"Here is what we've gathered from the intel overseas," reported Agent Tobias Harrelson, on the video call from the FBI's Joint Terrorism Task Force, explaining his team's role in raiding Mikalovich's home in Sarajevo and his subsequent disappearance.

After listening quietly, Baker asked, "So, we blew both of the raids?"

Rizzo glared at Baker. Agent Harrelson cleared his throat, reciting Mikal's extensive resume for evading capture. Then he offered a new bit of information.

"The CIA ascertains that a retinal surgeon in Sarajevo reportedly used something called the 'Pascal laser' to repair Mikalovich's torn retina, after he orchestrated a failed bombing of the U.S. Embassy in Montenegro in 2018… They believe that is when Mikal learned lasers can create patterns in retinas… He likely utilized this laser technology while using women as carrier pigeons. After his messengers deliver the coded message to his teams on the ground here in the U.S., they're told they could come home, get paid, end of story. But he's obviously used these women and is now getting rid of them instead."

"I was skeptical, but after observing the suspect at the scene, I believe," Rizzo said.

"Terror plots at what? Five, six locations??" Hawks scoffed. "Bowl games and SpaceX? This doesn't make any sense."

"Bin Laden plotted and executed four plots on 9/11," Rizzo said.

"Sports and space are as American as apple pie," Thorn added. "Hit us in both, and the world will take notice." The room murmured at the mention of bin Laden's infamous attack, which all of the U.S.'s intelligence agencies had been unable to prevent.

"*Quiet.* Very dramatic rendition," said Baker. "But I concur with Agent Hawks; this is all based on circumstantial hearsay. Where's the *physical evidence*? Why would a group of terrorists want to target SpaceX satellite launches?"

Rizzo calmly explained how the first two murdered women (Uma and Sheila) had led them to the Starship bomb. "As for the bowl games, you're holding the evidence," Rizzo said.

Assistant Director Baker held up the black voice recorder sealed in a plastic evidence baggie.

"This is the device you recovered at the site?"

"Ms. Bortiach recovered it, ma'am," Rizzo said. "Play it."

Baker switched on the recorder.

Everyone listened silently as the Doktor calmly discussed his preparations to extract the code from Svanna's eye.

"So, this corroborates the pathologist's findings of a message in her right eye," said Baker. "What can we deduce from the only physical evidence we've managed to recover in this case?"

"We believe there were similar messages in the other girls' eyes, which were used to plant a disruptive code in Starship's engine software. Maybe in Starlink's, too," Rizzo said. "That's why the Torcher burned the evidence. We stopped him this time. Or, Svanna did."

"Rational *assumption*. What do we know about our dead suspects and that elderly lady at the scene?" Baker looked at Agent Harrelson, who read through their dossiers.

"Adnan Muhami: Ex-Hezbollah, and Wahhabi Islamist. He entered Mikalovich's atmosphere in 2005. Like the so-called 'Sarajevo Svengali,' he's been linked to bombings in Sarajevo, Yemen, Tunisia, but was never captured. We believe he entered the country through the Canadian border earlier this month. The boy and elderly woman are a total mystery: no socials, no birth certificates, no passports. No current or prior residences. Zero digital trail."

"Really? Nothing at all on the old lady?" Baker asked.

"Interpol has no record of her either. She's a ghost."

"A ghost who ate a cyanide tablet," added Dr. Deuterman.

"That's old-school spy-craft right there," Thorn added.

Jean Brouchet from the Behavioral Analysis Unit (BAU) had joined the call to offer her expertise from the FBI's Chicago office. "The woman is likely part of a sleeper cell implanted in the States years ago. She fits the profile of an embedded handler who oversees Mikalovich's young women while they are on their missions."

"Hate to bring it up," Rizzo said, raising her hand. "But anyone seen the Torcher lately?"

Officer Ronald Thibodeaux of the Louisiana State Police updated the FBI on their case. "Perp's gone. He evaded our choppers and roadblocks. The white Impala, which was rented under a false name, was found two blocks from the house—but the perp left a trove of evidence at the scene: a recorder, doctor's kit, tools. Possible DNA. Our forensic team's working with the FBI team, still sweeping the premises."

"You forgot to mention one of your SWAT boys, who should have been covering the outside of the house and allowed the perp to kill a good man," Rizzo said. You could hear a pin drop on the call; this was Rizzo's intention.

"*Holster it,*" Thorn whispered to her grieving partner.

Baker cleared her throat. "Thank you for reminding us of Agent Boyle's valor, Agent Rizzo. We all regret what occurred."

"Anyone tell his wife and kids?" Rizzo asked.

"It's handled, Jane," Baker said. "Back to the matter at hand. Anybody got a clue where the suspect fled?"

No one said a word.

"Clock's ticking," said Baker. "If this plot is the live wire you say it is, we're on the verge of a national tragedy that would make 9/11 look like a warm-up act."

Rizzo spoke up. "Suspect mentioned locating a 'wayward dove.'"

"Wayward dove?" Thorn repeated.

"Wrote down his exact words." Rizzo called up the Notes app on her iPhone. "*The Svengali* will help us recover the wayward dove. We must hurry."

"First I heard of that." Thorn looked over at Rizzo, her mind percolating—then it clicked. *"Elena is Mikal's girlfriend.* They're meeting up in Orlando."

Rizzo's eyes widened. "Citrus Bowl is right next to Cape Canaveral."

"The citrus rose blooms," Thorn said. "Whoa."

The two agents jumped up from the table.

"Where do you think you're going?" asked a confused Baker.

Rizzo announced, "To stop the fourth messenger."

(45)

Indian Harbour Beach, Florida

Jake paced outside the closed door of *The Eye Cruiser*'s master stateroom listening to the shower run, occasionally stopping to comb his black hair in a wall mirror like a schoolboy on class picture day. "Tell her how you feel," he encouraged his reflection. "Who cares if her ex-boyfriend is a psycho killer? This may be your last chance at love. Seize the moment, you *couyon*."

He heard a loud crash outside. Jake froze, waiting for a maniac to kick in the door and destroy the fantasy world he had been living the past twenty-four hours. Instead, he heard a group of female club members clearly still tipsy from last night laugh hysterically over a dropped cocktail tray at the Harbor Club. Staring at his panic-stricken reflection, Jake slumped his shoulders. *You're nobody's hero*, he thought. *Stop lying to yourself. Man, I need a shrink.*

Feeling defeated, Jake picked up a cordless wall phone shaped like a sea sponge and dialed.

"Mazel. Happy New Year," a man with a familiar voice answered.

"Ben?" Jake whispered into the sponge phone.

"Bubby?" Ben whispered back. "My favorite fugitive?"

"I need help."

"This we KNOW. The local news stations all ran stories on you." Jake could hear Ben shuffling down the stairs to his office and closing the door. "*You're a celebrity.* You may get a book deal. After you serve hard time, of course."

"That's great, just great," Jake said, distracted by the shower's trickling.

"How's the yacht?" Ben asked.

"Obscene." Jake dreamily ran his hand up and down one of the Italian window dressings, imagining Elena's wet back. "Steve must be embezzling from the clinic."

"*This we also know*—enjoy your New Year's? I took Ruthie to the Kosher Grill in Orlando. We had a wonderful early dinner and then spent midnight with the kids watching the ball drop in Times Square."

"We went to the Cape." He sighed. "Slept under the stars. Or I did."

"I can't tell if you're on your honeymoon or on the lam," Ben said.

"…Think I'm in deep." Jake inspected his slightly fitter frame, pinching his belly fat.

"She *is* gorgeous. Did Jake get his groove back?" asked Ben.

Jake walked into Steve's massive closet to find some clean clothes to wear. "No one tells you being a fugitive is an aphrodisiac…she's taking a shower now." Wanting to look good for Elena, he frowned; everything Steve owned was too flashy for his taste.

"What are you waiting for??" Ben oozed. "I'm schvitzing just thinking about it!"

"Ben, her boyfriend is that serial killer. You know, the one on the news?"

"And you've got a heart condition. Nobody's perfect."

"I can't believe you're joking at a time like this… Ben, I need a favor."

"*Another favor?* You sound like my brother-in-law."

"Will you come sit with Elena? Just an hour. Think I have a way out of this." Jake could tell by Ben's silence, he was tempted. He knew his big-city friend was bored out of his mind with his domestic life in Florida. Still, Ben played hard to get.

"I'm already an accessory; you want more??"

"I'm begging you, Ben… Please."

"I'm thinking, I'm thinking," Ben said in a hurried whisper, pacing the floor.

Putting on the least garish beach shirt he could find, Jake briefly flexed his muscles in the closet mirror but stopped when he got an idea. "Is the sciatica still acting up?"

"Oy. Always," Ben moaned.

"Bring your trunks. Yacht has a Jacuzzi."

"Take a soak?" Ben said. "At a time like this?? Who are you??"

"Why does everyone keep asking me that?"

"Because you've lost your mind!"

"I know, but will you come? Perhaps, uh, Elena will join you in the tub?"

Ben thought about it. "I'll be right over."

(46)

An hour later, Dr. Ben Silverman padded up the gangplank and rang the bell on the door. Jake buzzed him in. Ben appeared at the yacht's sliding glass door wearing Bermuda shorts, sandals, black socks, and a plaid bucket hat. Jake could not help but smile seeing the familiar face. "Ruth is pissed, let me in, let me in." Ben shuffled inside carrying a yellow beach bag.

"You two *idiots* planning on hitting the beach?" Elena asked sarcastically.

"Hello, Elena," Ben said in his sexiest voice. "I came to keep you company."

She crossed her arms, lowering her chin and narrowing her eyes at the interloper. She turned to Jake, gesturing with her chin at Ben. "You talk too much, cow eyes. Loose lips sink ships."

"You have pet names for each other already? *Adorable*," Ben said.

"I am no one's pet!" Elena got up in the two men's faces. "I take care of myself. Much better than Tweedledee and Tweedledum." She dismissed the men in front of her.

"Which one of us is Tweedledum?" Ben said.

"I get it." Jake raised his arms in the surrender pose. "You're right. I saw you puncture that goon's eardrum with my ballpoint pen."

Ben cringed at the imagery. "What have you two outlaws been up to?"

Elena looked Ben up and down, sniffing at him.

"Stand. I will frisk you."

"With pleasure." Ben giggled while Elena frisked him for weapons and checked his bag.

"Okay, you can stay, one hour. You have a trustworthy face. For Israelite."

"I'm touched," Ben said sarcastically. "I take it you are of Muslim descent?"

195

"Play nice talking geopolitics, you two," Jake said. "I'll be back soon. Just keep it down."

"You can count on me, bubala," Ben said with a big smile, plopping down on a sofa and caressing the Italian leather with his palms. "*Expensive.* Steve always seats me at the kiddie table."

Elena sat down in a leopard print plush club chair directly across from him and leaned forward, elbows on her knees. They stared at each other like two opponents over a chessboard.

"I feel so much safer with *big man* around," she scoffed.

"Point of order, Jake said nothing about sacrificing my life for you," Ben clarified.

"I will use you as human battering ram if they come for me." She spat at him.

"Kinky. Speaking of…" He rubbed his lower back. "My achin' back. Care for a spritz?"

"Stop talking," Elena said, straight-faced. "Or I'll staple lips to tongue."

"Hurt me, Elena, but *don't kill me,*" Ben teased, digging around in his beach bag. He held up a giant yellow one-piece from J.C. Penney that looked like it was purchased in the last century. "You can borrow one of Ruth's suits."

Elena smirked. "I'm not discount shopper." She showed off the designer outfit she'd borrowed from Amber's closet. "*Obviously.*"

"Suit yourself." Ben put away the swimsuit, grinning at his own pun. "Incidentally, I read about your background in *The Sentinel.* Tragic. The genocide of your people. I can relate… Jake may have mentioned."

"Cow eyes never speaks of you."

"I counsel quite a few new immigrants with post-traumatic stress disorder."

"My family was slaughtered in a war camp. I watched them die as girl."

"*I'm sorry.*" Ben's eyes subtly drifted down from her face to her V-neck sweater. "Are there any other childhood traumas you'd like to get off your… chest?"

Elena rolled her eyes.

(47)

"What in the world?" muttered Bobby Ainge, a freckled member of the Eau Gallie Yacht Club to his sunbathing wife, Eileen, as the retired couple sipped cold beer on the deck of their sailboat four slips down from the Azimut yacht. He picked up his pair of binoculars.

"Will you look at this? Steve's got company."

"Stop spying, Bobby; everyone deserves their privacy," said Eileen, applying La Mer fluid to her sun-spotted arms.

"Big guy. But he moves well." Bobby adjusted his binoculars and sat up in his deck chair, craning to spy on Jake warily sneaking off the yacht. He focused on Jake's borrowed Tommy Bahama shirt. "He's even wearin' Steve's clothes?" Putting down the binoculars, Bobby picked up his cell.

After five rings, a hungover male picked up. "Not feeling too chipper, Bobcat."

"Landry, you and the little lady still at Disney World?"

"Gawd. Don't remind me… Amber got us kicked out of Trader Sam's Grog Grotto last night for cussing out an employee. She's sleeping it off."

"Well, son, hate to ruin your New Year's, but you know you got some hot chick and a big ol' boy squatting on your yacht?"

"Big ol' boy?" Landry sat up, banging his head on the top of a tanning bed. "*LaFleur.*" He swore and yanked off his sun goggles. "I'll be right there!"

Jake speed-walked down to the dirty yellow Hummer parked in the back lot, trying to blend in with the other mostly hungover club members on their way to the tennis courts, poolside bar, or to a late breakfast at the Harbor Grill. Squeezed like a sausage into another tight shirt from Landry's colorful beachwear collection (which looked more appropriate for South Miami Beach), he stuck out like a swollen floral neon thumb, if anyone were paying attention. Few were, except a man parked two rows behind the Hummer in a white rental car.

"You did well to track her," the Doktor said into his cellular phone.

"I use Pegasus spyware on American's phone," said Tarek.

"Bring the dove to the secure location."

"Arriving now. What about the American?" Tarek asked, turning the black van into the Eau Gallie Yacht Club parking lot with Khalid.

"I shall deal with him myself." He hung up, slipping on a pair of brown leather driving gloves to conceal his scratched hands.

(48)

Orlando, Florida

Jake gently pushed on the glass entry doors of Dr. Brennan's ophthalmology clinic at 1282 Sand Lake Road in Orlando. As expected, the office was closed for New Year's Day; the lights were off, but curiously the doors were unlocked. *I guess it's open for me*, Jake thought, walking down the hallway of the small clinic. He thought he had known all the retina specialists in Orlando. He never heard of Dr. Brennan.

"Doctor Aria?" Jake called out. "It's Jake." There was no answer. His phone pinged; it was Cindy. She'd called several dozen times since yesterday morning. He answered, "Mom. I'm okay."

"So now the big shot fugitive decides to answer? Where've you been? With that woman, I suppose? You're out of food, by the way."

"I have plenty of Weight Watchers in the freezer."

"Stone Phillips says you were never loved as a child," she accused him.

"Don't watch those shows, Mom. I'm turning myself in today, I swear. I'm innocent."

"I was a bad mother." Cindy began to cry. "When your father died, I didn't—"

"*Mom*. Don't. You're not a bad—" He heard something move. "Gotta go. I'll call later."

"You're killing your mother."

Jake ended the call, feeling a lump grow in his throat as he walked down the dark hallway. Listening for voices, he heard only the hum of the air conditioner. Jake called out Farshid's name again. No answer. Something was wrong. The butterflies in his stomach told him so.

A shadow moved behind the fogged glass window in the lobby. He opened the door slowly, feeling a rush of primal fear. *Am I about to get whacked?*

Jake's heart pounded. He said a Hail Mary to himself, even though he had not been to church in twenty years. *Calm down*, he said to himself. *Breathe… Be brave.*

"Farshid? …You in here?" he said.

Suddenly, he felt a hand on his shoulder. Jake jumped like a cat.

"You scared me!"

"So anxious you are." Dr. Farshid Aria appeared from the hallway.

"Where did you…? I wasn't sure you'd come. I called."

"My phone battery is low. How are you, my friend?" Farshid seemed nervous to Jake. *But who wouldn't be nervous meeting a fugitive?* he rationalized.

"I've been better," he said. "Thank you for meeting me. Why is it so dark in here?"

"The office is closed. Where is this strange girl you're with?" Farshid looked around.

"She was too frightened to come. But I brought high-resolution photos of her eyes."

"Too bad. From what I've read in the papers, she seems quite headstrong."

"…That's an understatement," Jake said.

"Remember, think with your head, not your heart. May I see the photos?"

Jake pulled the images up on his iPhone and showed them to Dr. Aria.

"I can't lie, it's been tough." He sighed.

"Beauty will do that." Farshid put on his eyeglasses and zoomed in on the photos. "Remarkable. This work is exquisite; your photos as well. Very detailed."

"A Pascal laser did this, right?" Jake looked over Farshid's shoulder.

"I believe so… The bar code is fascinating. How bizarre."

"What does the Arabic say?" Jake asked.

Farshid switched over to the photo of the left eye.

"It is difficult to translate… As you know, I speak Farsi. This is Mashriqi Arabic, an eastern dialect spoken in Syria, Lebanon, Palestine, but rarely in western Iraq where I am from… I assumed you knew the difference."

"Well, I didn't."

Farshid removed a brown leather notebook from his breast pocket and began jotting notes. "Most curious. I'd surmise this is a quote from the Quran. Although I am unable to translate." Jake watched his old friend closely. He translated the message into numerals and English words of some order. Jake waited for Farshid to show him his work. Instead, Farshid snapped the notebook closed.

"I see you wrote down some… Will you, uh, share whatever you have?" Jake asked.

Farshid sighed, putting the notebook back in his breast jacket pocket. Jake noticed Farshid had deep scratches on his right hand.

Jake gestured to Farshid's cuts. "What happened to your…?"

"Ah, it is of no consequence." Farshid removed a pair of brown driving gloves from his pocket. "Jake, you must stop running and turn yourself in."

"Like I said. Once I know what the message says, I will bring it to the police."

"Regretfully, I cannot help you—what about the girl?"

"She's safe," Jake nervously replied.

"Are you certain of that?" Farshid lowered his head to put on his gloves, never taking his eyes off Jake.

"Uh, I think so." Jake noticed a slight twitch in Farshid's left eye and a small scratch on his forehead. "Did you get in a fight or something?"

"I am fine… I fell. I am getting old." He shrugged. "Do you love this woman?"

"…I don't know."

"Her affection could be a hazard to your health," said Farshid. "From what I have read, everyone around her appears to perish quite tragically."

Jake felt Farshid's avuncular demeanor turn sinister. Normally warm and inviting, the air suddenly went cold around his old mentor. Jake felt his heart rate spiking. *Why is Farshid acting like this?*

"I think I need to go now. Sorry for bringing you down here."

"You cannot save her, Jake. Save yourself." Dr. Aria took his hands from his tweed jacket pocket and moved toward Jake, who stared at the brown driving gloves. He felt a chill run down his spine.

"I really gotta go… Cindy's making moussaka."

Jake turned and speed-walked down the hall and out the front door.

"*Jake, don't go*," Farshid called out. "You are in grave danger!"

Jake's heart raced as he started up the Hummer and threw it in reverse. *Am I being paranoid? Is he going to turn me in?? Was this a trap?? … Elena!*

———————•———————

Back at the yacht club, Dr. Steve Landry pulled up in his orange BMW 750, parking sideways in the empty spot where his Hummer should be. "What the hell?" He hopped out of his car, still in a pair of trademark sweatpants, slippers, and robe from the Ritz-Carlton resort in Orlando. "Where's my Hummer? Where's the security in this stupid place!" he bellowed while he scanned the parking lot and spotted a familiar blue Honda Accord parked in the back of the half-empty lot. He scowled. "LaFleur!"

Dumbfounded, he ran through the club grounds, ranting about his stolen vehicle to every passing valet, tennis instructor, or waiter carrying a tray of drinks. "Call the police, I've found him! Call *Dateline*! Call *Sixty Minutes*!" He ran up to his private dock and punched in the security code, letting himself through the metal gate. Furious, he leaned down to pick up the key hidden under the welcome mat. "I know you're in there!"

The sliding glass door opened. Dr. Landry stood up. He was suddenly face-to-face with a terrifying-looking man with a neck the size of an offensive lineman and three days' growth of facial hair. A tall, thin Middle Eastern man in a cowboy hat loomed over his shoulder. "May I help you?" asked Tarek with a thick foreign accent.

Landry stared at the two men, wondering if his hangover was causing hallucinations.

"This is my yacht!" Landry snapped out of it, bullying his way inside. "You're not the boys I'm looking for—where's LaFleur??" Landry looked around. A beautiful woman and a fat bearded man sat tied up and gagged on his Italian leather sofa. Elena let out a muffled cry, signaling to him with widening eyes. Landry took the cue and turned around. THWACK! Tarek clubbed Landry in the head with the butt of his Glock pistol. He dropped to the marble floor like a sack of sunburned potatoes.

"This my boat now," Tarek said.

Khalid appeared behind him. "Why your boat? I like ocean; I am Pisces." Tarek looked at Khalid; he had traded his cowboy hat for Landry's white captain's hat.

"Take that ridiculous thing off," Tarek said.

49

Indian Harbour Beach, Florida

"ELENA!" Jake sprinted through the open door of *The Eye Cruiser* in a panic. He darted around the living room; it was trashed: chairs knocked over, glasses shattered, vases broken, the contents of Ben's beach bag scattered across the marble floor. Someone had put up quite a fight in here. He knew who. "Elena…" He called out hopelessly, cautiously going room to room to check for intruders. "How could I be so stupid?" His mind reeled. *Did Farshid really lure me away from the yacht?* He thought about how his old mentor had dropped off the face of the earth the past two years and about his recent flurry of lectures scheduled throughout the country. *At dinner he mentioned he had recently come from Los Angeles and Austin. That's where the two dead girls were found.* Jake didn't know what to think.

Suddenly, a commotion came from the master stateroom. He pushed open the door. It wasn't Elena—it was Dr. Steve Landry wearing nothing but a purple Speedo and his white captain's hat, hog-tied and gagged, writhing like an oiled-up pig with a bright pink sunburn, flat in the middle of his clam-shaped rotating bed, which was (somehow) rotating. Jake stared as the bizarre sight went round and round. Landry squealed, his eyes begging for him to be released. Jake stopped the bed from rotating and ungagged him.

"You're so fired, LaFleur!" Landry raged.

"Who did this to you?"

"Some foreign maniacs! I'm pressing charges on all of you!" He squinted at Jake's outfit. "Are you wearing my clothes?"

Jake looked down at his neon orange and yellow ensemble. "I promise I'll have it dry-cleaned."

"I promise I will have them *burned*, LaFleur! *Untie me!*" Landry sputtered.

"Did you, by chance, see a beautiful woman onboard before they tied you up?"

"Untie me, dammit! You'll never run my clinic! You'll never practice medicine in this town again! No communist sleeps under my roof!"

Jake tried to get a word in edgewise. "Steve. Steve. I'm not—Never mind." Jake put the bandana gag back in Landry's mouth and left him on his bed squealing.

"I'm borrowing your car. I'll fill it up."

"LaFleuuuuuuur!!!" Landry mouthed out around the bandana.

Jake sprinted onto the walkway by the Indian River, weaving through club members preparing for an afternoon sail. Elderly snowbirds jumped out of his way, like he was a chubby first responder to some unknown emergency. Next to the parking lot was a boat ramp into the Indian River, where a sunbaked member and his guest fishing guide were putting their Bass Tracker into the water to fish, even though everyone knew the Indian River lagoon contained the blue-green algae toxin microcystin, so *eating* the fish they caught was out of the question. Tom Romero, now sporting a jaunty black eye patch, watched Jake barrel his way through the crowd like a neon battering ram. He squinted with his one good eye. "Raiders of the Lost Ark."

"What?" Red tried turning his head, but his camo neck brace prevented it.

"That fella there." Tom pointed at Jake. "'Member that scene where Indy's running from that big boulder? That guy's the boulder."

"I'm too hungover for levity," Red said, guiding the boat off the trailer.

"*Hey*. That's that tofu-eatin' doctor who fixed my eye," Tom explained.

Red turned his body to see. "I know that ol' boy."

"Ain't he the one that went Karate Kid on your voice box?" Tom asked.

"Reckon so. Nice fella though. Paid for my medical expenses. He better slow down or he's gonna have another heart attack."

"Well, shoot, man, ain't you sore at him??" Tom said. "Didn't we see him on the news?"

Jake stumbled down a small grass hill near the putting green, waving his arms to keep upright. He was running right at them.

"Hey, Doc! What, are the police chasing ya?" shouted Tom.

"Kinda. Hey, boys!" Jake yelled back, out of breath.

Tom whispered to Red. "Heard there's a re-ward for his hide."

"I wouldn't if I were you," Red muttered, gingerly touching his neck brace.

"Hold my beer." Tom handed his can of Old Milwaukee to Red and blocked Jake's path. "Sorry, Doc! But gonna have to hold you." Tom held up his arms stiffly like a traffic cop.

Jake barreled through Tom like a fullback for the Miami Dolphins, landing a powerful blow to his other eye with his shoulder. Tom went flying back like a featherweight.

"Stop by the office and I'll fix that for you!" Puffing like a steam engine, Jake raced past Red like a rampaging bull. "Hey, Red!"

Red tipped his trucker cap and slowly turned to Tom, writhing in pain on the pavement.

"Agh, my other eye," moaned Tom.

"You never listen." Red shook his head as he helped Tom stand up.

50

Gasping for breath, panicked, Jake slammed the Hummer door shut, wracking his brain for answers. He started up the engine, wondering if he'd ever see Ben or Elena again. *Who kidnapped them? Those goons at the airport?* Jake gulped nervously, feeling like everyone at the club was observing him. *Is her serial killer boyfriend watching me right now? … Breathe!*

Jake's eyes darted around the parking lot. He saw no sign of danger.

He considered driving to the police station and turning himself in. *I never translated the code; I have no leverage. What would Jason Bourne do? THINK!*

The *Mission Impossible* theme song rang out from his yellow shorts. He fumbled his phone out of the cargo pocket. Caller ID said: Federal Bureau of Investigation.

Is this the end? Jake steadied his nerves and answered the call. "…Hello?" he squeaked with an upward lilt.

"LaFleur." He heard a husky woman's voice. "This is Special Agent Jane Rizzo of the Federal Bureau of Investigation."

"Oh. Hi? … Can I, uh, help you?"

"You are in extreme danger. Listen to me carefully. We know you're in Melbourne with Smilovic. Turn yourself in to the Orlando Police immediately, and we will put you in protective custody. *Do not trust anyone.*"

"Umm. Can you be more specific?"

"Elena's lying to you. She's a terrorist. Her boyfriend's a butcher. He's coming to kill you both. Don't trust a word she says." She paused as Jake remained silent. "You're in danger, dumbass!"

Jake ducked down in the driver's seat, sure that he was being watched by God, the Feds, cops, hit men, and serial killers all at once. While Agent Rizzo warned him further about the precariousness of his situation, he angled down the vehicle's rearview mirror to look behind him. He noticed something familiar, disturbing—a white Impala idling in the parking lot fifty feet away. "I know that car..." he murmured.

Jake squinted, trying to look inside the tinted windows. He couldn't believe what he saw. *What is he doing here? ... Is it true?*

Jake interrupted Rizzo. "Ma'am? Ma'am? The bad guys, they took Elena."

"What? When?"

"*Now*! I'm going after her," Jake said.

"Bad idea, LaFleur," Rizzo shouted. "Don't be a hero!"

Jake hung up the phone and sent a hundred-yard stare into the rearview mirror.

Does he know where Elena is?

———————•———————

Dr. Farshid Aria sat exhausted in the parking lot of the Eau Gallie Yacht Club behind the wheel of his rental car, monitoring the movement of his young friend, who, in a tragic twist of fate, had gotten mixed up in Aria's secret life. He rubbed his salt-and-pepper beard, unsure of his next move. He had lost control of the situation. After following his former student from the ophthalmology office on Sand Lake Road, he could tell Jake was not thinking straight. Farshid empathized. *He can't possibly know who he's dealing with*, he thought. *Whose woman he had run off with...and what was at stake.*

Farshid observed Jake sprinting from the dock, back down the walkway, past a woman holding the hand of a small girl. The girl wore red ballet slippers. He stared at her little satin shoes. Pangs of regret hit him in the gut. Farshid remembered it was January 1, his daughter's twenty-fifth birthday. *I haven't seen Irfa on her birthday in...*

He could not remember the last time. Farshid had never seen his daughter dance. Eudora had taken her to every ballet class, as he traveled the country lecturing nonstop, working on his research treating retinal diseases with the Pascal laser, and then executing his secret duty as a Persian national. He had missed her entire childhood. Now Irfa was a prima ballerina for the Boston Ballet, while he had blood on his hands that would never wash off. Farshid longed to hug his estranged daughter, but his family had stopped speaking to him years earlier, when they said he had become too militant in his religious beliefs and dogmatic in his behavior. *Perhaps they were right.*

He stared at his scratched face in the rearview mirror. Farshid had not slept all week. He was haunted by terrible flashbacks of violent struggles with the young women in New Orleans, Los Angeles, and the Texas woods. *So much blood when you remove the eyes.* His victims were all his daughter's age. *What have I become?*

Dr. Farshid El-Fayed (aka Aria) had forgotten who he was before he was recruited as an Al-Qaeda operative. Seeing the little girl in the ballet shoes triggered his humanity. It was all coming back now… He had become a monster in the name of Allah. Farshid thought about how he had told Irfa as a little girl, "If you do anything in life, never be second best."

How far had that gotten him? He was not cut out for murder.

Farshid was a surgeon, a thinker, a man of faith who had got in too deep. He took his eyes off the little girl and watched Jake barrel over a man wearing an eye patch. *Poor boy, he's out of control, like me.* He shook his weary head and removed a bottle of chloroform from the glove compartment. Farshid knew his orders. Eliminate the American, then deliver the message. *It's Jake, or me… Mikal will see to that.*

Farshid knew he was a dead man for Baton Rouge. *They will never forgive me for losing the Sugar Bowl code. The SCO has no mercy.*

Once Farshid handed over the fourth messenger's code, which he had transcribed from Jake's photo of Elena's eye, he was certain he would be executed, whether he eliminated Jake or not. A text buzzed on his phone. He looked down.

It was Mikal. He could feel his presence nearby.

Gazing at Jake's head through the back window of the yellow truck, Farshid's life flashed before his eyes… *I've had enough.* He put down the bottle of chloroform and handkerchief. He reversed out of the parking spot. *They can get someone else.*

On the one-hour drive west on US-192 to the secure location in Kissimmee, Dr. Farshid Aria drove in anguished silence. The highway miles blurred by. He tried to remember how his secret life had started. What makes a surgeon a murderer? It was not ideology, dogma, nationalism, or the hatred of the West. It had all started as a favor, a well-paying one. Then he became their slave. *How did I get here?* Lost in thought, the tired old man failed to notice the yellow Hummer three cars back.

51

Saint Petersburg, Russia

The diminutive but highly respected Holy Cleric Hassan Rouhani leaned his grey beard close to the podium microphone, his stern brown eyes absorbing the collective gaze of the dignitaries inside the packed ballroom of the Four Seasons Lion Palace Hotel in Saint Petersburg. Holding the moment like a showman, he proclaimed in a commanding tone, "Tonight we offer allegiance to you, our comrades, in the fight against Western Imperialism. Together. From this day forward, we shall no longer be menaced by the American *bully*." He emphasized "bully" with disdain, then stood back as the opulent ballroom swelled with applause.

Down a gilded hallway a few meters away from the main event, Dr. Farshid El-Fayed sat at a marble table in a private conference room, feeling underdressed in his wrinkled khaki suit. He monitored Rouhani's speech on a large screen along with two other Persian men; one was small, handsome, and dapper, the other was the size of an American refrigerator.

Farshid looked uncomfortable. Called away at the last minute from a medical conference in Prague where he had been speaking on the latest advances in laser retinal procedures, he was unsure why he'd been invited to this event. *There are other Al-Qaeda operatives permanently stationed in Europe*, he thought.

At fifty-eight, Farshid had not been on a holy mission in many moons, and he had found that he rather fancied being semiretired. For the past fourteen months, while living in an empty apartment in Orlando, which he had been forced into after separating from his wife, he had often prayed that he was aging out of "jihadism" so he could spend more time on his work and with his family. Farshid sighed. *Martyrdom is the only resignation letter Allah accepts.*

He listened to the holy cleric's staged vitriol, while calmly cleaning his spectacles. *What irony*, he thought. *Rouhani threatens the West, but to be understood by an audience of America's enemies, he speaks English?* Wearing a traditional muam'am (turban), the bespectacled Rouhani concluded his speech by slamming his hand repeatedly on the podium. "We stand united today with our comrades. We shall join the Shanghai Cooperation Organization! Down with the American dogs! Death to the United States!"

The crowd passionately applauded. Iran is officially joining SCO, an anti-NATO alliance including Russia, China, Pakistan, India, and other former Soviet-bloc countries. Farshid pretended to be riveted as Russian president Vladimir Putin and Chinese president Xi Jinping approached the podium for handshakes and photos with Rouhani, their latest ally.

It is all a sideshow, Farshid thought to himself as the livecast concluded. The doktor glanced over at the elegant Persian gentleman with the handsome bearded face who smelled of expensive cologne. Farshid did not know Hussein al-Rifai (chief aide to the Iranian president) personally, but he was well aware of his breeding, his education at Oxford, and his ruthless reputation. Yet in person, the he felt Hussein looked more like an executive at Google than a mujahideen.

Hussein wears French cologne and bespoke suits. Tsk tsk. Young Persians like him claim to despise the West, while they adopt its culture… I fear Irfa's soul has been lost. I have not seen her dear face in so long. Hussein's iPhone rang.

Farshid felt a sinking in his stomach, unsure what came next. Nervous, he consumed one of the dates on display with other dried fruits on the conference table. After a few quietly exchanged words in Farsi, Hussein put away his phone and stood up.

"It is time," he intoned.

Hussein's massive bodyguard, Ali, led the men outside the Four Seasons into the damp winter night, passing by two marble lions still guarding the nineteenth-century palace since the days of Imperial Russia. Ali opened the door of a black Mercedes limousine idling by Alexander Park and across from St. Isaac's Cathedral, and the two men climbed inside the warm vehicle.

They drove to the center of downtown and parked in a dark, hidden brick alley.

"These are serious people, old one," Hussein quietly warned Farshid with his posh British accent as they exited the vehicle. "What we talk about here stays with you. You will be given your task. Our people expect you to carry through without question."

"You have not brought me here for my personality," Farshid replied.

Hussein looked at him with dead black eyes. "We do not find many humorists in our line of business, doktor."

"Praise be Allah." Farshid nodded demurely. "My organization stands with you."

Hussein knocked on a metal door numbered 114 in the alley, located along a row of closed shops. The alley smelled like rainwater and rubbish from a nearby dumpster.

Farshid heard squeaky footsteps on wooden floors coming toward them, and he saw someone on the other side of the door examining them through a peephole. The door opened. His breath quickened as a young European man with neatly gelled brown hair and fashionable tortoise-framed glasses ushered them in out of the cold. The man explained in Farsi that he was their facilitator and translator, if needed, as he led them through a dimly lit hallway to a sparse kitchen where two Eastern European men sat at a small wooden table under an antique hanging light fixture.

The young men stood as Hussein and Farshid entered, introducing themselves as "Mikal" and "Dakar" in English and inviting them to sit down. The translator stood by the door.

Farshid took a seat on a wooden chair across from Hussein, inspecting the two Europeans, who were both in their thirties and dressed stylishly in black jackets, mock turtleneck shirts, and pants. The one called "Dakar" was taller with short-cropped blond hair and a square jaw, while "Mikal" was younger, darker, whip-thin, and with angular features. But what was most notable to Farshid were his eyes—they were an amazing shade of steel grey, intense, intimidating even. *Who is this one?* Farshid tried to place the man. *I know those eyes.*

Dakar asked with a faint Russian accent, "Do you gentlemen speak English?"

Hussein and Farshid nodded.

For the next seven minutes, Mikal spoke deeply, deliberately explaining an elaborate plot to attack the United States on New Year's Day two years from now. He reported that China's "MSS" (Ministry of State Security) had discovered that the U.S. government was developing a massive network of satellites that would be used by the NSA and CIA to spy on their enemies' encrypted communications in every corner of the world. "Someone must punish this act of deception," Mikal said. "That someone, comrades, is me."

Farshid was astonished by what he was hearing from this arrogant young man.

The plot Mikal described was impossible, something out of a Hollywood movie: six simultaneous bomb sites, two spacecrafts, four football stadiums, all televised on American television on New Year's Day. *Hundreds of thousands of civilians will be killed*, he thought. *Women. Children. It's MADNESS. Could Putin, Xi, or Rouhani possibly have approved of this?*

Mikal insisted his sponsors from the SCO were not some group of underfinanced rogue religious extremists but a select group of well-funded government leaders from various nations.

"Consider this an *off-the-books* covert multi-government operation," Mikal explained.

Farshid rubbed his cold hands under the table, his mind racing. *If this plot succeeds it would certainly be taken as an act of war against those who perpetrated it. Can I be part of this?*

"Once our teams are in position, it will be as simple as pressing a button. Then, *poof*."

Mikal smiled wickedly. "There goes the imperialist infidels and their latest toys."

The small kitchen fell silent. Farshid cleared his throat and glanced over at Hussein, who had a wry smile on his face. *The Boy Wonder likes what he hears.* The he turned to look into Mikal's steel eyes. *Who are you?* Farshid thought he recognized a flaw in Mikal's left iris, possibly from shrapnel, as the facial scars around his eye indicated.

Feeling the older man's discriminating gaze, Mikal removed a roll of hard candy, Certs mints, from his jacket pocket and gingerly slipped one in his mouth.

Mint candies. It all came back to Farshid. *Bosnia.*

When their paths crossed fifteen years ago, Mikal Mikalovich was still a malnourished teenaged soldier who had become a star in the "Bosnian Mujahideen" during the war. Then after the war, he helped found a group called the "Active Islamic Youth" (AIO), whose mission was to awaken religious feelings in Bosnian Muslims who had been deprived of "the real Islam" by the Communist regime of the former Yugoslavia. But the group's altruistic purpose was just a front. Mikal's genius was the ability to recruit and train militant Muslim boys to perform crippling terror attacks all over Europe, Asia, and Africa. His success soon drew the interest of the Iranian "Mojāhedin-e Khalq" ("Mujahideen of the People"), who had sent Dr. Farshid El-Fayed to meet and train this young freedom fighter for larger global jihads.

In Sarajevo in the autumn of 2004, Farshid mixed inconspicuously with other elder Islamic missionaries and Arab volunteers who were teaching the real Islam to Mikal's young Bosniaks. Getting to know the nineteen-year-old who had taken up residence downtown in a bombed-out high-rise, Farshid sensed the Bosnian war had never ended for Mikal, and never would.

He learned the boy had grown up in a Serbian refugee camp—which explained his fascination with eye gouging, bombings, and torture—so while teaching him about Islam, Farshid instructed Mikal and his men in various ocular torture techniques, to inflict pain and stress the optic nerve. He became adept at enucleation, removing eyes from the eye socket. After many late-night conversations, the doktor began to feel a fatherly kinship toward this angry boy. He empathized with the orphan, though he did not agree with his lifestyle. A war hero in the Bosniak community, Mikal was allowed to revel in earthly pleasures that were against Muslim code; he drank alcohol, wore fine clothing, held court in nightclubs, and always had beautiful women following him around who had nothing to do with the holy purposes of the AIO. Farshid also observed that when Mikal was anxious, he obsessively consumed mint candies. To curry favor with him, Farshid made a supply of American mints available for Mikal in Sarajevo. This had led to rumors among some of the Islamic missionaries that Farshid was a member of the American intelligence. After living in the States so many years, perhaps Farshid's "American" was showing and after a month he was abruptly sent home by his handlers, but Mikal had never doubted his allegiance.

"Do you remember this face, old doktor?" Mikal asked, snapping Farshid back to reality.

Farshid coughed to cover his anxiety. "You have grown strong."

"Just a few more scars. Care for a glass of water?" Mikal asked cordially.

"Thank you, yes."

The man in the tortoiseshell glasses placed a bottle of water in front of Farshid on the wooden table. Farshid slowly drank as Mikal and Hussein al-Rifai watched the old man carefully, looking for any indication that he was a traitor. Farshid excused his interruption. "It was a long day's travel."

"I read about your work, with the Pascal laser, good Doktor, in one of the scientific quarterlies. I had the laser completed on my left eye after a trauma. Then I recalled that you were kind to me once as a young man."

So. That is why I am here.

"Praise be Allah. I am most flattered," Farshid replied humbly, his mind in a spin. *They will kill me if I show emotion. Keep your composure. You have come too far.*

"I have a special job for you." Mikal explained Farshid's pivotal role in the plot. Farshid's face went pale.

"Do not furrow your brow. No blood will be on your hands. You can read laser codes imprinted in the eyes, yes?" Mikal asked.

Farshid thought a moment. "Yes… With the proper tools."

Sensing his skepticism, Hussein al-Rifai interjected, "He is the world's preeminent expert in the technology. There is no better man for the job… Am I correct, doktor?"

The four men shifted their gaze to Farshid, who took another sip of water. He wanted no part in this insane scheme, but they knew where he lived; where his wife lived. They even knew Irfa's address in Boston. If he refused, they would kill everyone he loved. Farshid swallowed his fear and put down the empty glass.

He sighed. "I shall see to it personally."

———————●———————

A driver in a dark blue Silverado laid on its horn. Farshid was driving too slowly on the Florida highway.

"Okay! *Haroom Zade*!" ("Bastard" in Farsi) Farshid shouted at the driver of the truck behind him. Rattled, he pulled his white Impala off US-192 West, making a left turn at the Neptune Road exit in Saint Cloud. He found a strip mall and parked near a closed bar called the Drunken Parrot Saloon. With the sun beating down on him, he was covered in cold sweat.

He turned his AC off and typed a number into his cellular phone. The phone rang. He listened to his daughter's cheerful voice on her voicemail.

"Dearest," he stammered. "It is your father. We have not spoken in many months, too many. I just want to express how proud I am of you, my dear... I have not been a good father to you, I know this. I hope to make it up... But...if I do not see you again...know that I love you so much. And that I want only the best for you in life. Be happy, my dove... Be loved. You are in my heart... I will always be watching over you."

Farshid hung up, his tired brown eyes wet with tears. His phone buzzed. He looked down at the caller ID, hoping it was Irfa. It was Jake. Disappointed, Farshid let the call go to voicemail, started his engine, and pulled away.

Hidden in the back of the parking lot, a yellow Hummer crept behind him.

52

Melbourne, Florida

Agent Jane Rizzo bounded down the stairway of an FBI Gulfstream jet onto the windswept tarmac at the Melbourne-Orlando Airport, brushing wisps of hair from her eyes. It was crunch time, and after dragging their heels for a week, her superiors in the FBI were in scramble mode. Assistant Director Baker bet on Rizzo's detective work and got approval from Director Sheldon Cole to order the National Terrorism Advisory Board to issue an elevated threat "code red" lockdown of the Rose Bowl, Citrus Bowl, Orange Bowl, and Sugar Bowl. Nationwide, APBs had been issued for Mikalovich and his ring of terrorists. The case had also experienced another unexpected development on this eventful New Year's Day while Rizzo and Thorn were in the air.

The FBI in LA had arrested a software engineer named Xang Xi at LAX trying to board a British Airlines flight to Shanghai. Rizzo had begged her superior (Agent Hawks) to arrest Xi a week ago for writing a "backdoor" into the architecture of SpaceX's network. This is what Sheila used to nearly blow up Starlink. Rizzo felt some form of vindication for being right about this one.

After fifteen years of feeling underappreciated in the Agency, Rizzo gave Thorn a rare smile. "The cavalry is here." She pointed to a squad of eight law enforcement vehicles speeding down the tarmac with their sirens flashing. Brevard County sheriffs, Melbourne PD, FBI SUVs, and even a SWAT van from the FBI's Hostage Rescue Team had been scrambled to back up Agents Rizzo and Thorn in their case.

"We got their attention now," Thorn replied.

Rizzo took charge of her team like she was still in the army. "Listen up, everyone! We have less than six hours till the launch and kickoffs. Time's running out to secure the locations and find Mikalovich. Everyone got their assignments?"

Officer Olivine Williams from the Brevard County Sheriff's Department updated Rizzo and Thorn on another break in the case. "We got eyes on your Bonnie and Clyde. The good doctor's been hiding out with Smilovic at a yacht club right under our noses, a few miles from his own office. Officers are responding to the scene."

"Give me LaFleur's cell number," demanded Rizzo.

"He's not answering."

Three minutes later, Rizzo was yelling into her phone. "LaFleur! Don't be a hero! ... LaFleur?"

Rizzo looked at Thorn and Williams in disbelief. "Fool hung up. Said he's going after Elena."

"We're working on his exact location. Orlando PD received a call from some fisherman who got punched out by him in the parking lot of the Eau Gallie Yacht Club a few minutes ago."

"He's not going anywhere," said Sheriff Clark Roy, monitoring a laptop in his vehicle. "We'll have him soon."

"I'll intercept him before he gets himself killed," Rizzo said. "Text me the address of this yacht club and send units, make sure Elena's not there."

"Already on route," replied Sheriff Roy.

"Thorn, you track down Menard." Rizzo dashed off to get into a black FBI Suburban.

"Agent Rizzo!" shouted Agent Chris Portis of the FBI's Helicopter Unit. "Traffic's a mess today." He pointed to a converted tactical Sikorsky UH-60 Black Hawk on the tarmac a few hundred yards away. He grinned. "You get airsick?"

Rizzo slammed the Suburban's door. "Not a chance."

She climbed into the Black Hawk as it fired up its blades and rotor and lifted into the air. Rizzo gave Thorn a military salute as all the cops watched.

"Show-off." Thorn smiled, then glared at the cops who were standing around the tarmac.

"You know your assignments, let's go!"

53

Cape Canaveral, Florida

Following Agent Rizzo's orders, a phalanx of law enforcement vehicles arrived outside SpaceX's Complex 40 at the tip of Cape Canaveral with a warrant to sweep the premises for a bomb. Since the company had promoted it's Starlink satellites as "the day the most remote parts of the world will get free Internet and global encrypted satellite communications," the team ran into a throng of media jockeying for the best shot of the big event. Seeing the production vans from every major TV network jamming up Centaur Road, Sheriff Roy grumbled, "You'd think the Pope was going to the moon." He picked up his CB radio and bellowed through his squad car's PA system. "Clear a path! This is a police emergency!"

He hit his sirens.

A half mile down the Cape at SpaceX's "Launch and Landing Control Center," Agent Thorn pushed open the glass entrance doors of the one-story building, flashing her FBI badge to anyone who got in her way. Speed-walking down a maze of winding halls in the same cross trainers she had worn for a week, she found the Control Room where SpaceX's CORE engineers and the richest man in the world were staring up at a wall of monitors showing the police cars surrounding the Falcon 9 rocket hangar at the center of Complex 40.

"Doesn't the Director of IT Security answer the phone?" barked Thorn.

Gemma Arbor, Menard's British admin, ran interference. "Excuse me. He's been busy all day."

"He has time for us." Thorn shoved past Gemma.

"Why is THAT on our launchpad?" Menard pointed at the monitors.

"'Cause we arrested that Chinese coder of yours at LAX trying to flee the country. Xang Xi? The one you said was a waste of time?"

219

"Your sirens are interrupting our live feed," Menard insisted.

"Wake up, Xi confessed. He corrupted your code architecture—another one of your spaceships is about to go boom. Thought you'd like to know."

"How many times must we go through this?? That was a glitch," Menard countered.

"A glitch that nearly Hiroshima'd LA."

"Listen," Menard said, avoiding eye contact with Thorn. "My lawyers have advised me not to speak with you people. So unless you have a warrant, this is private property. I have an interview with Wolf Blitzer in seven minutes."

Losing patience, Thorn jammed a search warrant in Menard's face.

"Edward Menard, you are hereby ordered to postpone this launch. If you refuse to let us search your premises for explosives, you will be detained by these fine-looking federal marshals." Two huge, intimidating federal marshals with shaved heads appeared in the doorway.

Menard narrowed his eyes. "Your timing is amazing. Bring Franklin in here."

Gemma gave the federal marshals a nervous look as she dialed SpaceX's lead counsel.

"I'd say our timing's right on time." Thorn pointed to the Falcon 9 rocket on the monitors. "If those thirty-two Raptors you got warming up out there explode on takeoff? You said it yourself back in LA—it will set off a blast the size of sixty-four atomic bombs. You could level half of Florida!"

"Or it could fall harmlessly into the Atlantic." Menard smirked. "If you are speculating."

"You playing games? You really willing to risk all those lives for some TV ratings?"

"Safety is our first priority," Menard replied stiffly. "Look, I don't want to see anyone hurt, but this launch is bigger than you and your partner trying to make names for yourself on TV."

"Time's up." Agent Thorn instructed the two marshals closing in on Menard, "Detain him."

The marshals reached for their sidearms.

"Wait." Menard held up his hand. "I can prove our urgency. Gemma, get me the AG."

"Of the United States??" Thorn scoffed. "It's his day off. He's in Kenne-bunkport or Martha's Vineyard, or something."

"He'll take my call," Menard said.

Thorn shook her head. "Your cronies can't bail you out of this... *Two minutes*."

Menard and Gemma slipped out a side door to confer.

Thorn rolled her tight shoulders and stalked into the hallway. Milton Franklin squeaked past her. "Fugitive went that way, Milt." She pointed.

Thorn called Agent Rudy Russo, the senior agent leading the search at Complex 40. "Russo, Thorn. Menard's stalling. Sweep the hangar. Look for a rootkit device with Chinese symbols on it. We're bringing in Menard. ... *That's right.* I'll take the heat... Just do it, huh?"

$$\textbf{(54)}$$

Pasadena, California

S crambling to lock down four national college bowl games at the eleventh hour, tensions were running high as the FBI, ATF, Homeland Security, and state and local police rushed to coordinate a response. While thousands of football fans streamed into the Rose Bowl, Sugar Bowl, Citrus Bowl, and Orange Bowl stadiums, police installed reinforced security gates to withstand suicide bombing vehicles at all the entrances, while bomb-sniffing Belgian Malinois patrolled the grounds. "Brings back some bad memories," muttered veteran patrolman Sergeant Barry Carrol of the Pasadena Police Department, ambling his creaky knees past a long line of USC fans waiting to get through security checkpoints. Hearing over his walkie-talkie that the FAA had just established a "no-fly zone" over the Rose Bowl, he remembered working the game after 9/11 when some of the fans carried gas masks in their bags and anxiously held their breath whenever a plane flew too close to the stadium. He sighed. "Gonna be one of those days."

In a country obsessed with football, even the FBI did not have the power to cancel four bowl games unless a threat is irrefutably imminent. To avoid alarming fans, it was decided that a public warning would not be issued. As a result, none of the civilians in the Rose Bowl on this gorgeous New Year's Day suspected that a terror attack could possibly strike "the grand-daddy of them all," the longest-running bowl game in America. Their only concern was who would win the BCS Championship Game between the #2 USC Trojans and #1 Ohio State Buckeyes—and who would cover the point spread—as the heavyweights began their warm-ups on the field.

While star middle linebacker Xander Lopez stood on the USC sideline in his scarlet and yellow uniform getting over Sheila's murder by posing for selfies with a group of attractive fans, the Rose Bowl was being breached. A faded yellow "City of Pasadena Waste and Recycling" truck pulled into the "Employees Only" south tunnel and halted at the security gate. Two bearded men in matching yellow jumpsuits handed their "Department of Public Works" employee ID cards to Officer Griffith, a grey-haired security guard.

"Dropping off the new recycling cans," the driver announced.

Officer Griffith looked at the logo on the side of the green waste management truck; it read "City of Pasadena: Zero Waste by 2040." He had just read in the newspaper about the Pasadena City Council approving a new ordinance that would levy excessive fines for any facility that did not use the new service, which by 2040 claimed it would recycle one hundred percent of all waste products in the city.

Officer Griffith peered into the cab to get a look at their faces. "Saving the planet, are we?"

"Somethin' like that," replied the driver with a perfect southern California accent.

"Uh-huh." Officer Griffith frowned at the logo on the side of the truck.

"Just doing our jobs, dude," said the driver.

"You gonna let us in or what?" whined the second man.

Officer Griffith handed them back their ID cards. "All right. Move along." He waved the truck into the south entrance and watched it go.

"Tree-huggin' liberals," Officer Griffith complained.

The driver of the recycling truck parked behind three other waste trucks that looked just like theirs. Dimitri, the driver, pulled out his satellite phone and texted Mikal:

ROSE IS IN THE SOIL.

Ivan, the thin man in the passenger seat, slipped through the metal partition into the back of the truck. It was loaded with one hundred brand-new green plastic recycling receptacles.

Ivan walked over to one, lifted its lid, and looked inside. It was loaded with an "RDD," a radiological dispersal device containing one hundred sticks of dynamite and one hundred green tubes of radioactive material. He punched in the twelve-key Eastern Arabic detonator code on a keypad affixed to the RDD. The timer on the detonator began ticking down.

3 hours 14 minutes 22 seconds…21 seconds…20 seconds.

Dmitri slid open the rusty back door of the truck as light poured in. Ivan looked up at him and uttered the only American sports phrase he knew.

"Davay poigrayem v myach." ("Let's play ball" in Russian.)

———————•———————

The mercenaries efficiently unloaded ninety-nine of the new recycling cans with the "Zero Waste by 2040" logos on them like they were seasoned garbagemen on their routes. Once finished, the two men gently carried the final special receptacle by its plastic handles over to a door, carefully slipping the recycling can inside, and walking it up a flight of stairs that led onto the lower bowl concourse.

The terrorists did not realize they were being observed by Sergeant Carrol, who was buying his favorite game day snack, a spicy churro at a concession stand, a few feet from the stadium's Hall of Fame display.

"Funny," Sergeant Carrol said, watching the trashmen gingerly lug what appeared to be the most delicate trash receptacle in history. "Why they bringing full trash cans in, and not out?"

Jen, the concession stand employee, shrugged and went back to dusting churros.

Carrol wiped the cinnamon and sugar from his mustache and dropped the barely eaten churro into a wastebasket, to follow the suspicious men carrying the recycling can. He followed them into a secure "Employees Only Area" that led into the catacombs of the stadium, where he knew the trash and recycling bins were stored. Turning a corner of the dark cement hallway, which smelled of stale beer, the two men disappeared behind a second door. The veteran sergeant trailed after them, silently cracking open the door. He winced at the stench of rotten hot dogs and nacho cheese as he observed Dmitri and Ivan unload something metallic, beeping and full of wires (in the shape of a smiley face) from the recycling can. Carrol squinted to get a better view of the device. Without his transitional frames, it looked kinda like a robot's face. *These men ain't carrying trash*, he thought. His heart in his throat, he quietly closed the door and picked up his walkie-talkie.

"This is Sergeant Carroll," he said in a wavering baritone. "I got a situation here. Two suspicious trashmen poking around where they shouldn't be under the lower bowl. They're handling a suspicious metal box in a recycling can."

"You sipping on the job again, Sergent?" replied a female officer from his walkie-talkie.

"Don't mess with me, Peggy. They got a possible explosive device. Get me some backup, pronto."

"10-4."

(55)

Kissimmee, Florida

With his ex-girlfriend holding the final detonator code in her eyes and that fool doktor late to their meeting to extract it, Mikal paced the cement floor of an abandoned recycled electronics warehouse in Kissimmee, like a caged tiger.

"Više ne možete pronaći dobru pomoć" ("You can't find good help anymore"), he muttered to himself in Bosnian, sucking on a peppermint to ease his worried stomach. Since Elena's betrayal had forced him to come to America, Mikal decided to plant the Orlando bomb himself along with the "Citrus team," made up of Tarek and a four-man terror cell from Beijing that had incredibly arrived on time.

Plans had not gone so smoothly elsewhere. The "Orange team," led by the Russian extremist Yuri X, had been detained by Miami police after participating in a vodka-fueled New Year's Eve bar scrum with a pack of Hell's Angels. This came only hours after the "Sugar team" in New Orleans had been sent packing because Farshid had lost its detonator code in the shootout in Baton Rouge.

Disgusted with his team's incompetence, Mikal wished he could gouge out every last one of their eyes. To let off steam, he petulantly emptied the clip of his "lucky" Makarov pistol into a cement wall a few meters away from Tarek, who was hunched over as he assembled the Citrus bomb with the Chinese terrorist Huang. No one reacted to Mikal's outburst for fear of being pistol-whipped, or worse. No one except Elena, who laughed at his tantrum.

Mikal glanced angrily over at his former lover, who was tied to a metal assembly table, arms bound by leather straps, her face caked with blood from a cut above her eyebrow. Mikal walked over and stroked her brown hair.

"Ako moram platiti životom. I ti ćeš." ("If I must pay with my life. So shall you.")

Elena opened her swollen eyes and met his gaze. "You lied to me."

"You are lying whore," Mikal said. "Who is American fat man, huh?"

"Idiote." Elena spit into his face. "Ubit ću te." ("I will kill you.") Spittle dripped down his chin. Mikal gave her a cold smile and wagged a scolding finger at her.

His iridium encrypted satellite phone buzzed.

Wiping his face with the back of his hand, he read the text: *ROSE IS IN THE SOIL.*

He looked relieved.

"Neko radi svoj jebeni posao" ("At least someone does their freaking job"), he said, looking back at Elena. "I have one last message for you to deliver."

(56)

What does a rookie field agent do when a company like SpaceX blows off your search warrant? Thorn stared at the clock in the hall, considering her options. She felt helpless as Menard huddled with his legal team far longer than the two minutes she had allowed him. Wanting to prove herself, she resisted the urge to call Rizzo for advice.

Her iPhone rang. It was Agent Hawks.

"Director Cole has weighed in," Hawks announced. "You and Rizzo did admirable work piecing this together. But this is coming from up on high: Back off."

Thorn was astonished. "Back off? What are you saying to me, Harry!"

"AG persuaded the judge to recall the warrant."

"Recall? Based on what?!"

"Hands are tied. Let it go," instructed Hawks.

"Last time I checked, there still were three branches of government?" Thorn asked.

"Don't be flippant, Agent Thorn."

"Brevard County sheriffs hacked into LaFleur's phone. He and Smilovic spent last night by SpaceX's launchpad. She's guilty as hell."

"Smilovic works there, yeah? Could've been a date. It was New Year's," he retorted.

"Sir, please, subpoena the SpaceX security video; see if she snuck in there last night to plant a rootkit, like Sheila did."

"Here's how this works. When 'Justice' says stand down, we stand down. Stick to finding the Torcher and securing the Citrus... Welcome to the field, Agent Thorn."

Hawks abruptly hung up.

Thorn stomped her Nikes in frustration. Her phone rang again. She picked up.

"What now!"

"Thorn," she heard a woman say. "It's Assistant Director Baker in New Orleans."

"Oh…*sorry, ma'am*, I am having a day over here," said Thorn.

"You and me both," Baker replied.

"I've been ordered to let Menard go," Thorn sighed.

Baker paused. "It's out of my hands," she said.

"Excuse me while I throw up. Any good news to share?"

"Baton Rouge PD pulled a set of prints from Bortiach's windowsill. Your Baton Rouge doctor's got a name: Farshid Fayed Aria. Sixty, Persian. Eye doctor. Recently gave lectures in LA, Austin, and …*Orlando*."

"You're kidding me," Thorn exclaimed.

"I have no sense of humor; Aria's your serial killer."

"Isn't that LaFleur's mentor?" Thorn processed it. "LaFleur's nurse mentioned a Doctor Aria who gave him all the books on Islam. *Shoot*. We had the answer days ago."

"I don't know about that, but BAU suspects LaFleur's a pawn for Smilovic. Aria somehow slipped by the Baton Rouge police and we think he got on a private plane to Orlando. He's coming for Elena. So is Mikal," Baker said.

"Rizzo's got eyes on LaFleur. I'm pulling out."

Agent Thorn hung up and poked her head into the Control Room. Menard was back with his legal counsel, both wearing smug looks of satisfaction.

"Y'all may want to put your hazmat suits on now, boys," Thorn said, turning on her heel and leaving the room.

57

Pasadena, California

"Open up! Police!" An LAPD team bullied their way through the barricaded Sanitation Room door like a team of armored linebackers. Sergent Carrol stood back behind a cement pillar, eyes wide, his nine-millimeter, never fired in the line of duty, trembling slightly in his sweaty grip. He kept his eyes glued on the broken-down doorway, smelling the rotten trash and expecting one of the trashmen to come out guns blazing. He heard men shouting inside the room, and time slowed down—Carrol's brown eyes drifted to the graffiti scrawled on the pillar in front of him: "Sally + Art," "Zeppelin 4-ever," "Trojans Suck," "Emily Loves Esteban." He thought about all the college students who snuck down into the catacombs over the years to etch their imprint on the stadium. Then he focused on all the students outside streaming into the stadium. *Those kids got no idea how much danger they're in*, he thought.

Pop! Pop! Pop! Pop! Pop! Pop! Shots went off inside the room. Then shouting. Then silence. The firefight was over. The LA County Bomb Squad rushed in while Carrol holstered his nine-millimeter and joined his team from the Pasadena PD in locking down the area. Ten minutes later, two members of the bomb squad outfitted in demolition suits exited the splintered doorway. They gingerly carried the same green recycling receptacle, encased in padding, up a ramp and out of the stadium. They passed Sergeant Carrol, who would later learn that after taking four slugs in his chest, one of the terrorists fired his Glock at the "smiling bomb," trying to detonate it with his last breath. Dmitri missed by an inch, burying a slug in the cement wall, instead. The 92,542 people filing into the Rose Bowl never knew how close they came to annihilation; Sergeant Barry Carrol of the Pasadena Police Department would never forget.

(58)

Kissimmee, Florida

Dr. Farshid Aria made a left into the Kissimmee Industrial Park and drove slowly past a row of single-story cement-block buildings neatly land-scaped with Canary Island palms. Each building (an auto-repair shop, a flooring and tile store, a marketing and printing company) had an oversized rolling steel garage door with an adjacent business office. He pulled his Impala up to the last building in the complex and parked under a faded sign that read: "Recycle Electronics Depot." Farshid stepped out of the Impala, trudging through the afternoon sun to the office carrying a black bag and looking like a beaten man. He knew he had one more job to do and then his fight was over. He had done enough for the cause. It was time to put his family back together.

Trailing a few hundred yards behind Farshid, the yellow Hummer followed him into the industrial park. It pulled behind a large brown dumpster sitting outside of the printing company thirty feet away. *What am I doing here?* Jake nervously shifted his weight in the leather seat of the Hummer. He watched Farshid ring the office doorbell. The door opened and Jake squinted to see an irritated-looking younger Asian man smoking a cigarette, who waved Farshid into the office.

Jake felt bile rising in his throat. *What are you up to, old friend?* He couldn't believe his eyes. He didn't want to believe his old mentor could be part of anything criminal. *There has to be a simple explanation.*

The *Mission Impossible* theme song rang out from Jake's cell phone. It was Agent Rizzo again. *Should I answer?* he wondered. Knowing he was a fugitive, he let it ring.

———•———

Rizzo dropped her phone in frustration, shaking her head.

"LaFleur's got no idea what he's got himself into."

She was frustrated; she should've already been in Kissimmee to arrest Mikal, Elena, and the man suspected to be "The Eye Torcher," but her Sikorsky UH-60 Black Hawk had run into mechanical issues midair, and they were ordered to return to Patrick Space Force Base, forty-two miles away. "You gotta be kidding me?!" Rizzo berated pilot Portis over the whooshing sound of the smoking blades as they made an emergency landing near Cocoa Beach. Rizzo called to update her partner.

"Tell me you got 'em," Thorn said.

"*Nope*, so much for bringing this flying bazooka to a knife fight," Rizzo growled. To make up for lost time, she ordered an escort from two Brevard County deputy sheriffs. Their motorcade headed west on US-192, sirens and lights flashing. Up the coast, Agent Thorn and the FBI were stuck in SpaceX traffic, while the Orlando PD and Orange County sheriffs were rushing to lock down the Citrus Bowl. In those precious forty-five minutes, no one had a bead on Mikal, Elena, or the Doktor. No one, that is, except an overweight eye surgeon from Melbourne with a bad heart and dangerously high cholesterol.

Jake checked his heart rate on his Fitbit. *Breathe... Don't pass out.*

Sweat rolled down his cheeks. He opened the Hummer's center console, looking for a bottle of water. His eyes widened as he carefully pulled out a custom gold-plated Sig Sauer P365. Jake handled the gaudy weapon with respect. He recalled how Landry had once complained that he'd bought Amber a "golden gun" for protection, but she refused to touch it. Now here it was, like a gift from above.

Growing up in Louisiana, Jake's father had taught him how to handle handguns and hunting rifles. From the age of ten into his early twenties, Jake and his dad had made yearly hunting trips for whitetail deer in Texas. He was a decent shot, but he hadn't fired a gun in years. More of a pacificist, he never actually liked shooting or killing a deer—but he'd done it to bond with his father. Feeling the weight of the gun in his hands and knowing its terrible killing power, his hand trembled slightly.

He had to remind himself, *this is really happening.* He took a breath and depressed the magazine's release button with his thumb. The clip popped out the bottom of the handle. Jake inspected the magazine: a single stack with twelve nine-millimeter rounds. He pulled back on the slide with his left hand; the chamber was empty.

He slipped the clip back into the handle and took another calming breath.

He surveyed the lot. *Is Elena or Ben in there? Is Mikal the...serial killer?*

Swallowing his fear, Jake stuck the nine-millimeter into the waist of his shorts and exited the Hummer. He crept up to the warehouse, looking for an entry point. He ducked down alongside Dr. Aria's now-dirty white Impala. The garage door was not fully closed. He eyed the three-foot opening.

He ran over, dropped to his knees, and peered under the door. It was dark inside. He saw large treaded tires from what could possibly be a garbage truck parked in the back of the garage bay. "Come out to the coast," he whispered to himself, imitating John McClane from *Die Hard*. "We'll have a few laughs."

Then he heard a woman's scream echo through the garage.

Elena. He froze. He imagined her face and what he would do to anyone who hurt her. Jake felt a rush of anger; a bead of sweat dripped off his forehead onto the cement. *This is it,* Jake thought; he knew there was no turning back if he snuck inside the building. *Think thin.* He breathed a silent prayer, sucked in his gut, and rolled his thick torso under the garage door as gracefully as he could, bear-crawling on the cool cement floor over to a stack of old computer monitors lining the right wall. Thankfully, no one saw him enter. He hid behind the computers.

Through the gloom, he spied a door in the back of the garage cracked open like a crescent moon, its faint light barely illuminating the back of the garage bay. Muffled voices came from behind the door. He bear-crawled again alongside rows of metal shelves full of discarded computers, stereos, and CD and DVD players to the back of the garage, until he had a clear view of the vehicle.

It was a kelly-green City of Orlando Waste Management service truck like those he'd seen almost every day since living in Central Florida. *What are they doing with this thing?* Confused, he crawled up to the truck to check it out. In the dark, his hand touched what felt like a leather shoe. Jake recoiled his hand. *Dead body!* Tentatively, he reached out and felt the shoe, then a thick leg, then a thicker body. A man lying on his side. *What the—?* He pulled out his iPhone and lit up the man's face. He was stunned.

"Ben?" Jake whispered.

Ben's face was badly beaten; his eyes were swollen shut.

"Jake," Ben whispered, managing to exhale a small amount of air. "Jake, help me."

"I'm here. Just stay quiet. I'm going to get you out of here."

"They have Elena," Ben moaned.

'I know." Jake placed his hand on Ben's shoulder. "Hang tight, pal." He heard a cry come from behind the cracked door. He felt himself starting to shake again. *Can I do this?*

"Hold still!" a man commanded from behind the door. Jake heard a loud slap. Elena was sobbing. A flash of rage rushed through Jake, who pulled the Sig P365 from his waist.

He stood up behind the truck and crept to the door quietly, angling his body sideways to peer through the crack unnoticed. *They're killing her.*

(59)

The small storage room in the back of the garage was dimly visible. A tall metal gooseneck lamp had been placed beside a reclining medical exam chair, illuminating Elena's face. She was supine, lying at a forty-five-degree angle, unconscious and barely breathing, her arms tied to the cold metallic arms of the chair. A clear plastic bag filled with Diprivan hung above her body, steadily dripping into an IV tube. Dr. Farshid Aria checked the intravenous needle inserted into a vein in the back of her hand. He checked her brown almond-shaped eyes; they were widely dilated. His eyes moved slowly over her placid face, her light brown hair, and smooth white skin.

He shook his head. She was so young and beautiful. *What a waste.* But he had no choice. *She will serve her purpose.* He monitored her breathing closely. He knew excessive anesthesia could cause hypoxia and respiratory failure; if she died too quickly, he would not be able to retrieve the message. He only needed her asleep for a few minutes. A creaky door opened from the office; light flowed from the hallway.

Tarek leaned his head in. "Get you anything?" he asked

"I told you, I am not to be disturbed," Farshid shot back.

Tarek nodded and closed the door. Farshid wondered if Mikal's young soldiers even knew how to follow orders. The charming young Bosniak's plan had been well designed, but his execution lacked precision. Farshid had been working with these men for the past two weeks, but he hardly knew them. Now one of them was dead. His mind drifted as he waited for the drugs to fully sedate Elena. *What will happen to Jake?* he wondered. *He's gotten too close to this girl. He is a loose end Mikal will not allow to dangle...* He pondered his own fate and swallowed. Farshid decided the best course of action would be to finish retrieving the message from Elena and get back to Melbourne and warn Jake that he was in danger.

If Mikal allows me to live, he prayed.

Jake's eyes peered through the crack in the door. He stared at his old friend standing over Elena; it was a surreal experience. He knew he had to do something, but there were armed killers in the adjoining room, and there was no way he could get Elena and Ben out of the building safely without getting caught. He felt himself hyperventilating. He ducked away from the door to check on Ben and gather the courage to make a move.

Farshid glanced at his watch; it was time. He opened Elena's right eye with his left thumb and index finger and placed a thin wire spider lid speculum under her upper and lower lids. He lifted an ophthalmoscope from his case and positioned it on his head. A powerful light beamed out from the instrument, filling the dark room. Farshid raised a powerful lens inches from Elena's cornea and beamed the light from his headset directly into her eye. He examined the optic nerve, retinal vasculature, and macula; they were pristine in this young woman. He turned his attention to the peripheral retina. There was a bar code beautifully lasered on Elena's retina.

Farshid leaned down over Elena, now opening her left eye with the speculum. He recognized the twelve Eastern Arabic numerals needed to engage the dirty bomb. Farshid wrote the code down on a yellow notepad; finally Elena's message had been delivered.

Overcome, he briefly stepped away from Elena to reflect on his mission, his passion for his beliefs, and the trust that had been placed in him. An image of his cherished daughter and wife entered his mind and his eyes began to tear. He knew that he would be responsible for the deaths of thousands of people; he knew his life was over. He hoped they would not go after his family too. He gathered himself to finish the job.

Tarek knocked and peered around the door. "All done?"

Farshid nodded. Tarek flipped on the overhead lights and entered the office with Khalid and Huang, the smoking Chinese man who had assembled all of the dirty bombs. Farshid turned off his ophthalmoscope, oddly relieved to be finished. He felt guilty for what he had done to Elena and the other messengers who gave their lives, and there was nothing he could do to save these women now. But his guilt would not allow him to kill Elena; someone else would need to kill her.

He handed Huang the detonator code. "I presume your work is in order."

"This is *my* specialty," Huang scoffed, insulted. "Like you with the eyes. No more questions! The explosives will flatten the Citrus Bowl like a pancake, and the virus will be released as the people scramble. The wind is blowing from the west today. I will position the dirty bomb appropriately. You do not need to be concerned. More important to my country is that she was able to place the rootkit."

"The wayward dove has delivered your message," Khalid said as he joined them, patting Huang on his back. "We have proof of delivery."

"Smoke another cigarette, Huang, you seem tense," Mikal said, walking through the doorway wearing a black turtleneck. Seeming satisfied, Huang blew a plume of smoke into the air and sauntered over to the trash truck to arm the bomb.

"You feel we are unprepared, eh, old doktor?" Mikal circled Elena, staring down at her sedated body until he came face-to-face with the much shorter Farshid.

"I do not question. My job is complete," Farshid said quietly, eyes down.

"If you had only done the same in Baton Rouge, we might be in better shape."

"I could not have predicted a federal ambush," Farshid replied.

"Do I seek retribution?" Mikal put his arm around Farshid's shoulders. "What's past is past."

Elena stirred, gradually awakening. "Učinio sam ono što si tražio od mene." ("I did what you asked of me," she moaned in Bosnian.)

Turning away, Mikal instructed Farshid, "You may dispose of her."

Farshid put his ophthalmoscope gently back in its case. "You assured me no blood would be on my hands."

"What can I say?" Mikal shrugged. "I lied. What is one more life, old man, when you've taken to killing with such relish?"

He stared at Elena, relishing her helplessness.

"I am finished killing in God's name," Farshid said softly.

Elena glared up at Mikal with blurry eyes, waking from the sedative. "Sad me PUSTI." ("Let me GO.")

"Very well." Mikal smiled, stroking Elena's hair. "Out of all my doves, I loved you the most… You betrayed me for, what? A fat American? … My ego." He slapped his chest. "It hurts."

"This is funny way of showing love," Elena said, seething with her eye still stretched open by the speculum. Mikal plucked at the wire speculum playfully as if he were teasing a pet.

He gazed down at her. "You shall redeem yourself in the eyes of Allah. I have one final task for you."

"You promised Mia would see me again," Elena moaned.

"But she *shall*. Your jihad WILL BE TELEVISED." Mikal gestured to Tarek and Khalid. "Load her into the truck!"

Tarek shot Khalid a concerned look. He held out his satellite phone.

"Šta? Šta je sad?" ("What? What is it now?") Mikal asked, annoyed.

"West Coast," Tarek said.

Mikal took the phone. His bravado vanished as he stalked out into the dark garage shouting at someone on the other line. Tarek and Khalid followed him out, leaving the door wide open.

Jake retreated from the door until his backside hit a cement pillar. He strategically inched his large body around the pillar to avoid detection. He saw that he had a clear view through the open door. Farshid was carefully removing the speculum from Elena's face. Then the Farshid did something unexpected. He casually unfastened the leather restraints binding Elena's arms. Jake's eyes grew wide. *He just let her go.* Farshid gave Elena a knowing look. "Forgive me," he whispered.

Elena tentatively sat up, rubbing her wrists, stunned to be set free.

Get out of there: run, Elena, run! Jake thought as if he were talking to a movie screen.

SLAM!! Jake jumped. Behind him, the sanitation truck was being pounded by Mikal.

"BUDALO! (Fool!" in Bosnian.) Mikal kicked the door shut. "They had one job! ONE!!" He doubled over in pain as if he'd been socked in the gut. "This cannot be happening."

Tarek approached Mikal, pleading for calm. "Please. We still have one more truck. One more bomb."

Mikal kicked the door again and again, tearing it from the hinges.

"Šta je to važno?? Četiri meta su izvan ploče! Prerezali smo grlo!" ("What does it matter? Four targets off the board! We have slit our own throats!" he shouted in Bosnian.)

"Our friends in Shanghai would like words with you," Huang intoned, holding his own sat phone. He extended the device to Mikal. Mikal looked at it for several seconds. Then he angrily slapped it out of Huang's hand.

"К черту своих друзей в Шанхае!" ("Screw your friends in Shanghai!" he said in Russian.) Huang smirked as he got up close in Mikal's face. A bizarre argument in Bosnian, Russian, and Mandarin erupted among the three terrorists.

Hidden in the dark garage bay, Jake watched the commotion. *Get her while they're distracted,* he urged himself. He tried to move. *Where is your courage?! Your wife left you because you were a wimp. You've been a fat loser most of your life. You're pathetic!* He turned his gaze to Elena—he swore their eyes met. *She sees me.* His heart swelled. Jake stared down at the golden gun as if it were attached to someone else's body. His inner self coached: *You've lost eighty pounds. You box at Floyd Mayweather's fitness class. You're training for a freaking marathon. You're not a loser, you're a doctor! You know how to use a gun. Go!*

Mikal towered over Huang. "My plan was flawless. Your Xi and Vlad, they saddled me with incompetents."

"Not so flawless," Huang replied coolly. "My team did not fail you."

"Jebeni fijasko! Sve to!" ("Freaking fiasco! All of it!") Frustrated, Mikal shoved Huang and stalked back into the storage room, angrily destroying Farshid's metal gooseneck lamp as it crashed to the floor.

Farshid gave Elena a quick glance as he decided to try something.

"You treat my tools with disrespect?" he goaded Mikal.

"Your tools??" Mikal directed his anger at Farshid. "What about my detonator code?! You have some nerve, old doktor!"

"I did my duty. I want out."

Mikal's eyes widened in surprise as Farshid revealed he was brandishing a three-inch steel needle like a weapon. Mikal laughed.

"Who's giving the orders here?" He reached for the six-inch blade hanging in his belt sheath. "There is no out. We are all dead men. Four targets failed: Starship, Sugar, Orange, and now, Rose... I would execute myself if I were them."

"Allow me to do it for you," Huang muttered from the garage, firing his Glock G 18 at Mikal's head, grazing his left ear and then hitting Khalid square between the eyes. Wearing a stunned look, Khalid and his black cowboy hat fell lifelessly to the cement as Mikal darted out into the dark garage, firing back at Huang. Jake pushed his back up against a pillar to shield himself as bullets ricocheted off the walls, and Huang took cover behind the garbage truck. Tarek ducked as bullets flew over his head—some of Mikal's piercing the truck. *DING! DING! DING!*

Tarek waved his meaty arms. "Ostanavlivat'sya! Tíngzhǐ! ("Stop! Stop!" in Russian and Chinese.) Everyone knew a bullet could set off the bomb, but Mikal no longer seemed to care as he emptied his clip.

Out of bullets, he furiously threw his pistol to the ground.

Tarek ran toward him. "Kontroliraj svoju narav!" ("Control your temper!" in Bosnian.)

Farshid looked over at Elena, gesturing with the needle. With all of his might, he charged forward and horse-collared Tarek by the neck. Taken by surprise, Tarek dropped his gun to throw Farshid off his back. Huang lit a cigarette and calmly emerged from behind the truck, amused to see the old doktor wrestling with Tarek. For a moment, everyone had their guards down.

Elena narrowed her eyes. In a flash, she ran out and snatched up Tarek's pistol and fired off two precise shots… A second later, Huang fell to the ground.

Jake watched in shock as Tarek looked down, his leather jacket with Disneyland patches slowly blooming with blood. "Son of a …" He fell to his knees and toppled onto the floor next to Farshid, who stared at the stunned look on Tarek's dead face.

Elena's a sharpshooter?? Jake couldn't believe his eyes.

A slow clapping came from out of the darkness. Mikal stepped into view. "You get rid of my accomplices for me? … *Brava.*"

"Stay back!" Elena spat, pointing the gun at Mikal, her hands shaking.

Mikal approached Elena, palms out, holding his six-inch knife. "I would never hurt you. You did excellent work. Now. Give me the gun, and we'll go get sushi." He smiled jovially.

"Put it down!" she shouted.

Mikal laid on his Svengali charm. "It is over, my love. You don't believe me? We'll stay at the Four Seasons. We'll go to Disneyland."

"Screw Disneyland!" Elena shouted.

"You are my courageous dove. This is *me* you're talking to. I would never lie to you."

"Hah!" Her hands shook even more.

Shoot him! Jake thought. *What are you waiting for??*

Mikal walked closer and closer. But Elena could not kill her former lover.

"That's enough. Stop it right there, cowboy." Jake finally stepped out from his hiding spot, aiming his gun at Mikal's head—he had a clear shot. Mikal turned and smirked.

"There he is," he said in a perfect American accent. "*The man with the golden gun.*"

With all eyes on Jake, Farshid rose to his feet behind Mikal. Jake watched his old friend raise his three-inch needle and run at Mikal's back, who pivoted to meet him.

"Old fool! *Enough*!!!" Mikal slit Farshid's throat with one flamboyant sweep.

Farshid's body fell backwards. Mikal let out a sharp cry. Looking down he saw with horror Farshid had stabbed him in the crotch with the syringe.

"You are the infidel," Farshid seethed on the ground, choking, blood spurting from his neck.

Jake's eyes welled. "NOOOOO!!!" He fired a wild flurry of shots at Mikal, missing him completely.

Elena ducked. "Cow eyes! Stop it!!"

Jake stopped firing. "Sorry." He looked at Elena with ambiguous bravado. "Can't get rid of me."

"You are dumber than you look, Boy Scout," Elena quipped, her eyes dancing.

Seeing Jake and Elena lock eyes, Mikal yanked the needle out of his crotch and laughed. "Cow eyes?? That is your pet name for him???" Grabbing his knife by the blade he whipped the handle toward Elena's gun hand. *KLANG!* The weapon fell to the cement. Mikal lunged, pulling her into a bear hug and picking up Tarek's pistol. "If I'm a martyr, you're coming with me!"

He struck Elena again and again on her face and neck.

Jake grimaced, pointing his shaking gun at Mikal's head.

"Don't shoot, cow face!" Mikal shouted. "You may hit someone you care about!"

Jake didn't hesitate. He pulled the trigger. *Click*. He fired again. *Click*. The Sig was empty. He had fired all twelve shots.

"Always check your weapon first, cow face!" Mikal cackled, firing off two shots at Jake, sending him ducking and rolling out of the way.

Using Elena as a shield, he dragged her over to the garbage truck and tossed her in the back like a piece of trash, after tying her hands behind her back. Shocked to be out of bullets, Jake checked his clip as Mikal started the engine and peeled away, callously running over Huang's body with the rear tires. Using the truck's grill, Mikal rammed through the garage door and sideswiped the Impala. Jake watched helplessly as the radioactive garbage truck drove away with Elena inside. He ran to Farshid's limp body, crumpled in a red pool, blood still spurting from his neck. Jake applied pressure to his throbbing carotid artery. "My friend...why?"

Farshid stared up at him with fading sorrowful eyes. "Irfa," he gasped.

With his free hand Jake began to dial 9-1-1, but Farshid went limp; it was too late. Tears and sweat dripped off Jake's nose onto Farshid's face. He delicately laid his old friend down on the ground. Still in shock, Jake ran over and untied Ben, who sat up, rubbing his swollen face.

"I saw everything," Ben moaned. "You shoot like a girl, bubby."

"Get up. Let's go!" Jake helped him to his feet.

$$\textbf{(60)}$$

Jake supported Ben as they staggered together out of the warehouse and into the late afternoon sun. They were both covered in blood and shaking from adrenaline fatigue. Jake helped Ben into the passenger seat of Landry's Hummer. "You stole his yellow chariot? You outlaw." Ben attempted a smile. "We'll get blood on this fancy leather interior."

"Screw it." Jake looked around and spotted the Waste Management truck tearing onto North Stewart Avenue. He threw the Hummer into gear and screeched as he drove into the street.

"How did two guys like us get mixed up in this?" Jake exclaimed. "This is insane."

"You said you wanted adventure," Ben replied weakly.

The *Mission Impossible* theme song rang from Jake's pocket. He pulled it out, hoping it might be Elena. He frowned. "Well, what now?"

He accidentally answered it and put in on speakerphone. His mother Cindy's voice came through the receiver. "Honey, I bought a roasted chicken. Will you be home for dinner, or are you already in jail with *that woman*?"

"Can't talk, Mom!" Jake shouted, making a sharp left onto West Mabette Street.

"You're killing your mother!" Cindy cried, as he threw the phone at Ben's feet.

Jake looked at Ben. "She's worried."

"You mensch." Ben tried to smile.

The sound of the *Mission Impossible* theme song ran out again.

"Maybe Elena got free?" Jake pointed at the phone.

Ben glanced down at the Caller ID. It read "Federal Bureau of Investigation."

Ben picked it up and showed it to Jake. "You may want to take this one."

Jake took the phone. "Sorry. Are you pissed? I can explain!"

243

"Surrender, LaFleur," Agent Rizzo shouted. "This is the FBI!"

Jake heard the sound of sirens but saw nothing in the rearview mirror. He handed the phone to Ben.

"It's for you." Jake stomped on the gas.

Ben fumbled, putting the phone to his ear. "Hi. I'm, uh, Jake's therapist. Is there something I can help you with?" Ben asked mildly, wiping dried blood off his face with a wet nap he found in the console.

"This is the FBI, you idiots! Where's Elena and Mikalovich!"

"Tell her Mikal's got a bomb! He's driving a Waste Management truck!" Jake shouted. "I'm following him. He's on Sand Lake heading towards International Drive."

Rizzo corrected him. "The target is the Citrus Bowl. We'll handle this!"

"Seems like he's headed towards Disney," Jake said as Ben spotted a sign that read: "Disney Springs, 5 miles."

"He's headed to Disney Springs," Ben repeated.

"That's not what I said!" Rizzo shouted.

Jake swerved the Hummer right, cutting off two vehicles next to them. The drivers cursed them and leaned on their horns.

"Tell your pal he's being played! Elena's no victim. Turn yourselves in!" Rizzo shouted. Ben handed the iPhone back to Jake. "I don't think she likes your new girlfriend." Jake took the phone and listened to Agent Rizzo.

"This is a police matter, LaFleur! Do not intervene or we WILL SHOOT YOU."

"Got it! Got it! But I can't do that." Jake hung up on Rizzo mid-sentence.

"That was the FBI you just hung up on??" Ben asked.

"…Yeah." Jake looked at him, terrified and exhilarated.

"You're my hero." Ben smiled a bloody-toothed grin.

(61)

Lake Buena Vista, Florida

Desperately steering a weapon of mass destruction through holiday traffic, Mikal's forehead glistened as he wiped perspiration from his eyes. The Citrus Bowl swarming with federal agents, and with his terror team in disarray, he prepared for his martyrdom. He recalled the specs he gathered on the McNeilus garbage truck he now commanded: it weighed fifteen thousand pounds and could reach a speed of fifty miles per hour. At top speed, it could plow through anything. Its momentum would increase the impact and explosive value to a maximal lethal capacity.

Looking up into the flawless blue sky, he saw a helicopter tailing him.

"You put a gun in both our mouths!" he shouted over his shoulder at Elena. "We'll enter the gates of heaven together."

Tied in the back of the garbage truck, she cringed as each passing speed bump jostled the trash can with the explosives inside. Elena closed her eyes and thought about her life. She prayed God would spare her and allow her to see Mia again; she told Mia she was sorry.

"What about SpaceX and Starlink?!" Elena pleaded. "I did what you asked of me!"

"You betrayed me!" he shouted.

Elena looked desperately around her for a way out, contorting her body to pull a pin from her messy hair. She used it to try and pick the lock of her handcuffs. Mikal turned his head and saw her. "Nevaljala djevojka." ("Naughty girl.") He swerved the wheel—Elena held on as the trash cans slid back and forth.

Suddenly, they heard a loud car horn honking from the right side of the truck. Mikal glanced to the passenger-side mirror—a boxy yellow blur was gaining fast. He squinted; it was that garish Hummer—to him, an overwhelmingly disgusting symbol of America.

"Why won't you die, cow face?!" he raged, his eye scar pulsating with every heartbeat. Elena smirked. *My Boy Scout's alive.*

Behind the wheel of the Hummer, Jake's round face lit up like he was mainlining Red Bull. "I see you, bastard!!" Jake growled, fully in superhero character.

"You're going too fast!" Ben exclaimed, clutching at the grab handle, worried he was careening to his death. Jake floored it, glancing at his Fitbit. His heart rate was through the roof.

"Whatever you do, don't die. Breathe through your nose!" Ben yelled.

Jake gnashed his teeth. "*This is personal. No wimping out—not this time!*"

He pulled the Hummer up alongside the dump truck. Mikal rammed the side of the Hummer with sadistic glee, pushing it across two lanes to a crescendo of honking horns. The Hummer vanished amid the wake of upset traffic.

Mikal looked in his side mirrors. "You wanna play rough? Let's play!"

He drove under a road sign that read: "Disney Springs next left."

A smile spread across his face. Early planning for their plot to attack America, Disney Springs had been suggested as an option to place explosives and create maximum casualties. He looked back at Elena.

"What do you say we shove it up the Mouse's ass?!"

Mikal made a hard right off Epcot Center Drive and onto East Buena Vista Drive.

———————————•———————————

"Take the wheel on my cue. I've got an idea," Jake directed Ben as he hit the gas.

He sped up, pulling the Hummer side by side with the dump truck.

"Bloated pest!" he heard Mikal say, raging through the open passenger window.

Jake waved playfully at Mikal, then looked over at Ben. "Don't let him run us off the road, okay?" Jake grabbed Amber Landry's gold-plated handgun from his lap and loaded a fresh twelve-round clip he'd found stashed in the center console.

"Okay?? What, pray tell, are you planning to do??" Ben exclaimed.

"I'm taking out the trash," Jake sneered. He chambered a nine-millimeter round and rolled down the window of his driver's-side door. Warm Florida wind blew through the cab as Jake began hoisting himself out the window legs first, his heart monitor pinging furiously.

"Now!" Jake shouted.

In shock, bruised, and in pain, Ben lumbered over the center console and slid behind the wheel, just as Jake leapt out of the moving vehicle, grabbed the side handle of the dump truck, and landed on its running board.

Ben couldn't believe his eyes. "You're *Indiana Jones*, in person!" Ben steadied the wheel and pumped his sandaled foot on the gas, grinning like this was the best day of his life.

Jake hung onto the side of the weaving truck like a well-fed veteran trashman as the moving traffic on East Buena Vista Drive honked at him, some (no doubt) wondering if this was a chase scene being filmed for a Disney movie.

"Sorry! Sorry!" Jake apologized to the angry drivers as they shouted obscenities at him. He wondered if Elena was still alive inside the truck as he looked around at the passing scenery that he knew so well.

He gripped the gun, gathering his courage. "It's go time." Wind whipping through his hair, he flung open the passenger-side door, theatrically shouting, "Say hello to my little friend!!"

He fired off two shots—and badly missed both times.

"Crazy American!" Mikal shouted as he used his Makarov handgun to return fire at Jake, who ducked out of the way, leaving him dangling off the truck by one arm like a bloated stuntman.

"I'm full of surprises," Jake muttered, swinging himself back up and firing again, this time hitting Mikal in the right shoulder, causing him to drop his gun on the floorboard. Jake instantly had a clear shot at Mikal's head. He aimed. *Do it! Kill shot!* he told himself. But he couldn't shoot an unarmed man, not even a vicious murderer.

"STOP!" he shouted.

Mikal made a hard right turn into the Disney Springs parking lot, trying to throw Jake off the truck. The centrifugal force caused Jake to slip off the truck's running board; he held on to the sturdy sideview mirror with all the strength of his two hands. Mikal focused his eyes straight ahead to the road;

he spied a clear path through a nearby parking lot leading to the busy Disney Springs entertainment and shopping area. Using all of his might, Jake pulled himself back to the truck's door and lunged through the open door at Mikal, gabbing at his neck, growling like a wrestler.

The two men locked arms as they struggled for control of the wheel.

Fifty yards behind them, Ben slowed the Hummer. He could only watch as the out-of-control trash truck veered through the packed Watermelon and Mango Parking Lots at top speed. It careened through parked cars and cleared a swath of stunned pedestrians as it slammed through a cement security barrier and onto the Disney Springs sidewalk. Its momentum continued as Mikal approached the Cirque du Soleil Theater.

"This ain't good," Ben said, watching the tourists scatter like ants as the dump truck bounced up a wide set of stairs and smashed through a fifteen-foot-tall plate glass wall on the side of the theater and finally came to an abrupt halt.

———●———

"Land this thing!" Agent Rizzo shouted over the helicopter blades to the pilot.

"Where?! Lots are full!" Portis circled around, looking for a clearing outside the packed park. Rizzo picked up her radio to give play-by-play to the response team.

"Suspect has plowed into the Disney Springs theater! We're looking for a landing spot! All units respond!" She added, "It's showtime."

Inside the theater, a full house was enjoying Cirque du Soleil's "Drawn to Life," a performance highlighting classic artwork from Disney movies set on a stage that resembled a giant animator's drawing table.

Suddenly there was an ear splitting *SMASH!!!!*

The theater shook as a kelly-green garbage truck crashed through the stage backdrops depicting sketches of Tinker Bell and Peter Pan. Children tumbled off their grandparents' laps and the crowd erupted in screams as performers dressed like pencils and paintbrushes jumped to safety. The smoking truck twisted over onto its side, streaming a shower of sparks in its wake, until it came to a squealing stop in the middle of the stage. There was a moment of suspended animation as the shocked crowd gawked wordlessly at the enormous truck, then screams exploded as everyone ran in terror for the aisles. Massive fire sprinklers rained down, drenching the fleeing crowd. The back door of the dump truck opened, smacking down on the stage with a booming metallic thud. In the second row of the VIP section, Congressman Parker and his grown son Kip cowered behind the seats in front of them.

"Think this is part of the show?" the congressman asked Kip. Kip peered over a seatback just as plastic trash barrels tumbled like jumping beans out the back of the truck onto the stage, toward him. One barrel wedged into the lip of the stage inches away from Kip's head. He saw it had a rectangular digital display with nine flashing red numbers. Next to the display was a lit Bluetooth logo. Terrified, Kip looked at his dad.

"It's no show! It's a bomb! RUN!"

The two men bolted past parents and kids stampeding for the exits as security guards and ushers herded everyone out. With the evacuation demanding all the attention of Disney's security team, Jake and Mikal tumbled out of the dump truck's driver-side door, falling to the stage. The two men both slowly stood up faced each other. Mikal's legs wobbled as he threw a right fist at Jake, who ducked under the punch. Using his strong legs from marathon training for leverage, Jake plowed his right shoulder into Mikal's gut, lifting him up and pancaking him onto the floor. Jake hit the stage hard with his forehead. Seeing stars, he let go of Mikal and rolled over on his backside.

Stuck in a bottleneck of tourists making frenzied efforts to exit the theater, Kip turned to see the action. He lifted his eye patch to get a better look. "Yo, it's that karate man eye doctor!"

Mikal made it to his feet. He looked down at Jake, whose head was still reeling.

"Read this, cow face!" Mikal grabbed an oversized prop pencil from Geppetto's workshop and smashed it over Jake's head. But the blow from the Styrofoam pencil had an opposite effect on Jake. It actually cleared his mind enough to use a leg-sweeping yoga move to take out the back of Mikal's knees, who collapsed forward onto the stage. With both men on the ground, something shiny caught their eyes. It was Landry's golden gun, which had jettisoned out of the truck and slid to the front of the stage. It gleamed like a glistening movie prop.

Glancing at each other, they frantically crawled like animals toward it. Mikal clamped down on the golden gun first and pointed it at Jake.

"You need more cardio! Too much McDonald's," he sneered.

"I've gone vegan!" Jake said, standing up and raising his hands in defeat.

Mikal walked over to inspect the display on the bomb. He searched his back pocket for the Bluetooth remote control. It was missing. He looked back at the truck.

"Just shoot me!" Jake pleaded, realizing Mikal had dropped the remote. "Why kill all these innocent people?"

"Innocent?" Mikal turned to Jake, shaking sprinkler water from his wet hair. "INNOCENT! Your country is responsible for the murder, execution, and conquest of more innocent people than any other nation in history! Do you not know that? …What do they teach you in school? That you are heroes? The World's Big Brother? You are terrorists in swim shorts! Gestapo with gold cards!"

"Look out there!" Jake pleaded, pointing to the screaming crowd. "See the women? Children?"

"Your murderous country consumes women and children for breakfast!" Mikal countered. "For your ignorance and your obvious gluttony, YOU, my fat-faced friend, and all of these DISGUSTING PEOPLE are going to pay. On your knees!"

Hearing his words, tourists unable to get out of the theater turned to watch Mikal press the golden gun to Jake's temple as if it were a stage play.

"You stole my girlfriend, cow head!" Mikal raged.

"You killed my mentor!" Jake spat back. "What did you do to Elena??" Jake growled up at him.

"She's somewhere around here." Mikal gestured with his gun. "And the old man? … Pshaw…he was weak. Your friend murdered all those women." He went on, "Cut out their eyes. Sick stuff. How does that make you feel?"

"You lie!" Jake cried.

"Do I?" Mikal laughed.

Through the smoke and sprinkler rain, a shapely soaking-wet silhouette of a woman emerged from behind a hunk of smoldering metal. It crept up on Mikal like a wounded panther, dragging an impossibly large appendage, silver handcuffs dangling from her right wrist.

Jake closed his eyes and began a "Hail Mary."

Mikal chambered a round. "Go on. *Pray*. Your God won't save you!"

"…Holy Mary, Mother of God, pray for us sinners now and at the hour of our death. Glory be to the Father, and to the Son, and to the Holy—"

SMASH!!

Elena walloped Mikal in the head with the prop arm from a seven-foot wooden Pinocchio.

"Consider this your breakup call, you jerk," Elena said, as Mikal fell senseless into the orchestra pit like he'd been KO'd by Mike Tyson.

Jake crawled to the edge of the stage and peered down at his motionless adversary. He exhaled, rolling over on his back. He stared at the ceiling of the theater, trying to regain his strength. *My prayers were answered.* He struggled to his feet and limped over to Elena. Too tired to speak, he stared into her caramel eyes and put his arms around her. Some people still standing in the aisles, who had been watching the struggle, applauded.

"KISS HER," called a man.

Jake looked over Elena's shoulder. It was Ben, who had stumbled through the gaping hole backstage. He gave him a thumbs-up. "Better hurry. Cops coming."

On cue, Jake laid a passionate kiss on Elena at center stage.

"Hold that thought. I forgot something," he said. Jake walked over to the trash truck and climbed in front and found the blinking remote. He hit the cancel button on the Bluetooth device; the blinking red numbers on the barrel went black.

Ben checked the bomb's digital display. "It's off! It's a miracle!"

"My Boy Scout." Elena smiled as Jake walked over and kissed her again just like he'd dreamed. The crowd erupted in cheers. Twenty feet up in the air, even Trish, the tiny acrobat playing Tinker Bell, who had safely watched the whole melee from her perch, shed a tear of joy, still dangling from her giant red scarf swing. "So romantic," she sighed.

With everyone celebrating, Mikal silently crawled out of the orchestra pit, seething with anger. Bloodied and bruised, he laid eyes on Elena kissing Jake. Someone in the audience gasped as others filmed Mikal's resurrection with their iPhones. Ben heard the gasps. He turned to see Mikal on a broken ankle hobbling toward Jake. He still clutched the gold pistol.

"Look out, bubby!" Ben shouted. "Coming from your left!" He pointed.

"Old boy, every imperialist should know," Mikal shouted, pointing the pistol at the happy couple, "if you want to kill a cobra, you take off its head."

Elena jumped at the sound of her tormentor's voice. Ben looked up. Trish, the acrobat, was directly above Mikal. Ben and Trish locked eyes. She slowly lowered her scarf swing down over Mikal's head.

Elena turned around. Mikal's dead green eyes were staring at her as he aimed at her heart.

"Goodbye, Elena," he whispered through gritted teeth.

Her face went flush, then drained to an ash grey.

"Drop the gun! This is the Disney police!" shouted the chief of a group of security officers stampeding their way through the swell of tourists flooding the exit doors.

Mikal eyed the crowd and emitted a chuckle. "Disney police."

Above Mikal, out of the corner of her eye, Elena spied Trish's looped scarf lowering from above and reacted, snatching it and wrapping it around Mikal's neck in a flash—just as Jake punched Mikal square in the nose.

"Ow." Mikal looked like a poleaxed prizefighter. "You do not hit like girl after all."

Elena and Jake watched as Mikal was hoisted high up into the rafters by his neck. Offstage, Ben manned the scarf swing controls, pulling it as high as it would go. Mikal cried out, grabbing the scarf with one hand, as he twisted and pointed the gun down at Jake. Twenty feet above their heads, croaking through his fury, Mikal fired two wild shots.

Jake ducked. Mikal had missed—gargling as he dropped the golden gun to the stage.

Ben rushed over and brutally choked him until he lost consciousness.

Then Mikal's body went limp, and he swung from the rafters like a hanged man.

"Happy New Year from the good ole U.S. of A.," Ben shouted tauntingly up at Mikal.

The audience erupted in cheers. "USA! USA!"

Elena glanced at Jake, who was staring up in disbelief at Mikal. "You always get your man?" she asked, out of breath. She smiled and extended her long slender hand. Jake took it. "You saved my life. Again." They embraced warmly. Jake buried his face in her neck.

Gradually, he felt something warm and wet on his chest. He pushed away from her and looked down. His shirt was covered with fresh blood. It was not his, or Mikal's, or Farshid's.

"Elena!"

Her top was covered in blood.

"Elena. You're hit."

Her smile was radiant. "I don't feel a thing." She beamed at him, her body running on adrenaline alone.

Jake gently lifted her shirt. Above her black bra, there was a nasty four-inch wound from a large piece of truck shrapnel. It was bubbling blood.

Punctured lung, he thought. "*Yikes.*" He held her firmly as he applied pressure to her bleeding wound with a piece of costume fabric he picked off the stage.

"Funny how things turn out…hunh?" Elena stared down in shock at her bleeding chest, her eyes glassing over.

"Just lay, lay down now," Jake stammered, switching to doctor mode. Elena slumped down to the stage. "Somebody call an ambulance!" Jake shouted to the crowd, who were too busy texting and videoing with their iPhones to call 9-1-1.

Elena wheezed from the wound and broken ribs, her collapsed lung releasing air and blood into her chest cavity.

"Pretty good punch…for a cow," Elena whispered, coughing up blood. "…Tell Mia… I love her."

"Don't talk like that," he said, still applying pressure. "We may be going to jail, but you'll live." Jake said all the right words, though he wasn't sure they were true.

"I never meant…that anybody be hurt," Elena said, wheezing.

"I never told you I love you," Jake said, tears running down his cheeks. She leaned up and kissed him softly with blood-covered lips.

"I know…stupid."

She sighed and closed her brown eyes.

He laid her head gently back down on the stage.

"Ben! Call an ambulance! … I love you."

62

Thorn was the first agent through the massive truck-sized hole in the theater wall. Leading the charge of law enforcement, she helped evacuate the remaining tourists, including Congressman Parker and his ne'er-do-well son. EMTs rushed in behind her with their gear and attended to Elena. Jake was cradling her in his lap, keeping pressure on her chest wound, which had stopped pumping blood. He broke down when she was taken away. Jake wanted to ride with her in the ambulance, but the authorities would not allow it.

She was pronounced dead at 6:04 p.m.

The bomb squad forced everyone to clear the theater so they could dismantle Mikal's barrel and dispose of it safely. Scores of firemen and law enforcement evacuated all the restaurants, bars, and kiosks in the Disney Springs Entertainment Complex, including the world's largest Disney store, full of stubborn shoppers. On stage FBI agents lowered Mikal from the rafters. Remarkably, despite a crushed larynx he was still breathing and was taken into custody.

Outside, among the hundreds of bystanders being questioned, Dr. Jake LaFleur, Dr. Ben Silverman, and the tiny acrobat Trish sat motionless and exhausted on a Disney park bench under silver thermal security blankets, sipping water from plastic cups shaped like mouse ears.

"Hey, look, bubby." Ben pointed to the giant screen above the ESPN Zone sports bar. "The launches are today. Almost forgot."

"Me too," Jake said softly, grieving Elena.

The dual launch of Starlink and Starship was taking place as planned. ABC was broadcasting it live across every screen in the complex, though the theater area was now empty, except for witnesses, EMTs, FBI, and local law enforcement.

"Too bad we couldn't watch it this year," Ben said.

Rizzo and Thorn conferred with their bosses about what to do with the two doctors.

"Do we arrest them or pin medals on them?" Rizzo asked Agent Hawks on her phone. It was determined it would take a long investigation to sort out all that transpired. But for right now, Agents Rizzo and Thorn came over to question the so-called "heroes" of the day before letting them go home. After Jake and Ben gave their official depositions, Rizzo had one final question. "Still think Elena was innocent, LaFleur?"

Still emotional, Jake stood up to face Rizzo. "You're a real jerk, you know that?"

Rizzo smirked unapologetically. "Your girl was in on it."

"In on what? Nothing happened!" Jake shot back.

"Yeah! Thanks to us," Rizzo replied defensively.

"Says the agent who showed up late to every party," Jake said and sat back down.

"No reason to get personal, Doctor LaFleur. There's enough credit to go around. But he kinda does have a point, Jane," Thorn said, putting her hand on Rizzo's shoulder.

"Excuse me. Ma'ams?" Ben chimed in. "Can my patient have a minute? I'm his psychiatrist and he's just been through a traumatic event."

"You're both going to get plenty of therapy time in federal prison," Rizzo shot back.

"This man is a hero!" Ben stood up. "Check your social media! Everyone in there had iPhones!"

"Screw social media, you committed at least forty-seven felonies!" Rizzo insisted.

Jake only shrugged, defeated. Out of habit, he looked up at the Jumbotron to distract his racing mind.

"Today's SpaceX launches are coming at you LIVE from the Ports of Los Angeles and Cape Canaveral," announced an overhyped ABC reporter, who was counting down to the launch like it was New Year's Eve. "Let's listen in to SpaceX mission control."

"T-minus 10, 9, 8, 7, 6…"

Everyone in the Disney complex paused to look up at the Jumbotron to follow the countdown.

Rizzo glanced at Thorn. "Menard better pray he's right."

A split screen showed the two sleek silver rockets firing up their engines and taking off simultaneously in rumbles of billowing smoke and flames. In Los Angeles, Starship 1, with a group of billionaires onboard, rose successfully into the clear Southern California afternoon.

"We are watching history, folks. The first private citizens to take a trip around the moon! Wow!" warbled the on-air reporter.

Rizzo and Thorn then turned their attention on the second screen showing the Starlink rocket, which seemed like an ordinary takeoff.

"Who doesn't want free Internet? I sure do. I'm a web-surfing junkie!" quipped a female TV anchor as the ship ascended into the stratosphere. The launch appeared fine—so fine that Jake and the onlookers lost interest. Until a massive explosion engulfed the Starlink rocket. The response team at Disney reacted in shock. "OH!" "Whoa!" "*OH no*!"

The ship ignited to a fireball, falling from the sky and crashing into the Atlantic Ocean. Jake watched, numb; all he could think of was Elena.

A few feet away, Kip and Congressman Parker sat with the other survivors. "Whoa, Pops, what's happening?!" Kip shouted, savoring the chaos.

The ABC reporter recited a solemn play-by-play like he was watching the Hindenburg crash. A shaky camera cut to the SpaceX launch team on the viewing tower dropping their heads in disbelief.

Rizzo looked at Thorn. "We'll probably get blamed for that."

63

Washington, DC

"Explain yourselves, ladies, and speak slowly," ordered aging FBI Director Sheldon Cole, a few days later. Agent Rizzo nodded, as she walked into Cole's mahogany wood-paneled office in Washington, D.C., on a cold January morning. Rizzo had been told that Director Cole wanted to meet her so she could "explain herself personally." After their meeting, Cole intended to brief the National Security Director and the President of the United States before he flew to attend the G8 Summit in Oslo. Agent Tami Thorn (in her best custom sneakers) accompanied Rizzo in her best blue power suit, with a laptop full of analysis and top secret intel collected from Interpol, the CIA, NSA, and the FBI's Forensic Science Lab. Rizzo cleared her throat as she cued up a PowerPoint presentation that Thorn and Junior Intelligence Analyst Benji Weir had put together to connect the dots in Mikalovich's labyrinthian plot.

"His primary objective was the cyberattacks on SpaceX to take down the Starship and Starlink projects, to interrupt what the Russian and Chinese governments ostensibly believe is a U.S. communication spy satellite network being developed. Russia and China in particular are worried about SpaceX's mission."

"Chatter tells us they feel it threatens their security and sovereignty," Thorn added.

"Don't they want free Internet like the rest of us?" Cole asked, half kidding.

"Apparently not, sir," Rizzo replied. "We believe the secondary targets, the dirty bombs set to detonate at the bowl games on New Year's Day, were organized by a rogue group of anti-American extremists in the Iranian and Russian governments who were also involved. We are still unsure who

257

funded Mikal's multipronged operation. Our best intel says the bowl game attacks were distractions from the cyberattack on SpaceX."

"Some distractions," Cole said.

"Agent Rizzo's hunch was on point, after all," Thorn said.

"The exploding rockets also would have rained nuclear-contaminated debris down on Los Angeles and Orlando, killing and/or maiming thousands of innocent civilians. A double whammy for Mikalovich's team," Rizzo declared.

"Nasty sucker, ain't he?" Cole mused like an absent-minded professor. "But you got him."

"Yes, sir—and the college football game attacks were his cherry on top," Thorn added.

"Wiping out as many innocent civilians as possible on national TV. That's nine-eleven on steroids, sir, from a psycho looking to make a name for himself on the global stage," Rizzo said.

"I presume he did not act alone," Cole said. "Who put Mikalovich up to this?"

"We're still investigating, but we know he had help."

Thorn clicked her remote. A PowerPoint slide came up on the screen. The infographic illustrated how "Mikal's Angels," posing as college interns, were able to sabotage the two SpaceX rocket Raptor engines with a virus, after Xang Xi—the Chinese coder, who was in protective custody—corrupted SpaceX's software architecture with a backdoor.

"Xi is singing like a canary to avoid being sent back to China," Rizzo said. "He has confirmed that three interns with security access in separate SpaceX locations helped sabotage the rockets using rootkit software."

Intelligence Analyst Baris (calling in from the LA office) spoke up on the Cisco WebEx video call. "A rootkit is a malicious computer program designed to provide access to a computer without the knowledge of the systems owner or administrators while actively hiding its presence until it's too late."

"Baris, I read the report. I know what a rootkit is!" Cole scolded.

Baris sat back in his chair self-consciously and adjusted his thick black-framed glasses.

Agent Rizzo shot Benji an annoyed look. "Elena Smilovic was part of his three-person terror cell that had been secretly embedded in Menard facilities in Waco, Los Angeles, and Orlando. Each woman carried messages in their eyes, in the form of bar codes and detonator codes."

"In their *eyes*??" Cole repeated incredulously. "What the hell?" His voice crescendoed.

"Yes, sir," Rizzo replied. "A retina specialist in Sarajevo lasered the messages into their eyes. The first was a University of Texas student, Uma Gloten, who used the bar codes to implant a rootkit in a SpaceX database in Waco. Meanwhile a woman named Sheila Roustamov implanted a rootkit in the Starship Raptor rocket system in LA. Elena Smilovic then implanted a rootkit in the Starlink's rocket satellite system in Cape Canaveral on New Year's Eve after plying a local doctor, Jake LaFleur, with too much vodka."

Cole stirred uncomfortably in his high-backed leather chair. He stared at Elena's attractive passport photo projected on the screen.

"Lucky son of a gun, that doctor was. You sure he wasn't in on it?"

"Mm-hmm, one hundred percent," Rizzo said.

Cole fanned out the slide printouts in front of him. He stared at them, his brow furrowed, looking like he was trying to understand astrophysics. "And all these girls were murdered by that serial killer?"

"All but Smilovic," Rizzo said. "Mikal was disposing of his accomplices."

"What about this Svanna Bortiach, the woman from Baton Rouge?" he asked.

"She was the only one who was not directed to plant a rootkit," Rizzo relied.

"We suspect that's because she flunked out of her aerospace engineering program at LSU and lost her top-secret clearance at the SpaceX Rocket Lab in Alabama where she had briefly interned," Thorn explained.

"But she was carrying a detonator code from Bosnia in her right eye for the thwarted Sugar Bowl plot," Rizzo added.

"You did crack work in Baton Rouge, Agent Rizzo. Shame about Agent Boyle."

"Yes, sir. I am in touch with his wife," Rizzo said solemnly.

"But how do we position this as a win?" Cole asked. "We've spent nearly two million federal dollars to thwart these attacks and still lost one of our agents and a billion-dollar spaceship on national TV! It's giving me a migraine. What can I tell the President?"

"Well…there are silver linings," Rizzo calmly explained.

"Give me one," Cole demanded.

"We will give you six." Rizzo pulled up another slide illustrating their list of six biggest accomplishments from the case.

Thorn stood to assist in the presentation summary. "Agent Rizzo thwarted the Sugar Bowl attack and the Starship bomb with all those uppity billionaires on board."

"None of the bowl game dirty bombs went off," Rizzo said. "That's good, right?"

"It certainly is," Cole said. "Are they all accounted for?"

"Yep. Except for the, uh, New Orleans one."

"Oh. Well, get on that." He frowned. "What else?"

"We identified the Eye Torcher as a member of Mikalovich's team and a possible Iranian Al-Qaeda sleeper cell."

"Where is he now?" asked Cole.

"Dead—Farshid Aria was discovered at the Kissimmee warehouse. Throat slit. Along with other members of Mikalovich's crew," Rizzo said.

"Mikal was disposing of his accomplices," Thorn added. "Picking up where the Eye Torcher left off."

"Finally," Rizzo continued, "the Starlink rocket that blew up was carrying satellites, no passengers. Plus, it exploded so high in the stratosphere over the Atlantic, a catastrophic nuclear disaster was averted directly over Orlando." Rizzo put down her remote control.

FBI Director Cole leaned back in his leather chair and thought for a moment.

"Okay. Good work, agents... I think. Is Mikalovich talking?"

"Took a vow of silence—he's awaiting trial at Guantanamo Bay."

"I'll brief the President then. You ladies gonna take some time off? Hit the beach or whatever it is you do?"

Rizzo cringed being called a "lady." "I don't do time off. Respectfully."

"Me neither, sir," Thorn said. "This is my life."

"I like that kind of ambition. You'll go far with us. Just keep at it," said Cole.

"Tell our boss that," Rizzo said with a wry smirk.

"Where is Agent Hawks anyway?" Cole asked.

"Day off. Getting his teeth bleached, I believe, sir," Rizzo said with a straight face.

The two exhausted agents stood up to leave the meeting with Director Cole, feeling good about the lives they helped to save but wondering if they did enough to finally get the promotions they so desired, as well as respect among their peers. Only time would tell, but Rizzo and Thorn were now partners and media celebrities (of sorts) with book deals from Random House as the only two FBI agents in American history who had simultaneously caught a serial killer and thwarted a terrorist plot.

"Oh, wait. One final thing." Cole raised his hand.

"Yes, sir." Rizzo turned while strapping her leather computer satchel over her shoulder.

"You gals hear that Xi character had quite a story to tell?"

"Like what?" Rizzo said.

"Did you pick up any chatter about the 'Shanghai Cooperation Organization' in your investigation?" he asked them. The two agents shook their heads.

"The bombs and rootkits were made in China," Thorn said.

"So were Xi and Huang, who was one of the dead terrorists we found in the Kissimmee warehouse."

"But that's the CIA's business," Rizzo added. "Right, sir?"

"Right, right. Very good then. Go have a few sodas on the company dime." Cole waved them away like an indulgent grandfather.

———————●———————

To this day, no one could say for certain who was behind Mikal's plot. Through diplomatic back channels, the official response from the eight member nations in the Shanghai Cooperation Organization claimed no knowledge of a terrorist plot. In the months to come, the FBI's and CIA's anti-terrorist task forces would place official blame on a rogue splinter group of anti-American extremists within the eight governments of the SCO nations, led by Mikalovich, who remained in custody at Guantanamo Bay and held to a vow of silence.

His only external communication was with a fanatical following of young female fans who wrote him faithfully and often in prison.

(64)

Lake Buena Vista, Florida

Huffing his way through the humid air, Jake made the final turn to the finish line, passing by crowds of cheering fans who filled the stands at the last two hundred yards of the marathon. Jake's vision was blurred, but he could make out the oversized digital Disney World clock above the finish line: it read 3:58:32. *I can crack four hours, if I get it in gear.* His sunburned arms barely swinging, his thick legs cramping from hips to toes—he dug deep for the final push. The excitement of the crowd gave him the burst of energy he needed to power across the finish line in just under four hours. He had met his goal, a monumental achievement for a man who, a week earlier, had been ruled out for having a heart attack. Jake smiled as Minnie Mouse hung a medal around his neck and handed him a bottle of water and a banana.

But he hurt inside—he had spent most of the 26.2 miles listening to achy-breaky country music and thinking about Elena. No matter how many times Rizzo and Thorn showed him the evidence, he couldn't believe she willingly had been involved. But in quiet moments as he attended to patients or pursued his marathon training, he remembered her words. Her confession in the banana grove and on the yacht, and her asking for forgiveness when she was dying in his arms.

Jake had been questioned by the authorities countless times. He didn't know what to believe anymore. All he knew was that he loved a woman, and she was gone. He was certain that if Elena was knowingly involved, she only consented to do it for Mia, her little girl, as she said that night they kissed under the fireworks in Landry's Hummer.

During the week after the whole crazy affair, Jake had done some research and contacted Elena's Uncle Abi and Aunt Jula to make sure Mia would be cared for. He even got to talk to little Mia on the phone and tell her how brave her mother was. He promised to send her a big package from Walt Disney himself with lots of cool Little Mermaid gear.

But his pain was still there. Toweling off, he walked through the finishers' chute toward the parking lot, passing other runners proudly displaying their medals, snapping selfies, and congratulating each other. Jake gave enthusiastic high fives and fist bumps to complete strangers, like he was a kid again. Riding the runner's high as long as he could, he walked alone, but like soldiers who had been through a war he felt a camaraderie with the other marathon runners. They had all survived the same pain.

Cindy, who hated crowds and sporting events, was waiting back at Jake's condo, making him a special dinner. Ben could not be there due to an interview he was shooting on *Entertainment Tonight*. Ben and Trish, the Cirque du Soleil acrobat, had become overnight TikTok sensations. A video shot by someone in the crowd showed them lassoing Mikal by the neck and hanging him from the stage; of course it had gone viral. Surprisingly, Jake and Elena had somehow been forgotten by the mass media—though not by Jake's ex-wife, Didi, who had been so impressed by Jake's role in thwarting the terrorist attack, she had asked Jake to FaceTime her when he was at the finish line. He agreed but completely forgot about it since he was totally depleted mentally and physically. Being alone was fine with Jake. He had proven something to himself. He could run a marathon. And his heart could still love someone. It may be broken for now, but he was not finished living yet.

With his car invisible somewhere in the full Disney World parking lot, Jake hit his key fob, hoping the car alarm would give him a clue to its whereabouts. He followed the sound of his honking horn, hobbling along on stiffening knees.

Silently, a black Ford SUV glided up alongside him. The dark tinted rear window hummed downward. It revealed Agent Rizzo, smiling at him.

"Congratulations, Doc. Well done," she said.

"Thanks. Means a lot coming from a star athlete," Jake replied. "What brings you here, Agent Rizzo?"

"Just had to see you finish. I had you wrong from the beginning, LaFleur. You're a gutsy guy. No give-up in you."

Jake smiled and kept walking as the SUV crept alongside him.

"Know that she had no choice," Rizzo said emphatically, her eyes searching his tired face. "They were going to kill her daughter."

Jake stopped walking and turned to face the agent.

Rizzo opened the SUV door. "Get in. We'll drive you to your car."

She slid over and Jake gingerly shifted himself into the back seat of the SUV.

"Follow the honking horn," he told her.

Agent Rizzo updated Jake on the FBI's final report—explaining how Elena had been groomed, coerced, and ultimately drugged to in order to take part in Mikal's scheme. "She was trying to get away when she met you that night in the emergency room."

Jake listened quietly, head down, swiping away a tear from his eye, hoping that Rizzo hadn't noticed. "Thanks for telling me. I would've always wondered. Now I know what I believed in my heart... She will not be forgotten."

The SUV pulled up to Jake's old blue honking Honda. He stepped out of the SUV and pressed his key fob to stop the alarm. He went to open the door.

Rizzo leaned out and put her hand on his arm. "Doctor LaFleur, as I mentioned, I am very impressed by the way you handled yourself." She gazed at him earnestly.

"Thanks, Agent Rizzo."

"My superiors at the Bureau are even more impressed. You helped save thousands of lives. The FBI and the nation are in your debt."

"I feel like I fumbled into that whole mess and stumbled out the other side, without Elena. I failed."

Rizzo paused. "You did everything you possibly could have. You were incredibly brave. No way any other civilian would have done half of what you did."

Jake stared at the tinted windows. "Appreciate the pep talk."

"You can still help us," Rizzo continued.

Jake's heart jumped a beat. "Who, me? I'm a doctor."

"Keep your cover gig. With your knowledge of languages and your guts, we can use more operatives like you to help keep our country safe."

"You mean, like, a secret agent?" He stared at her.

"Whatever you want to call it." Agent Rizzo smiled warmly and cocked her head at him. "You game, Doctor LaFleur?"

"Uhh, I guess, I mean. You know I'm game, Agent Rizzo," he stammered, grinning.

He bounced back into the SUV. Rizzo motioned to the driver to keep going. "That's what I like to hear. Let's grab a beer and celebrate your marathon. I'll fill you in on the details."

Jake could not believe this was happening. His phone's *Mission Impossible* ringtone went off in his gym bag, interrupting the moment.

Embarrassed, he fished the phone out of his bag and placed it to his ear.

"Hi, Mom," he said softly.

"Well, my son, did you pass out on Donald Duck, or what?" Cindy asked.

"I finished. Under four hours."

Rizzo cracked a smile and shook her head.

"Good gracious. You must be hungry as a horse," his mother chirped. "When are you coming home?"

Jake paused and shot Rizzo a glance.

"Don't wait up, Mom… I'm working late, again."

ABOUT THE AUTHOR

Marcus Shore is a retired doctor. During his thirty-year career, he specialized in the medical and surgical treatment of ocular disorders. In addition to writing, he is an accomplished marathoner and triathlete, and he loves playing competitive tennis.

Although this represents his first effort in writing, he has a lot of stories to tell in his second career.

A free ebook edition is available with the purchase of this book.

To claim your free ebook edition:

1. Visit MorganJamesBOGO.com
2. Sign your name CLEARLY in the space
3. Complete the form and submit a photo of the entire copyright page
4. You or your friend can download the ebook to your preferred device

Morgan James
BOGO™

A **FREE** ebook edition is available for you or a friend with the purchase of this print book.

CLEARLY SIGN YOUR NAME ABOVE

Instructions to claim your free ebook edition:
1. Visit MorganJamesBOGO.com
2. Sign your name CLEARLY in the space above
3. Complete the form and submit a photo of this entire page
4. You or your friend can download the ebook to your preferred device

Print & Digital Together Forever.

Snap a photo   Free ebook   Read anywhere

9 781636 984179